R.A. MONTGOMERY PR

CHOOSE YOUR OWN ADVENTURE

JOURNEY UNDER THE SEA

WRITTEN BY

Andrew E.C. Gaska
E.L. Thomas

BASED ON THE ORIGINAL BY

R. A. Montgomery

ILLUSTRATED BY

Dani Bolinho

BACKGROUND ART BY

Leandro Casca

COLORS BY

PH Gomes

LETTERS BY

Joamette Gil

CHOOSECO

ONI PRESS

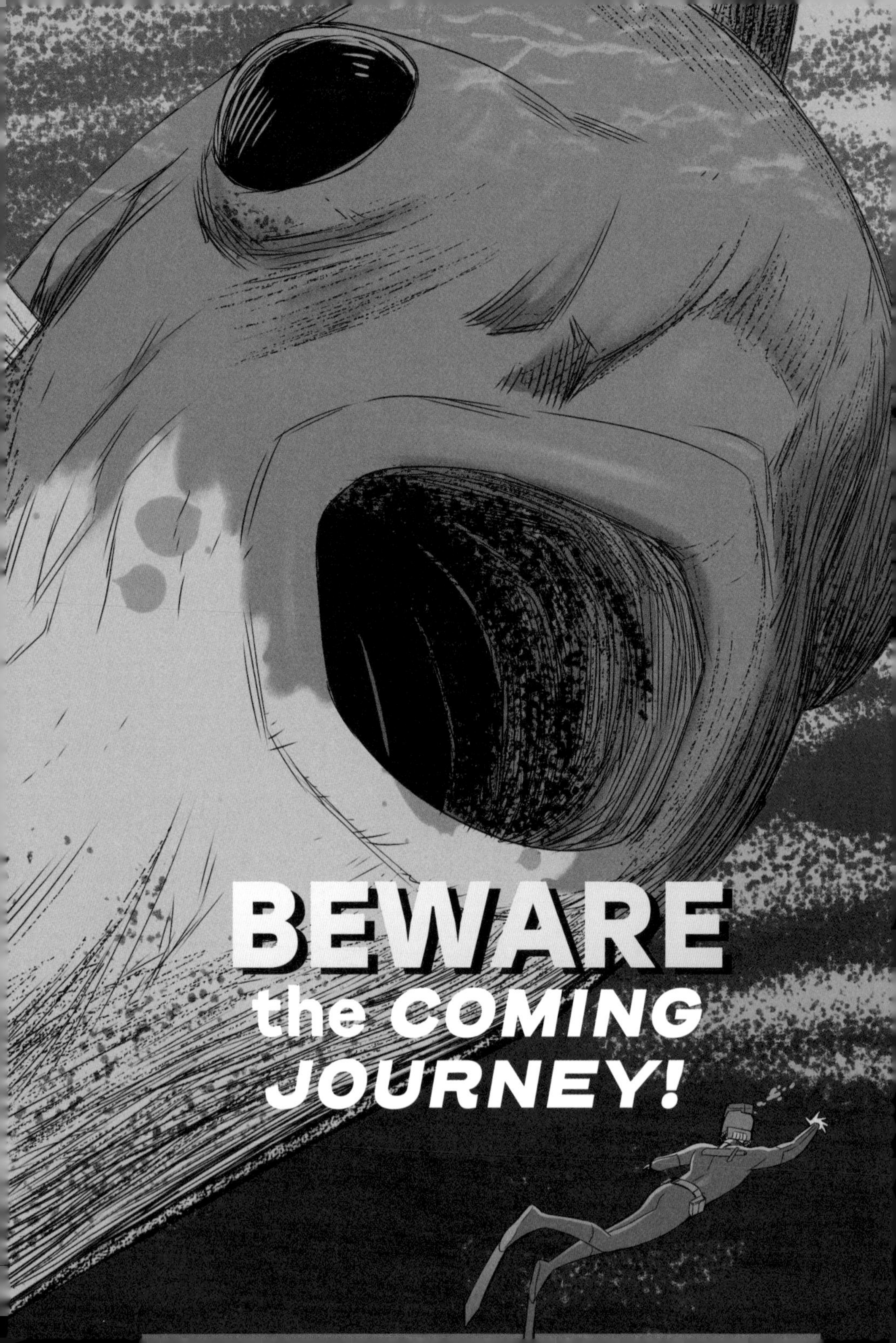
BEWARE
the COMING
JOURNEY!

This book will be different from others you've encountered,

for here, **YOU** and **YOU** alone are in charge of every decision and every pathway **YOU** take. How the story ends rests solely on **YOUR** shoulders.

The coming journey will take **YOU** deep below the ocean's surface, through harrowing and exciting experiences. A grand adventure that can lead to discovery or destruction. But never fear! At any time, **YOU** may go back and make another choice, this is **YOUR** journey and no one else's.

So dive! Dive into the mysterious world of ocean kingdoms, of sea monsters both big and small, of fantastical locals and perilous underwater caverns. Depending on the choices **YOU** make, **YOU** may never see the surface world again. But would that be so bad if **YOU** discover the magical and mysterious fabled underwater city of Atlantis? That is a decision for **YOU** and **YOU** alone to make.

COVER BY Dani Bolinho & Italo Silva
EDITED BY Desiree Rodriguez
ADDITIONAL EDITS BY Robert Meyers
DESIGNED BY Carey Hall & Hilary Thompson

SPECIAL THANKS TO Shannon Gilligan & Rachel Hullett

PUBLISHED BY ONI-LION FORGE PUBLISHING GROUP, LLC.

James Lucas Jones, president & publisher
Charlie Chu, e.v.p. of creative & business development
Steve Ellis, s.v.p. of games & operations
Alex Segura, s.v.p. of marketing & sales
Michelle Nguyen, associate publisher
Brad Rooks, director of operations
Amber O'Neill, special projects manager
Margot Wood, director of marketing & sales
Katie Sainz, marketing manager
Henry Barajas, sales manager
Tara Lehmann, publicist
Holly Aitchison, consumer marketing manager
Troy Look, director of design & production
Angie Knowles, production manager
Kate Z. Stone, senior graphic designer
Carey Hall, graphic designer

Sarah Rockwell, graphic designer
Hilary Thompson, graphic designer
Vincent Kukua, digital prepress technician
Chris Cerasi, managing editor
Jasmine Amiri, senior editor
Shawna Gore, senior editor
Amanda Meadows, senior editor
Robert Meyers, senior editor, licensing
Desiree Rodriguez, editor
Grace Scheipeter, editor
Zack Soto, editor
Ben Eisner, game developer
Sara Harding, entertainment executive assistant
Jung Lee, logistics coordinator
Kuian Kellum, warehouse assistant
Joe Nozemack, publisher emeritus

onipress.com
🇫 facebook.com/onipress
🐦 twitter.com/onipress
📷 instagram.com/onipress

CYOA.COM
🐦 twitter.com/chooseadventure
📷 instagram.com/cyoapub
🇫 facebook.com/ChooseYourOwnAdventure

First Edition: August 2022
ISBN 978-1-62010-984-7
eISBN 978-1-63715-054-2

1 2 3 4 5 6 7 8 9 10

Library of Congress Control Number 2021949911

Printed in China.

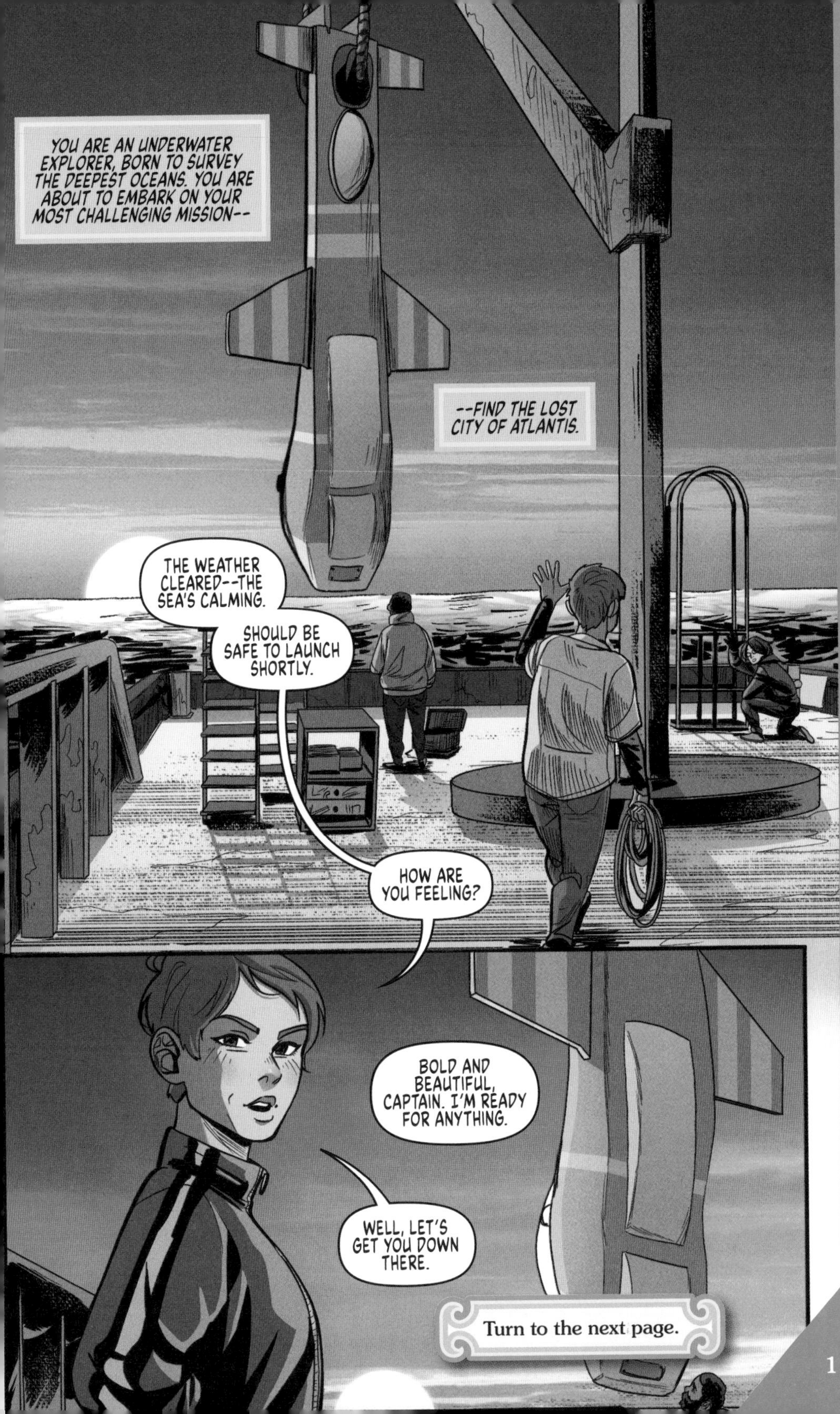
YOU ARE AN UNDERWATER EXPLORER, BORN TO SURVEY THE DEEPEST OCEANS. YOU ARE ABOUT TO EMBARK ON YOUR MOST CHALLENGING MISSION--
--FIND THE LOST CITY OF ATLANTIS.
THE WEATHER CLEARED--THE SEA'S CALMING.
SHOULD BE SAFE TO LAUNCH SHORTLY.
HOW ARE YOU FEELING?
BOLD AND BEAUTIFUL, CAPTAIN. I'M READY FOR ANYTHING.
WELL, LET'S GET YOU DOWN THERE.

Turn to the next page.

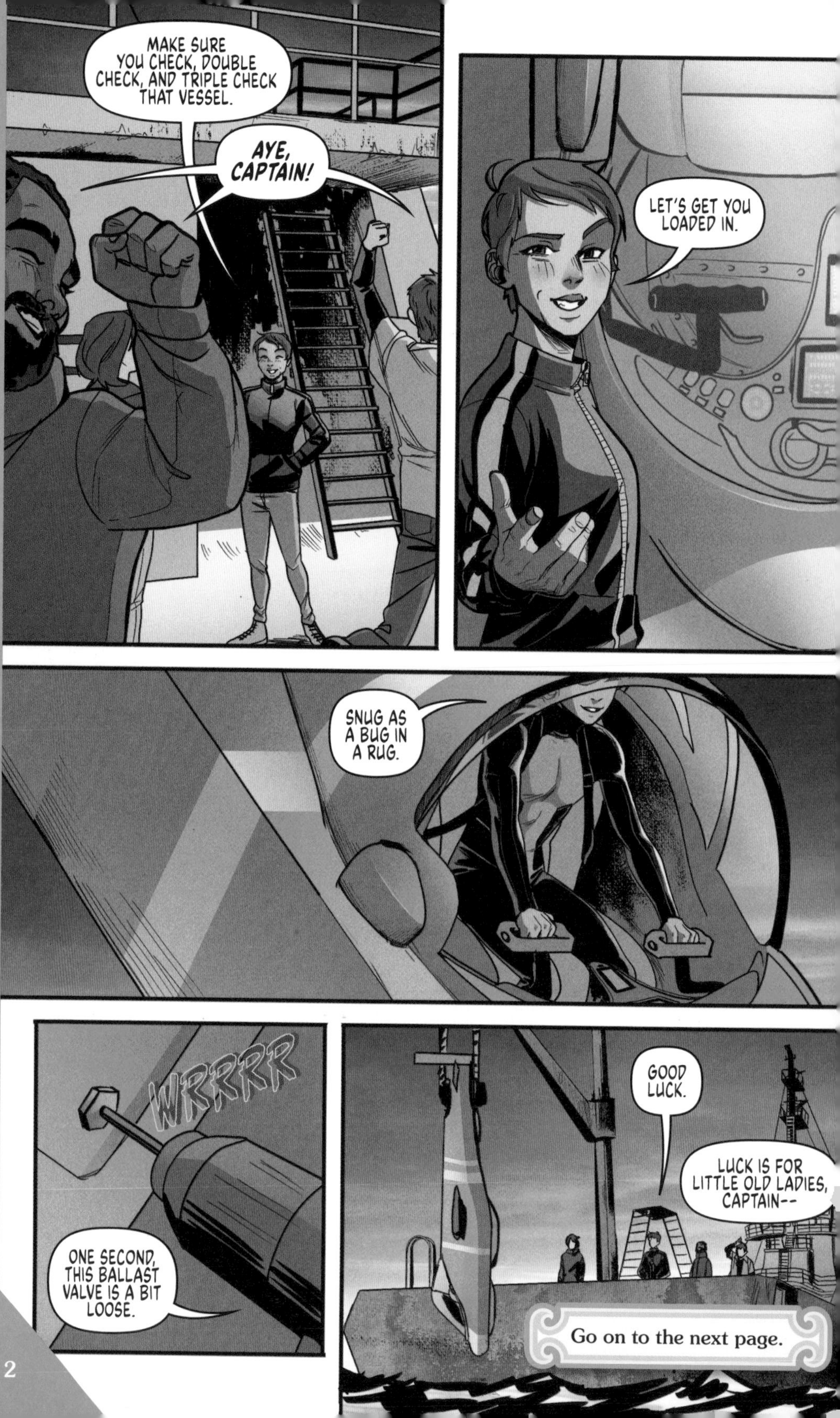
MAKE SURE YOU CHECK, DOUBLE CHECK, AND TRIPLE CHECK THAT VESSEL.
AYE, CAPTAIN!
LET'S GET YOU LOADED IN.
SNUG AS A BUG IN A RUG.
WRRRR
ONE SECOND, THIS BALLAST VALVE IS A BIT LOOSE.
GOOD LUCK.
LUCK IS FOR LITTLE OLD LADIES, CAPTAIN--

Go on to the next page.

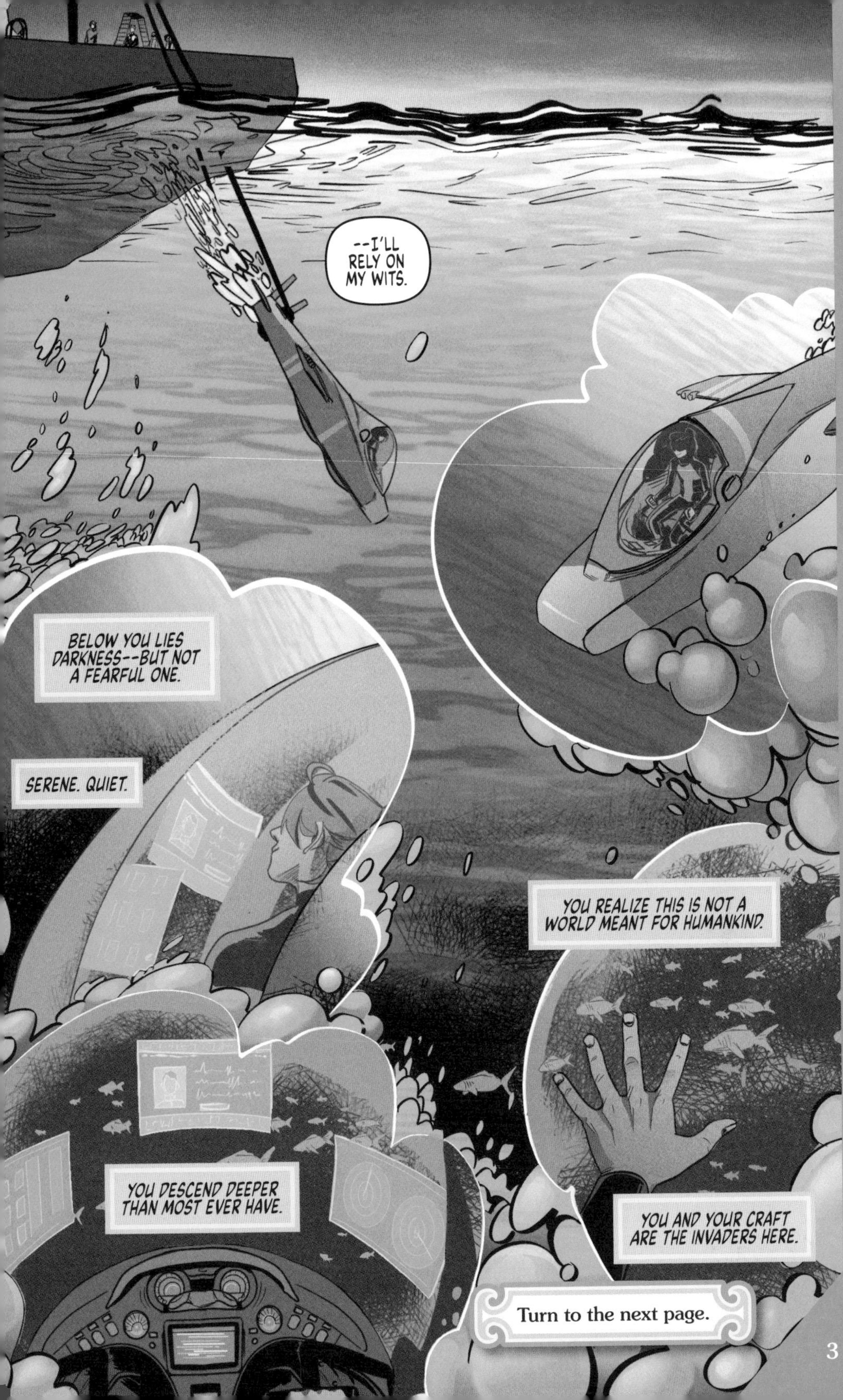
--I'LL RELY ON MY WITS.
BELOW YOU LIES DARKNESS--BUT NOT A FEARFUL ONE.
SERENE. QUIET.
YOU DESCEND DEEPER THAN MOST EVER HAVE.
YOU REALIZE THIS IS NOT A WORLD MEANT FOR HUMANKIND.
YOU AND YOUR CRAFT ARE THE INVADERS HERE.

Turn to the next page.

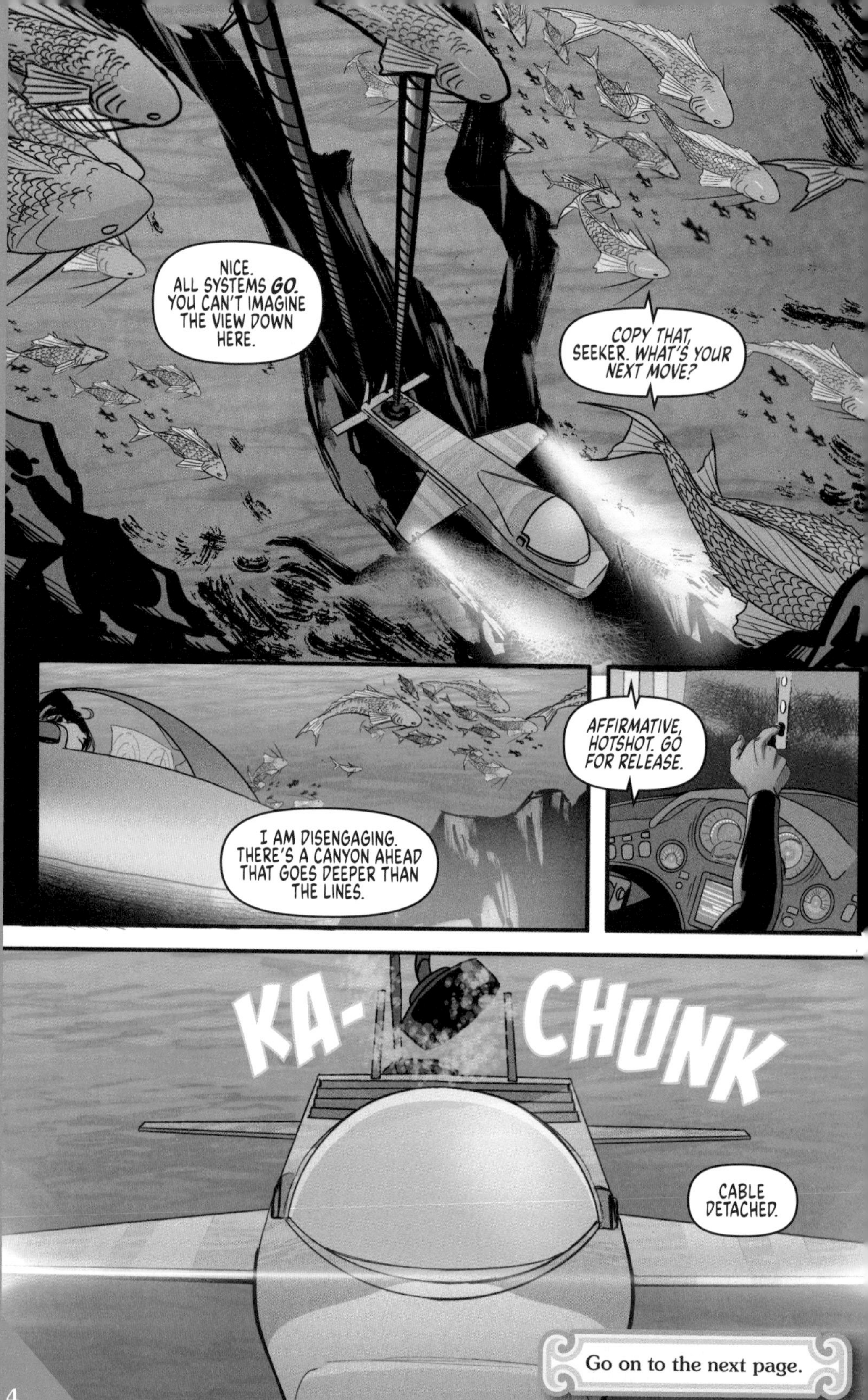
NICE. ALL SYSTEMS GO. YOU CAN'T IMAGINE THE VIEW DOWN HERE.
COPY THAT, SEEKER. WHAT'S YOUR NEXT MOVE?
I AM DISENGAGING. THERE'S A CANYON AHEAD THAT GOES DEEPER THAN THE LINES.
AFFIRMATIVE, HOTSHOT. GO FOR RELEASE.
KA-CHUNK
CABLE DETACHED.

Go on to the next page.

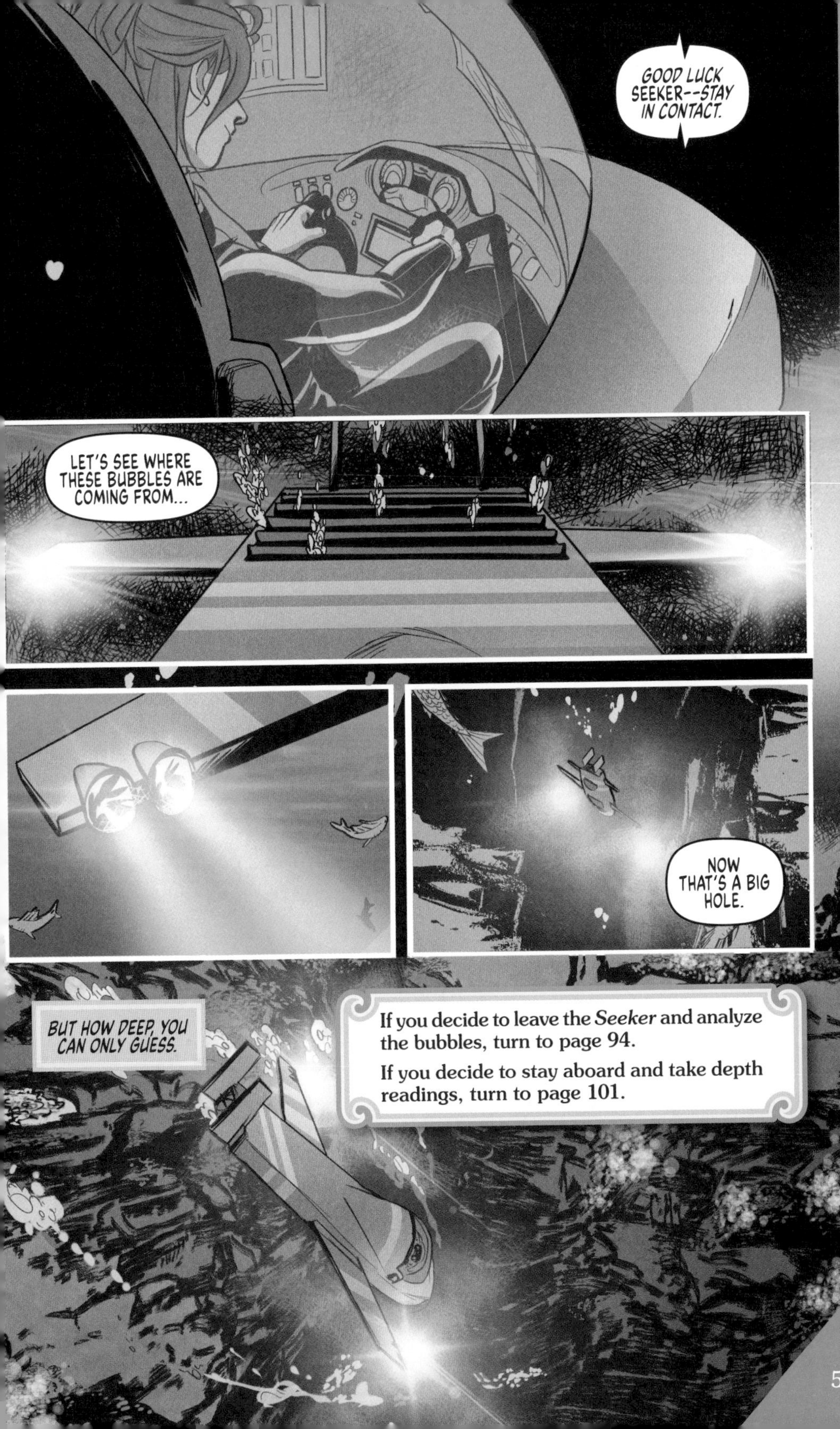
GOOD LUCK SEEKER--STAY IN CONTACT.
LET'S SEE WHERE THESE BUBBLES ARE COMING FROM...
NOW THAT'S A BIG HOLE.
BUT HOW DEEP, YOU CAN ONLY GUESS.

If you decide to leave the *Seeker* and analyze the bubbles, turn to page 94.

If you decide to stay aboard and take depth readings, turn to page 101.

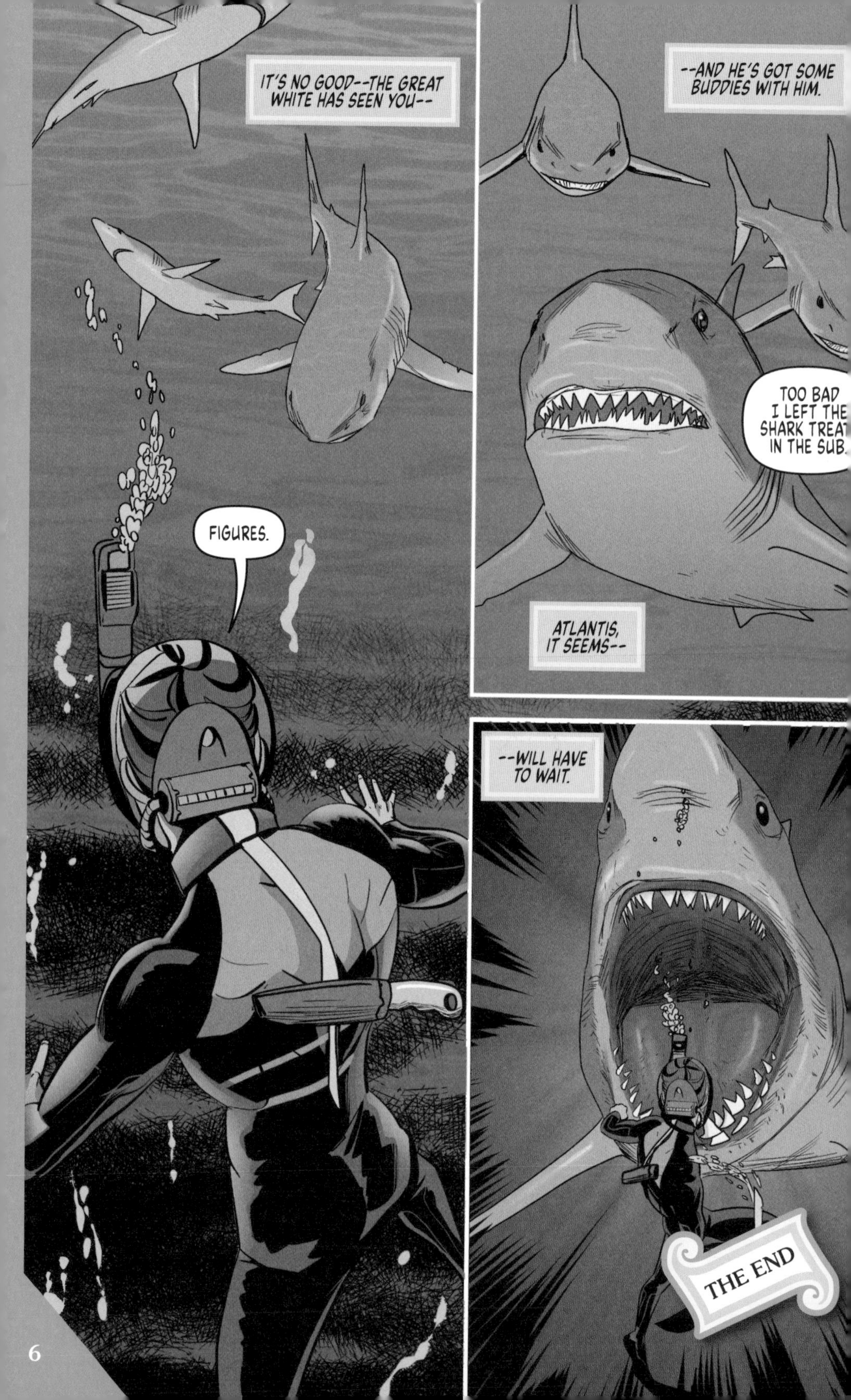
IT'S NO GOOD--THE GREAT WHITE HAS SEEN YOU--
FIGURES.
--AND HE'S GOT SOME BUDDIES WITH HIM.
TOO BAD I LEFT THE SHARK TREAT IN THE SUB.
ATLANTIS, IT SEEMS--
--WILL HAVE TO WAIT.
THE END

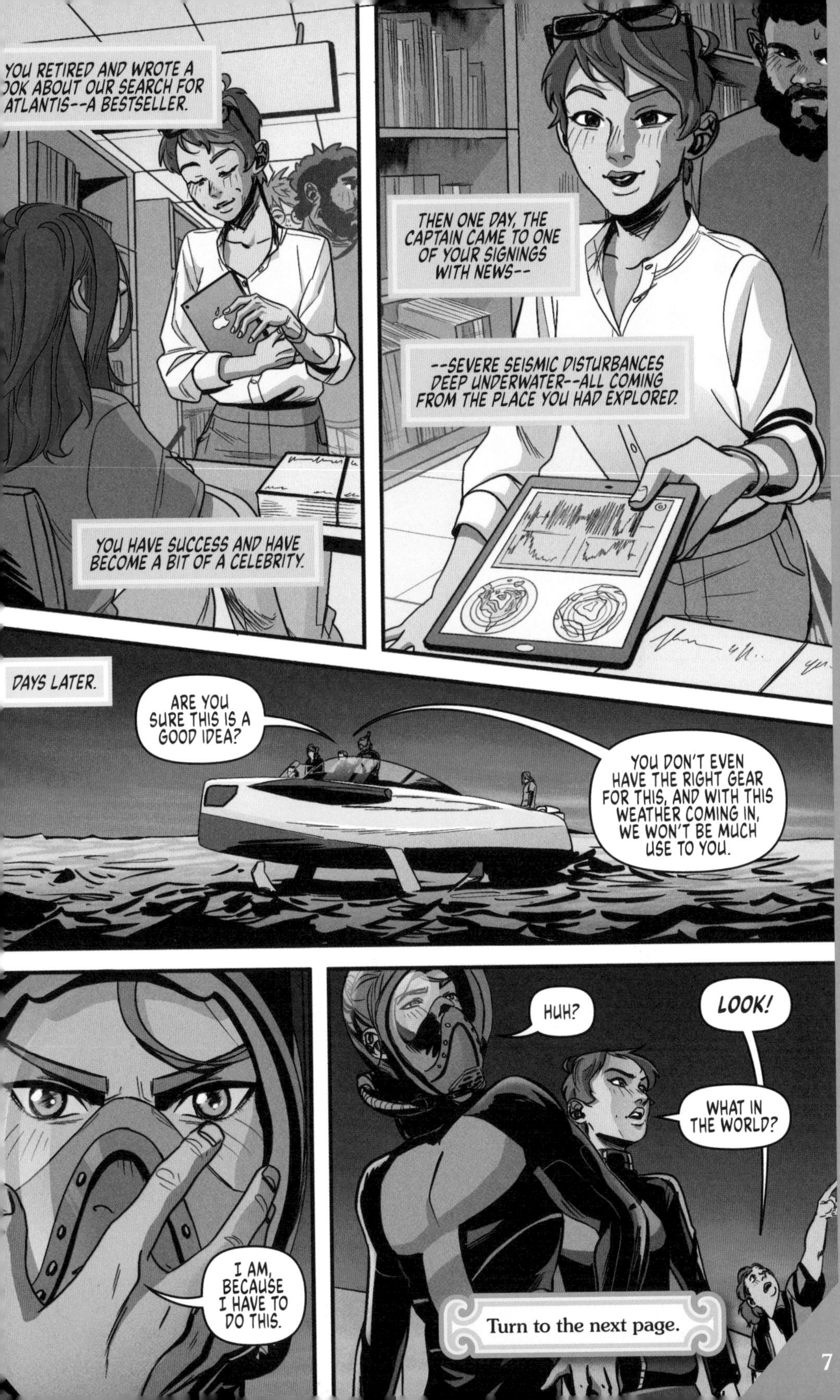
YOU RETIRED AND WROTE A
BOOK ABOUT OUR SEARCH FOR
ATLANTIS--A BESTSELLER.
YOU HAVE SUCCESS AND HAVE BECOME A BIT OF A CELEBRITY.
THEN ONE DAY, THE CAPTAIN CAME TO ONE OF YOUR SIGNINGS WITH NEWS--
--SEVERE SEISMIC DISTURBANCES DEEP UNDERWATER--ALL COMING FROM THE PLACE YOU HAD EXPLORED.
DAYS LATER.
ARE YOU SURE THIS IS A GOOD IDEA?
YOU DON'T EVEN HAVE THE RIGHT GEAR FOR THIS, AND WITH THIS WEATHER COMING IN, WE WON'T BE MUCH USE TO YOU.
I AM, BECAUSE I HAVE TO DO THIS.
HUH?
LOOK!
WHAT IN THE WORLD?
Turn to the next page.

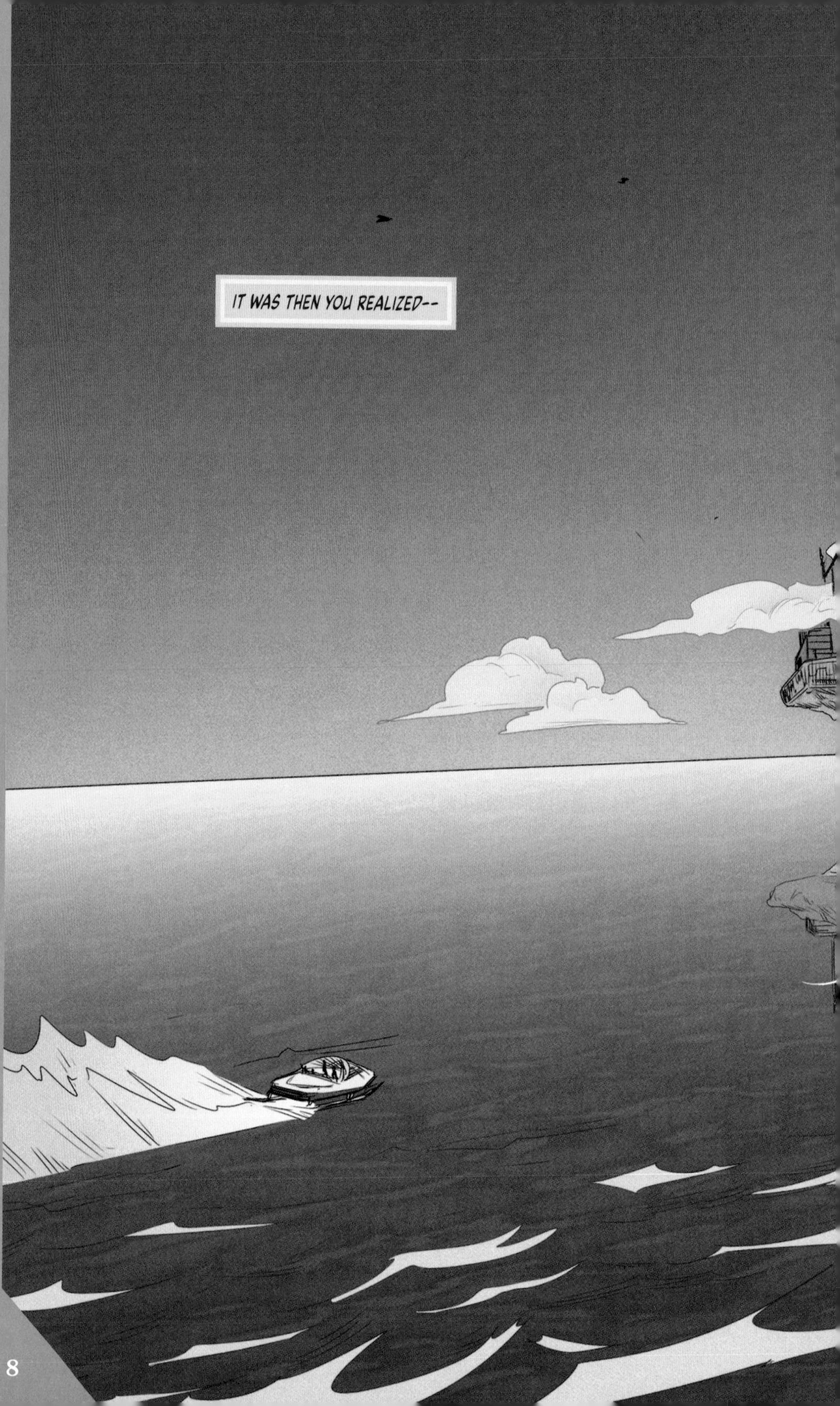
IT WAS THEN YOU REALIZED--

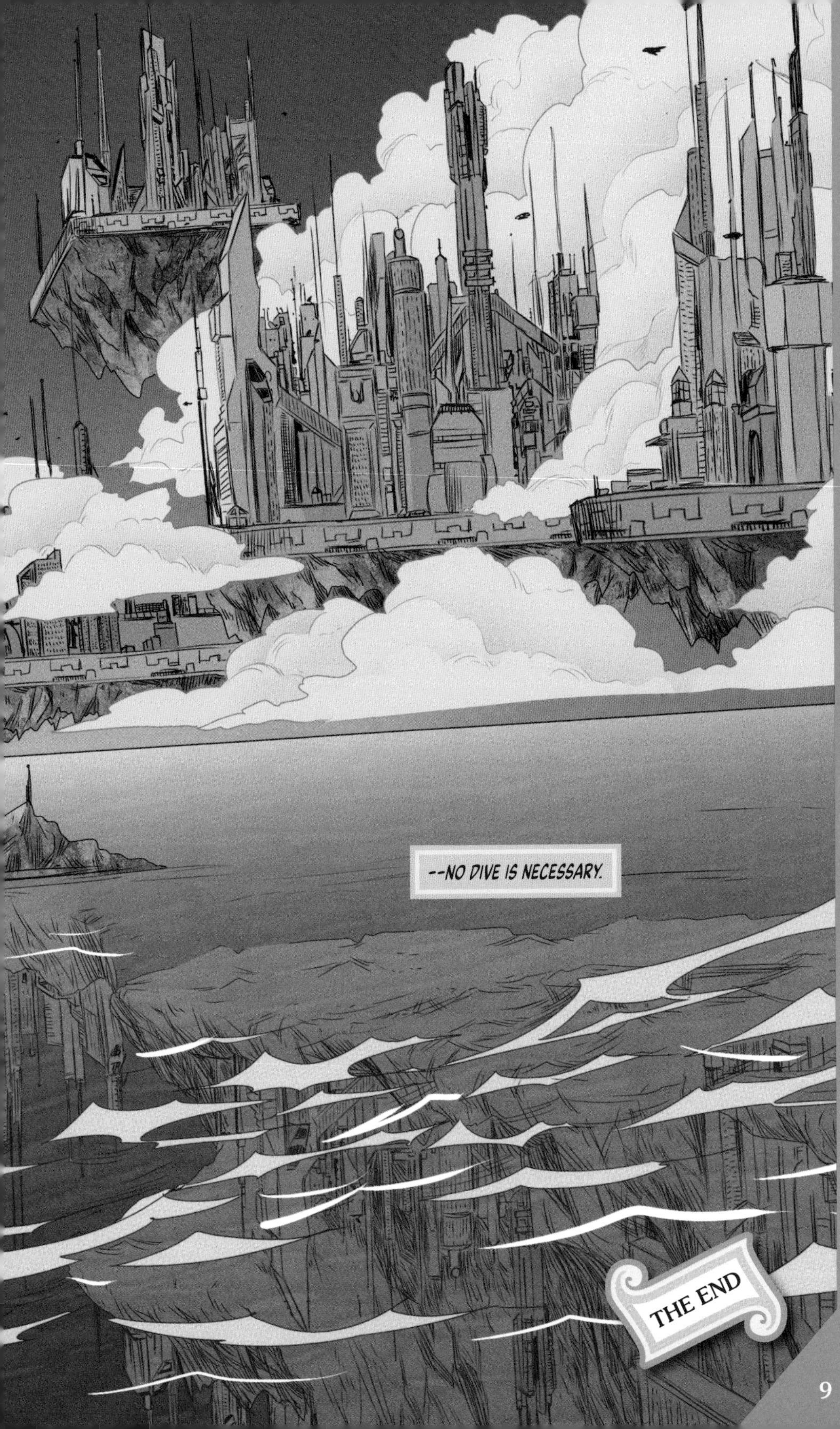
--NO DIVE IS NECESSARY.
THE END

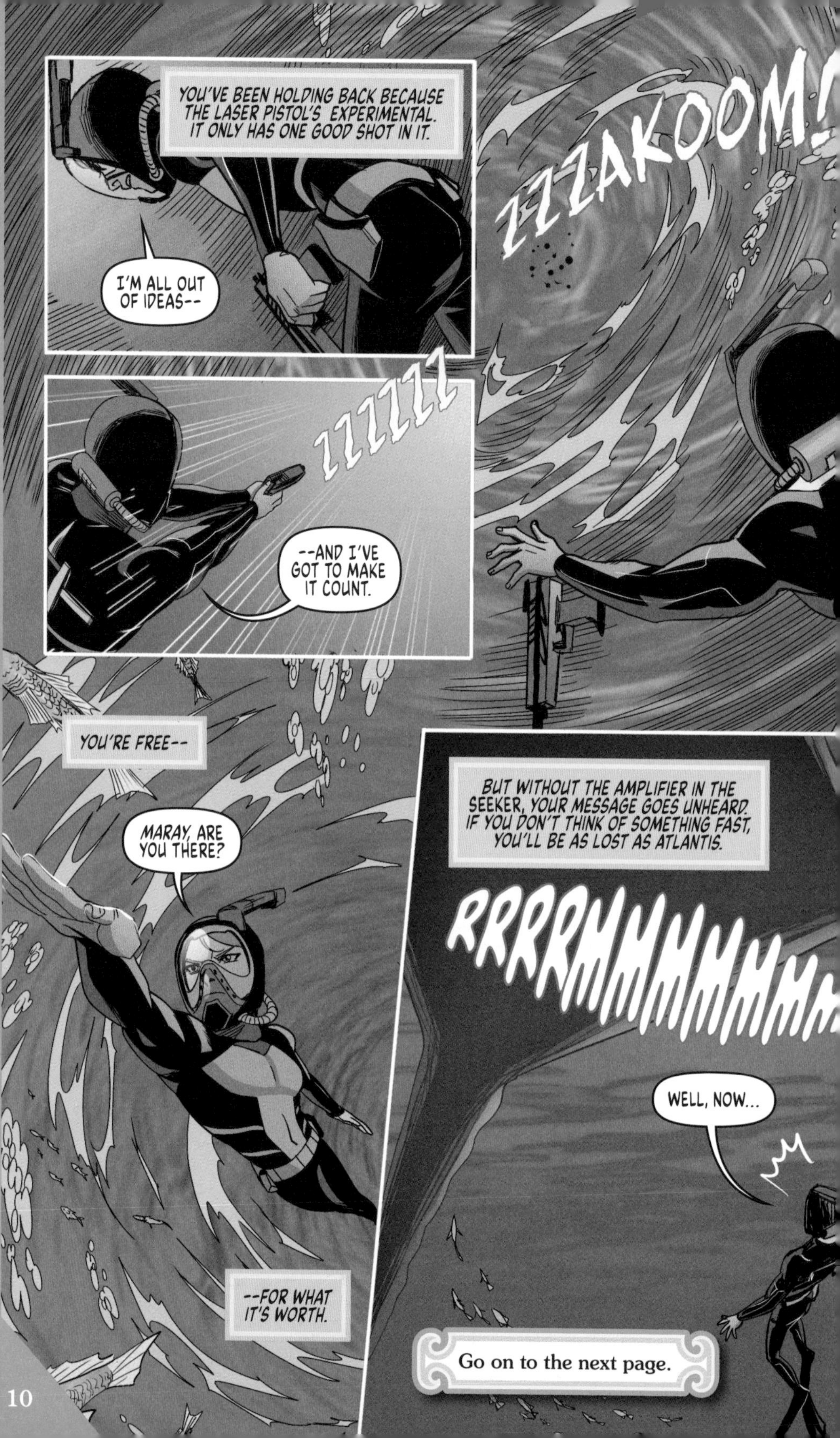

YOU'VE BEEN HOLDING BACK BECAUSE THE LASER PISTOL'S EXPERIMENTAL. IT ONLY HAS ONE GOOD SHOT IN IT.
I'M ALL OUT OF IDEAS--
ZZZZZZ
--AND I'VE GOT TO MAKE IT COUNT.
ZZZAKOOM!
YOU'RE FREE--
MARAY, ARE YOU THERE?
--FOR WHAT IT'S WORTH.
BUT WITHOUT THE AMPLIFIER IN THE SEEKER, YOUR MESSAGE GOES UNHEARD. IF YOU DON'T THINK OF SOMETHING FAST, YOU'LL BE AS LOST AS ATLANTIS.
RRRRMMMMMM
WELL, NOW...

Go on to the next page.

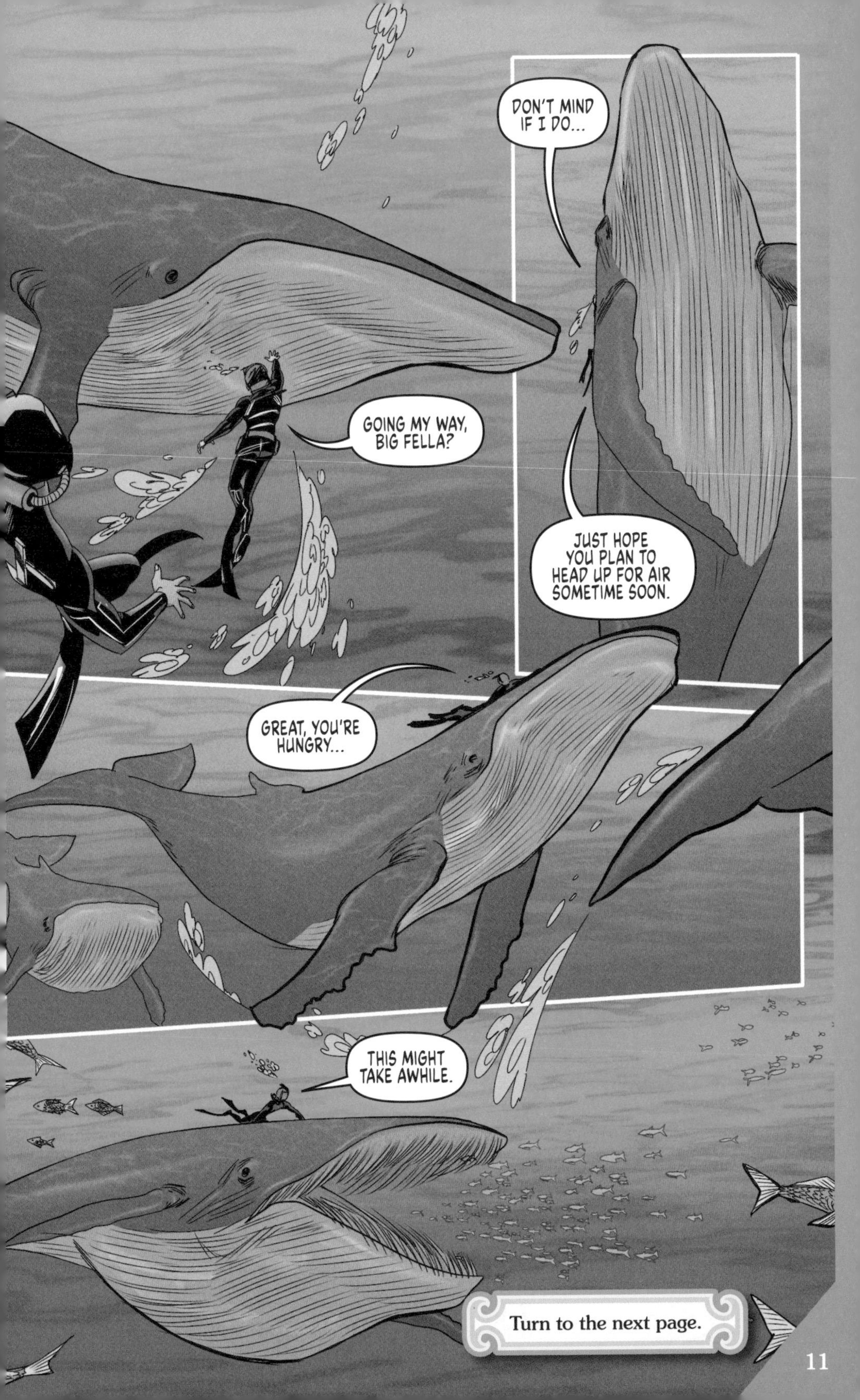
GOING MY WAY, BIG FELLA?
DON'T MIND IF I DO...
JUST HOPE YOU PLAN TO HEAD UP FOR AIR SOMETIME SOON.
GREAT, YOU'RE HUNGRY...
THIS MIGHT TAKE AWHILE.

Turn to the next page.

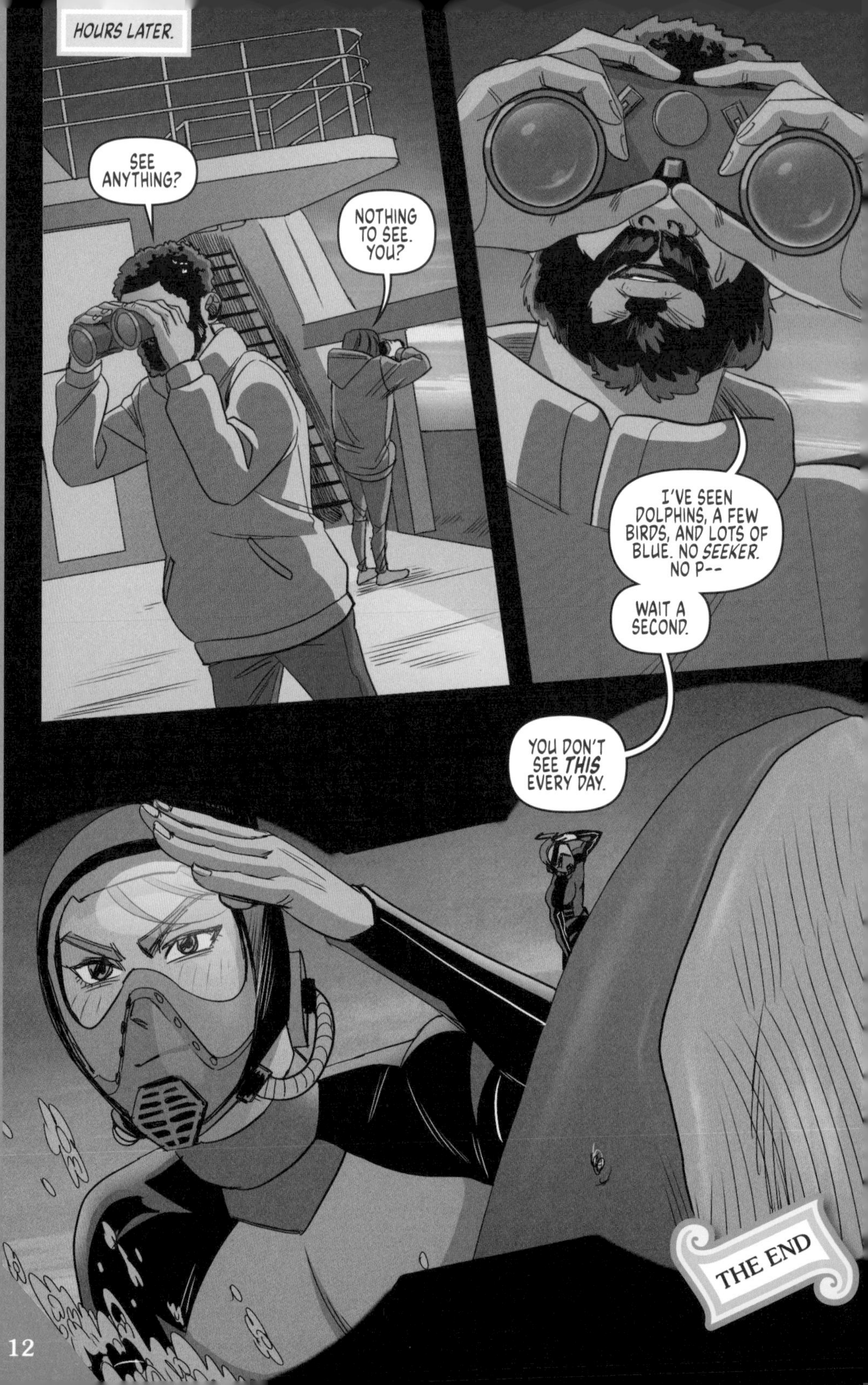
HOURS LATER.
SEE ANYTHING?
NOTHING TO SEE. YOU?
I'VE SEEN DOLPHINS, A FEW BIRDS, AND LOTS OF BLUE. NO SEEKER. NO P--
WAIT A SECOND.
YOU DON'T SEE THIS EVERY DAY.
THE END

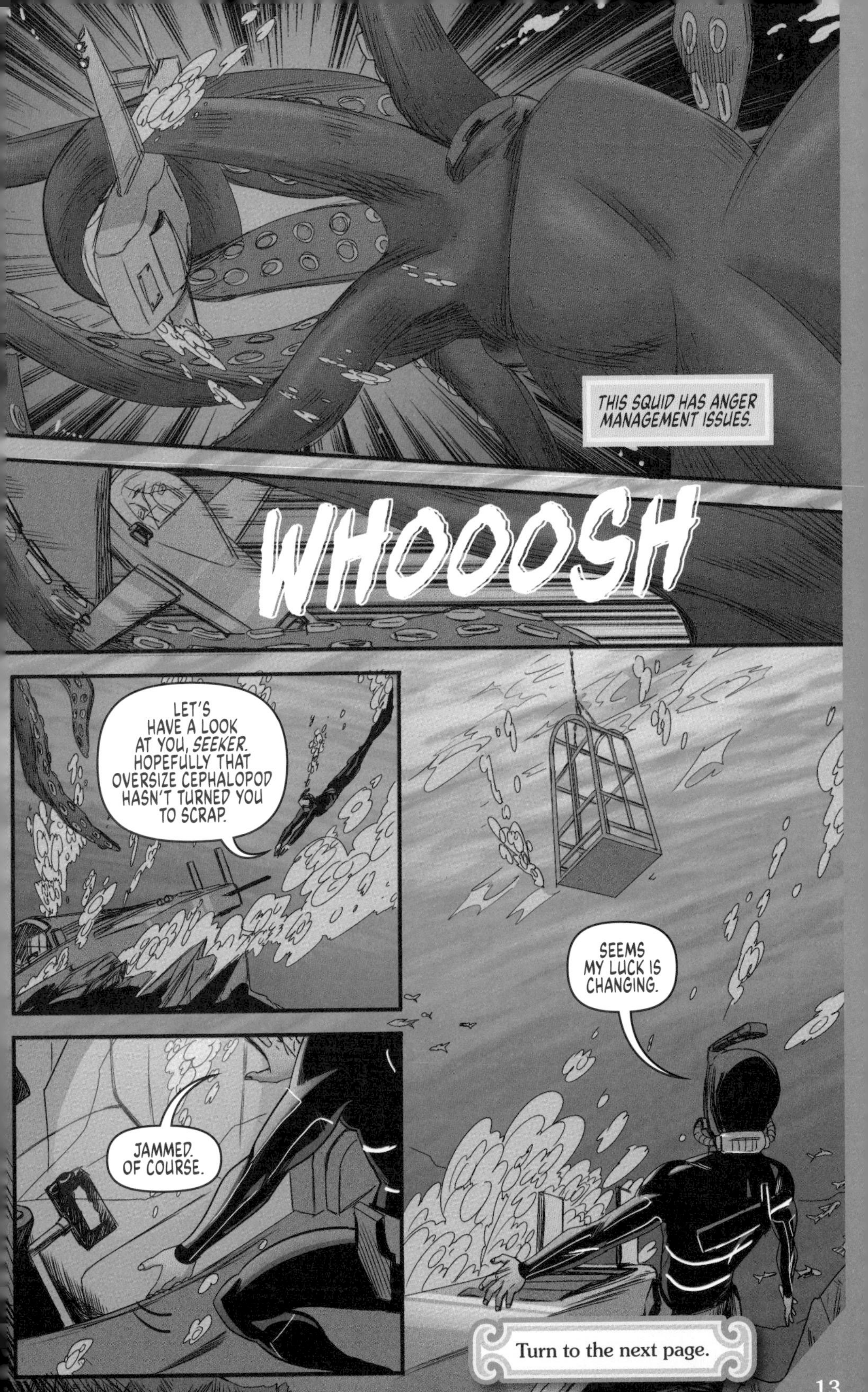
THIS SQUID HAS ANGER MANAGEMENT ISSUES.
WHOOOSH
LET'S HAVE A LOOK AT YOU, *SEEKER.* HOPEFULLY THAT OVERSIZE CEPHALOPOD HASN'T TURNED YOU TO SCRAP.
SEEMS MY LUCK IS CHANGING.
JAMMED. OF COURSE.

Turn to the next page.

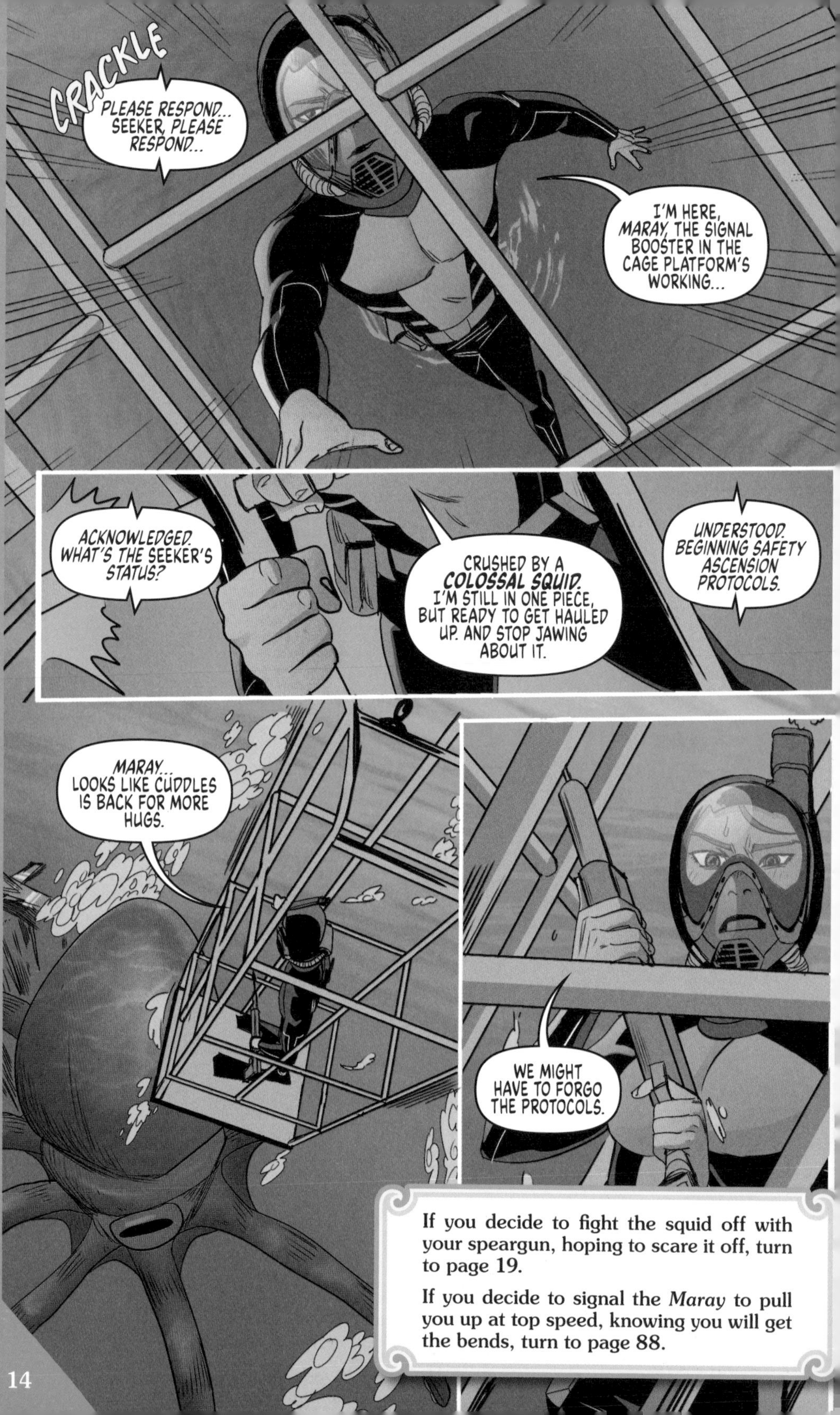
CRACKLE
PLEASE RESPOND... SEEKER, PLEASE RESPOND...
I'M HERE, MARAY, THE SIGNAL BOOSTER IN THE CAGE PLATFORM'S WORKING...
ACKNOWLEDGED. WHAT'S THE SEEKER'S STATUS?
CRUSHED BY A **COLOSSAL SQUID.** I'M STILL IN ONE PIECE, BUT READY TO GET HAULED UP. AND STOP JAWING ABOUT IT.
UNDERSTOOD. BEGINNING SAFETY ASCENSION PROTOCOLS.
MARAY... LOOKS LIKE CUDDLES IS BACK FOR MORE HUGS.
WE MIGHT HAVE TO FORGO THE PROTOCOLS.

If you decide to fight the squid off with your speargun, hoping to scare it off, turn to page 19.

If you decide to signal the *Maray* to pull you up at top speed, knowing you will get the bends, turn to page 88.

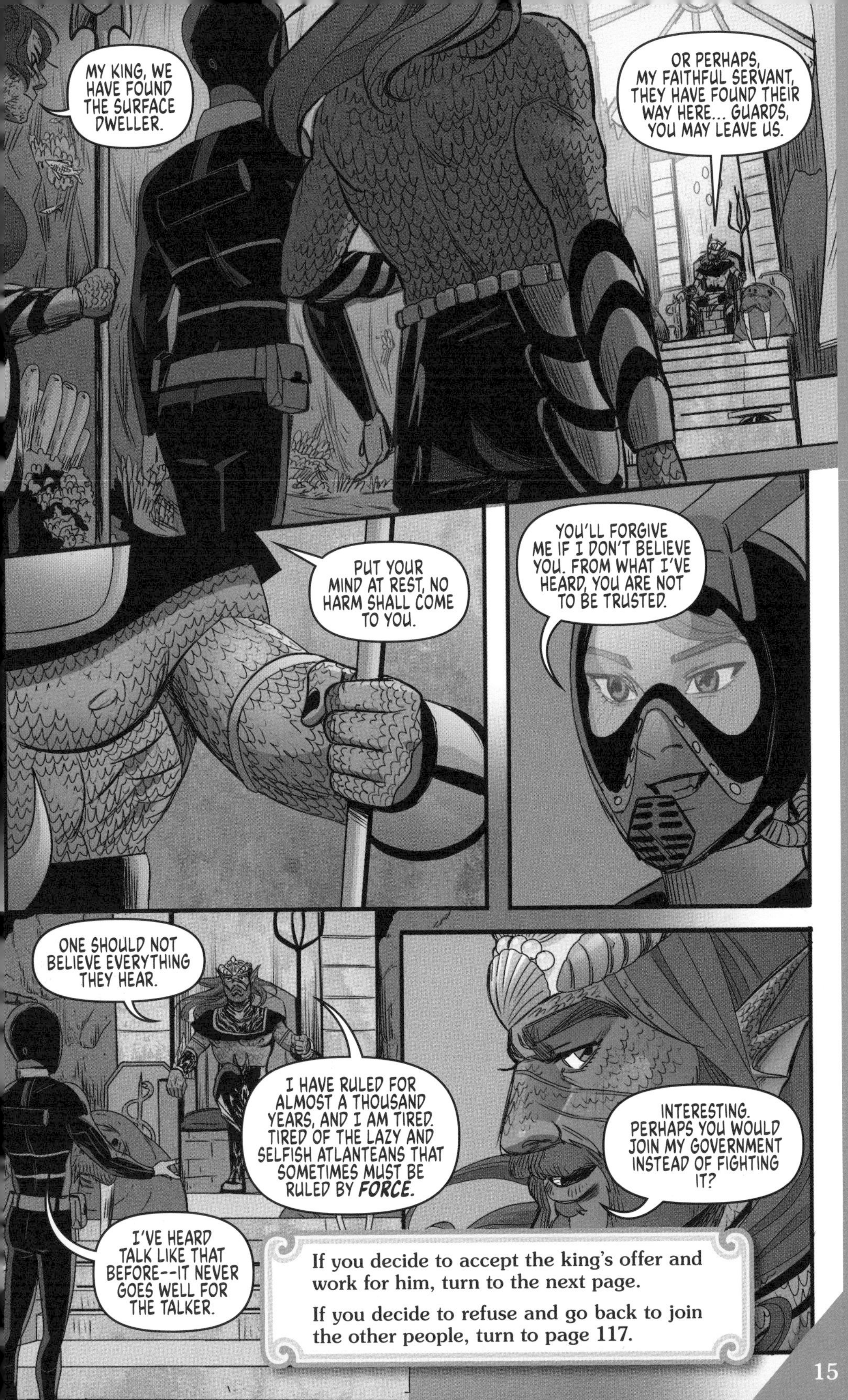
MY KING, WE HAVE FOUND THE SURFACE DWELLER.
OR PERHAPS, MY FAITHFUL SERVANT, THEY HAVE FOUND THEIR WAY HERE... GUARDS, YOU MAY LEAVE US.
PUT YOUR MIND AT REST, NO HARM SHALL COME TO YOU.
YOU'LL FORGIVE ME IF I DON'T BELIEVE YOU. FROM WHAT I'VE HEARD, YOU ARE NOT TO BE TRUSTED.
ONE SHOULD NOT BELIEVE EVERYTHING THEY HEAR.
I HAVE RULED FOR ALMOST A THOUSAND YEARS, AND I AM TIRED. TIRED OF THE LAZY AND SELFISH ATLANTEANS THAT SOMETIMES MUST BE RULED BY ***FORCE.***
I'VE HEARD TALK LIKE THAT BEFORE--IT NEVER GOES WELL FOR THE TALKER.
INTERESTING. PERHAPS YOU WOULD JOIN MY GOVERNMENT INSTEAD OF FIGHTING IT?

If you decide to accept the king's offer and work for him, turn to the next page.

If you decide to refuse and go back to join the other people, turn to page 117.

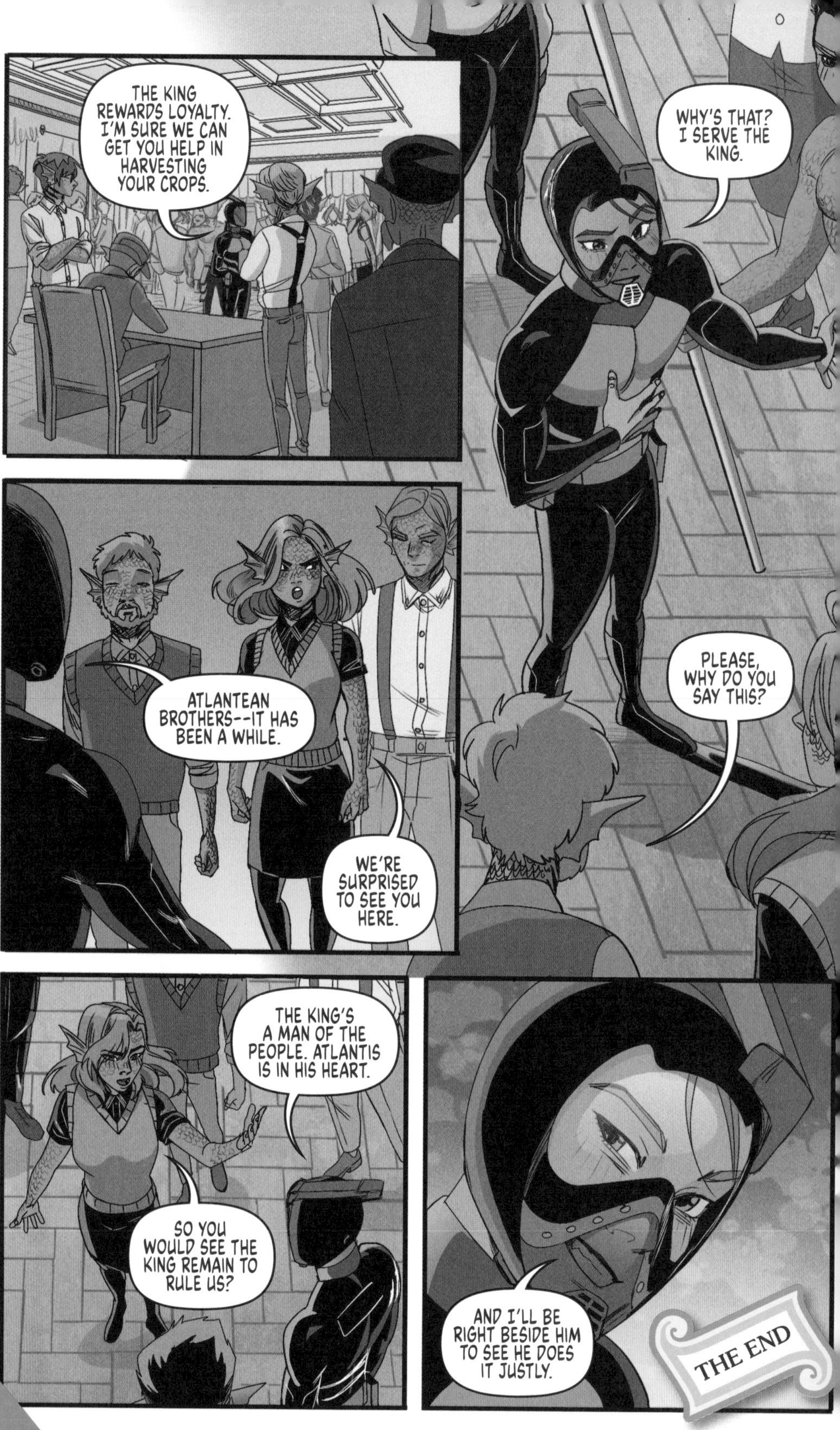
THE KING REWARDS LOYALTY. I'M SURE WE CAN GET YOU HELP IN HARVESTING YOUR CROPS.
WHY'S THAT? I SERVE THE KING.
ATLANTEAN BROTHERS--IT HAS BEEN A WHILE.
WE'RE SURPRISED TO SEE YOU HERE.
PLEASE, WHY DO YOU SAY THIS?
THE KING'S A MAN OF THE PEOPLE. ATLANTIS IS IN HIS HEART.
SO YOU WOULD SEE THE KING REMAIN TO RULE US?
AND I'LL BE RIGHT BESIDE HIM TO SEE HE DOES IT JUSTLY.
THE END

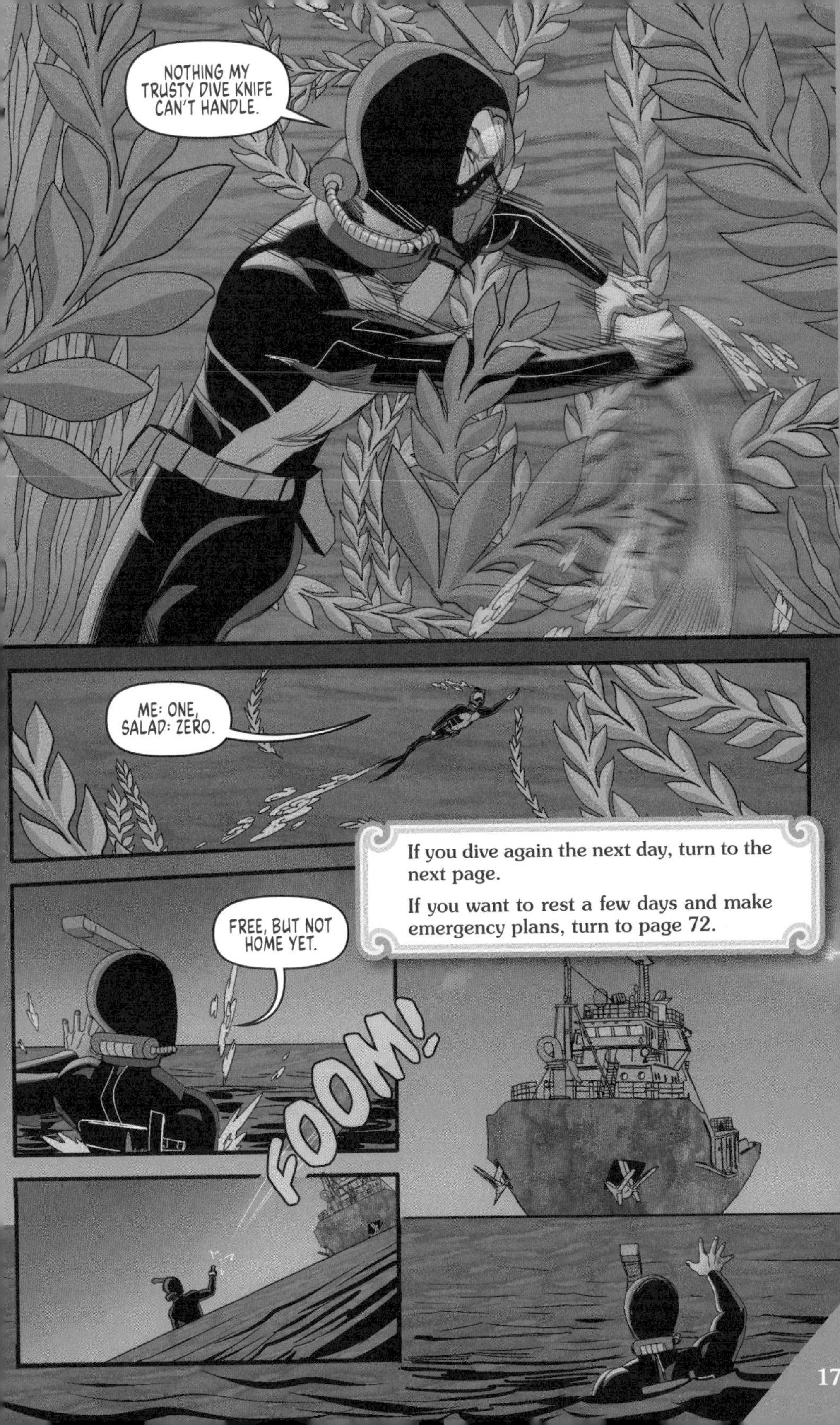
NOTHING MY TRUSTY DIVE KNIFE CAN'T HANDLE.
ME: ONE, SALAD: ZERO.
FREE, BUT NOT HOME YET.
FOOM!

If you dive again the next day, turn to the next page.

If you want to rest a few days and make emergency plans, turn to page 72.

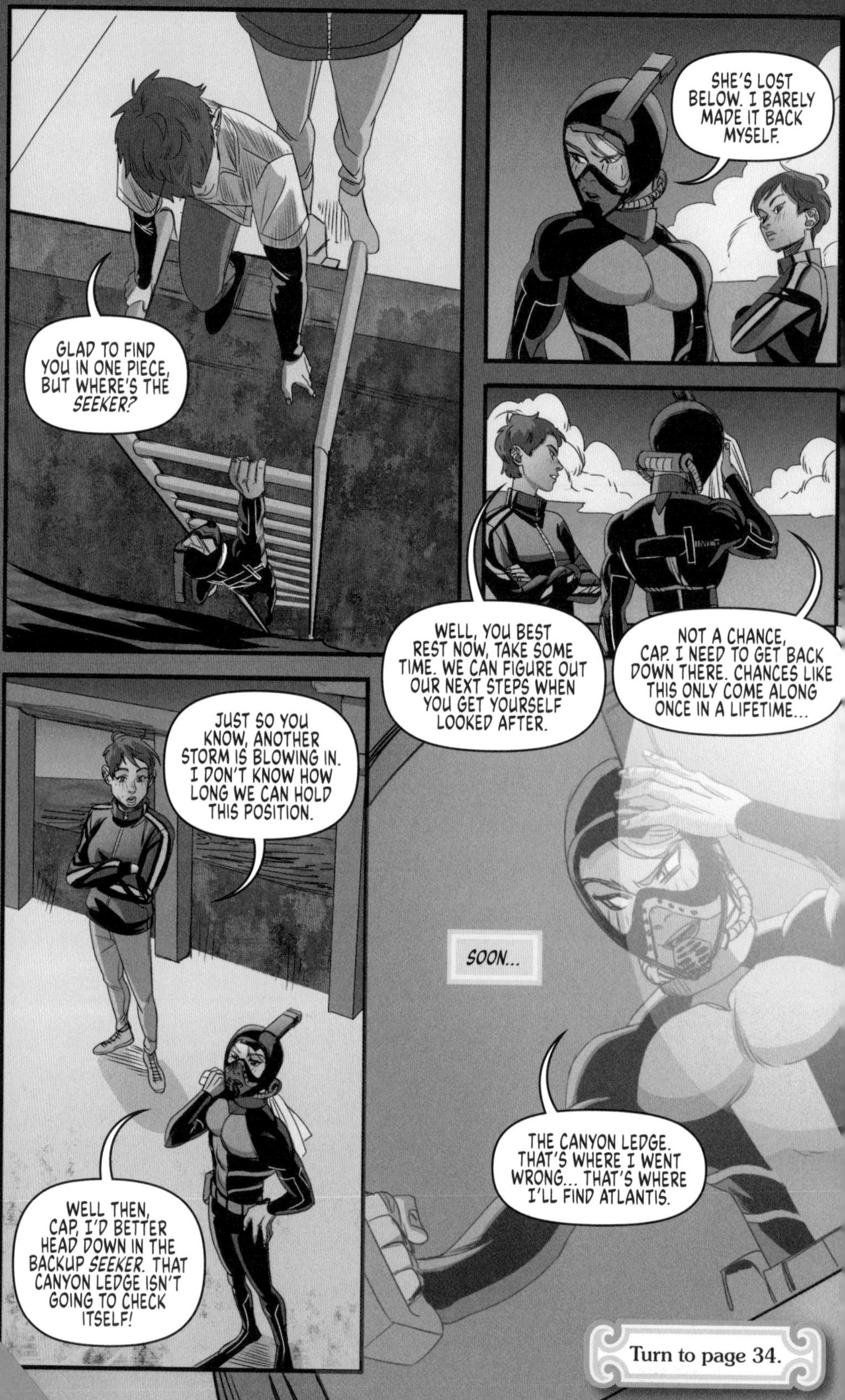
GLAD TO FIND YOU IN ONE PIECE, BUT WHERE'S THE *SEEKER?*
SHE'S LOST BELOW. I BARELY MADE IT BACK MYSELF.
WELL, YOU BEST REST NOW, TAKE SOME TIME. WE CAN FIGURE OUT OUR NEXT STEPS WHEN YOU GET YOURSELF LOOKED AFTER.
NOT A CHANCE, CAP. I NEED TO GET BACK DOWN THERE. CHANCES LIKE THIS ONLY COME ALONG ONCE IN A LIFETIME...
JUST SO YOU KNOW, ANOTHER STORM IS BLOWING IN. I DON'T KNOW HOW LONG WE CAN HOLD THIS POSITION.
WELL THEN, CAP, I'D BETTER HEAD DOWN IN THE BACKUP *SEEKER*. THAT CANYON LEDGE ISN'T GOING TO CHECK ITSELF!
SOON...
THE CANYON LEDGE. THAT'S WHERE I WENT WRONG... THAT'S WHERE I'LL FIND ATLANTIS.

Turn to page 34.

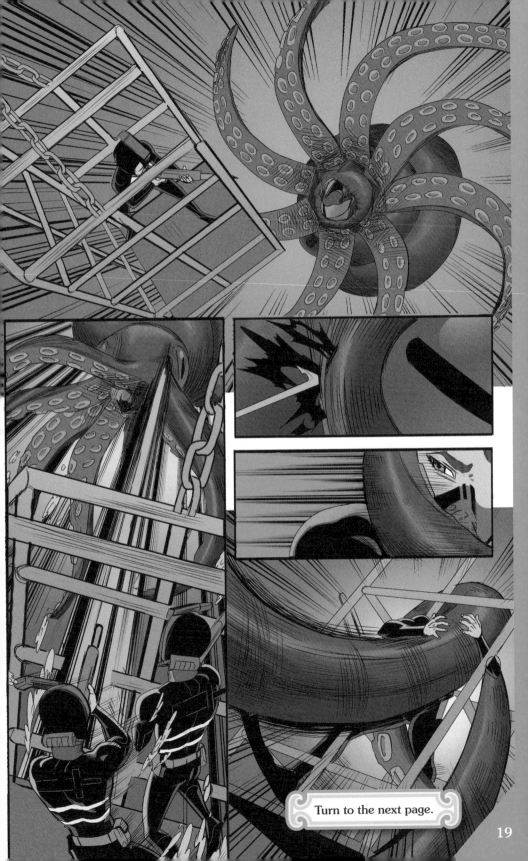

Turn to the next page.

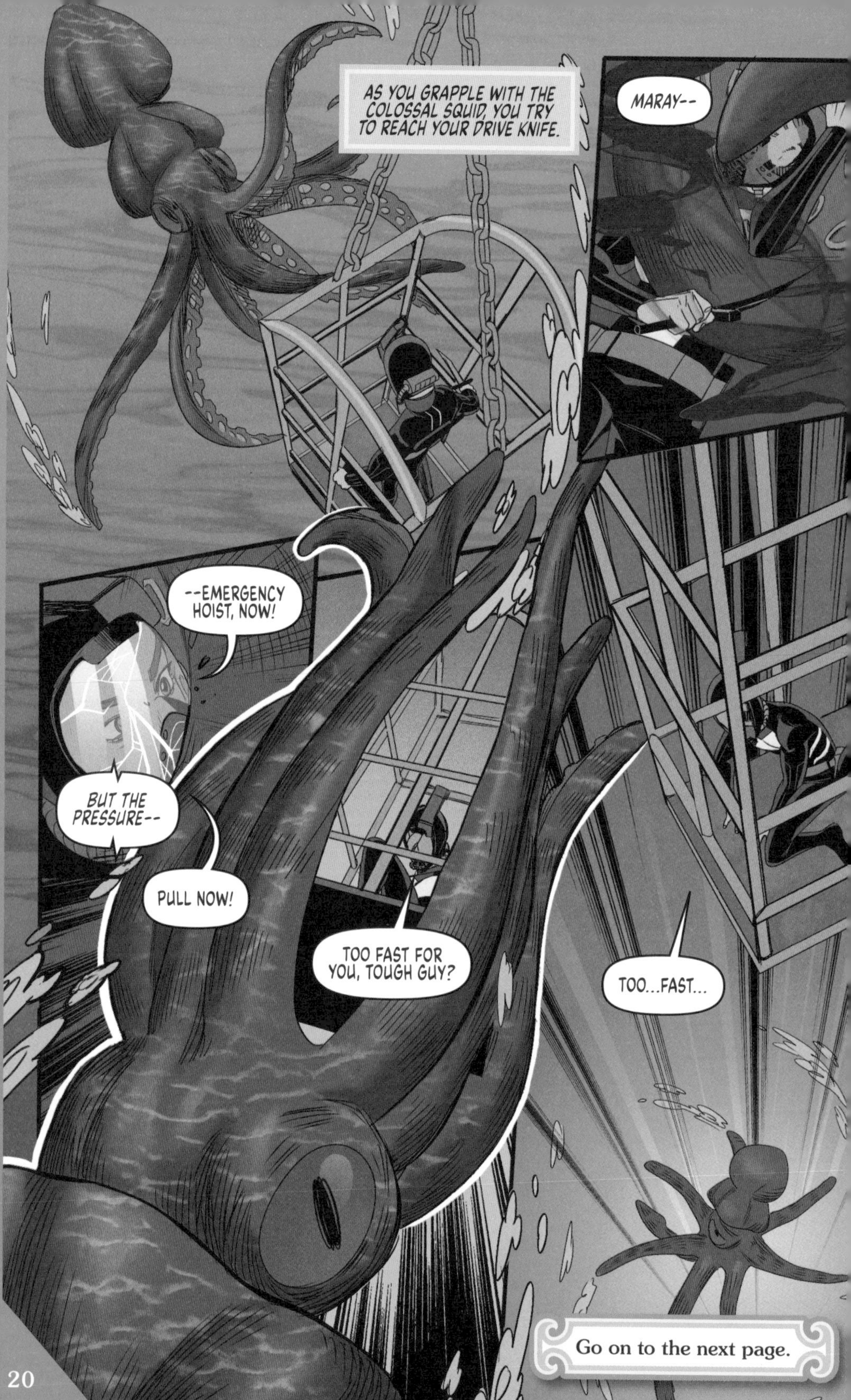
AS YOU GRAPPLE WITH THE COLOSSAL SQUID, YOU TRY TO REACH YOUR DRIVE KNIFE.
MARAY--
--EMERGENCY HOIST, NOW!
BUT THE PRESSURE--
PULL NOW!
TOO FAST FOR YOU, TOUGH GUY?
TOO...FAST...

Go on to the next page.

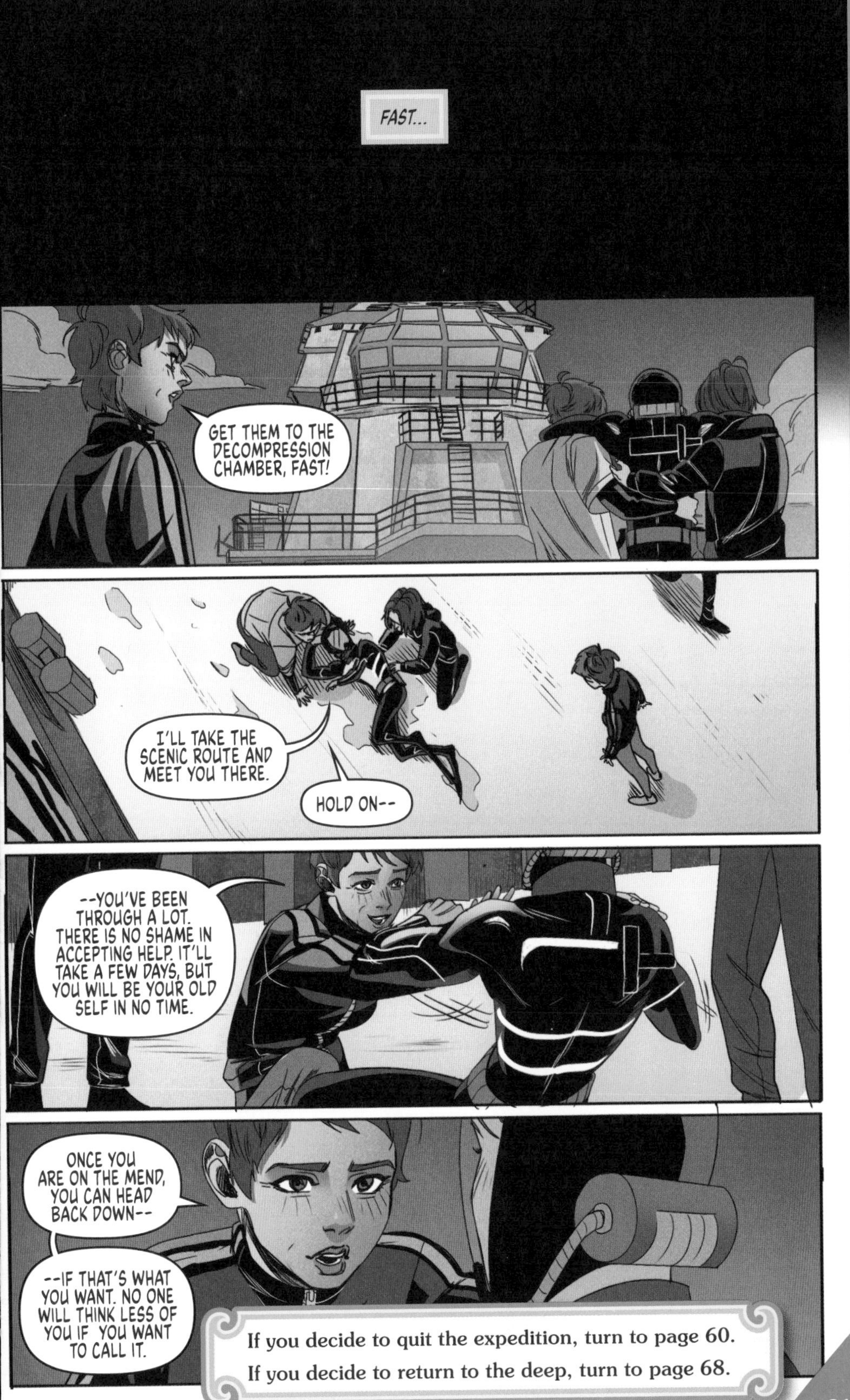
FAST...
GET THEM TO THE DECOMPRESSION CHAMBER, FAST!
I'LL TAKE THE SCENIC ROUTE AND MEET YOU THERE.
HOLD ON--
--YOU'VE BEEN THROUGH A LOT. THERE IS NO SHAME IN ACCEPTING HELP. IT'LL TAKE A FEW DAYS, BUT YOU WILL BE YOUR OLD SELF IN NO TIME.
ONCE YOU ARE ON THE MEND, YOU CAN HEAD BACK DOWN--
--IF THAT'S WHAT YOU WANT. NO ONE WILL THINK LESS OF YOU IF YOU WANT TO CALL IT.

If you decide to quit the expedition, turn to page 60.
If you decide to return to the deep, turn to page 68.

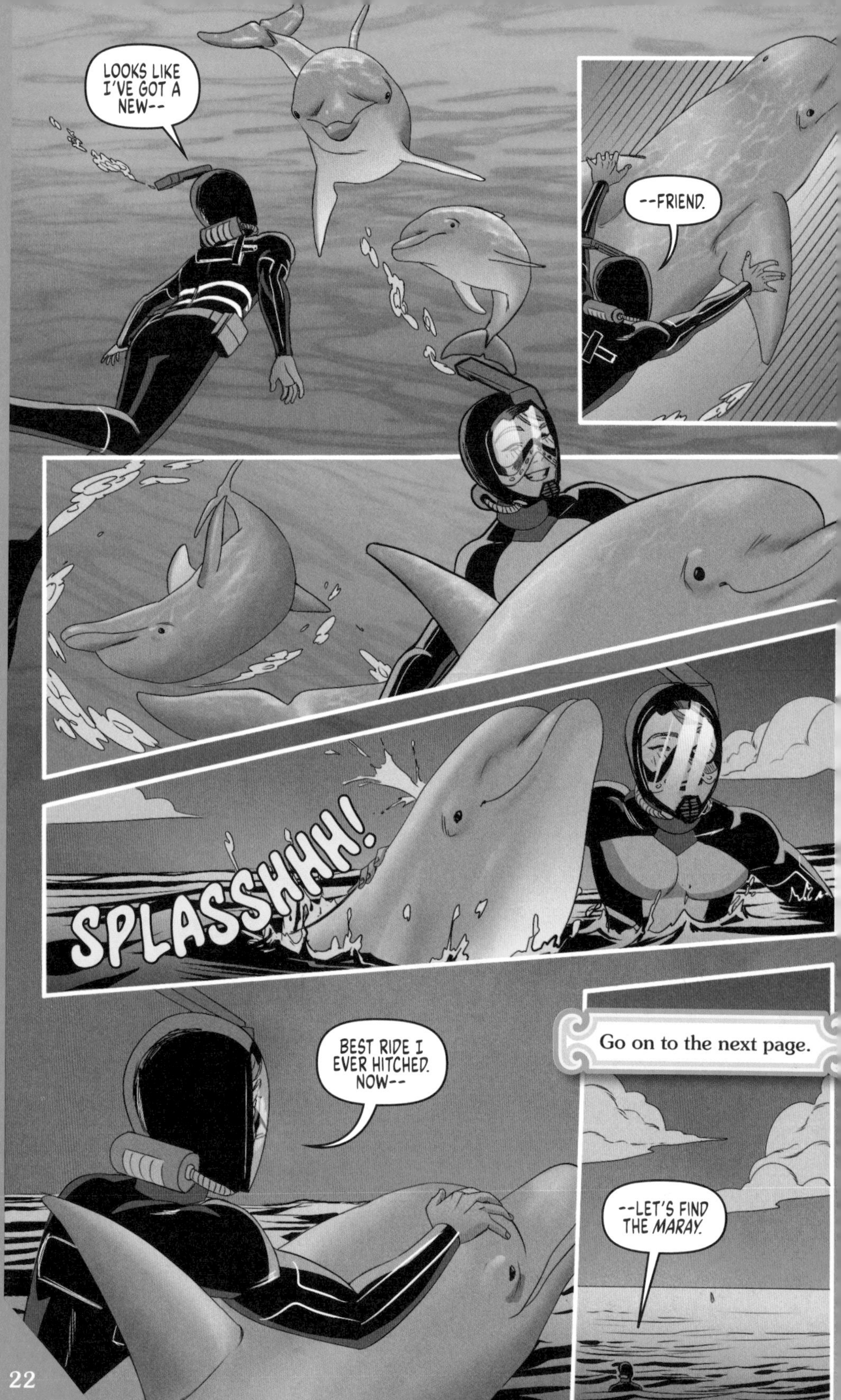
LOOKS LIKE I'VE GOT A NEW--
--FRIEND.
SPLASSHHH!
BEST RIDE I EVER HITCHED. NOW--
--LET'S FIND THE *MARAY*.

Go on to the next page.

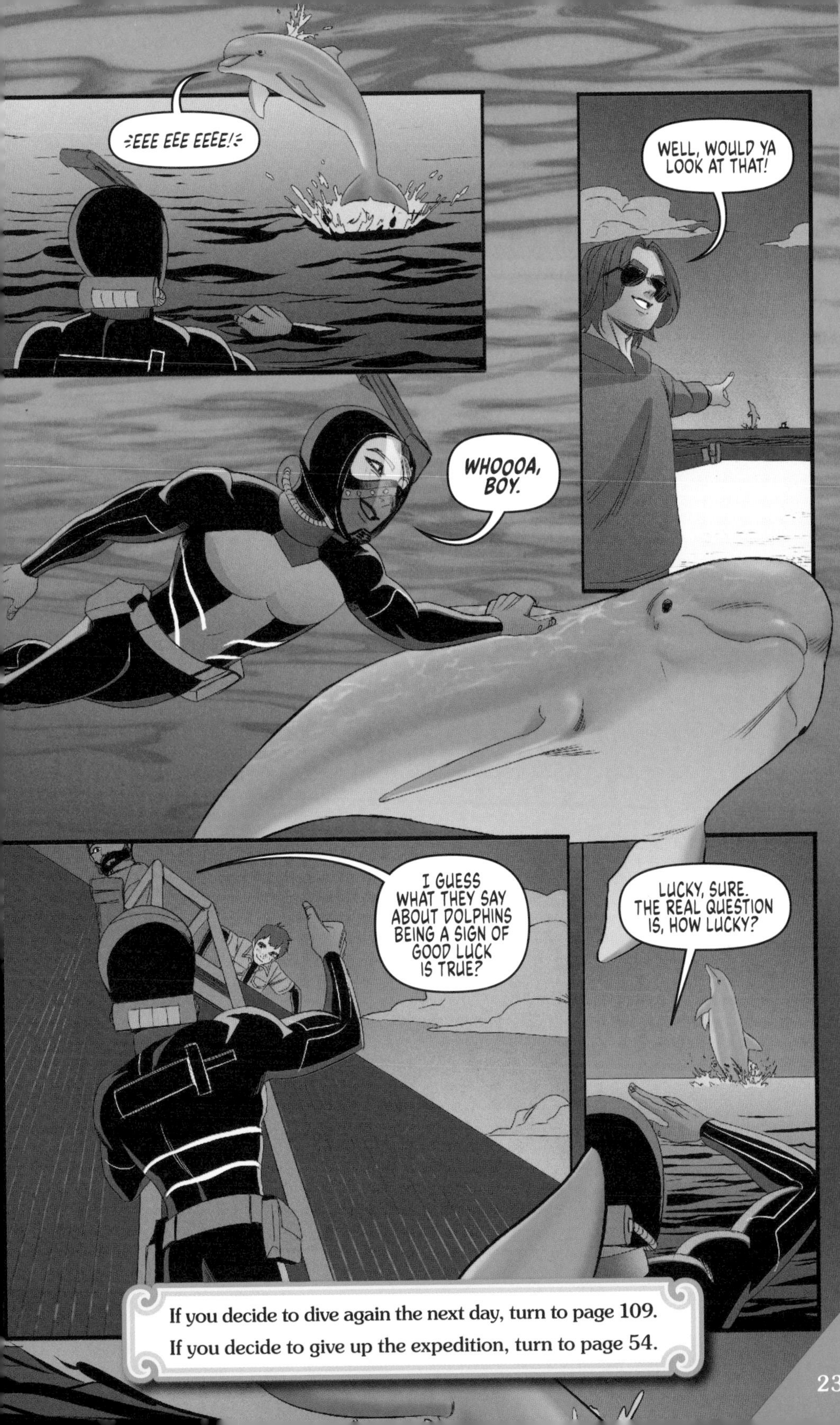
EEE EEE EEEE!
WELL, WOULD YA LOOK AT THAT!
WHOOOA, BOY.
I GUESS WHAT THEY SAY ABOUT DOLPHINS BEING A SIGN OF GOOD LUCK IS TRUE?
LUCKY, SURE. THE REAL QUESTION IS, HOW LUCKY?

If you decide to dive again the next day, turn to page 109.
If you decide to give up the expedition, turn to page 54.

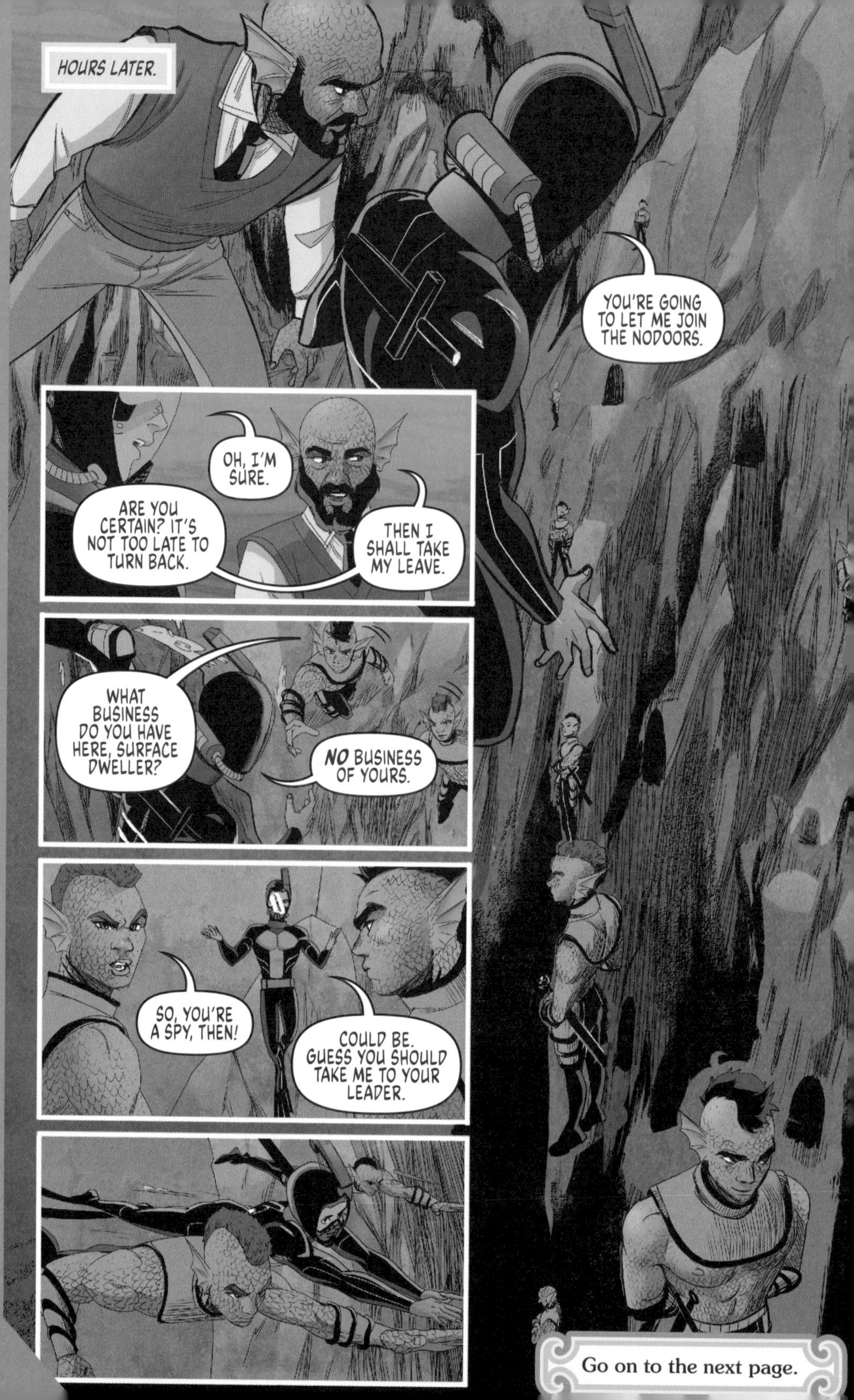
HOURS LATER.
YOU'RE GOING TO LET ME JOIN THE NODOORS.
OH, I'M SURE.
ARE YOU CERTAIN? IT'S NOT TOO LATE TO TURN BACK.
THEN I SHALL TAKE MY LEAVE.
WHAT BUSINESS DO YOU HAVE HERE, SURFACE DWELLER?
NO BUSINESS OF YOURS.
SO, YOU'RE A SPY, THEN!
COULD BE. GUESS YOU SHOULD TAKE ME TO YOUR LEADER.

Go on to the next page.

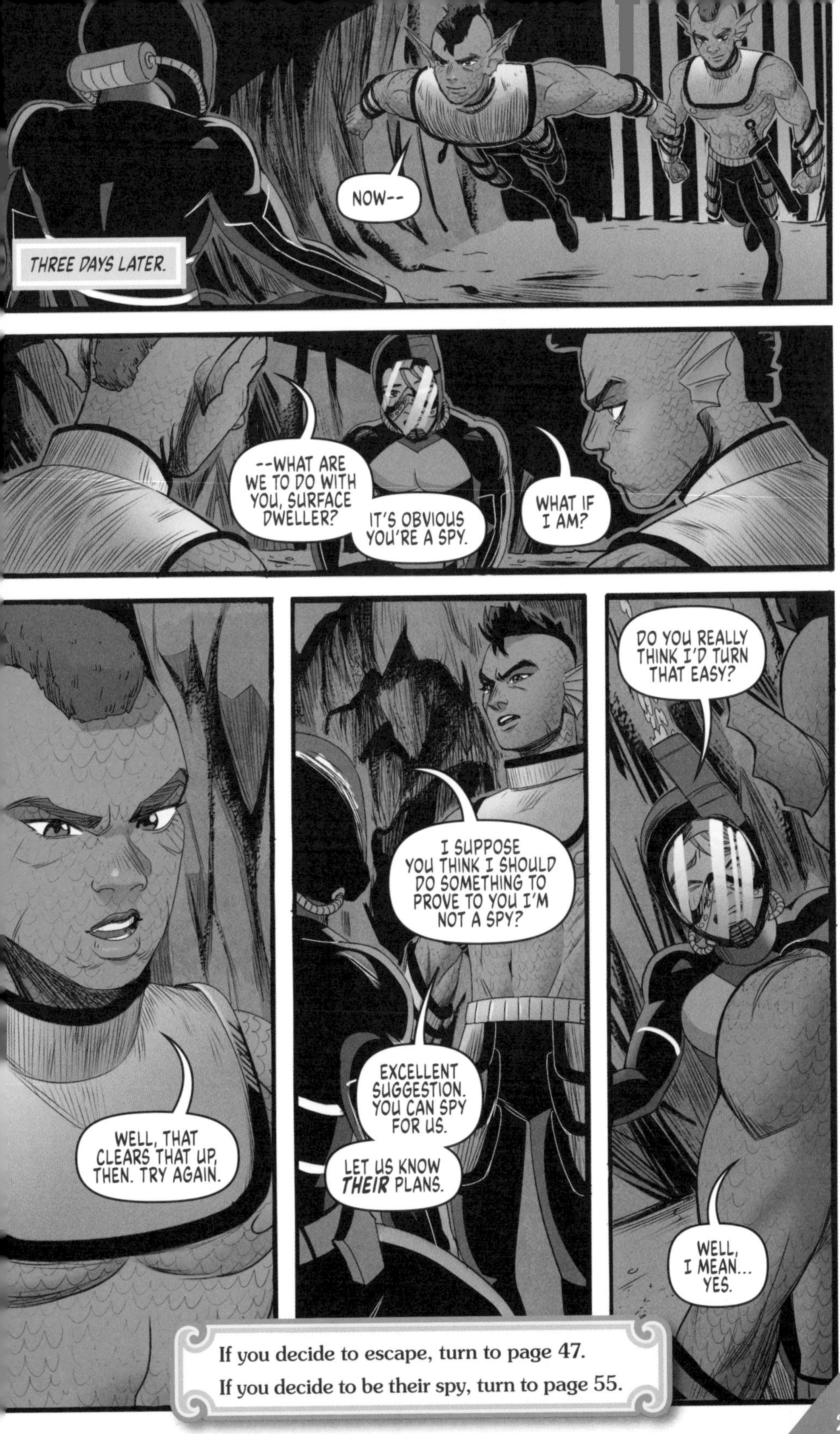

THREE DAYS LATER.
NOW--
--WHAT ARE WE TO DO WITH YOU, SURFACE DWELLER?
IT'S OBVIOUS YOU'RE A SPY.
WHAT IF I AM?
WELL, THAT CLEARS THAT UP, THEN. TRY AGAIN.
I SUPPOSE YOU THINK I SHOULD DO SOMETHING TO PROVE TO YOU I'M NOT A SPY?
EXCELLENT SUGGESTION. YOU CAN SPY FOR US.
LET US KNOW *THEIR* PLANS.
DO YOU REALLY THINK I'D TURN THAT EASY?
WELL, I MEAN... YES.

If you decide to escape, turn to page 47.

If you decide to be their spy, turn to page 55.

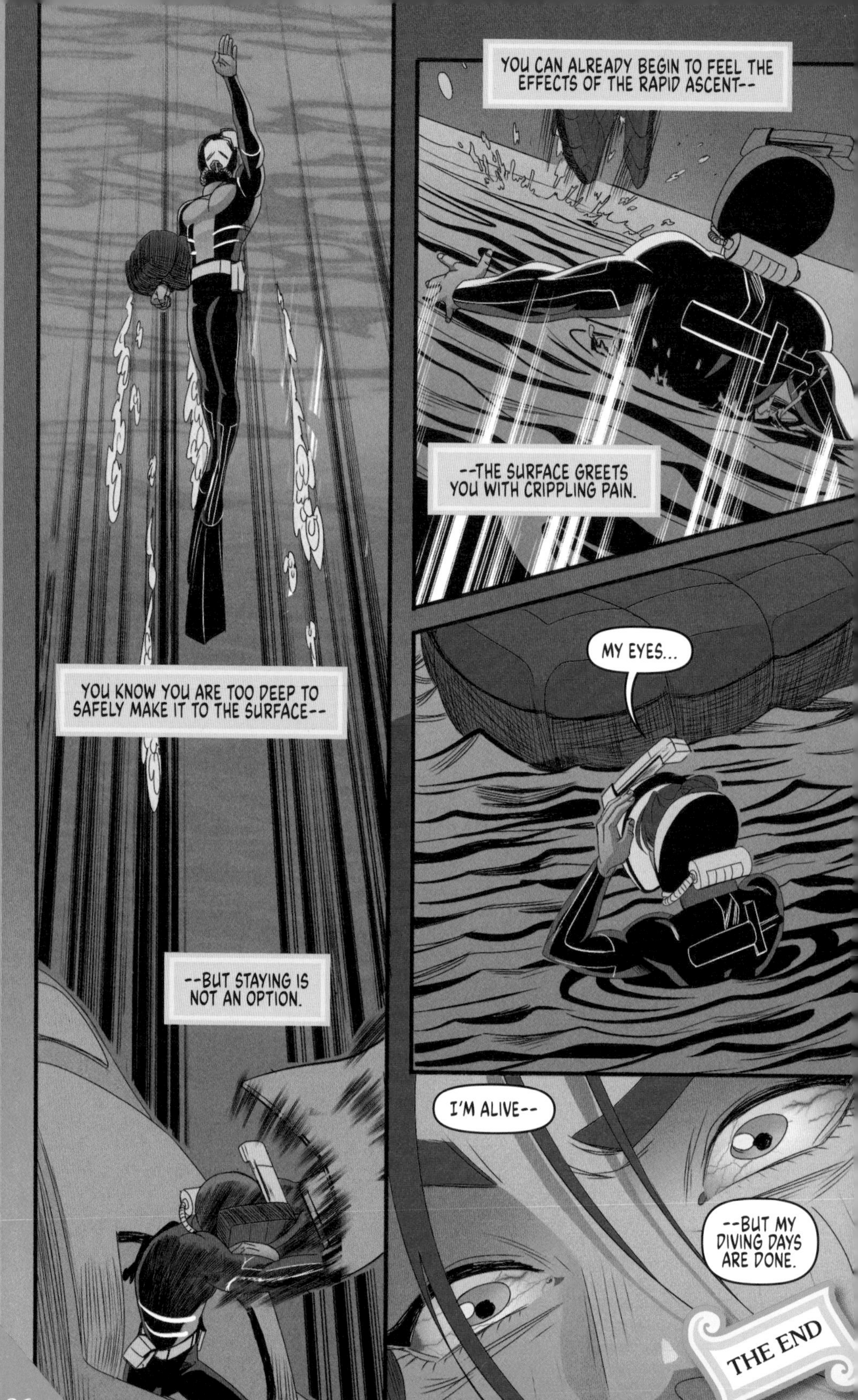
YOU KNOW YOU ARE TOO DEEP TO SAFELY MAKE IT TO THE SURFACE--
--BUT STAYING IS NOT AN OPTION.
YOU CAN ALREADY BEGIN TO FEEL THE EFFECTS OF THE RAPID ASCENT--
--THE SURFACE GREETS YOU WITH CRIPPLING PAIN.
MY EYES...
I'M ALIVE--
--BUT MY DIVING DAYS ARE DONE.
THE END

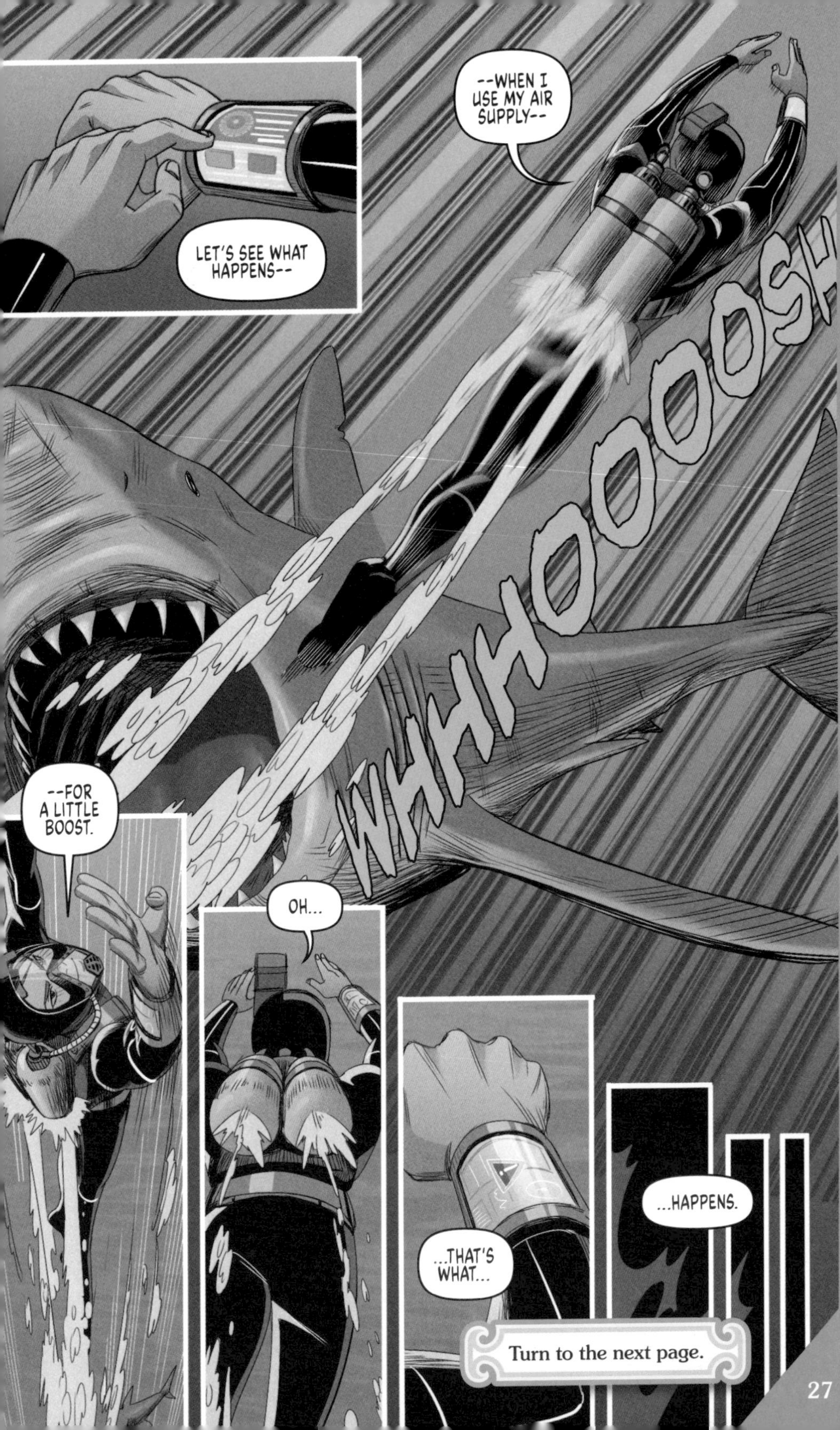
LET'S SEE WHAT HAPPENS--
--WHEN I USE MY AIR SUPPLY--
WHHHOOOOOSH
--FOR A LITTLE BOOST.
OH...
...THAT'S WHAT...
...HAPPENS.

Turn to the next page.

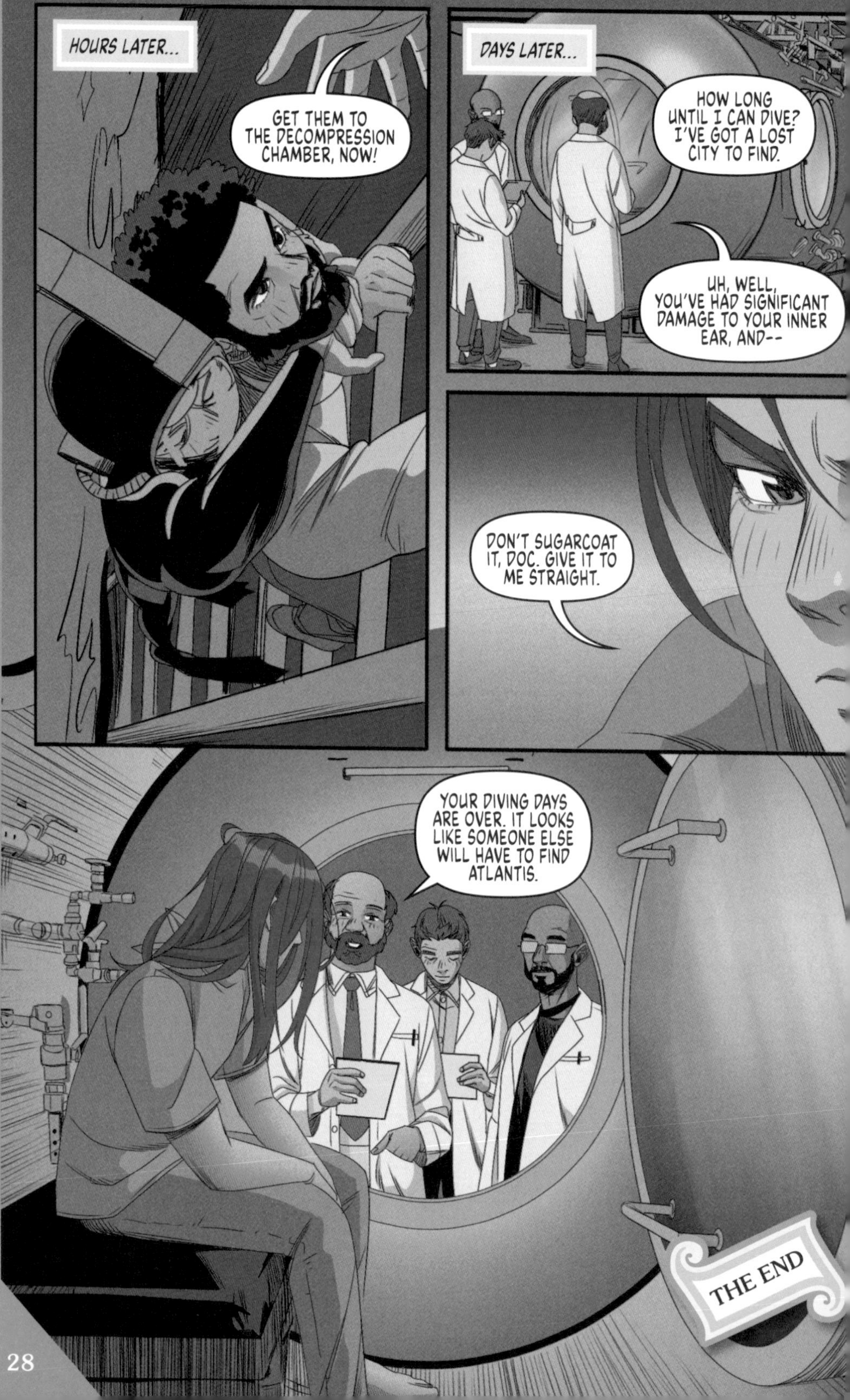
HOURS LATER...
GET THEM TO THE DECOMPRESSION CHAMBER, NOW!
DAYS LATER...
HOW LONG UNTIL I CAN DIVE? I'VE GOT A LOST CITY TO FIND.
UH, WELL, YOU'VE HAD SIGNIFICANT DAMAGE TO YOUR INNER EAR, AND--
DON'T SUGARCOAT IT, DOC. GIVE IT TO ME STRAIGHT.
YOUR DIVING DAYS ARE OVER. IT LOOKS LIKE SOMEONE ELSE WILL HAVE TO FIND ATLANTIS.
THE END

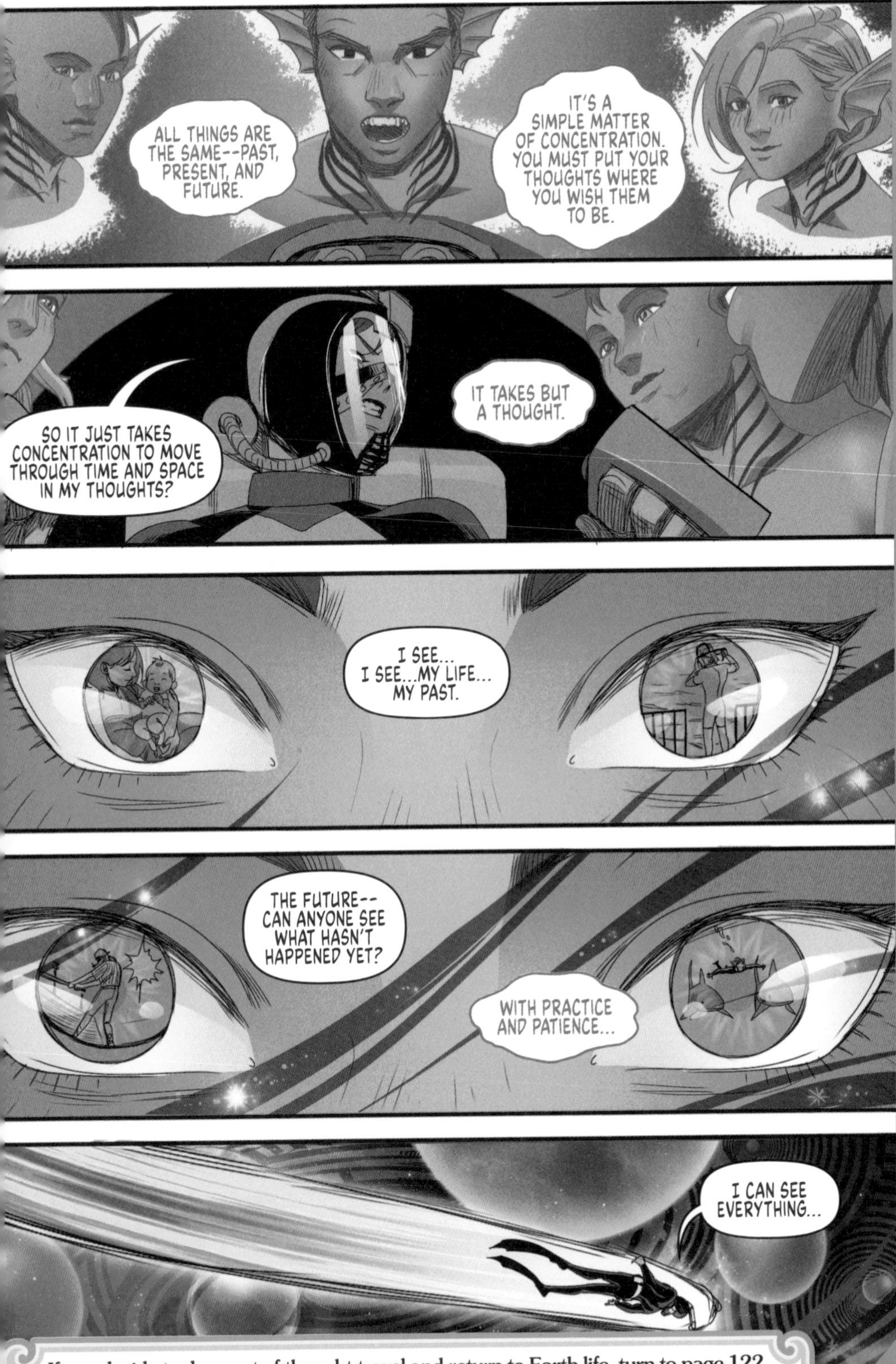
ALL THINGS ARE THE SAME--PAST, PRESENT, AND FUTURE.
IT'S A SIMPLE MATTER OF CONCENTRATION. YOU MUST PUT YOUR THOUGHTS WHERE YOU WISH THEM TO BE.
SO IT JUST TAKES CONCENTRATION TO MOVE THROUGH TIME AND SPACE IN MY THOUGHTS?
IT TAKES BUT A THOUGHT.
I SEE... I SEE...MY LIFE... MY PAST.
THE FUTURE--CAN ANYONE SEE WHAT HASN'T HAPPENED YET?
WITH PRACTICE AND PATIENCE...
I CAN SEE EVERYTHING...

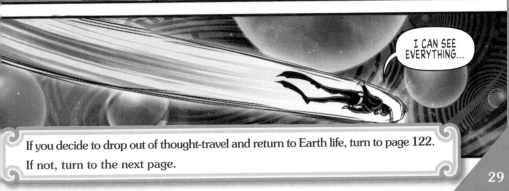

If you decide to drop out of thought-travel and return to Earth life, turn to page 122.

If not, turn to the next page.

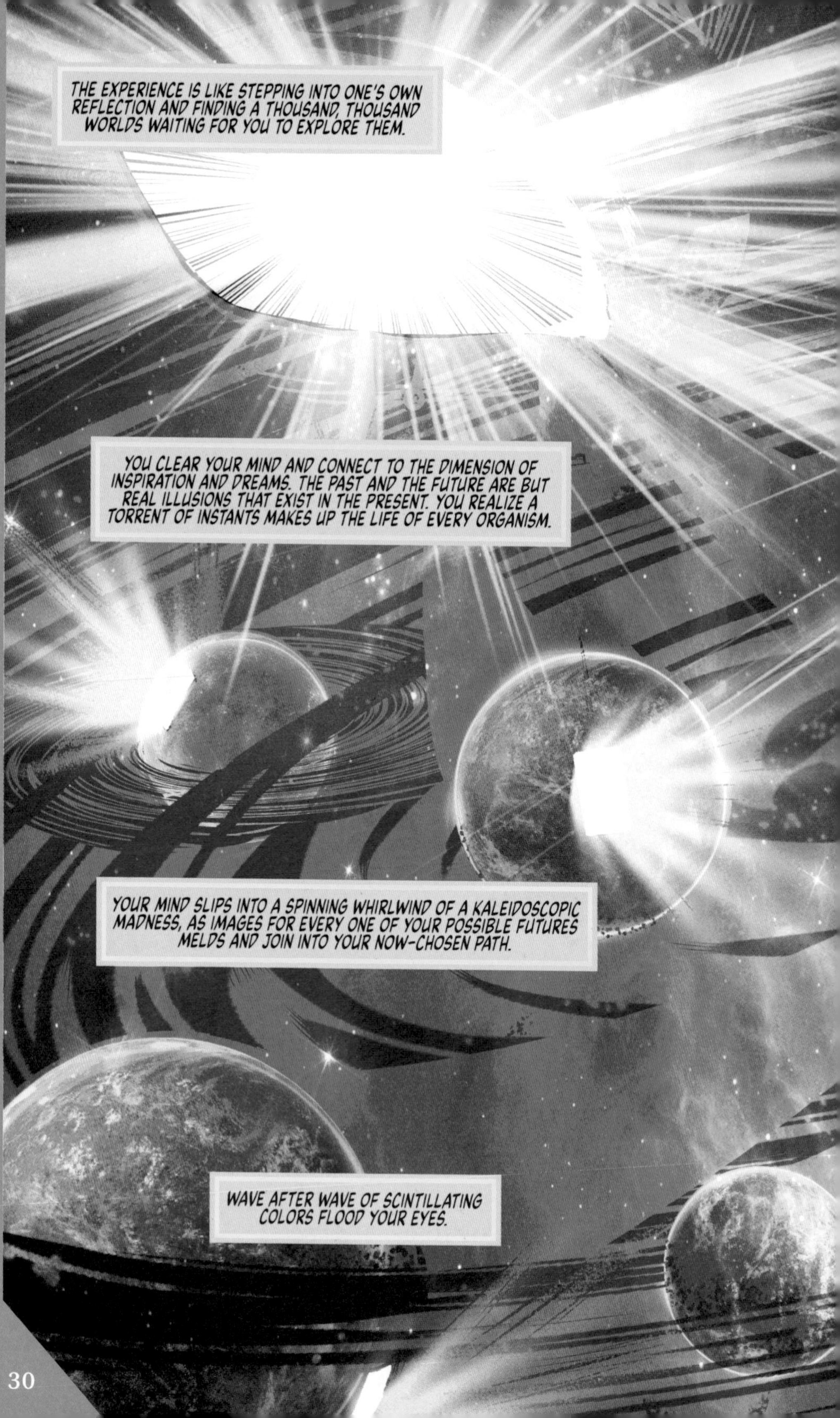
THE EXPERIENCE IS LIKE STEPPING INTO ONE'S OWN REFLECTION AND FINDING A THOUSAND, THOUSAND WORLDS WAITING FOR YOU TO EXPLORE THEM.
YOU CLEAR YOUR MIND AND CONNECT TO THE DIMENSION OF INSPIRATION AND DREAMS. THE PAST AND THE FUTURE ARE BUT REAL ILLUSIONS THAT EXIST IN THE PRESENT. YOU REALIZE A TORRENT OF INSTANTS MAKES UP THE LIFE OF EVERY ORGANISM.
YOUR MIND SLIPS INTO A SPINNING WHIRLWIND OF A KALEIDOSCOPIC MADNESS, AS IMAGES FOR EVERY ONE OF YOUR POSSIBLE FUTURES MELDS AND JOIN INTO YOUR NOW-CHOSEN PATH.
WAVE AFTER WAVE OF SCINTILLATING COLORS FLOOD YOUR EYES.

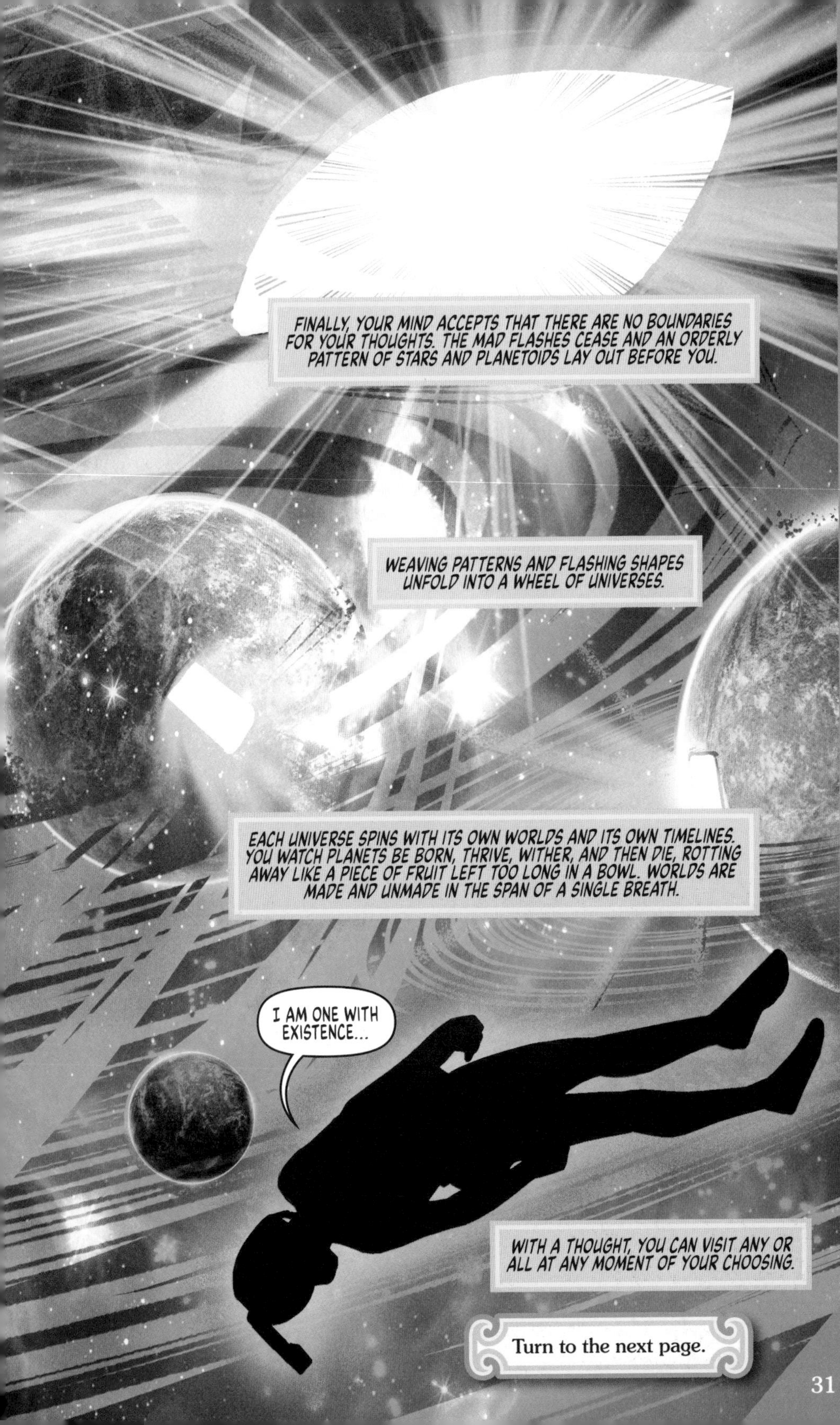
FINALLY, YOUR MIND ACCEPTS THAT THERE ARE NO BOUNDARIES FOR YOUR THOUGHTS. THE MAD FLASHES CEASE AND AN ORDERLY PATTERN OF STARS AND PLANETOIDS LAY OUT BEFORE YOU.
WEAVING PATTERNS AND FLASHING SHAPES UNFOLD INTO A WHEEL OF UNIVERSES.
EACH UNIVERSE SPINS WITH ITS OWN WORLDS AND ITS OWN TIMELINES. YOU WATCH PLANETS BE BORN, THRIVE, WITHER, AND THEN DIE, ROTTING AWAY LIKE A PIECE OF FRUIT LEFT TOO LONG IN A BOWL. WORLDS ARE MADE AND UNMADE IN THE SPAN OF A SINGLE BREATH.
I AM ONE WITH EXISTENCE...
WITH A THOUGHT, YOU CAN VISIT ANY OR ALL AT ANY MOMENT OF YOUR CHOOSING.

Turn to the next page.

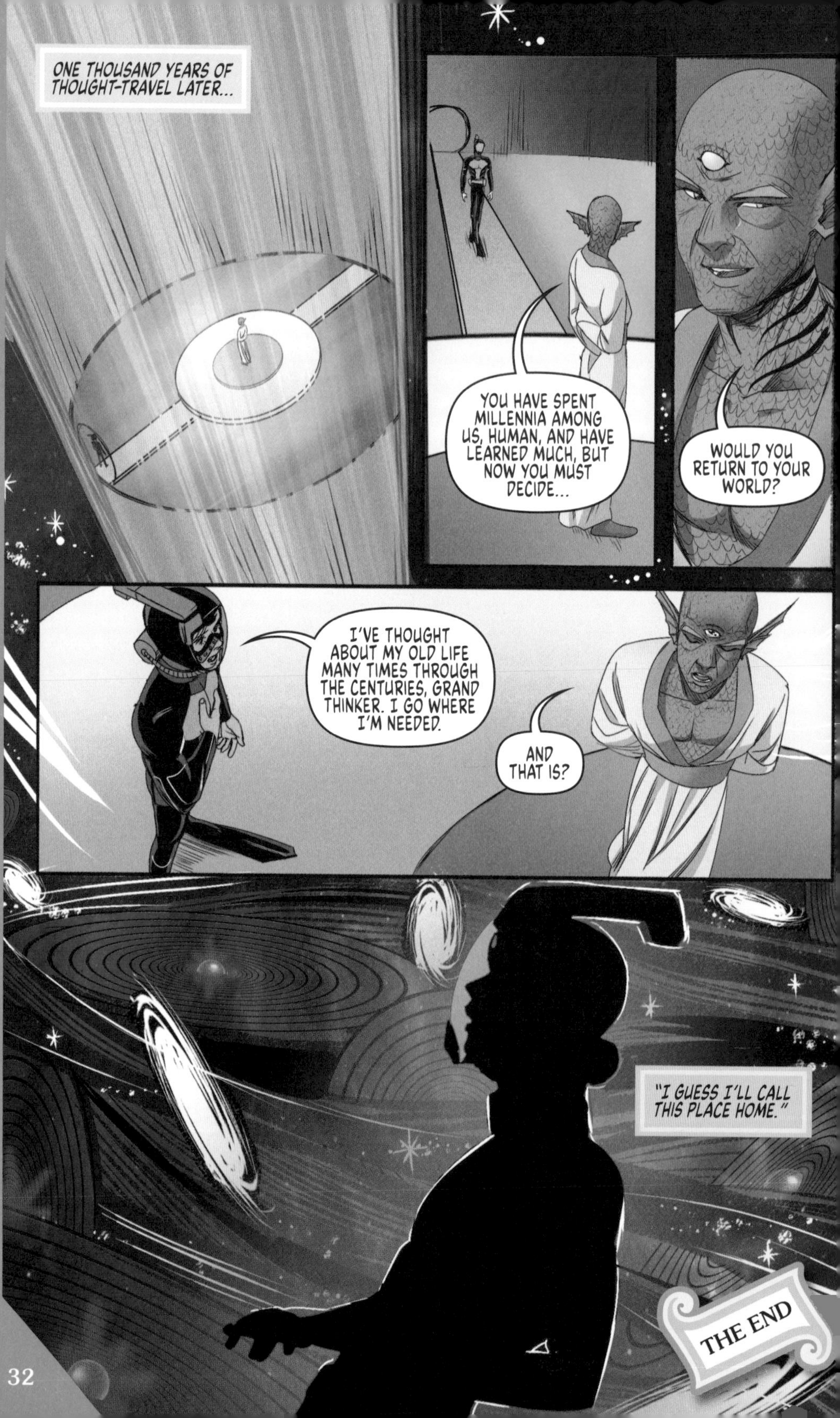
ONE THOUSAND YEARS OF THOUGHT-TRAVEL LATER...
YOU HAVE SPENT MILLENNIA AMONG US, HUMAN, AND HAVE LEARNED MUCH, BUT NOW YOU MUST DECIDE...
WOULD YOU RETURN TO YOUR WORLD?
I'VE THOUGHT ABOUT MY OLD LIFE MANY TIMES THROUGH THE CENTURIES, GRAND THINKER. I GO WHERE I'M NEEDED.
AND THAT IS?
"I GUESS I'LL CALL THIS PLACE HOME."
THE END

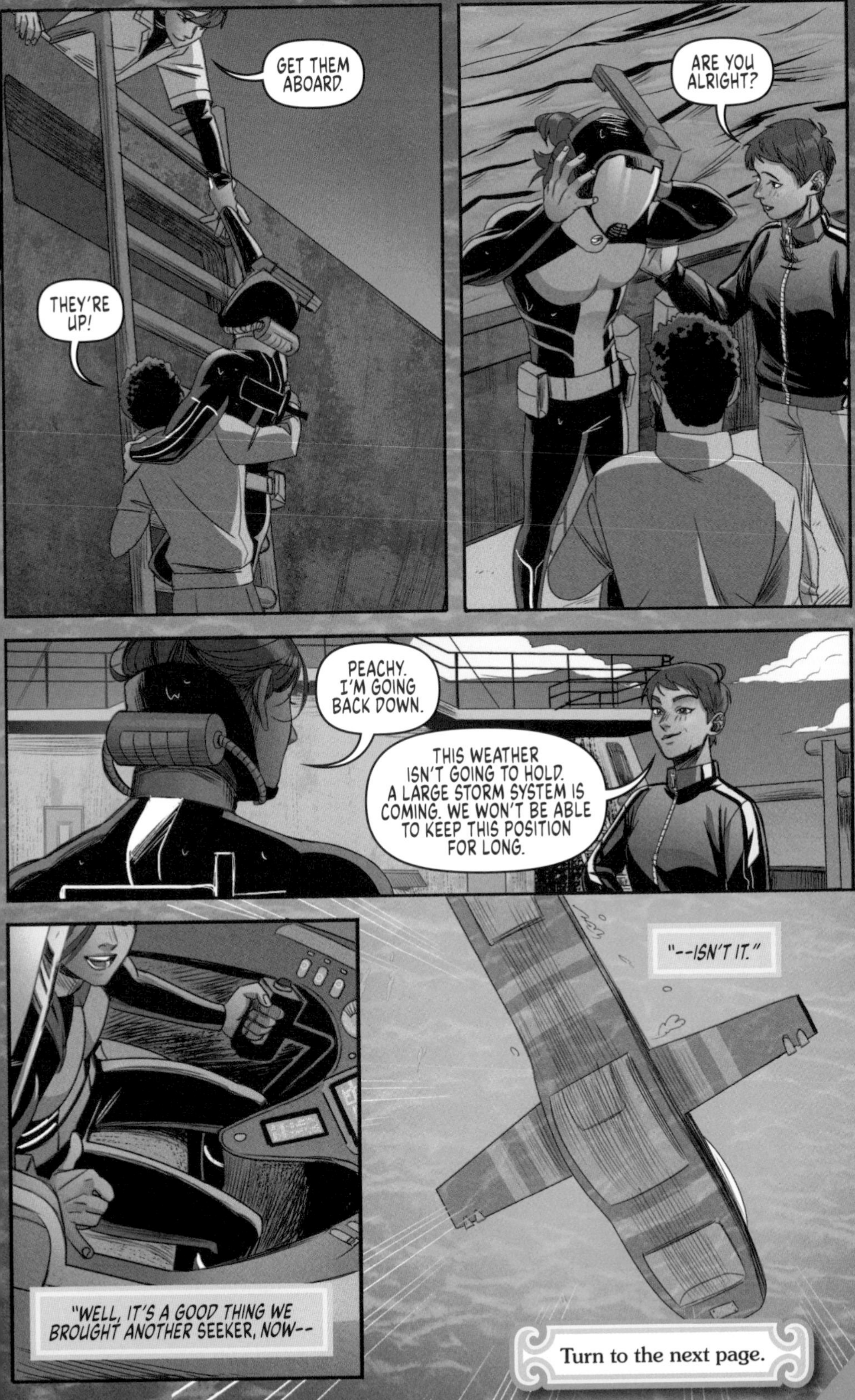
GET THEM ABOARD.
THEY'RE UP!
ARE YOU ALRIGHT?
PEACHY. I'M GOING BACK DOWN.
THIS WEATHER ISN'T GOING TO HOLD. A LARGE STORM SYSTEM IS COMING. WE WON'T BE ABLE TO KEEP THIS POSITION FOR LONG.
"WELL, IT'S A GOOD THING WE BROUGHT ANOTHER SEEKER, NOW--
"--ISN'T IT."

Turn to the next page.

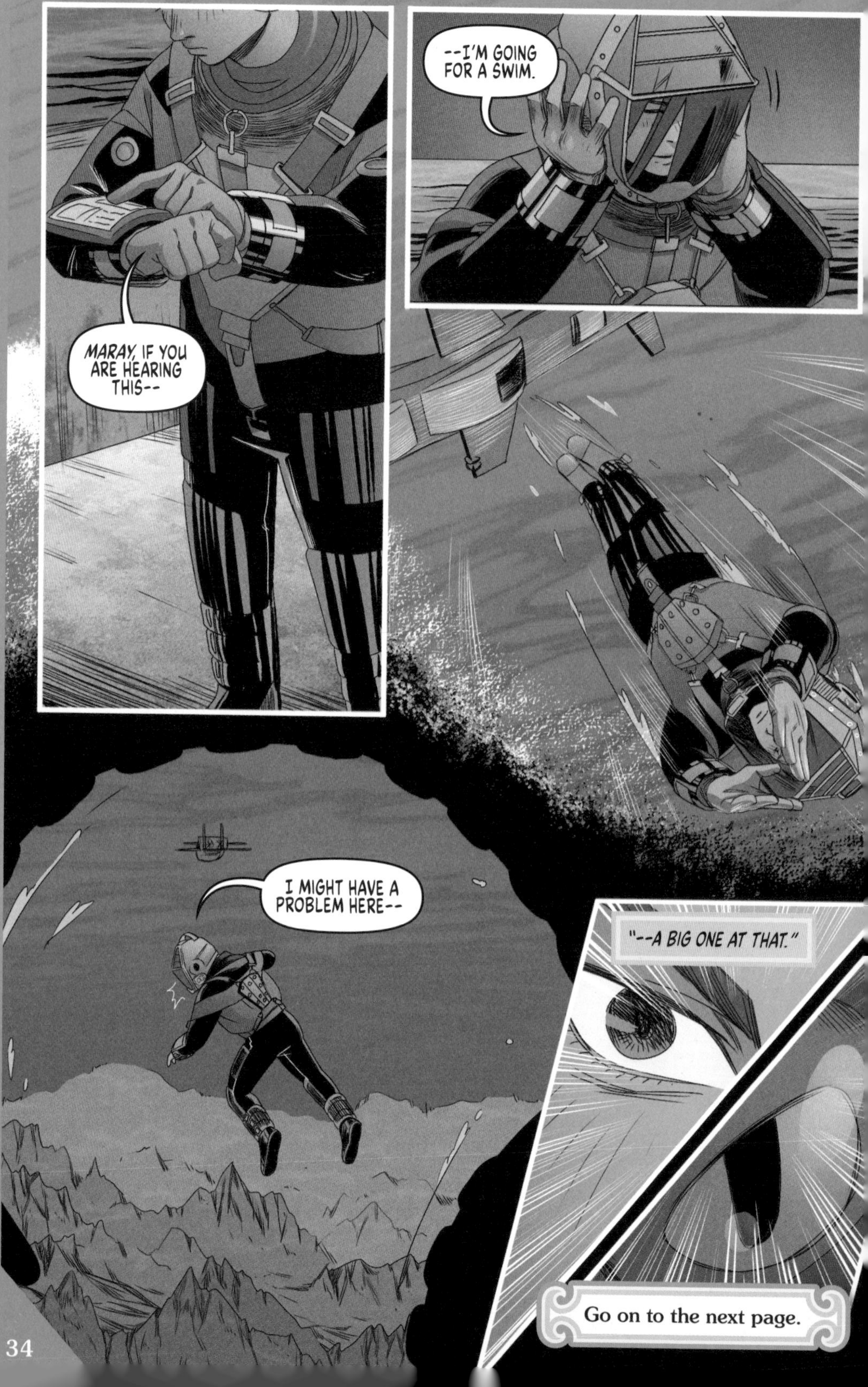
MARAY, IF YOU ARE HEARING THIS--
--I'M GOING FOR A SWIM.
I MIGHT HAVE A PROBLEM HERE--
"--A BIG ONE AT THAT."

Go on to the next page.

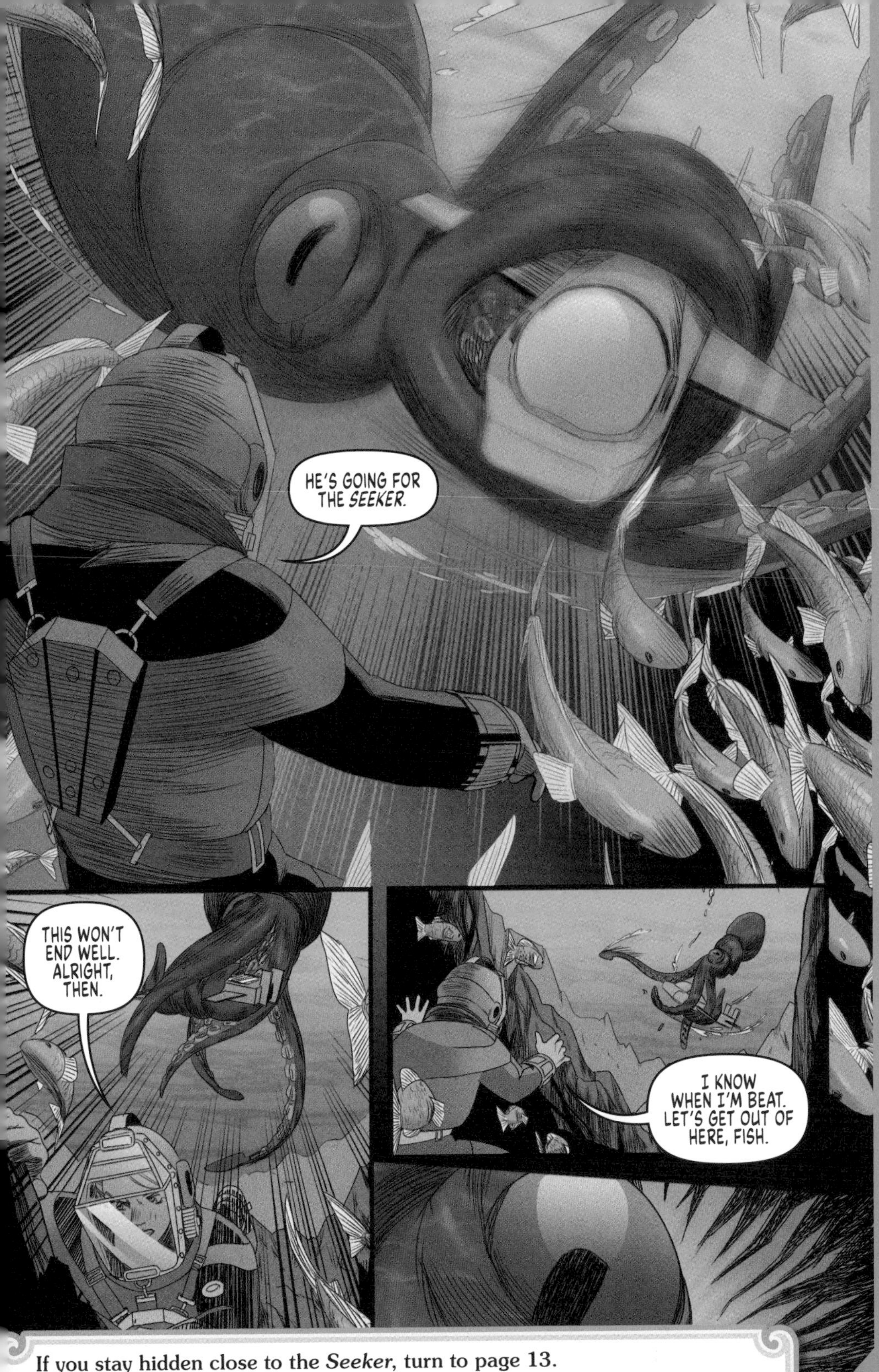
HE'S GOING FOR THE *SEEKER*.
THIS WON'T END WELL. ALRIGHT, THEN.
I KNOW WHEN I'M BEAT. LET'S GET OUT OF HERE, FISH.

If you stay hidden close to the *Seeker*, turn to page 13.

If you try for the surface in the hope that rescuers will see you, turn to page 70.

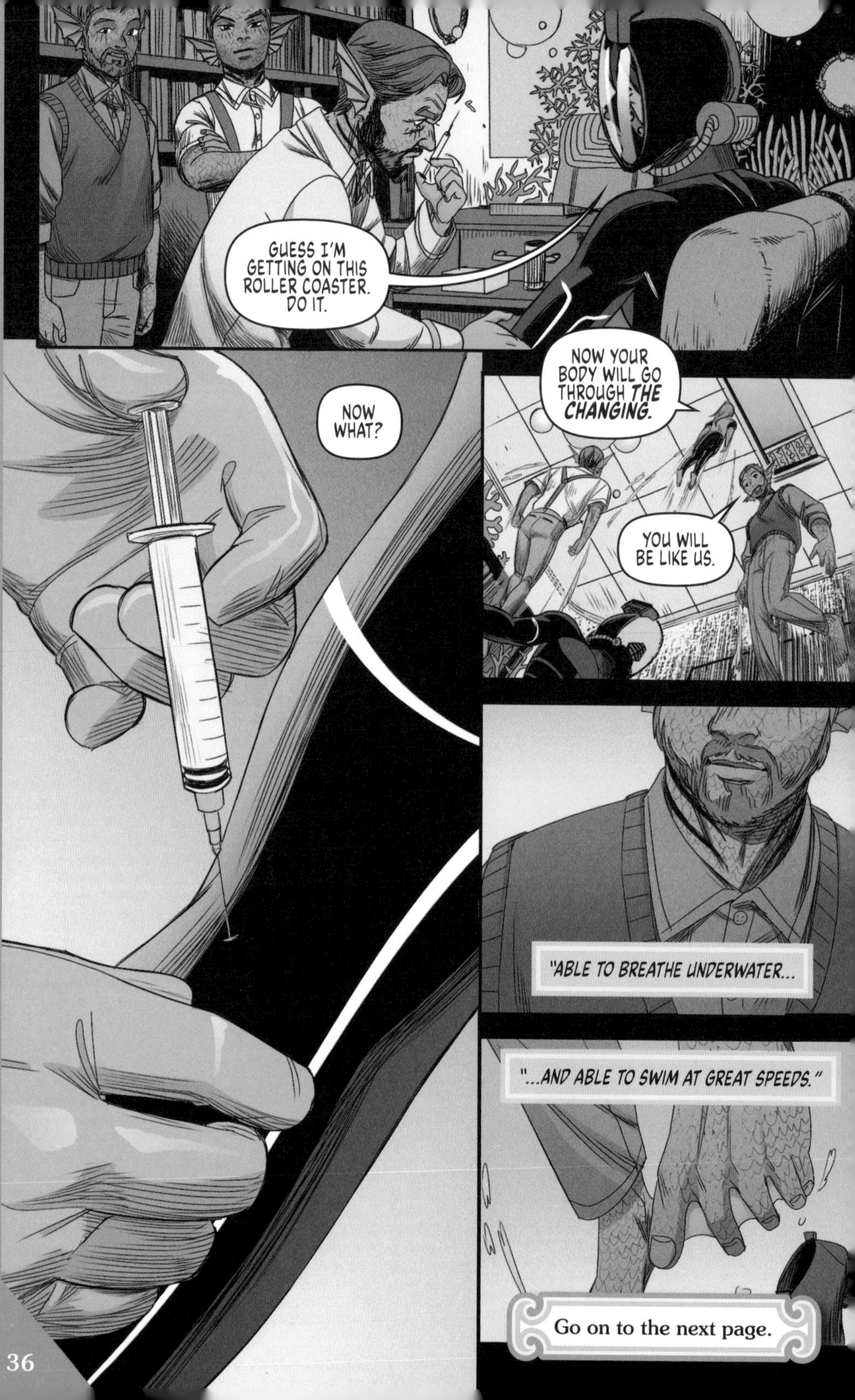
GUESS I'M GETTING ON THIS ROLLER COASTER. DO IT.
NOW WHAT?
NOW YOUR BODY WILL GO THROUGH *THE CHANGING.*
YOU WILL BE LIKE US.
"ABLE TO BREATHE UNDERWATER...
"...AND ABLE TO SWIM AT GREAT SPEEDS."
Go on to the next page.

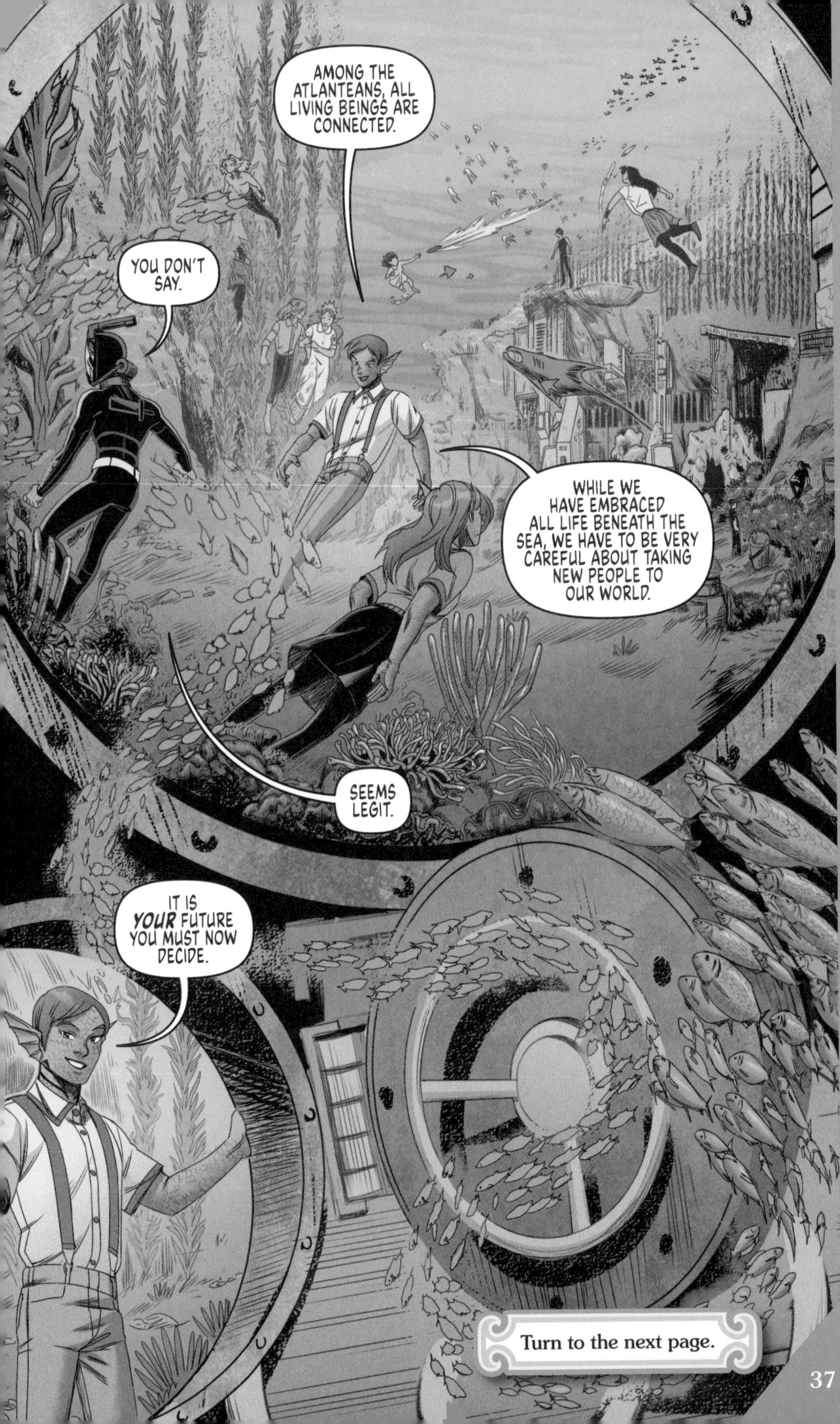
AMONG THE ATLANTEANS, ALL LIVING BEINGS ARE CONNECTED.
YOU DON'T SAY.
WHILE WE HAVE EMBRACED ALL LIFE BENEATH THE SEA, WE HAVE TO BE VERY CAREFUL ABOUT TAKING NEW PEOPLE TO OUR WORLD.
SEEMS LEGIT.
IT IS ***YOUR*** FUTURE YOU MUST NOW DECIDE.

Turn to the next page.

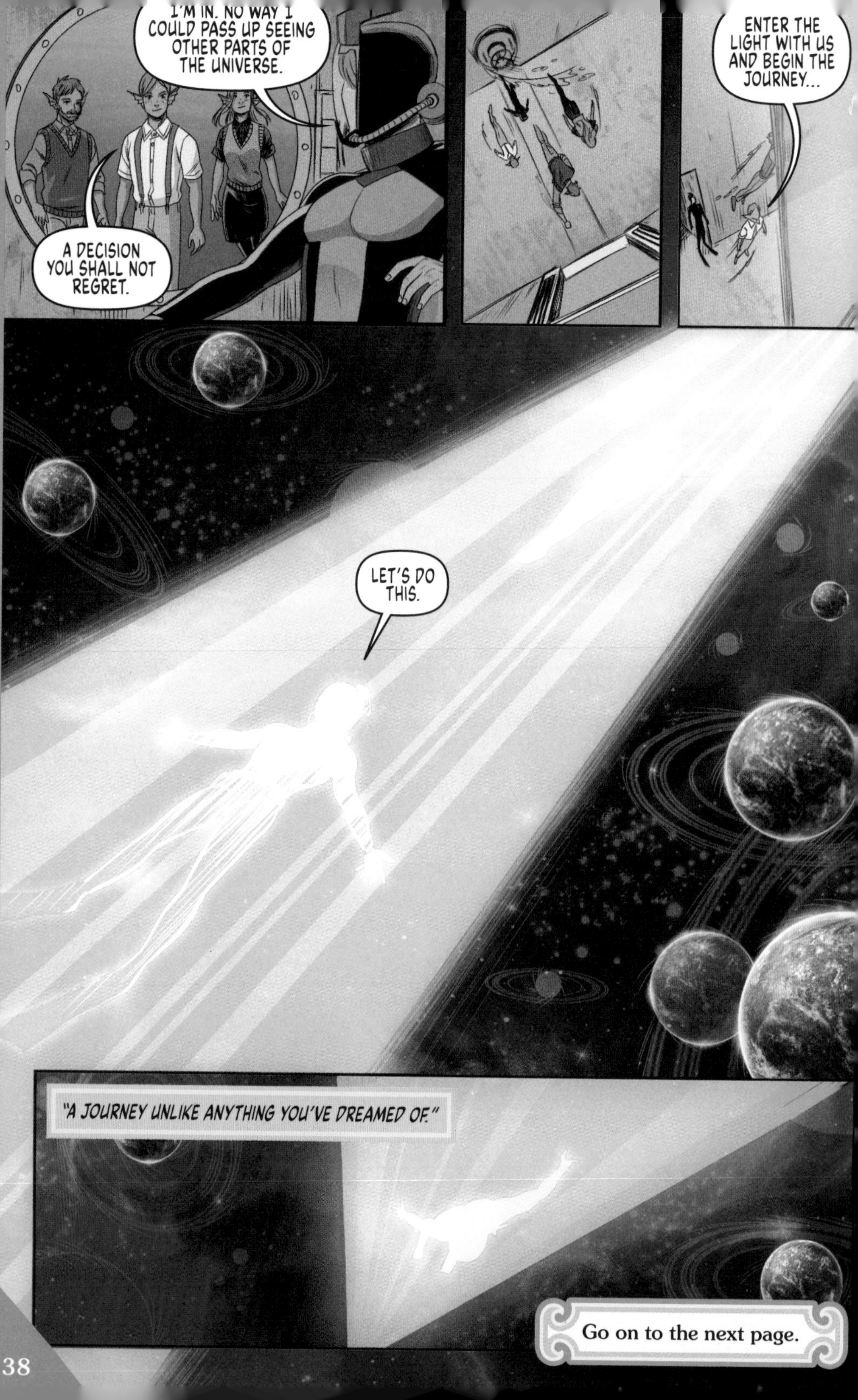
I'M IN. NO WAY I COULD PASS UP SEEING OTHER PARTS OF THE UNIVERSE.
A DECISION YOU SHALL NOT REGRET.
ENTER THE LIGHT WITH US AND BEGIN THE JOURNEY...
LET'S DO THIS.
"A JOURNEY UNLIKE ANYTHING YOU'VE DREAMED OF."

Go on to the next page.

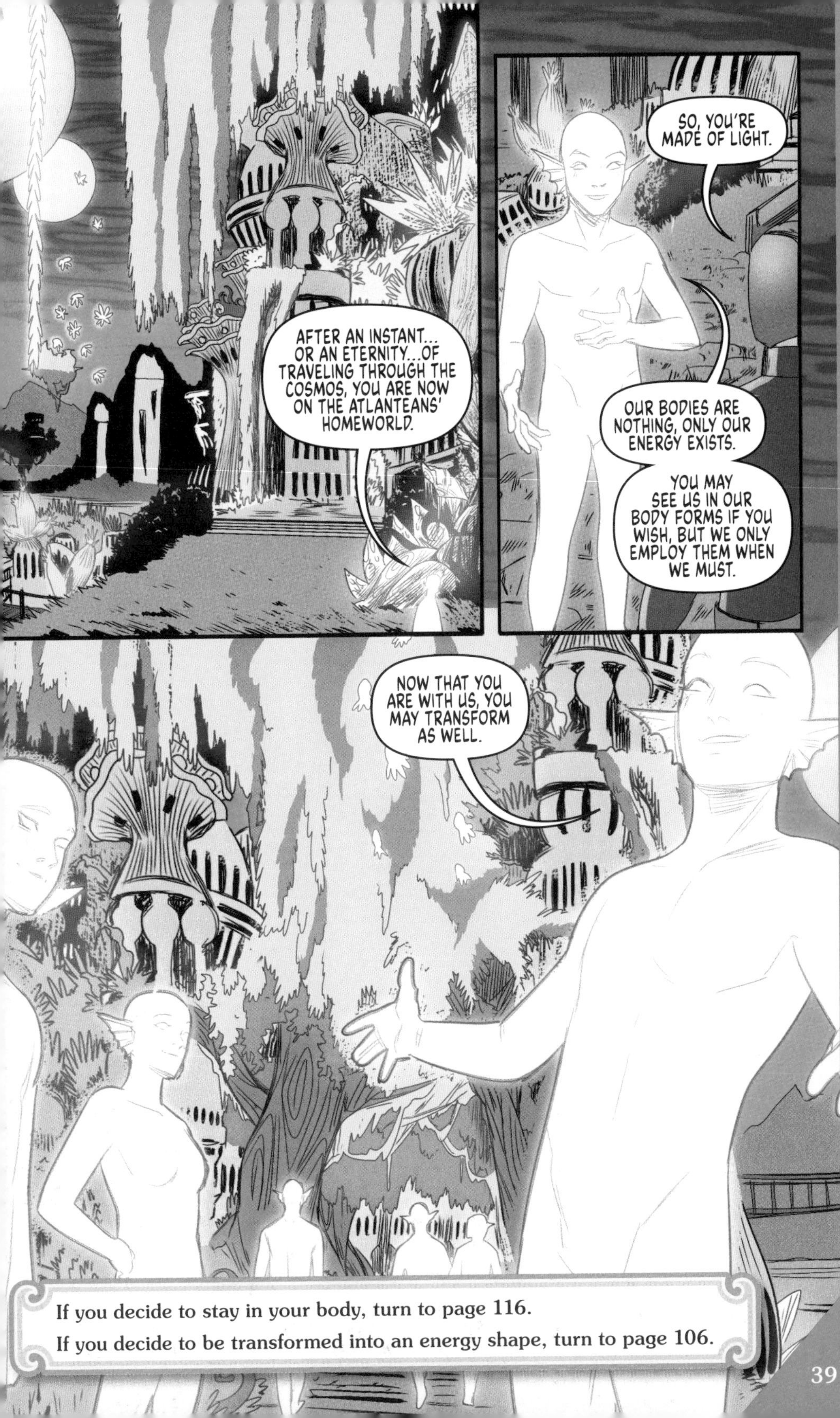
AFTER AN INSTANT... OR AN ETERNITY...OF TRAVELING THROUGH THE COSMOS, YOU ARE NOW ON THE ATLANTEANS' HOMEWORLD.
SO, YOU'RE MADE OF LIGHT.
OUR BODIES ARE NOTHING, ONLY OUR ENERGY EXISTS.
YOU MAY SEE US IN OUR BODY FORMS IF YOU WISH, BUT WE ONLY EMPLOY THEM WHEN WE MUST.
NOW THAT YOU ARE WITH US, YOU MAY TRANSFORM AS WELL.

If you decide to stay in your body, turn to page 116.
If you decide to be transformed into an energy shape, turn to page 106.

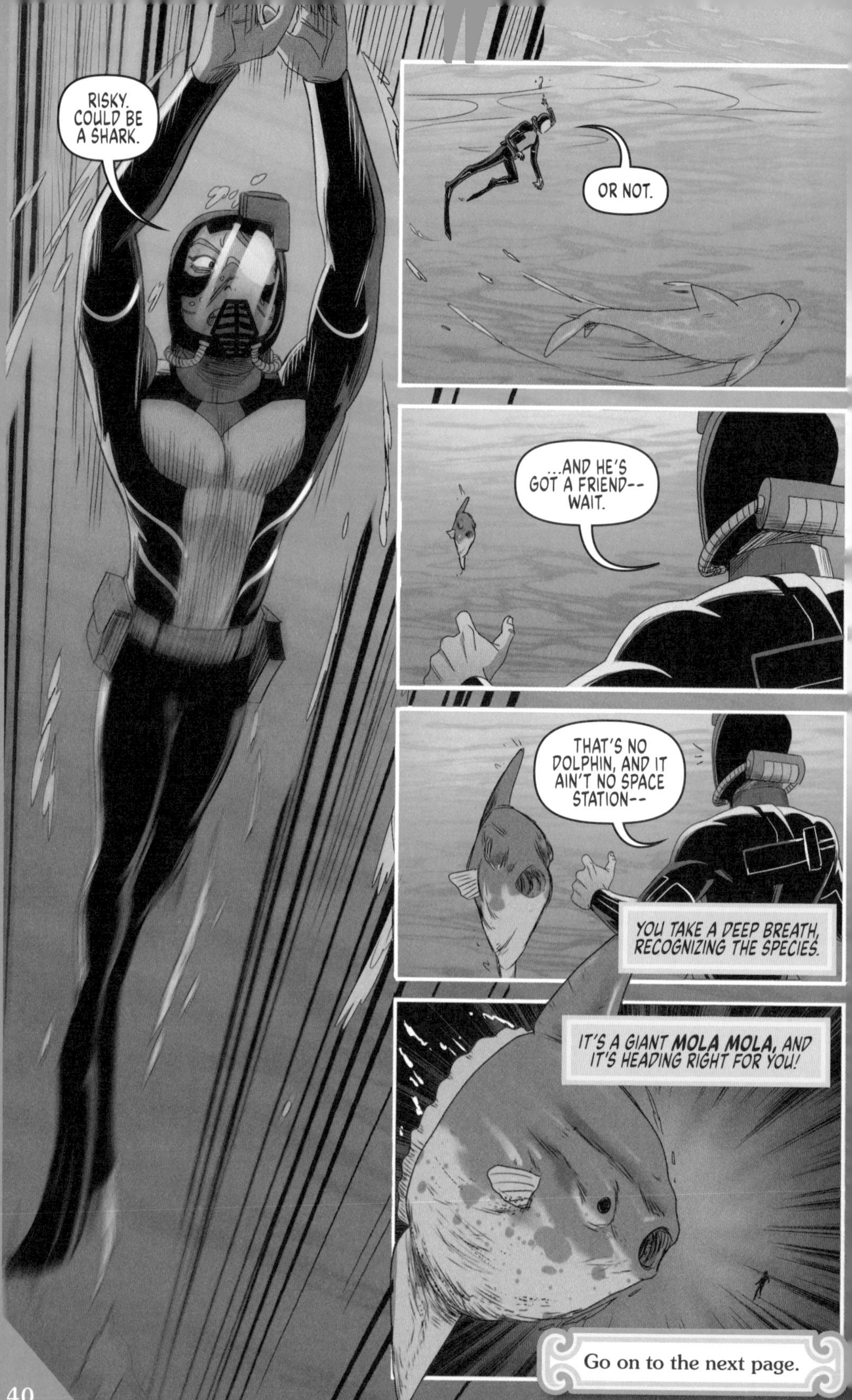
RISKY. COULD BE A SHARK.
OR NOT.
...AND HE'S GOT A FRIEND-- WAIT.
THAT'S NO DOLPHIN, AND IT AIN'T NO SPACE STATION--
YOU TAKE A DEEP BREATH, RECOGNIZING THE SPECIES.
IT'S A GIANT **MOLA MOLA,** AND IT'S HEADING RIGHT FOR YOU!
Go on to the next page.

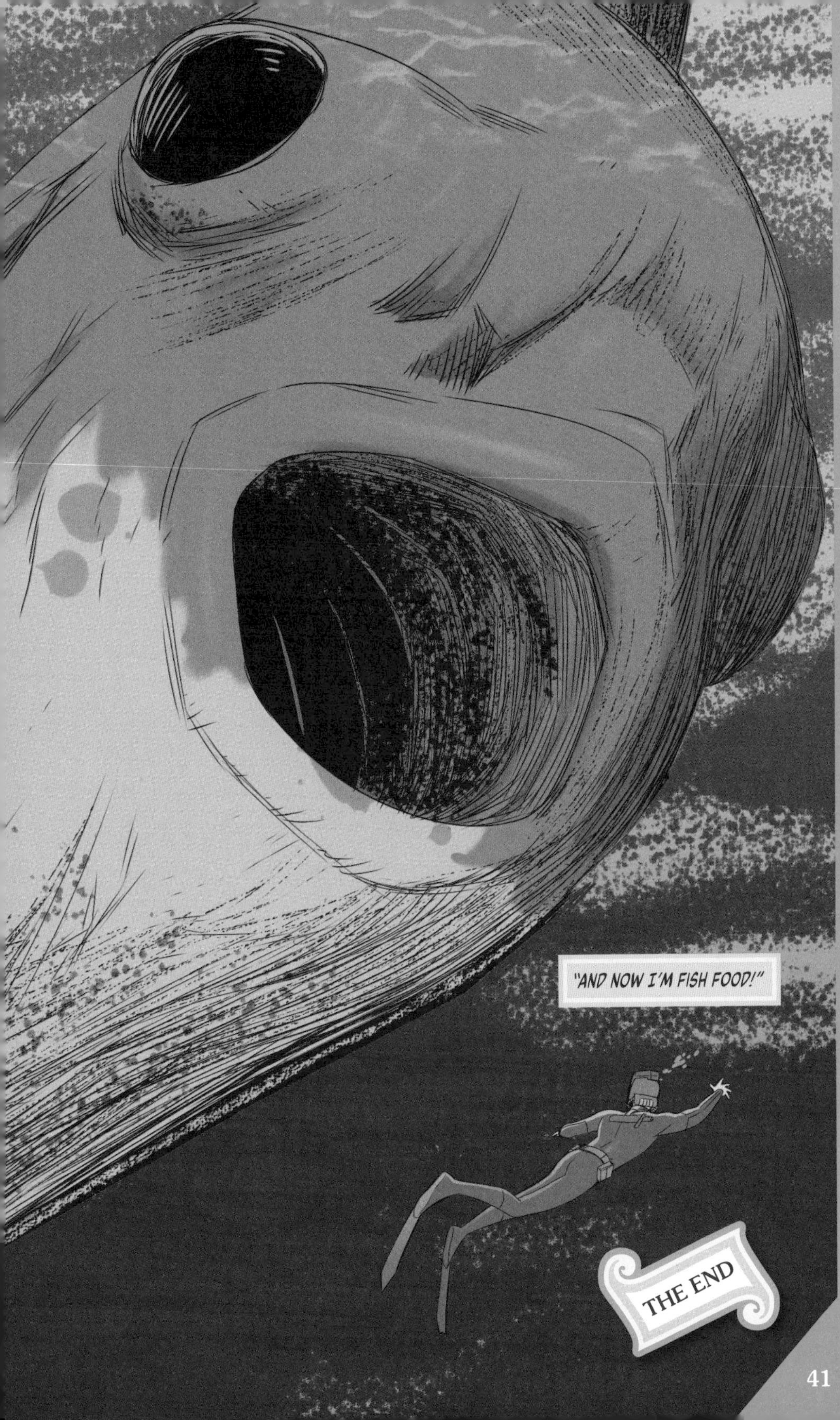
"AND NOW I'M FISH FOOD!"
THE END

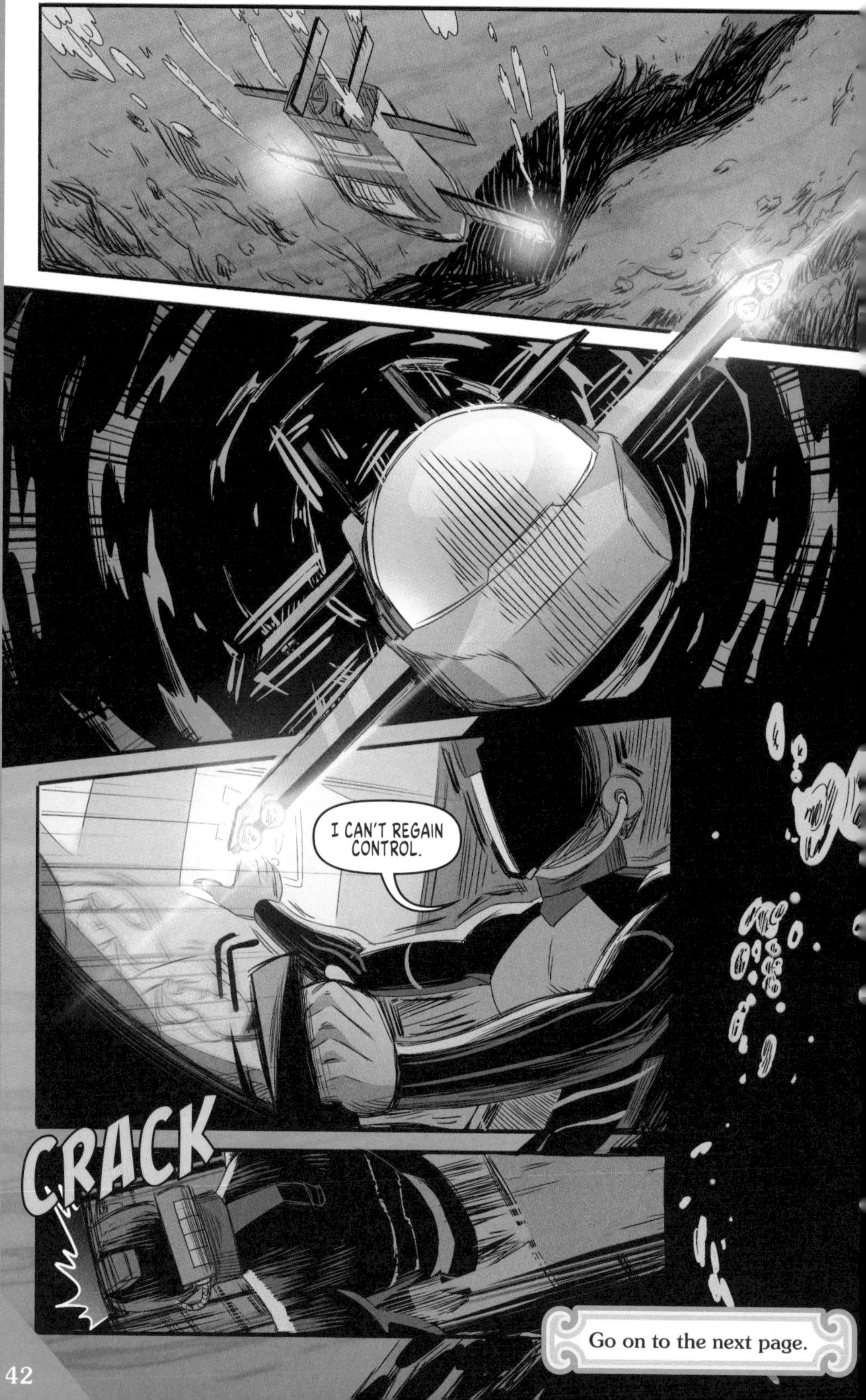
I CAN'T REGAIN CONTROL.
CRACK

Go on to the next page.

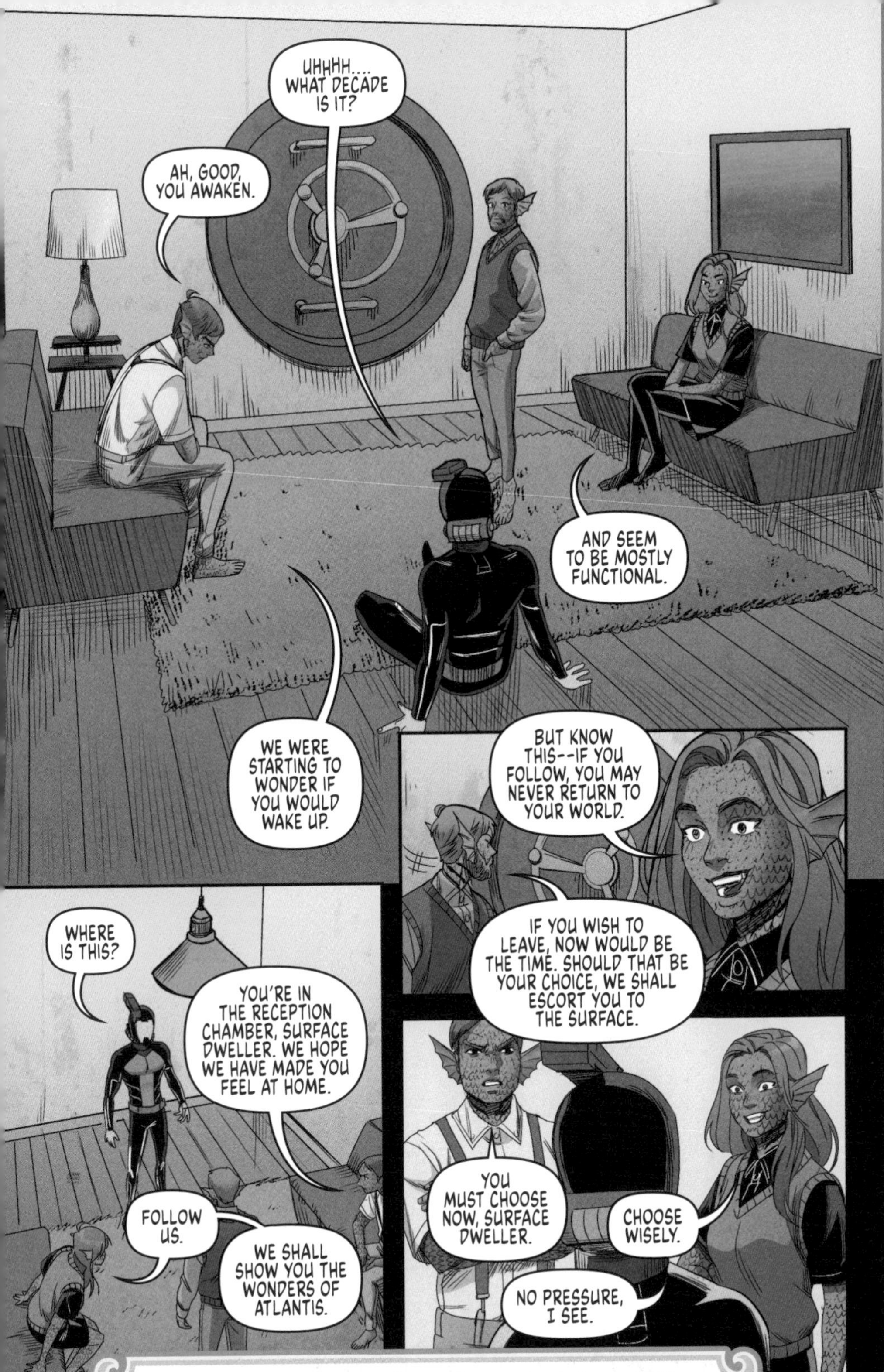
AH, GOOD, YOU AWAKEN.
AND SEEM TO BE MOSTLY FUNCTIONAL.
WE WERE STARTING TO WONDER IF YOU WOULD WAKE UP.
UHHHH.... WHAT DECADE IS IT?
WHERE IS THIS?
YOU'RE IN THE RECEPTION CHAMBER, SURFACE DWELLER. WE HOPE WE HAVE MADE YOU FEEL AT HOME.
FOLLOW US.
WE SHALL SHOW YOU THE WONDERS OF ATLANTIS.
BUT KNOW THIS--IF YOU FOLLOW, YOU MAY NEVER RETURN TO YOUR WORLD.
IF YOU WISH TO LEAVE, NOW WOULD BE THE TIME. SHOULD THAT BE YOUR CHOICE, WE SHALL ESCORT YOU TO THE SURFACE.
YOU MUST CHOOSE NOW, SURFACE DWELLER.
CHOOSE WISELY.
NO PRESSURE, I SEE.

If you decide to return to the surface, turn to page 124.
If you follow them into the city of Atlantis, turn to page 64.

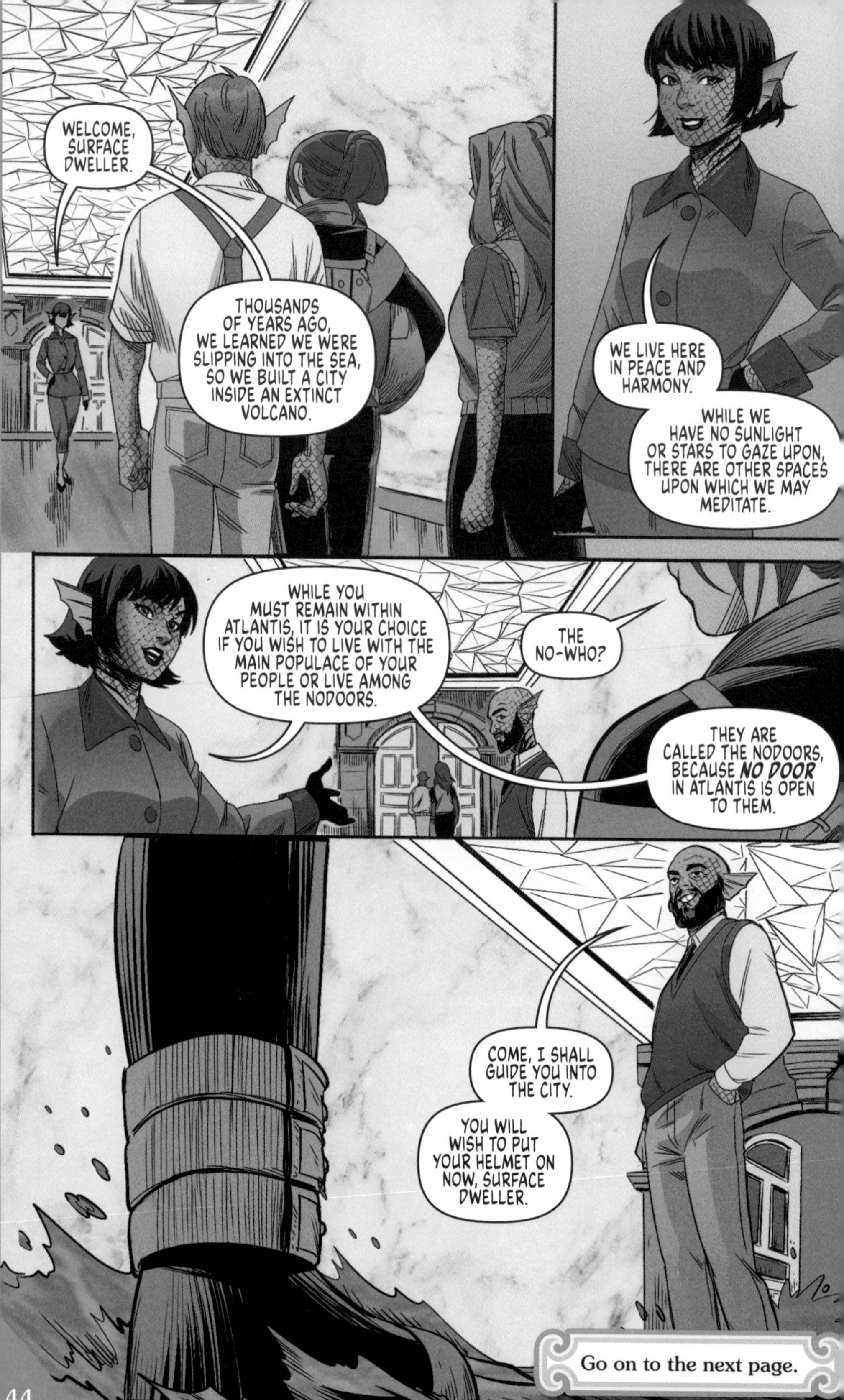
WELCOME, SURFACE DWELLER.
THOUSANDS OF YEARS AGO, WE LEARNED WE WERE SLIPPING INTO THE SEA, SO WE BUILT A CITY INSIDE AN EXTINCT VOLCANO.
WE LIVE HERE IN PEACE AND HARMONY.
WHILE WE HAVE NO SUNLIGHT OR STARS TO GAZE UPON, THERE ARE OTHER SPACES UPON WHICH WE MAY MEDITATE.
WHILE YOU MUST REMAIN WITHIN ATLANTIS, IT IS YOUR CHOICE IF YOU WISH TO LIVE WITH THE MAIN POPULACE OF YOUR PEOPLE OR LIVE AMONG THE NODOORS.
THE NO-WHO?
THEY ARE CALLED THE NODOORS, BECAUSE ***NO DOOR*** IN ATLANTIS IS OPEN TO THEM.
COME, I SHALL GUIDE YOU INTO THE CITY.
YOU WILL WISH TO PUT YOUR HELMET ON NOW, SURFACE DWELLER.

Go on to the next page.

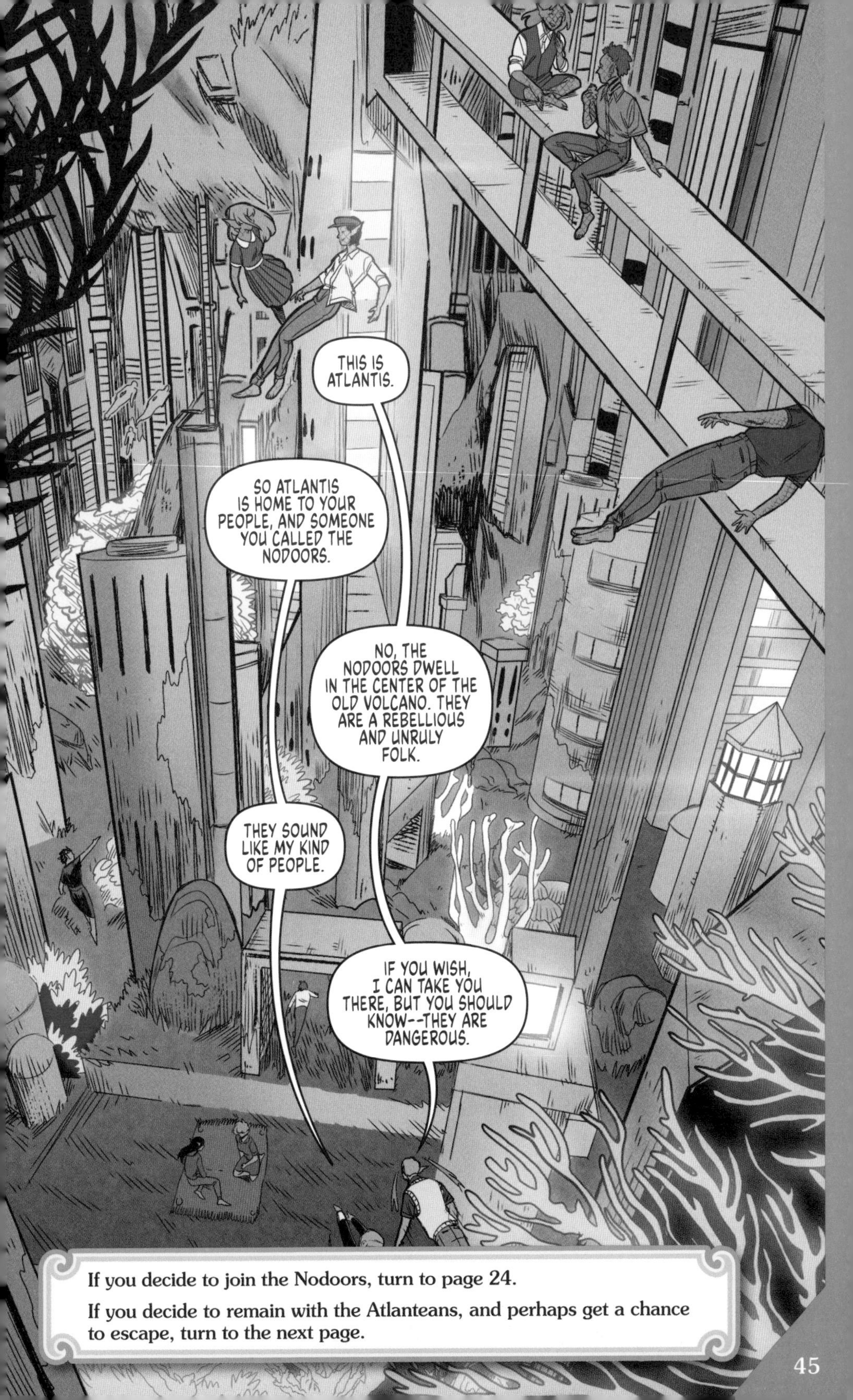
THIS IS ATLANTIS.
SO ATLANTIS IS HOME TO YOUR PEOPLE, AND SOMEONE YOU CALLED THE NODOORS.
NO, THE NODOORS DWELL IN THE CENTER OF THE OLD VOLCANO. THEY ARE A REBELLIOUS AND UNRULY FOLK.
THEY SOUND LIKE MY KIND OF PEOPLE.
IF YOU WISH, I CAN TAKE YOU THERE, BUT YOU SHOULD KNOW--THEY ARE DANGEROUS.

If you decide to join the Nodoors, turn to page 24.

If you decide to remain with the Atlanteans, and perhaps get a chance to escape, turn to the next page.

I THINK RIGHT HERE IS WHERE I'M SUPPOSED TO BE--

--FOR NOW.

TELL ME-- WHAT HAPPENED IN THE YEARS AFTER YOUR PEOPLE MOVED INTO THE VOLCANO--

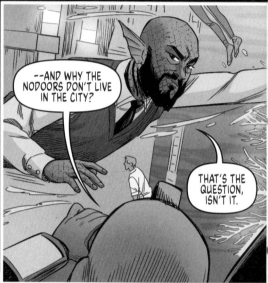

--AND WHY THE NODOORS DON'T LIVE IN THE CITY?

THAT'S THE QUESTION, ISN'T IT.

YOU HAVE A CURIOUS MIND, SURFACE DWELLER. THERE ARE WAYS YOU CAN SEE HISTORY FIRSTHAND...

LET ME SHOW YOU.

If you want or understand what was meant by seeing history firsthand, go to page 29.

If you decide to escape, turn to page 118.

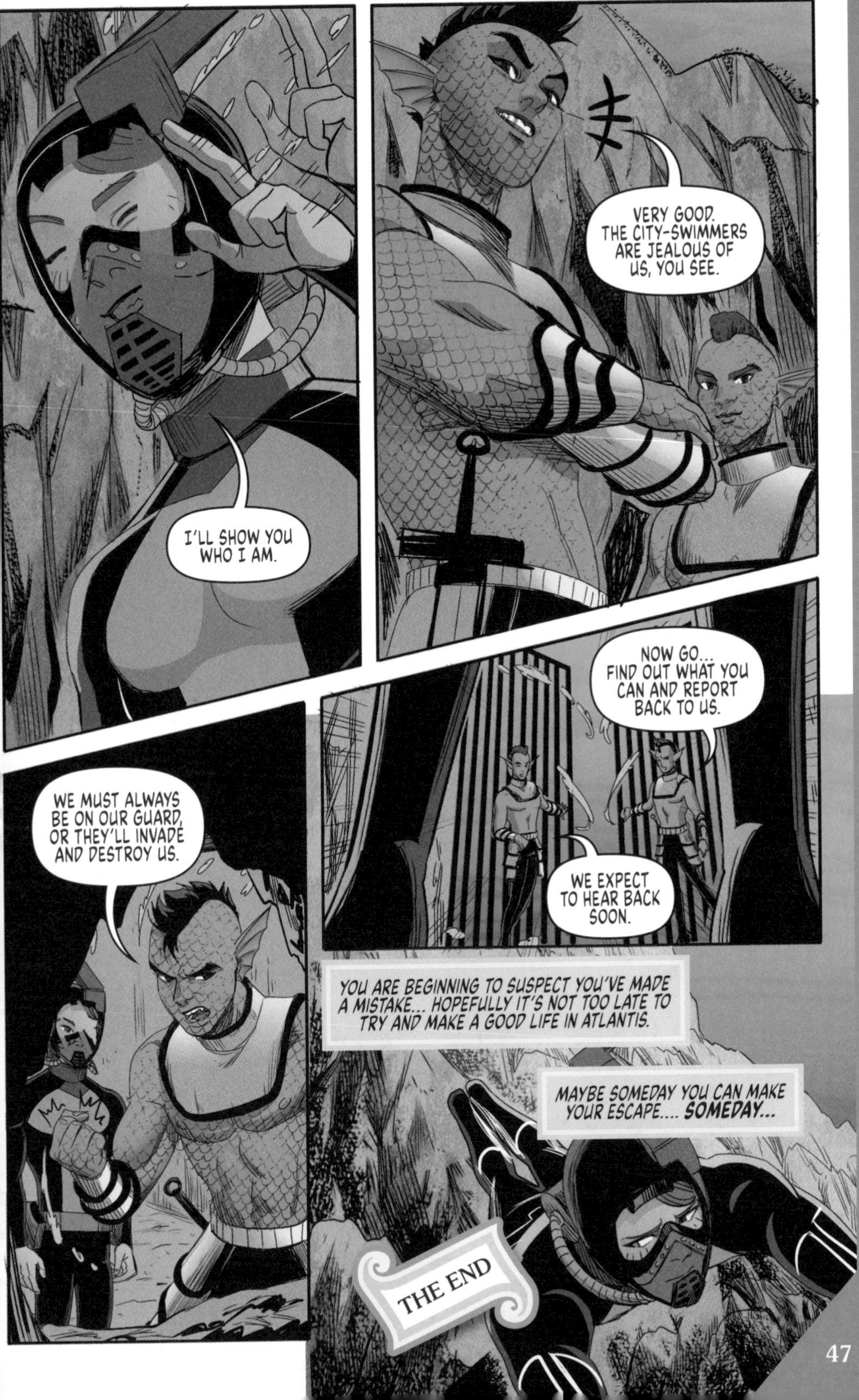
I'LL SHOW YOU WHO I AM.
VERY GOOD. THE CITY-SWIMMERS ARE JEALOUS OF US, YOU SEE.
WE MUST ALWAYS BE ON OUR GUARD, OR THEY'LL INVADE AND DESTROY US.
NOW GO... FIND OUT WHAT YOU CAN AND REPORT BACK TO US.
WE EXPECT TO HEAR BACK SOON.
YOU ARE BEGINNING TO SUSPECT YOU'VE MADE A MISTAKE... HOPEFULLY IT'S NOT TOO LATE TO TRY AND MAKE A GOOD LIFE IN ATLANTIS.
MAYBE SOMEDAY YOU CAN MAKE YOUR ESCAPE.... SOMEDAY...
THE END

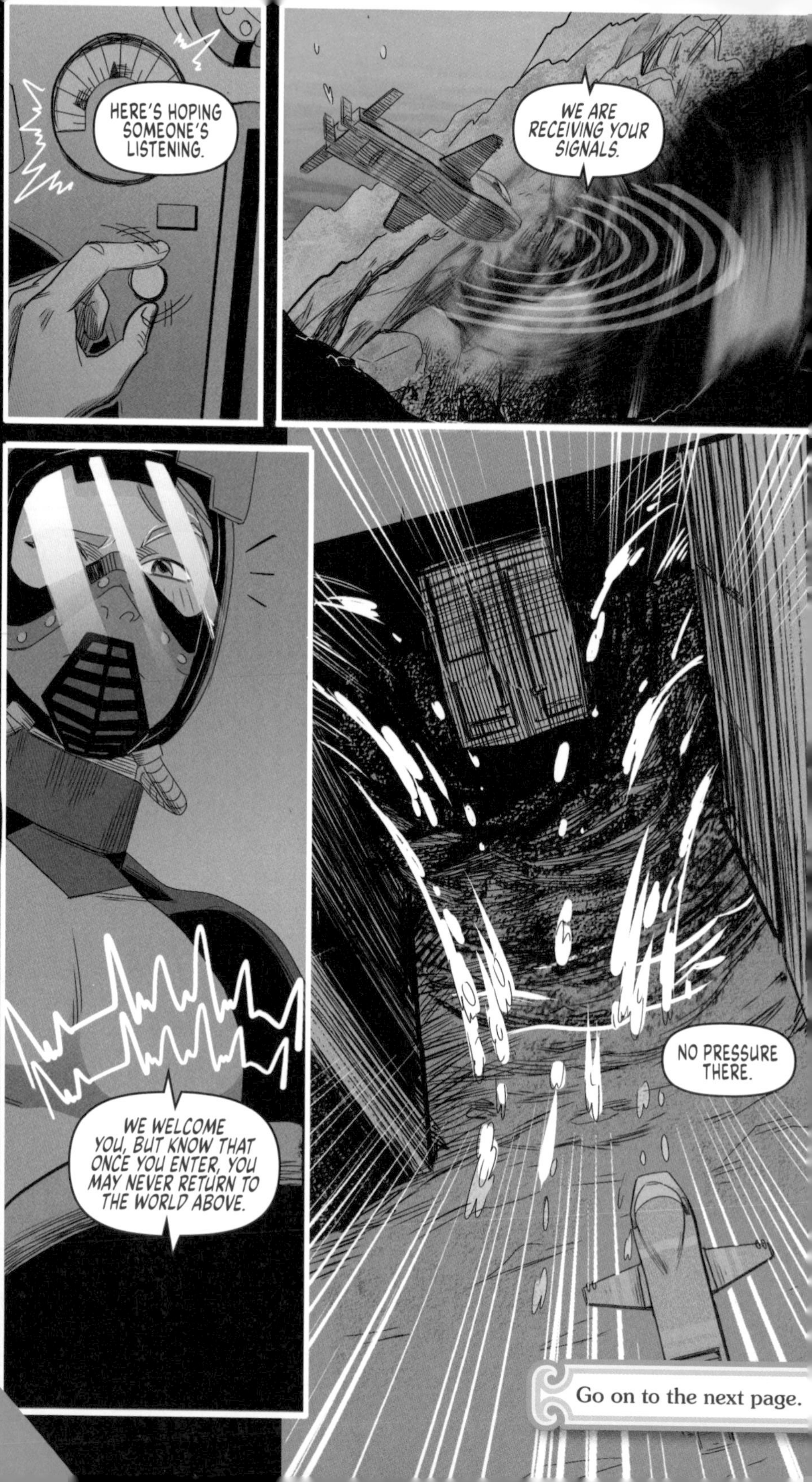
HERE'S HOPING SOMEONE'S LISTENING.
WE ARE RECEIVING YOUR SIGNALS.
WE WELCOME YOU, BUT KNOW THAT ONCE YOU ENTER, YOU MAY NEVER RETURN TO THE WORLD ABOVE.
NO PRESSURE THERE.

Go on to the next page.

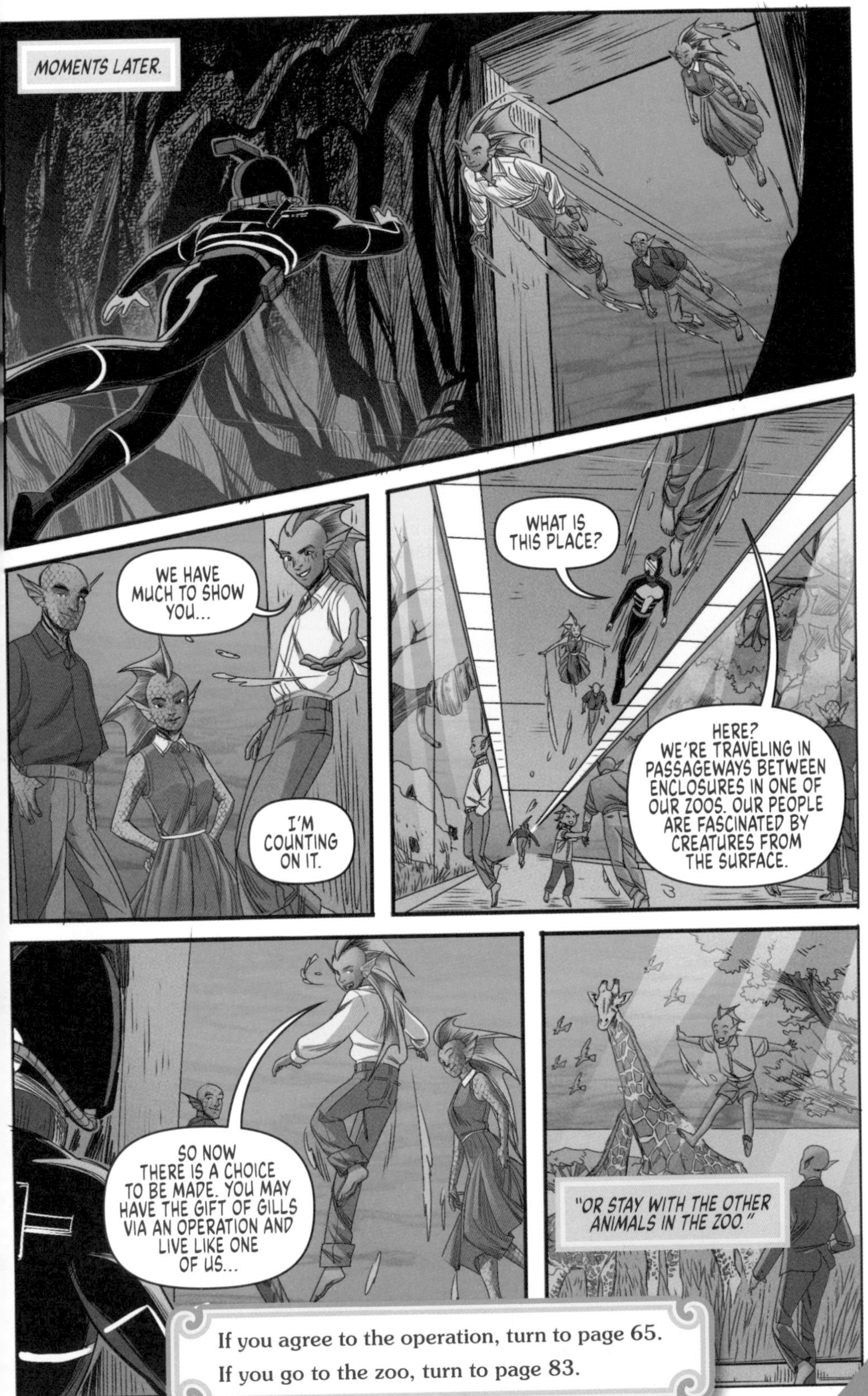
MOMENTS LATER.
WE HAVE MUCH TO SHOW YOU...
I'M COUNTING ON IT.
WHAT IS THIS PLACE?
HERE? WE'RE TRAVELING IN PASSAGEWAYS BETWEEN ENCLOSURES IN ONE OF OUR ZOOS. OUR PEOPLE ARE FASCINATED BY CREATURES FROM THE SURFACE.
SO NOW THERE IS A CHOICE TO BE MADE. YOU MAY HAVE THE GIFT OF GILLS VIA AN OPERATION AND LIVE LIKE ONE OF US...
"OR STAY WITH THE OTHER ANIMALS IN THE ZOO."

If you agree to the operation, turn to page 65.

If you go to the zoo, turn to page 83.

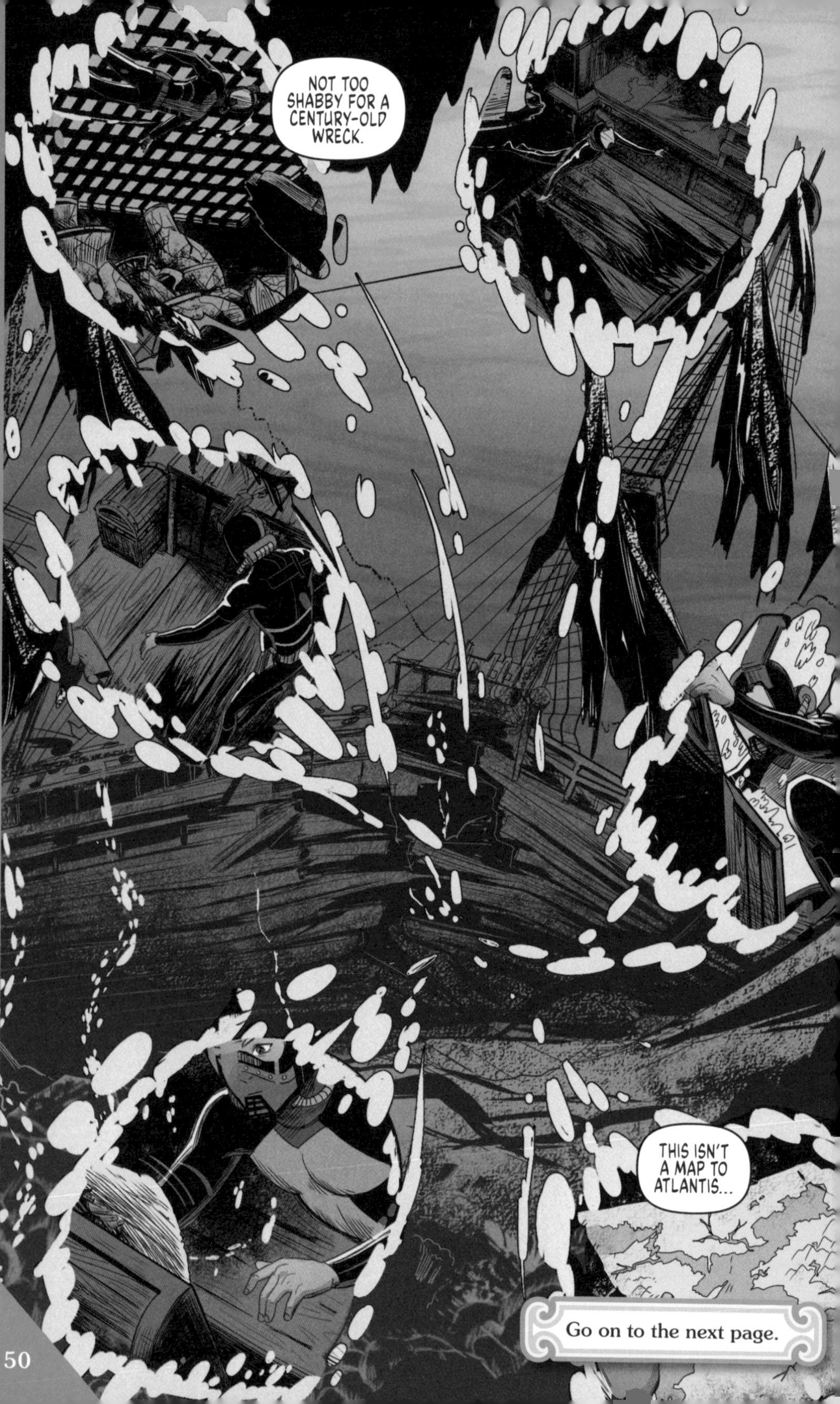
NOT TOO SHABBY FOR A CENTURY-OLD WRECK.
THIS ISN'T A MAP TO ATLANTIS...

Go on to the next page.

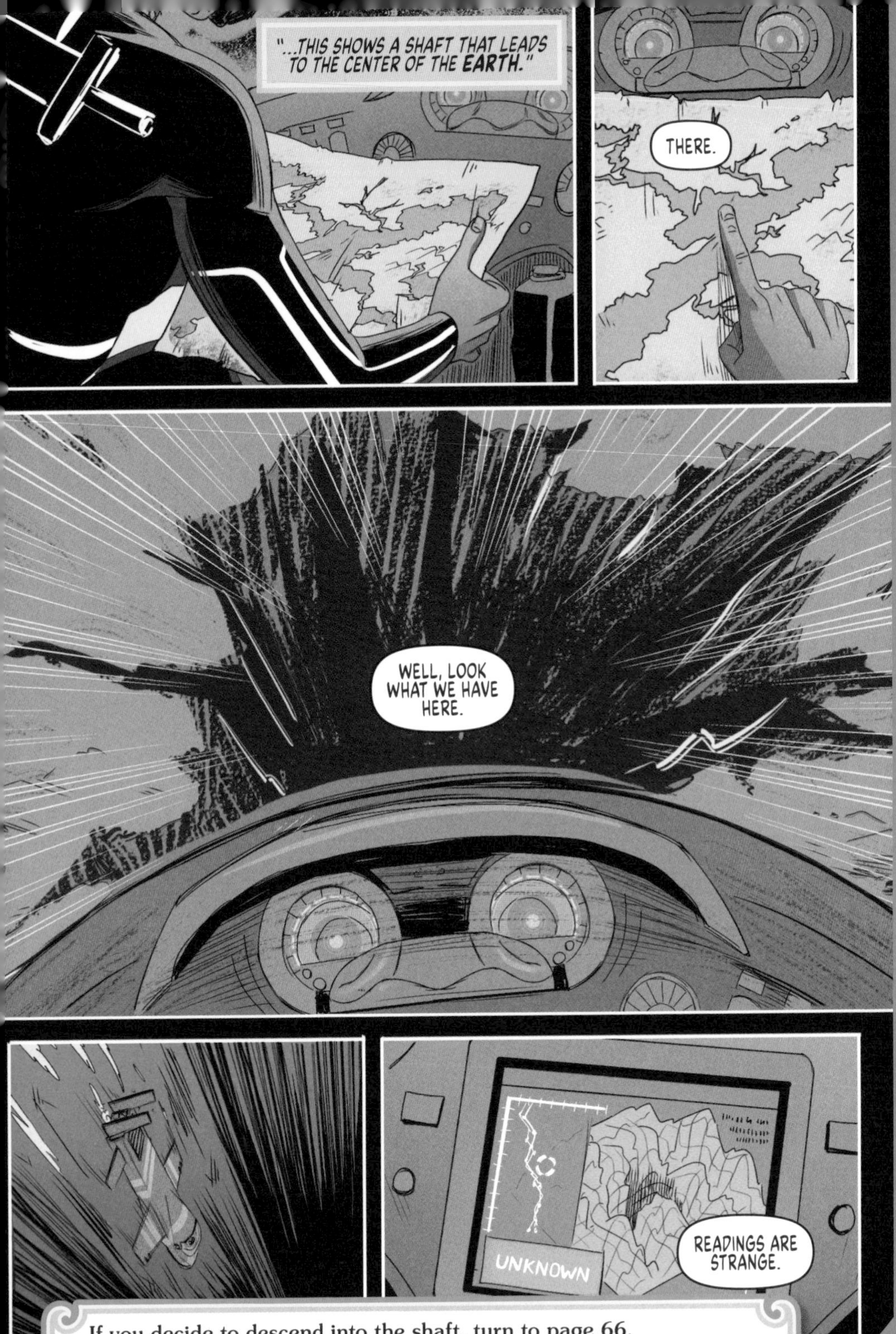
"...THIS SHOWS A SHAFT THAT LEADS TO THE CENTER OF THE EARTH."
THERE.
WELL, LOOK WHAT WE HAVE HERE.
UNKNOWN
READINGS ARE STRANGE.

If you decide to descend into the shaft, turn to page 66.
If you decide it is time to go back up to the surface, turn to page 59.

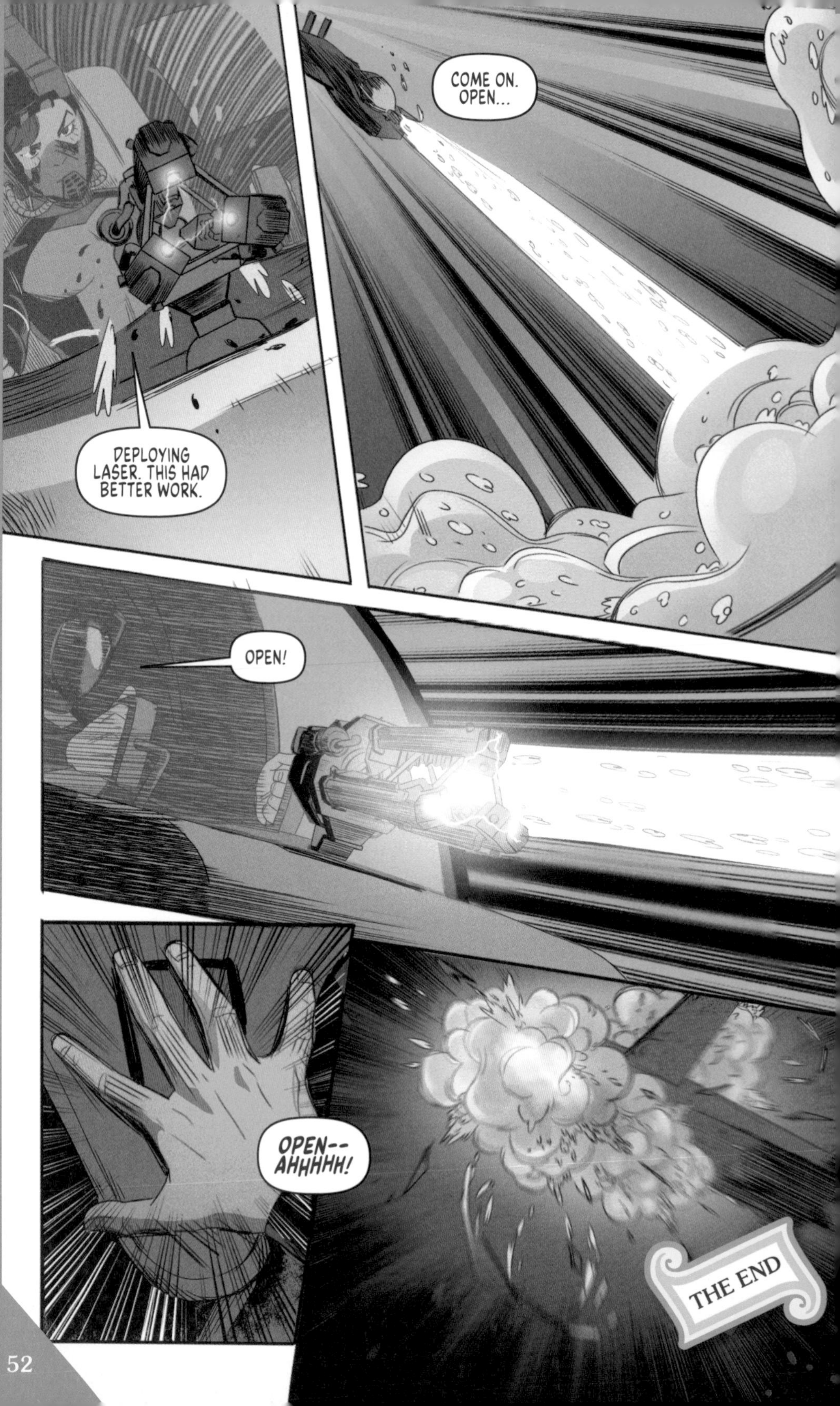
DEPLOYING LASER. THIS HAD BETTER WORK.
COME ON. OPEN...
OPEN!
OPEN-- AHHHHH!
THE END

MADE IT!

IMPRESSIVE.

ᲔᲙᲐᲩᲔᲕ ᲫᲮᲓᲒᲓᲔᲮᲚᲝᲜ

I GET THAT A LOT. THAT'S FAR ENOUGH FOR NOW.

WE ARE A GOOD AND PEACEFUL PEOPLE, BUT RULED BY A GREEDY, SELFISH, AND DANGEROUS KING. PLEASE, WILL YOU HELP US?

�6ᲛᲛᲮ ᲮᲔᲛᲛᲛ ᲜᲮᲜᲕᲣ,ᲛᲣᲮ--APOLOGIES-- WE NEEDED TO BE CERTAIN OF YOUR LANGUAGE. WE ARE HAPPY YOU RECEIVED OUR MESSAGE.

WAY TO CUT TO THE CHASE.

If you decide to leave your new friends and search for their ruler, turn to page 15.

If you decide to help your new friends escape, turn to page 87.

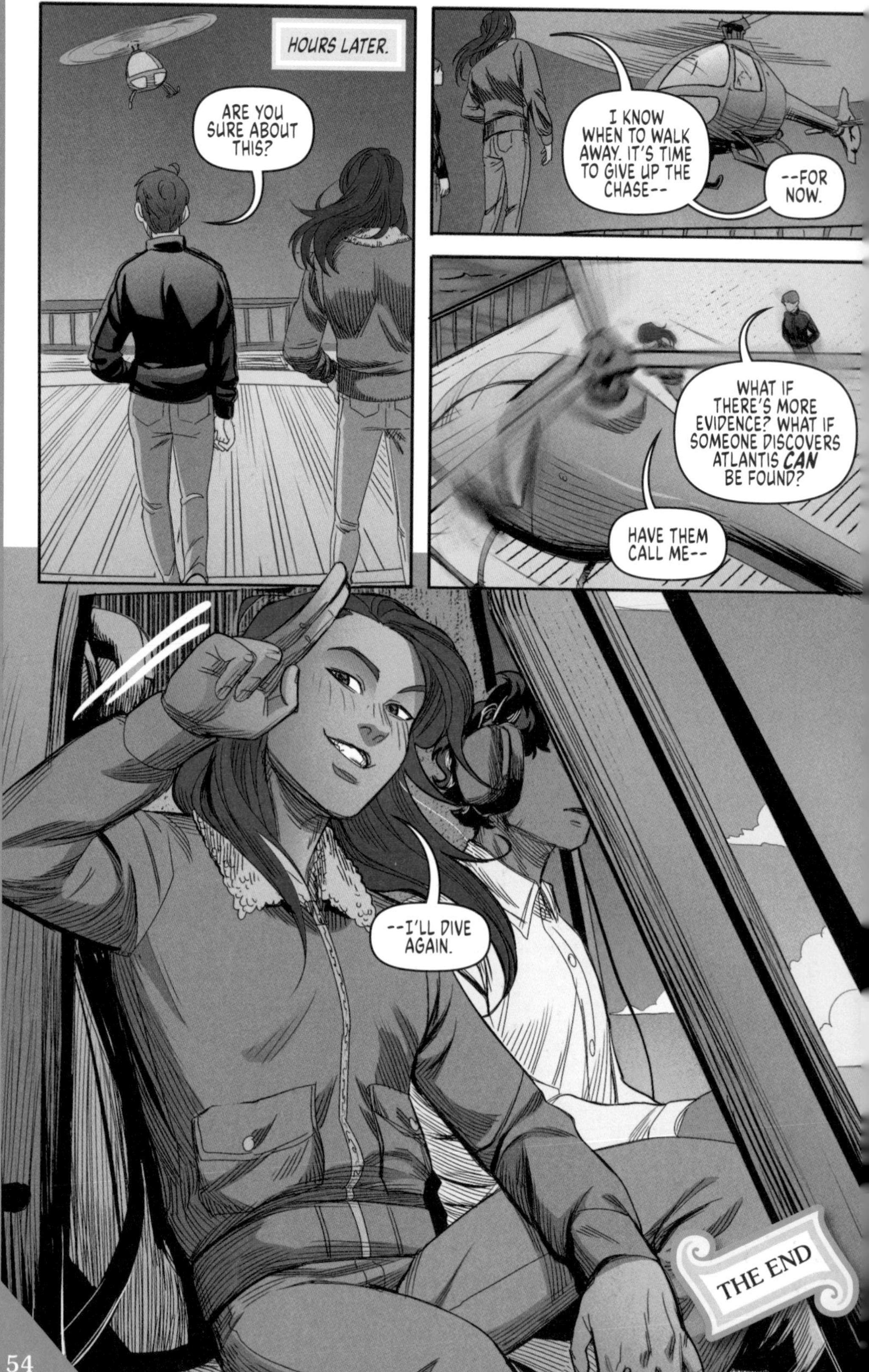
HOURS LATER.
ARE YOU SURE ABOUT THIS?
I KNOW WHEN TO WALK AWAY. IT'S TIME TO GIVE UP THE CHASE--
--FOR NOW.
WHAT IF THERE'S MORE EVIDENCE? WHAT IF SOMEONE DISCOVERS ATLANTIS CAN BE FOUND?
HAVE THEM CALL ME--
--I'LL DIVE AGAIN.
THE END

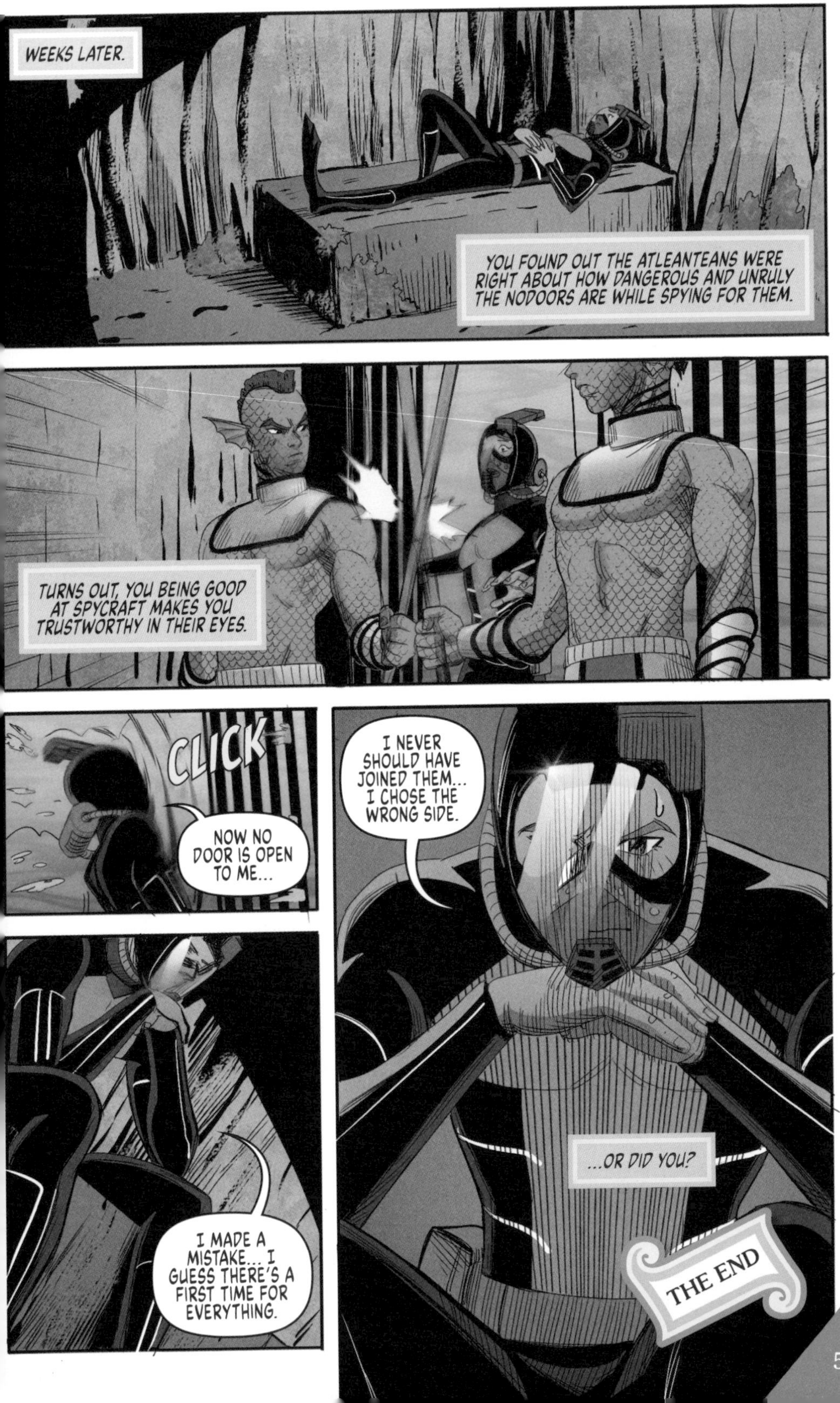
WEEKS LATER.
YOU FOUND OUT THE ATLEANTEANS WERE RIGHT ABOUT HOW DANGEROUS AND UNRULY THE NODOORS ARE WHILE SPYING FOR THEM.
TURNS OUT, YOU BEING GOOD AT SPYCRAFT MAKES YOU TRUSTWORTHY IN THEIR EYES.
CLICK
NOW NO DOOR IS OPEN TO ME...
I MADE A MISTAKE... I GUESS THERE'S A FIRST TIME FOR EVERYTHING.
I NEVER SHOULD HAVE JOINED THEM... I CHOSE THE WRONG SIDE.
...OR DID YOU?
THE END

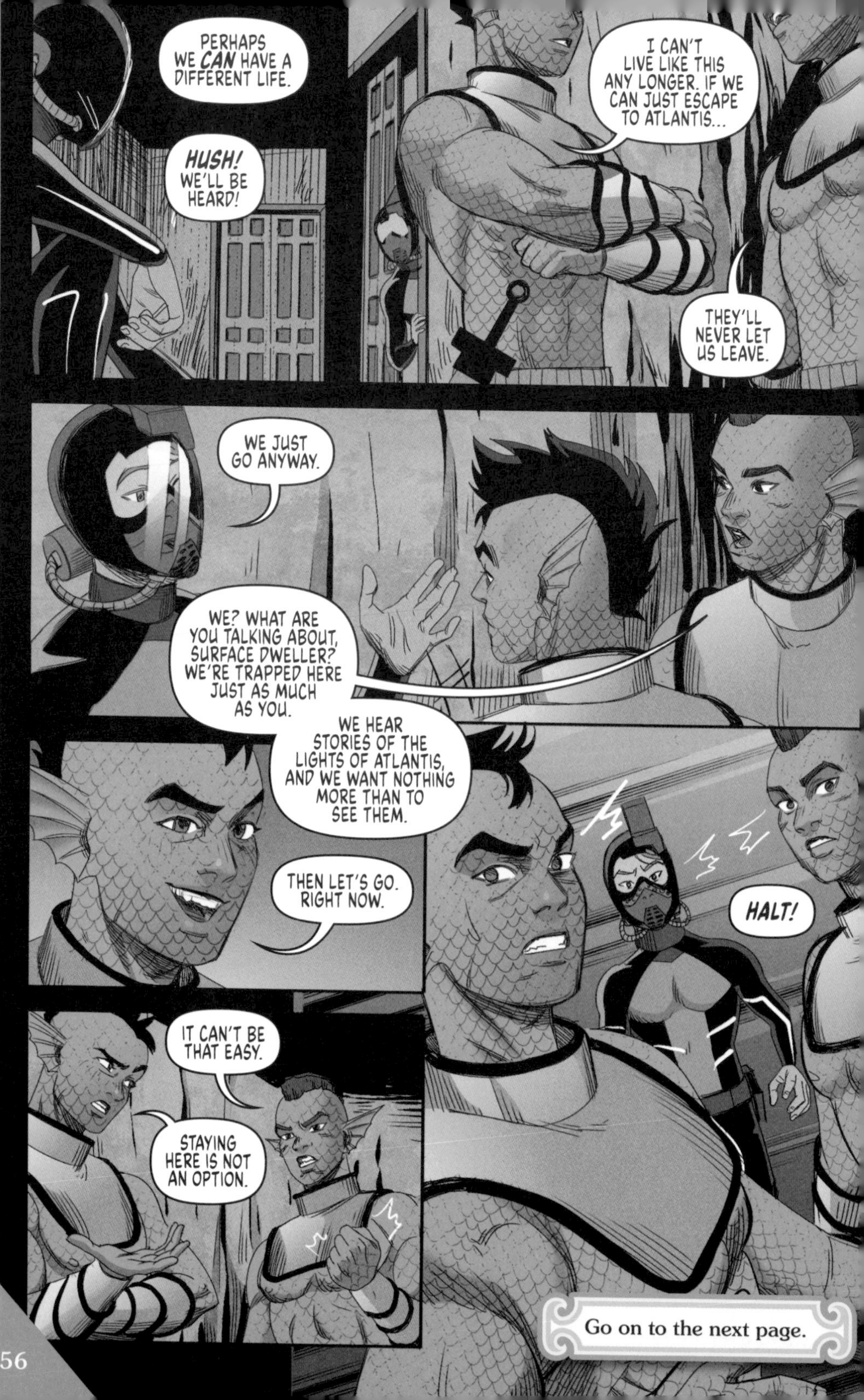
PERHAPS WE *CAN* HAVE A DIFFERENT LIFE.
HUSH! WE'LL BE HEARD!
I CAN'T LIVE LIKE THIS ANY LONGER. IF WE CAN JUST ESCAPE TO ATLANTIS...
THEY'LL NEVER LET US LEAVE.
WE JUST GO ANYWAY.
WE? WHAT ARE YOU TALKING ABOUT, SURFACE DWELLER? WE'RE TRAPPED HERE JUST AS MUCH AS YOU.
WE HEAR STORIES OF THE LIGHTS OF ATLANTIS, AND WE WANT NOTHING MORE THAN TO SEE THEM.
THEN LET'S GO. RIGHT NOW.
IT CAN'T BE THAT EASY.
STAYING HERE IS NOT AN OPTION.
HALT!

Go on to the next page.

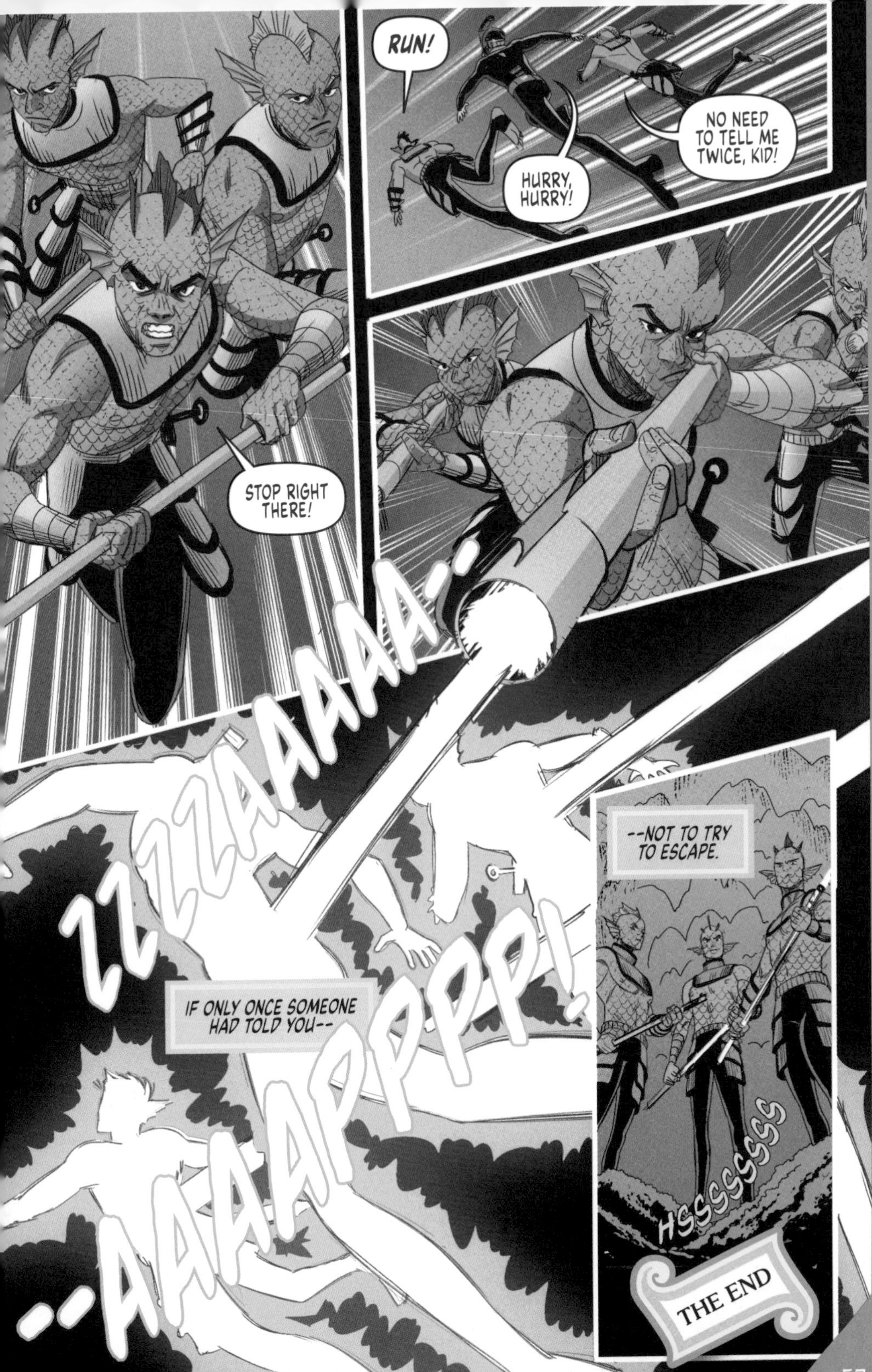
STOP RIGHT THERE!
RUN!
HURRY, HURRY!
NO NEED TO TELL ME TWICE, KID!
ZZZZAAAAAAA--
IF ONLY ONCE SOMEONE HAD TOLD YOU--
--AAAAAPPPP!
--NOT TO TRY TO ESCAPE.
HSSSSSSSS
THE END

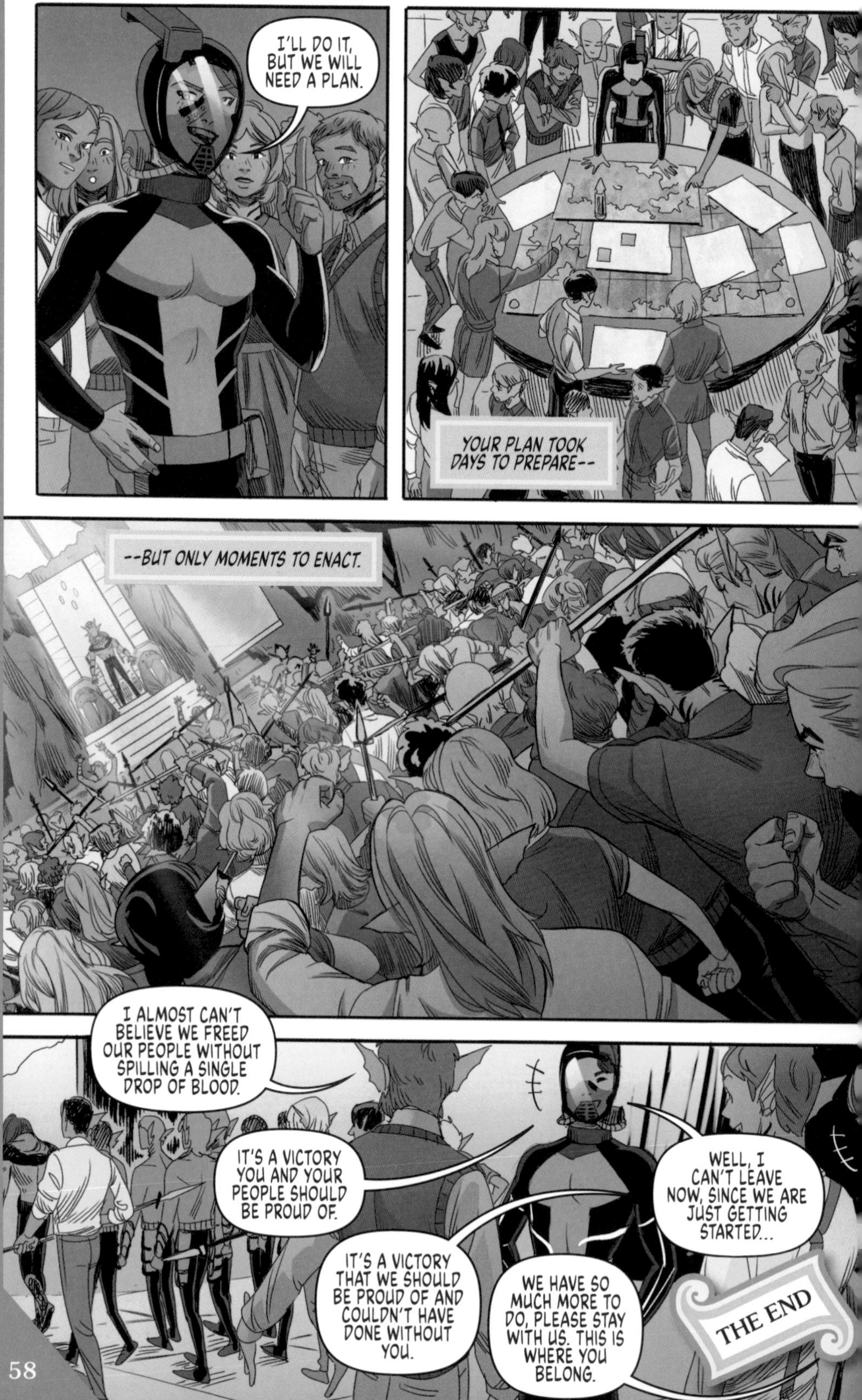
I'LL DO IT, BUT WE WILL NEED A PLAN.
YOUR PLAN TOOK DAYS TO PREPARE--
--BUT ONLY MOMENTS TO ENACT.
I ALMOST CAN'T BELIEVE WE FREED OUR PEOPLE WITHOUT SPILLING A SINGLE DROP OF BLOOD.
IT'S A VICTORY YOU AND YOUR PEOPLE SHOULD BE PROUD OF.
IT'S A VICTORY THAT WE SHOULD BE PROUD OF AND COULDN'T HAVE DONE WITHOUT YOU.
WE HAVE SO MUCH MORE TO DO, PLEASE STAY WITH US. THIS IS WHERE YOU BELONG.
WELL, I CAN'T LEAVE NOW, SINCE WE ARE JUST GETTING STARTED...
THE END

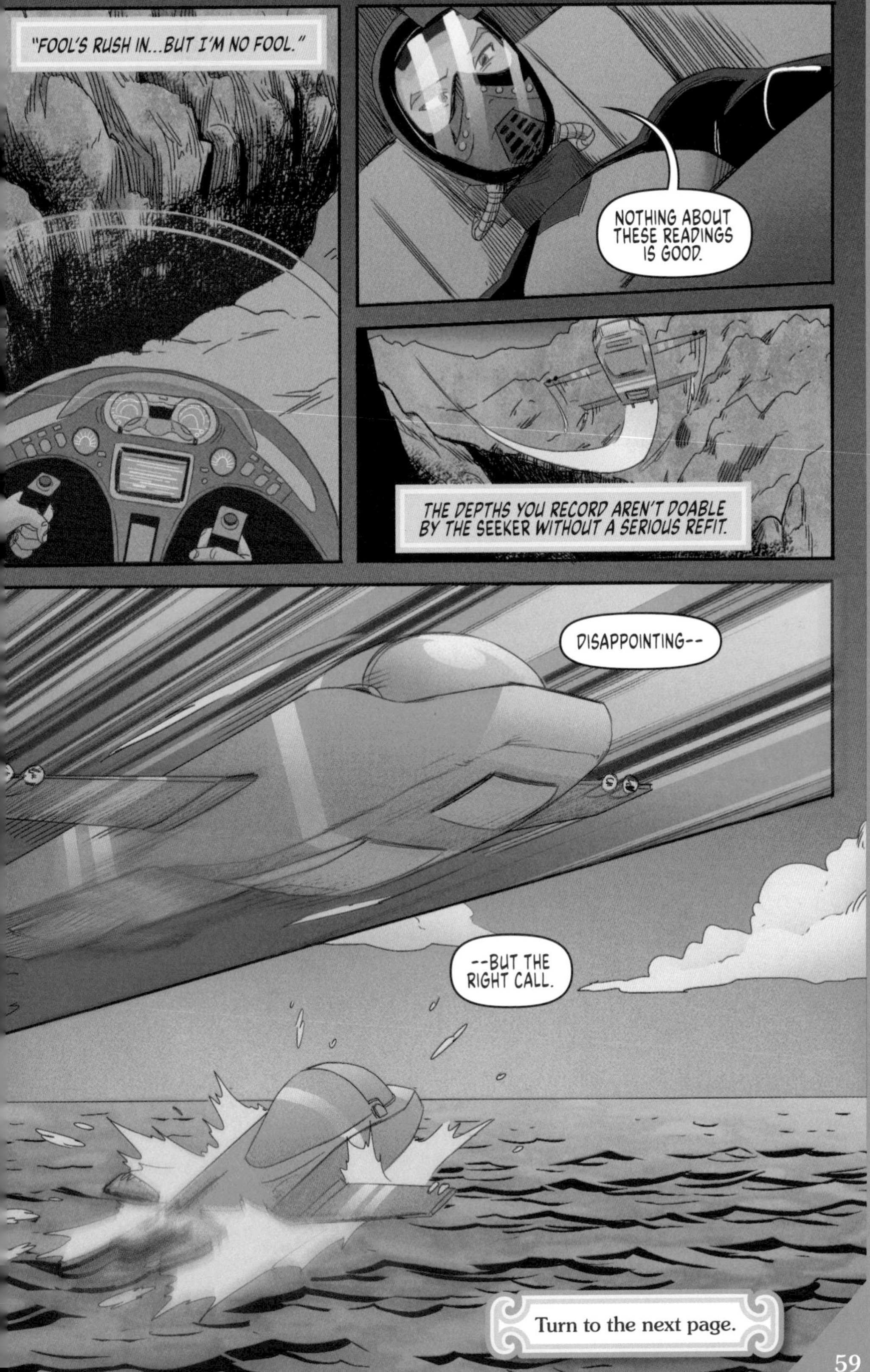
"FOOL'S RUSH IN...BUT I'M NO FOOL."
NOTHING ABOUT THESE READINGS IS GOOD.
THE DEPTHS YOU RECORD AREN'T DOABLE BY THE SEEKER WITHOUT A SERIOUS REFIT.
DISAPPOINTING--
--BUT THE RIGHT CALL.

Turn to the next page.

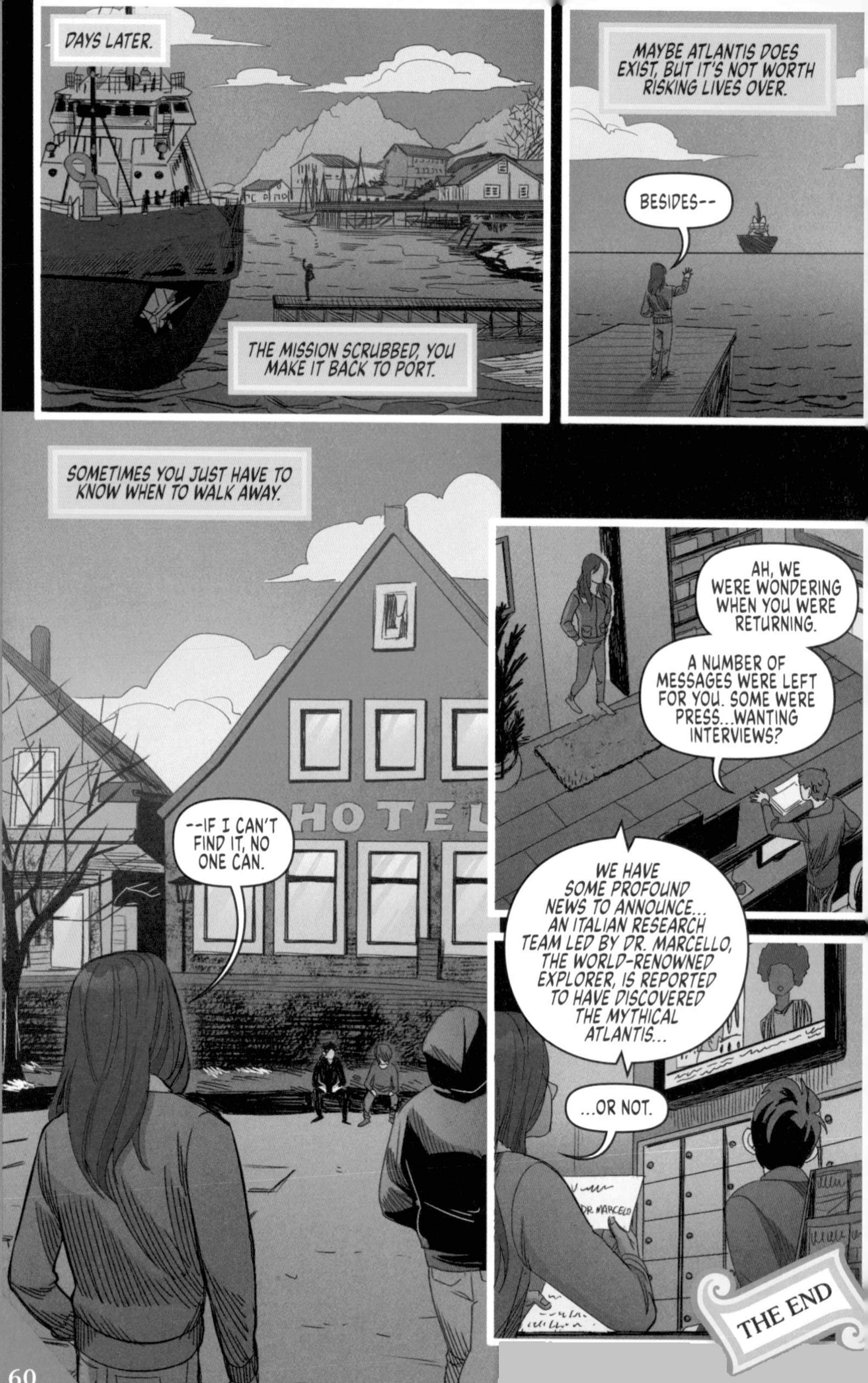
DAYS LATER.
THE MISSION SCRUBBED, YOU MAKE IT BACK TO PORT.
MAYBE ATLANTIS DOES EXIST, BUT IT'S NOT WORTH RISKING LIVES OVER.
BESIDES--
SOMETIMES YOU JUST HAVE TO KNOW WHEN TO WALK AWAY.
HOTEL
--IF I CAN'T FIND IT, NO ONE CAN.
AH, WE WERE WONDERING WHEN YOU WERE RETURNING.
A NUMBER OF MESSAGES WERE LEFT FOR YOU. SOME WERE PRESS...WANTING INTERVIEWS?
WE HAVE SOME PROFOUND NEWS TO ANNOUNCE... AN ITALIAN RESEARCH TEAM LED BY DR. MARCELLO, THE WORLD-RENOWNED EXPLORER, IS REPORTED TO HAVE DISCOVERED THE MYTHICAL ATLANTIS...
...OR NOT.
DR. MARCELLO
THE END

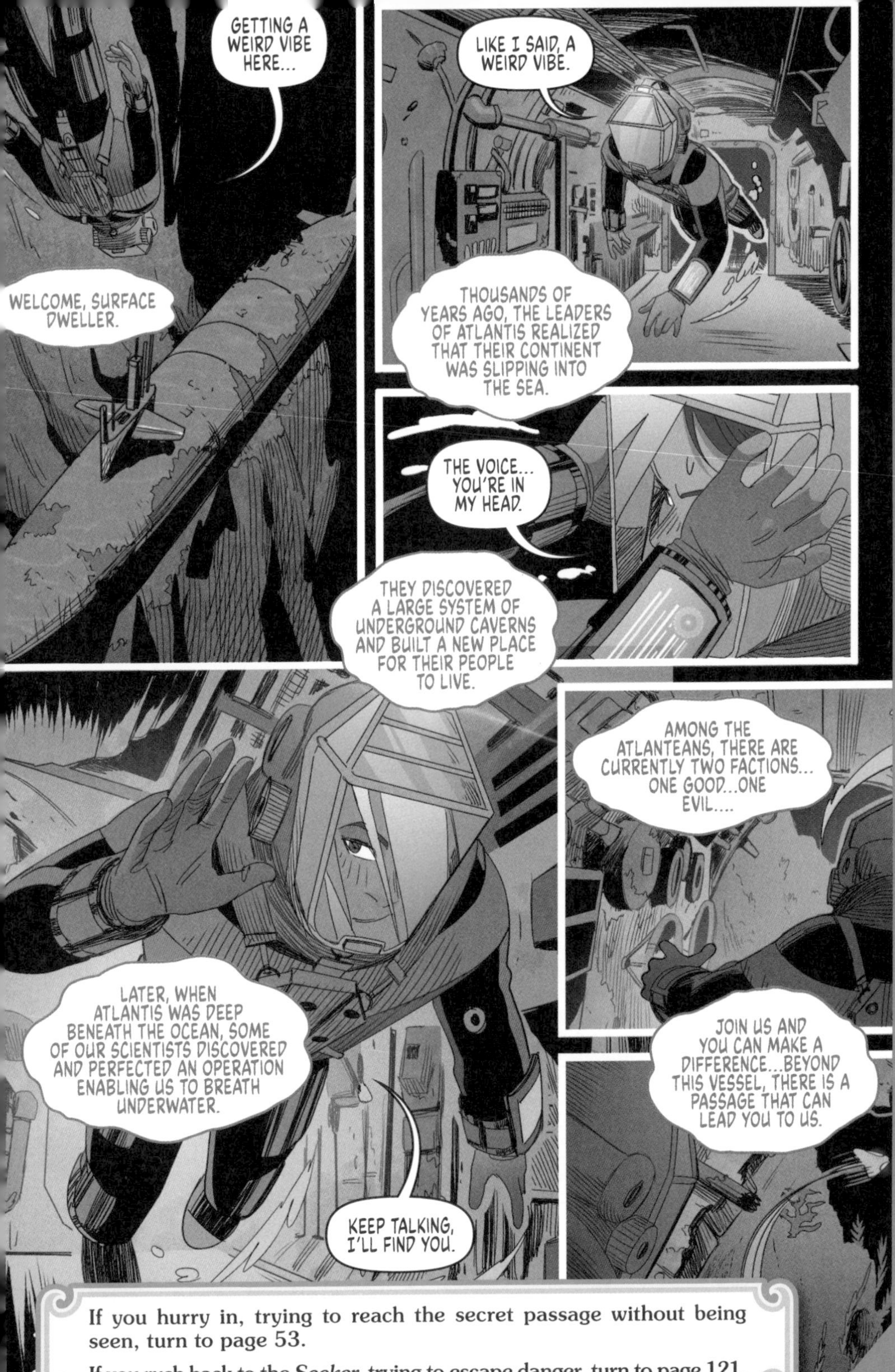
GETTING A WEIRD VIBE HERE...
LIKE I SAID, A WEIRD VIBE.
WELCOME, SURFACE DWELLER.
THOUSANDS OF YEARS AGO, THE LEADERS OF ATLANTIS REALIZED THAT THEIR CONTINENT WAS SLIPPING INTO THE SEA.
THE VOICE... YOU'RE IN MY HEAD.
THEY DISCOVERED A LARGE SYSTEM OF UNDERGROUND CAVERNS AND BUILT A NEW PLACE FOR THEIR PEOPLE TO LIVE.
AMONG THE ATLANTEANS, THERE ARE CURRENTLY TWO FACTIONS... ONE GOOD...ONE EVIL....
LATER, WHEN ATLANTIS WAS DEEP BENEATH THE OCEAN, SOME OF OUR SCIENTISTS DISCOVERED AND PERFECTED AN OPERATION ENABLING US TO BREATH UNDERWATER.
JOIN US AND YOU CAN MAKE A DIFFERENCE...BEYOND THIS VESSEL, THERE IS A PASSAGE THAT CAN LEAD YOU TO US.
KEEP TALKING, I'LL FIND YOU.

If you hurry in, trying to reach the secret passage without being seen, turn to page 53.

If you rush back to the *Seeker*, trying to escape danger, turn to page 121.

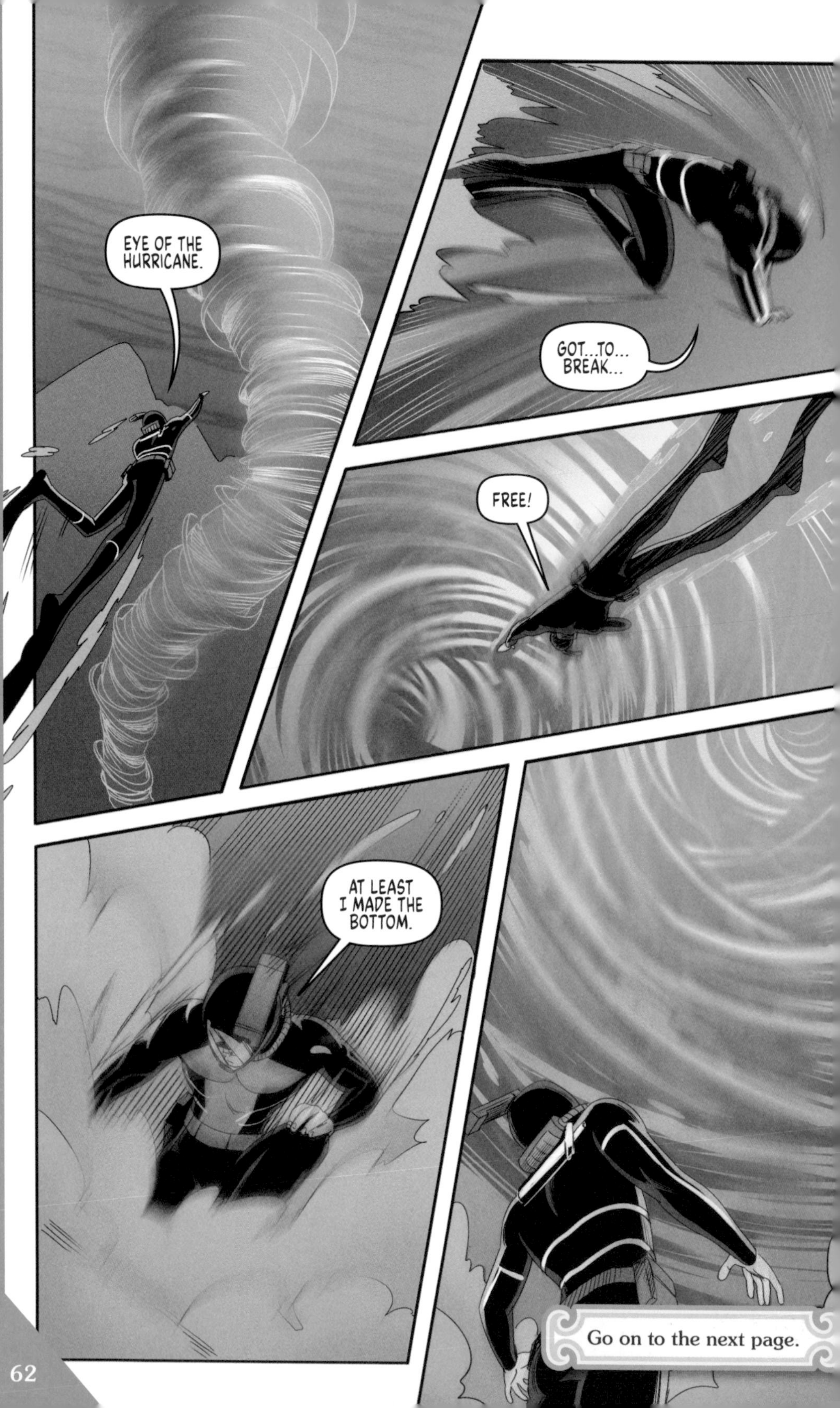
EYE OF THE HURRICANE.
GOT...TO... BREAK...
FREE!
AT LEAST I MADE THE BOTTOM.
Go on to the next page.

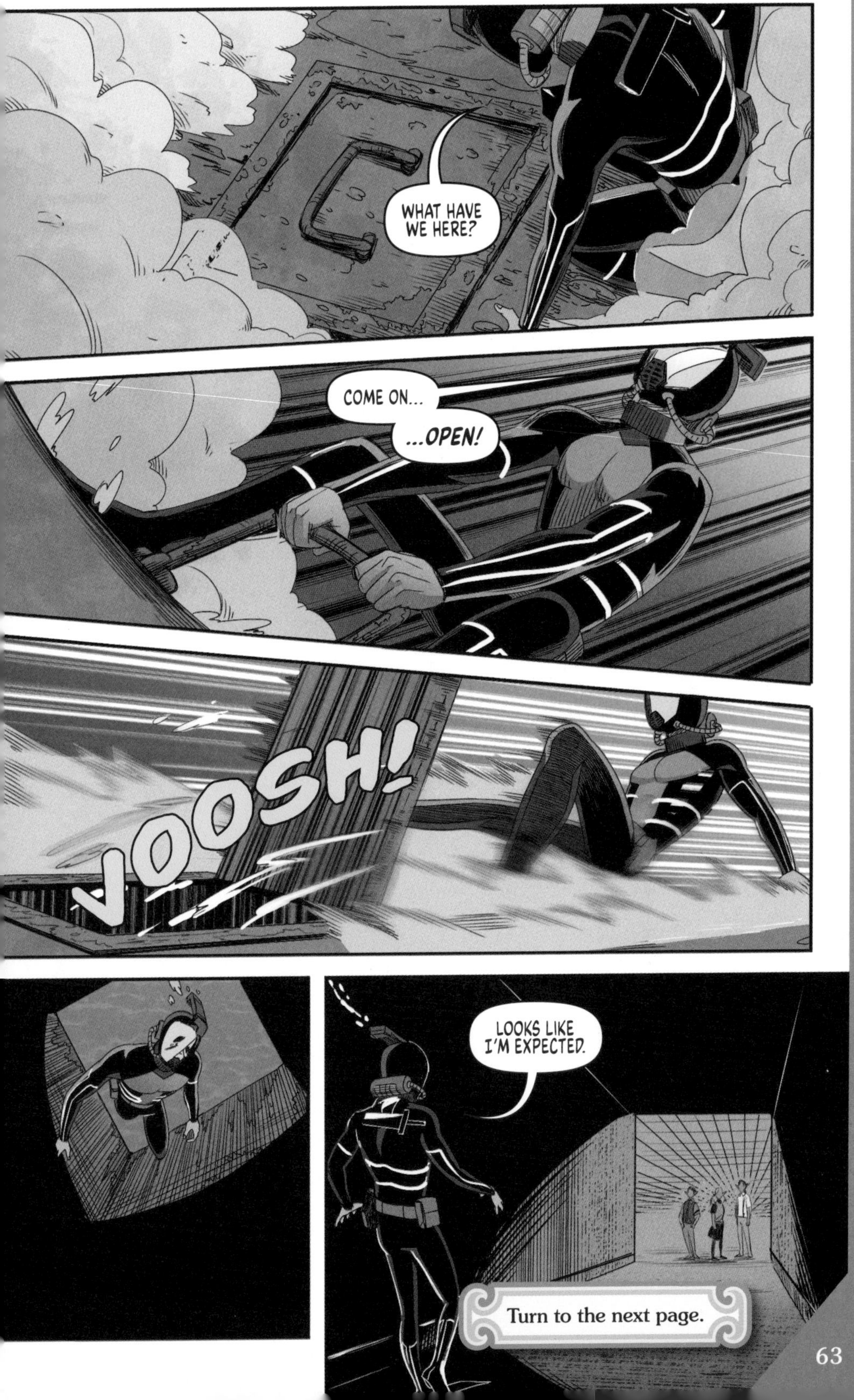
WHAT HAVE WE HERE?
COME ON...
...OPEN!
VOOSH!
LOOKS LIKE I'M EXPECTED.
Turn to the next page.

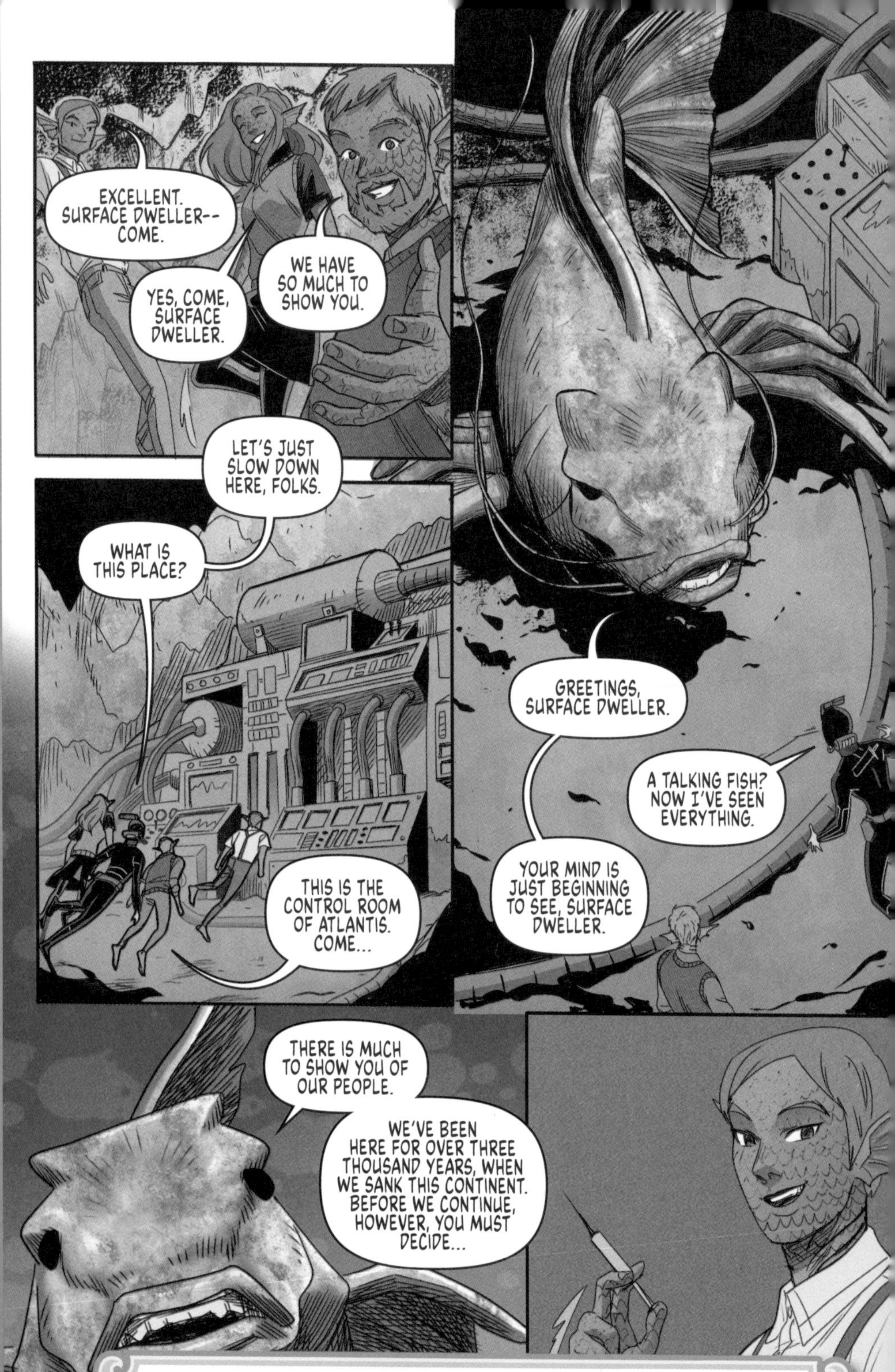
EXCELLENT. SURFACE DWELLER-- COME.
YES, COME, SURFACE DWELLER.
WE HAVE SO MUCH TO SHOW YOU.
LET'S JUST SLOW DOWN HERE, FOLKS.
WHAT IS THIS PLACE?
THIS IS THE CONTROL ROOM OF ATLANTIS. COME...
GREETINGS, SURFACE DWELLER.
A TALKING FISH? NOW I'VE SEEN EVERYTHING.
YOUR MIND IS JUST BEGINNING TO SEE, SURFACE DWELLER.
THERE IS MUCH TO SHOW YOU OF OUR PEOPLE.
WE'VE BEEN HERE FOR OVER THREE THOUSAND YEARS, WHEN WE SANK THIS CONTINENT. BEFORE WE CONTINUE, HOWEVER, YOU MUST DECIDE...

"...will you allow us to inject you with a serum to enable you to live down here?" Turn to page 36.

"Or will you be our prisoner?" Turn to page 78.

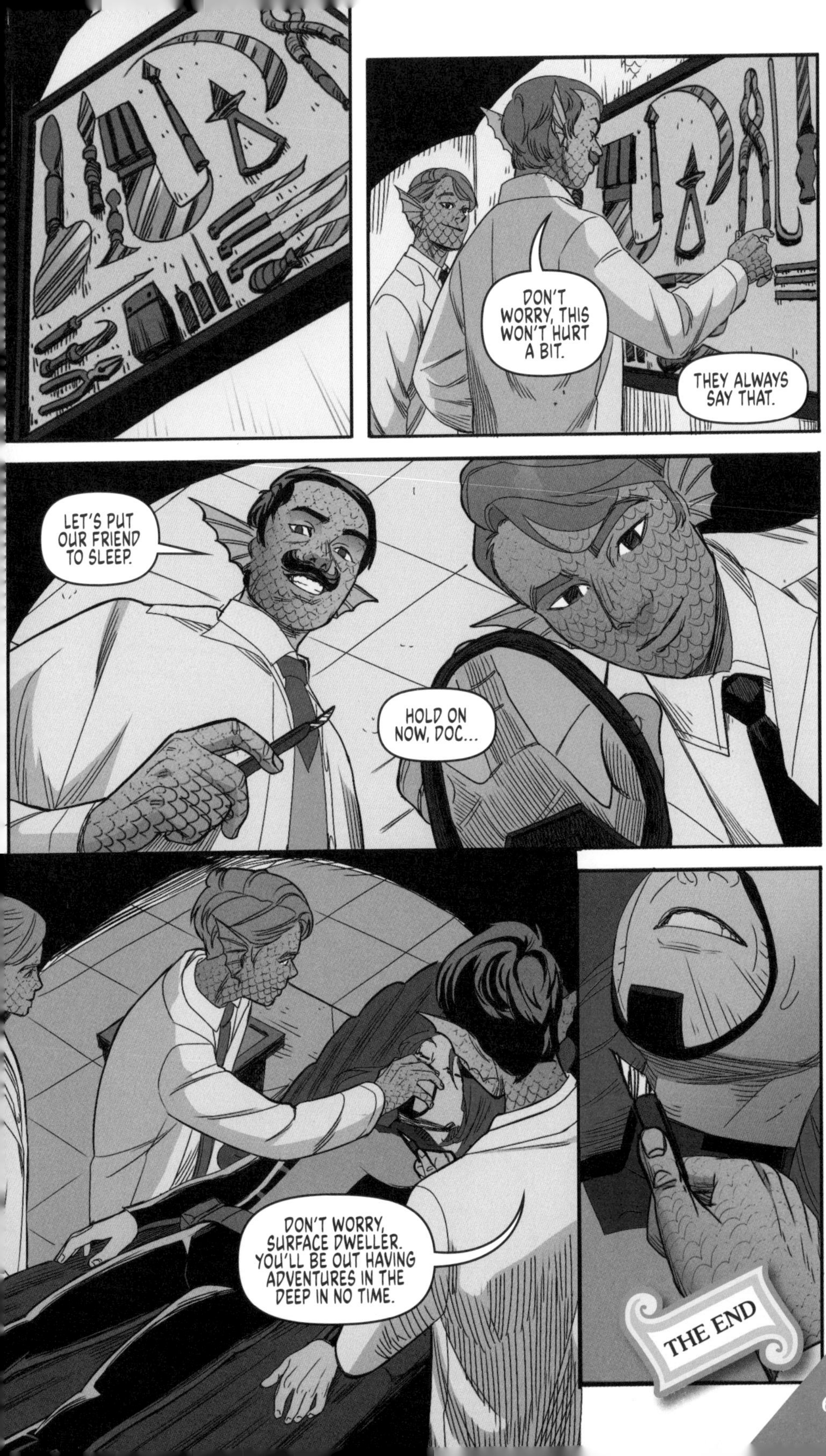
DON'T WORRY, THIS WON'T HURT A BIT.
THEY ALWAYS SAY THAT.
LET'S PUT OUR FRIEND TO SLEEP.
HOLD ON NOW, DOC...
DON'T WORRY, SURFACE DWELLER. YOU'LL BE OUT HAVING ADVENTURES IN THE DEEP IN NO TIME.
THE END

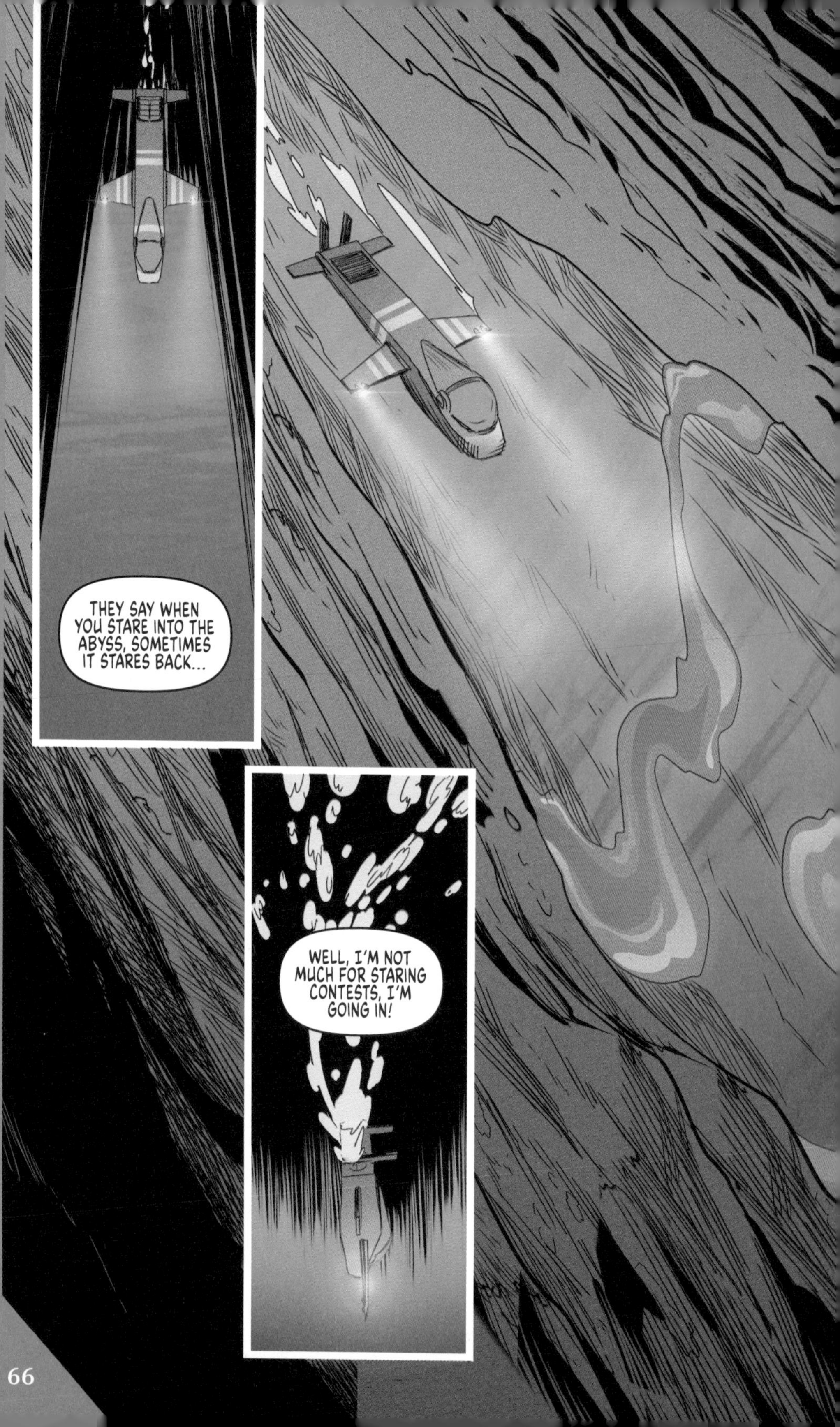
THEY SAY WHEN YOU STARE INTO THE ABYSS, SOMETIMES IT STARES BACK...
WELL, I'M NOT MUCH FOR STARING CONTESTS, I'M GOING IN!

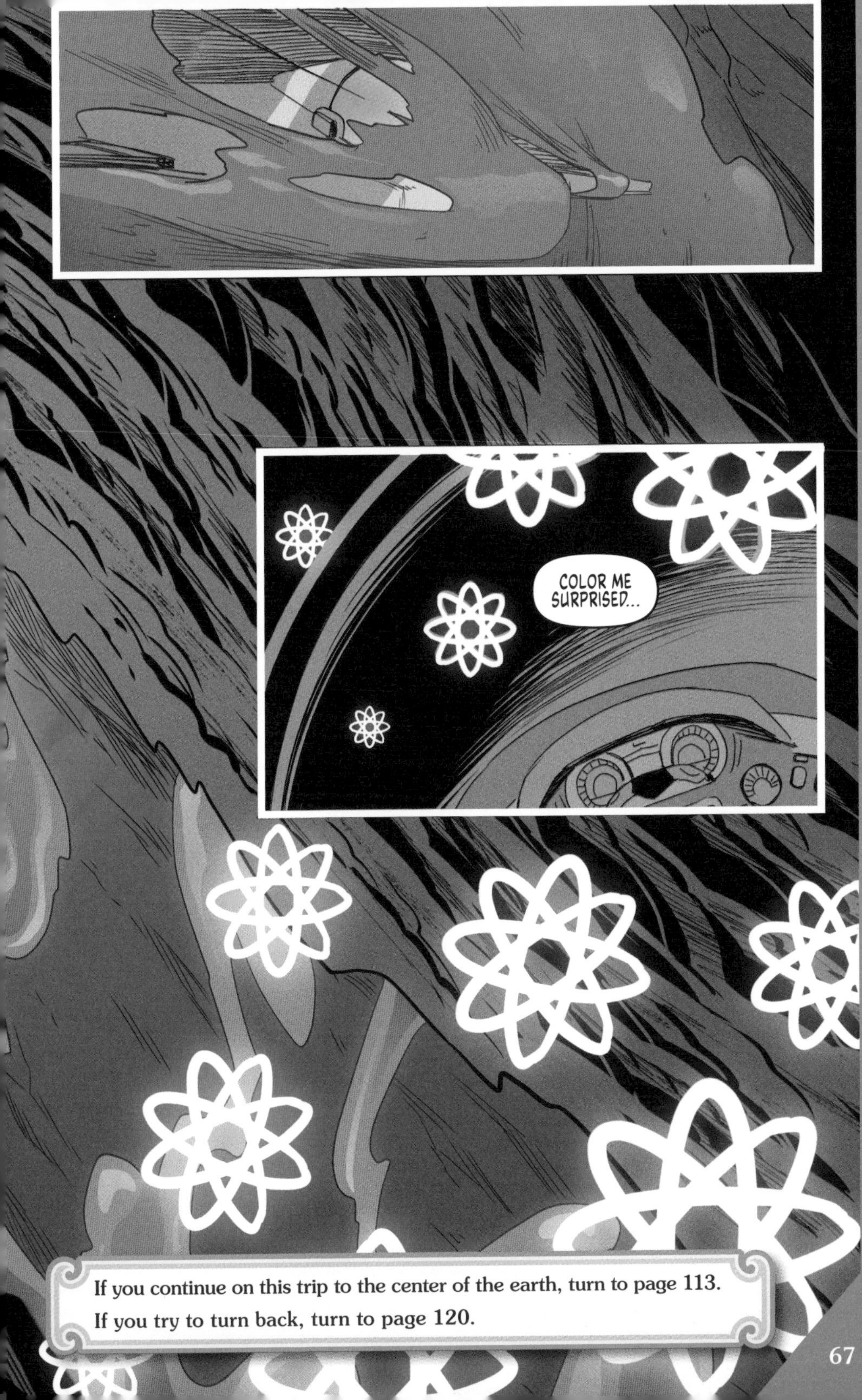
COLOR ME
SURPRISED...

If you continue on this trip to the center of the earth, turn to page 113.
If you try to turn back, turn to page 120.

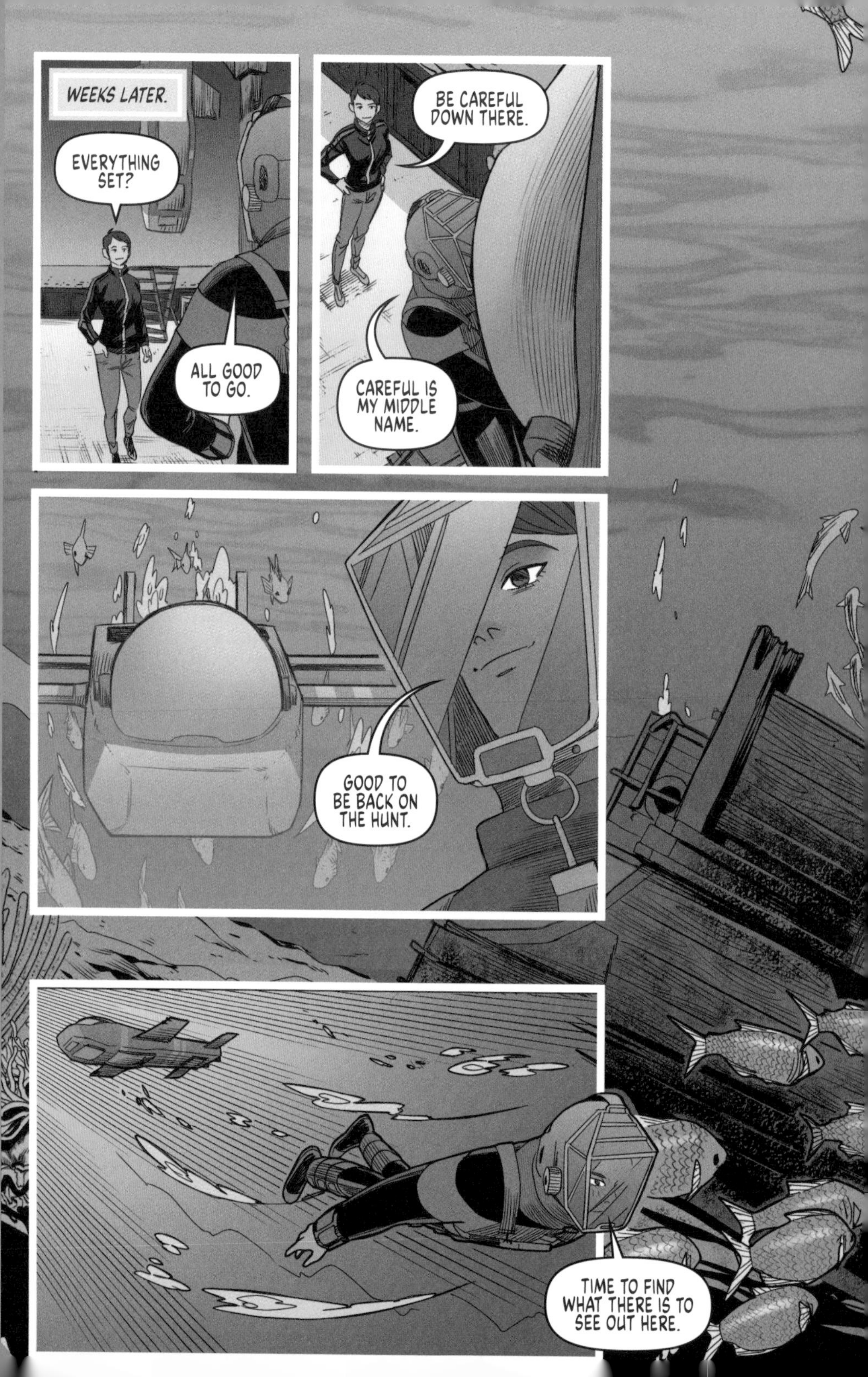
WEEKS LATER.
EVERYTHING SET?
ALL GOOD TO GO.
BE CAREFUL DOWN THERE.
CAREFUL IS MY MIDDLE NAME.
GOOD TO BE BACK ON THE HUNT.
TIME TO FIND WHAT THERE IS TO SEE OUT HERE.

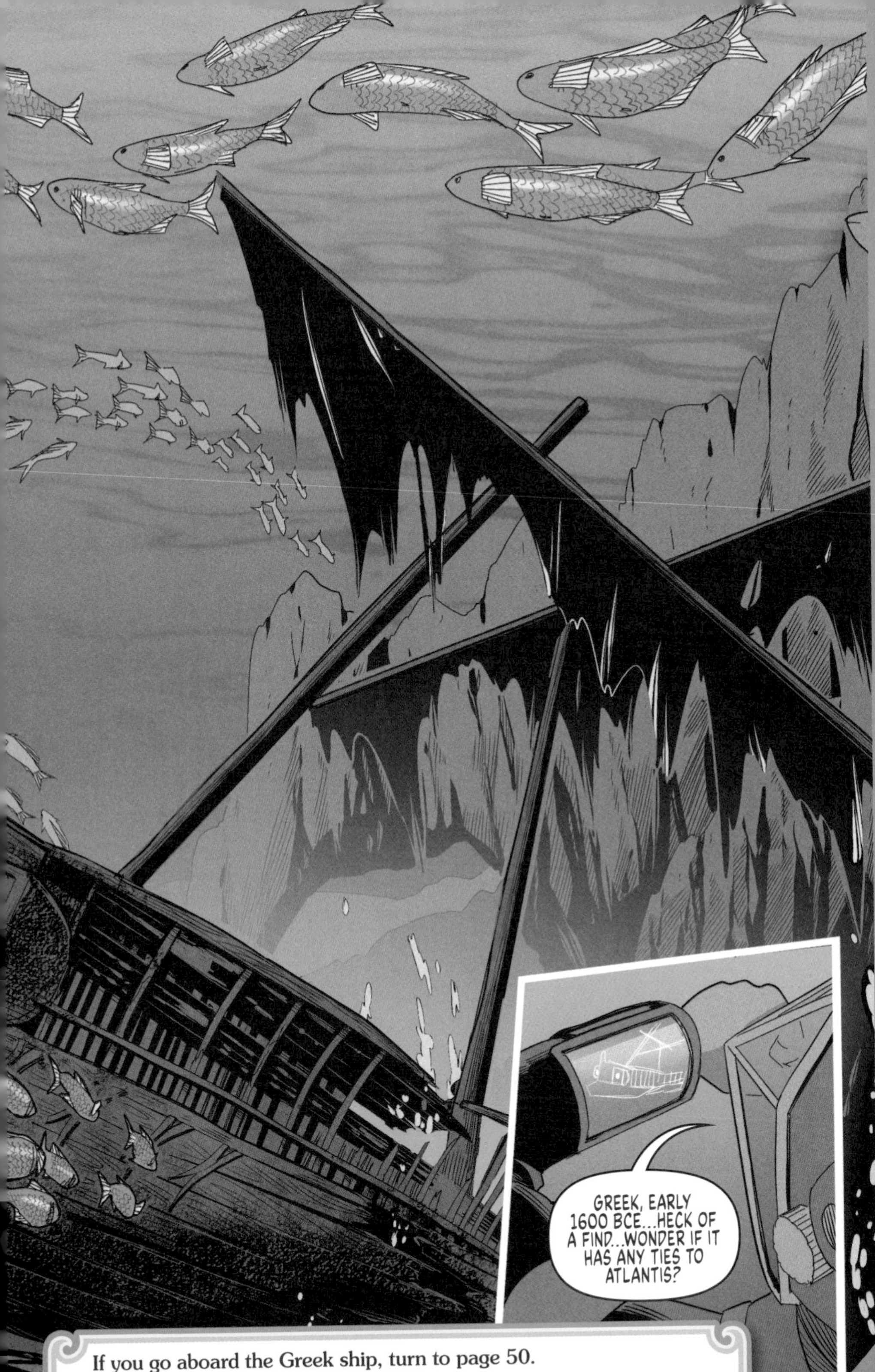
GREEK, EARLY 1600 BCE...HECK OF A FIND...WONDER IF IT HAS ANY TIES TO ATLANTIS?

If you go aboard the Greek ship, turn to page 50.
If you return to the surface to report your findings, turn to page 108.

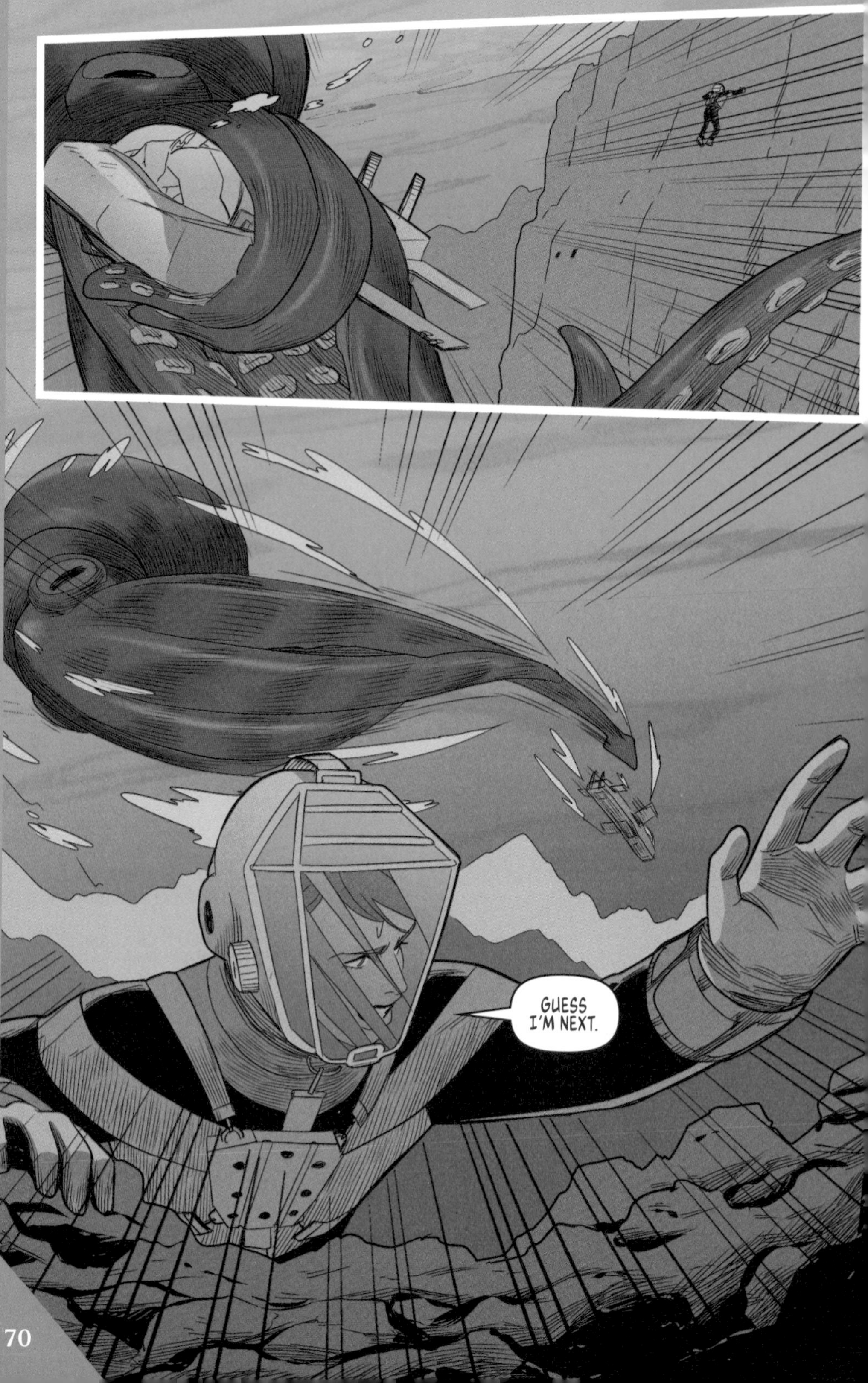
GUESS I'M NEXT.

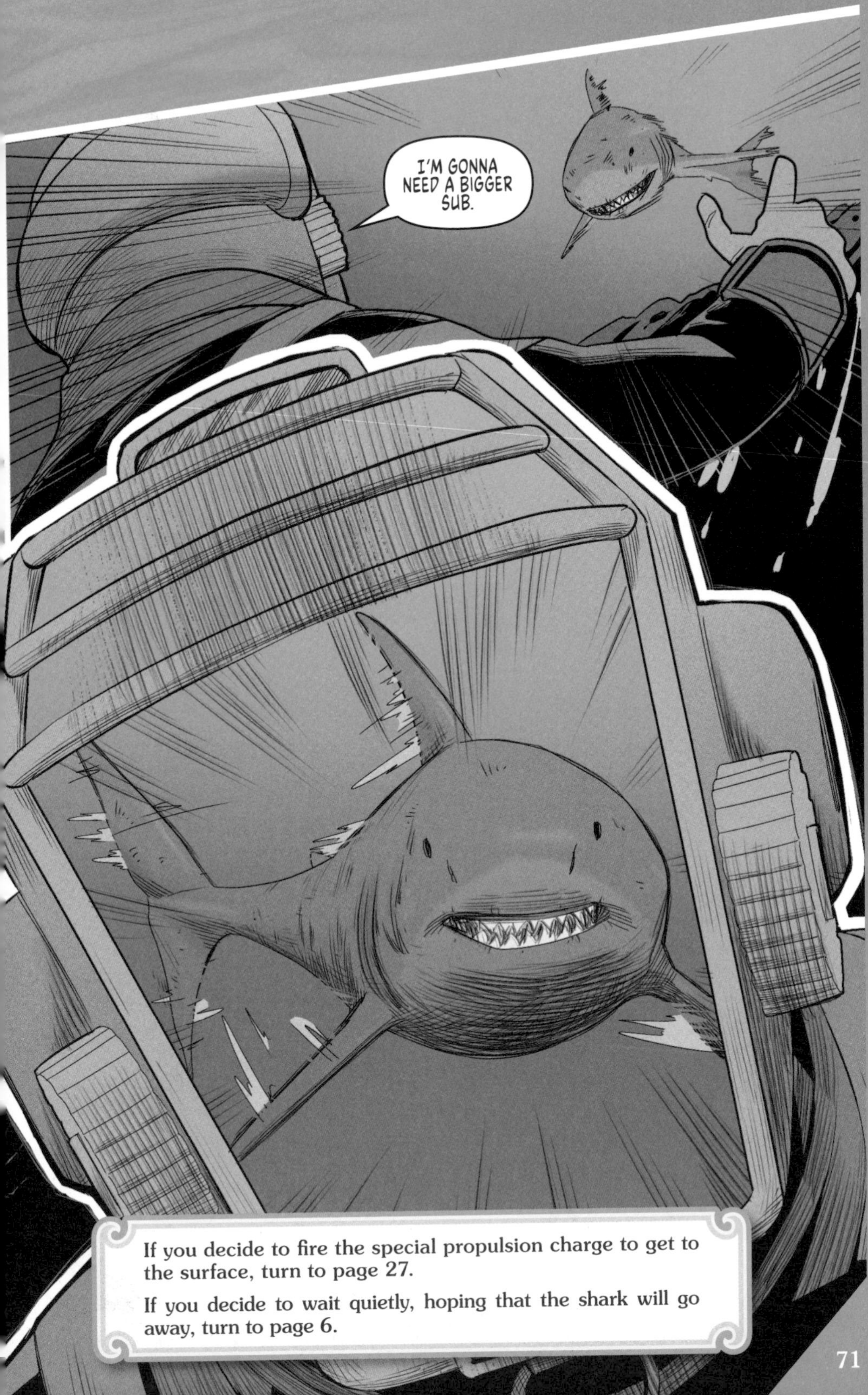
I'M GONNA NEED A BIGGER SUB.

If you decide to fire the special propulsion charge to get to the surface, turn to page 27.

If you decide to wait quietly, hoping that the shark will go away, turn to page 6.

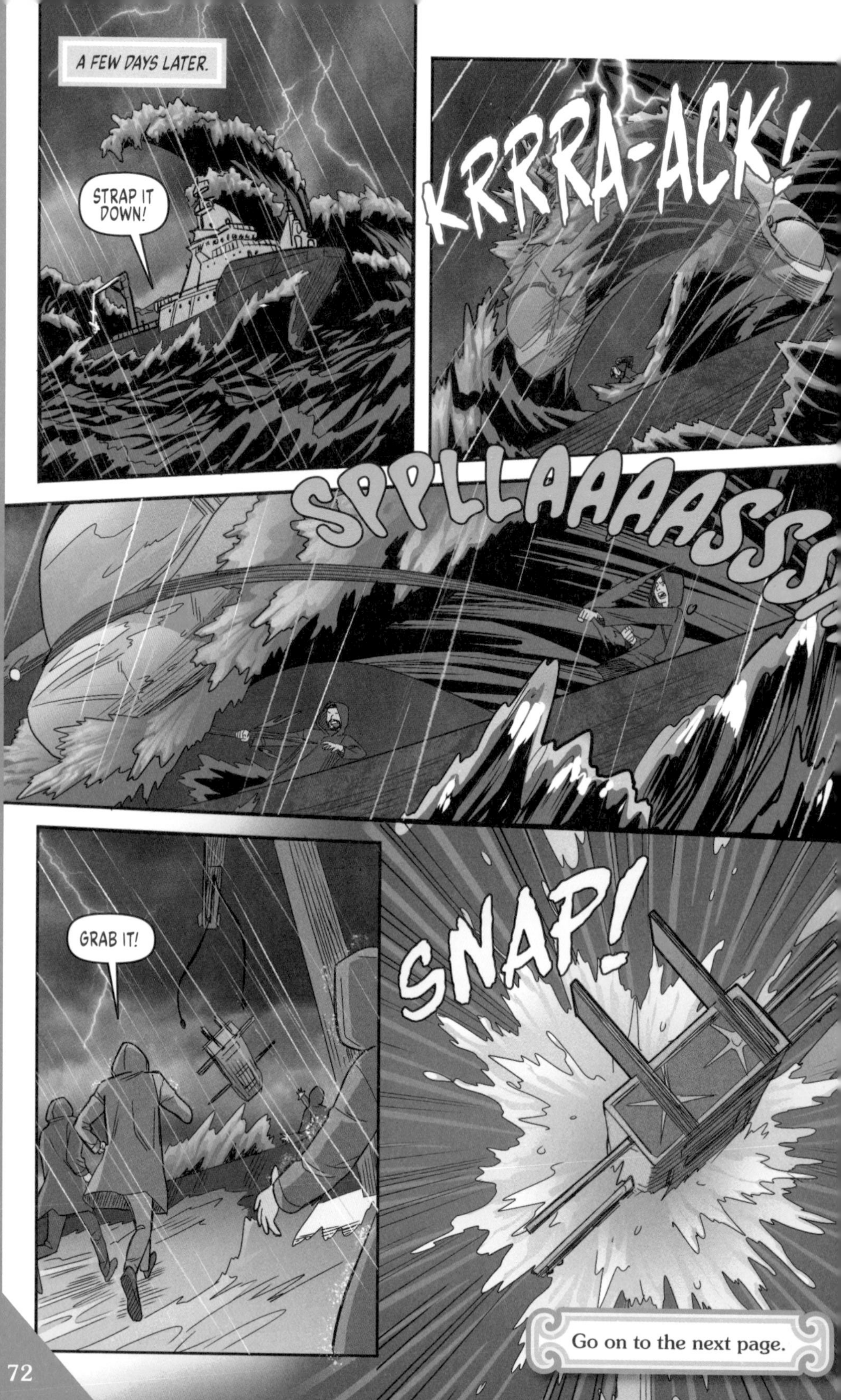
A FEW DAYS LATER.
STRAP IT DOWN!
KRRRA-ACK!
SPPLLAAAASS
GRAB IT!
SNAP!

Go on to the next page.

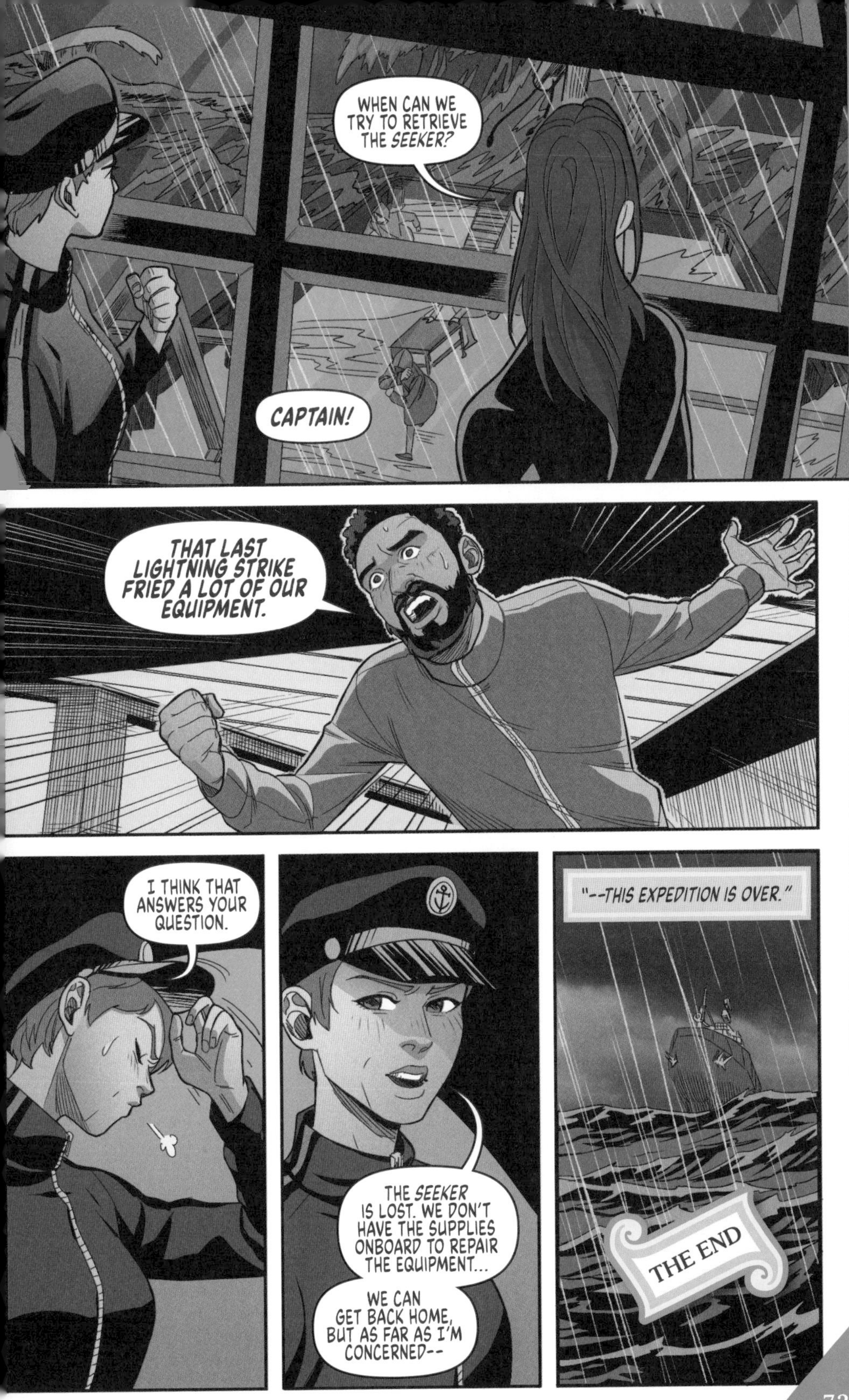
WHEN CAN WE TRY TO RETRIEVE THE *SEEKER?*
CAPTAIN!
THAT LAST LIGHTNING STRIKE FRIED A LOT OF OUR EQUIPMENT.
I THINK THAT ANSWERS YOUR QUESTION.
THE *SEEKER* IS LOST. WE DON'T HAVE THE SUPPLIES ONBOARD TO REPAIR THE EQUIPMENT...
WE CAN GET BACK HOME, BUT AS FAR AS I'M CONCERNED--
"--THIS EXPEDITION IS OVER."
THE END

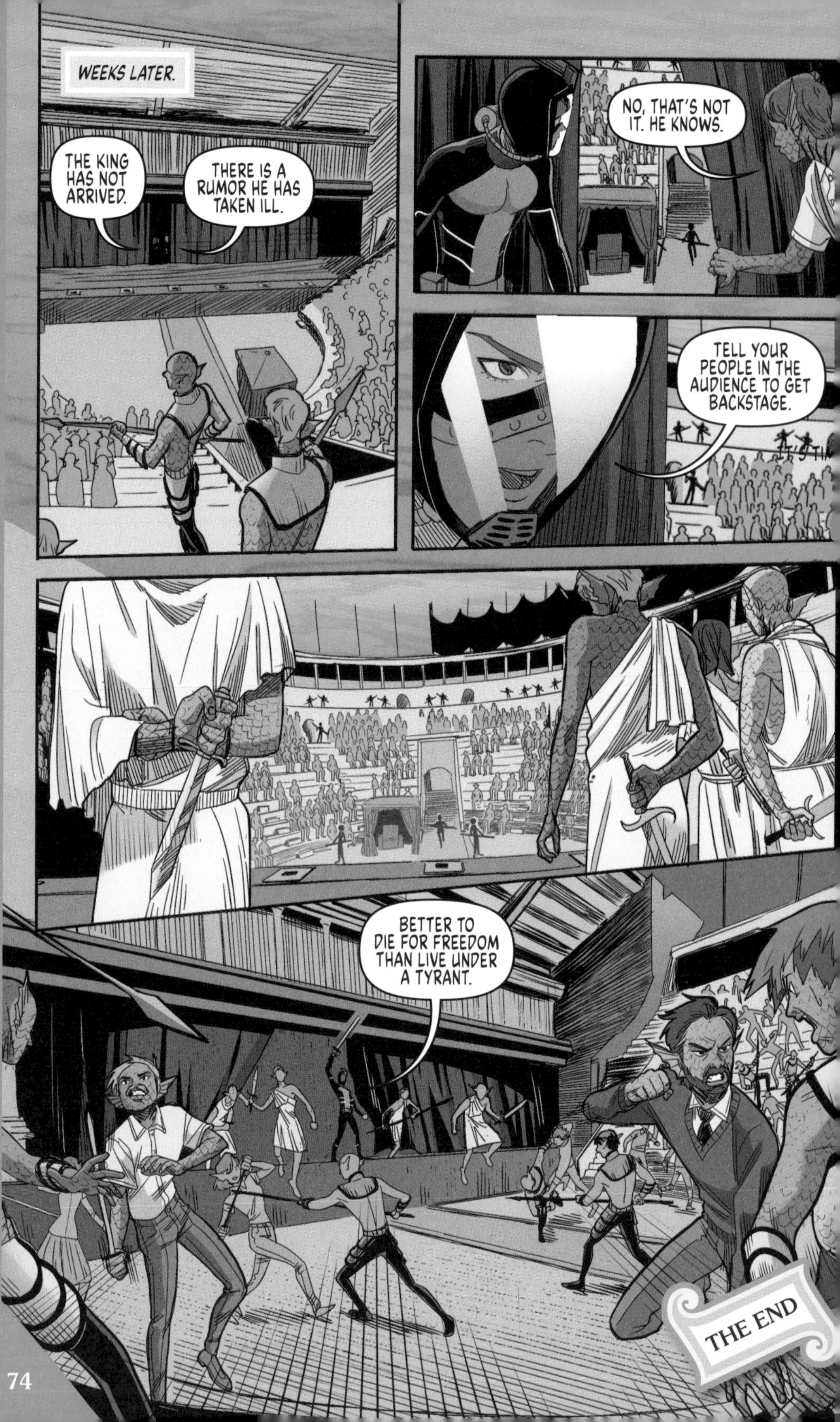
WEEKS LATER.
THE KING HAS NOT ARRIVED.
THERE IS A RUMOR HE HAS TAKEN ILL.
NO, THAT'S NOT IT. HE KNOWS.
TELL YOUR PEOPLE IN THE AUDIENCE TO GET BACKSTAGE.
BETTER TO DIE FOR FREEDOM THAN LIVE UNDER A TYRANT.
THE END

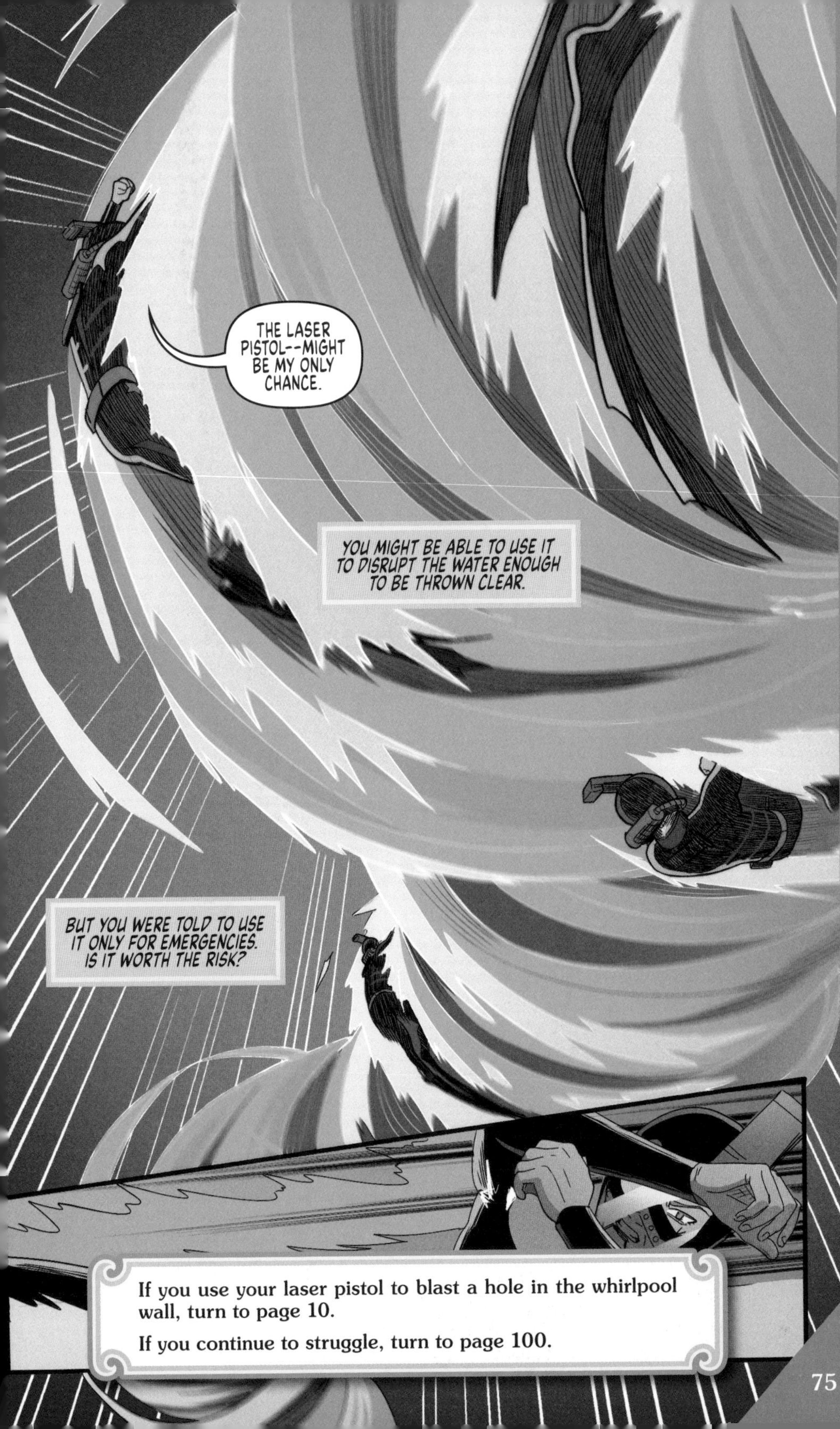
THE LASER PISTOL--MIGHT BE MY ONLY CHANCE.
YOU MIGHT BE ABLE TO USE IT TO DISRUPT THE WATER ENOUGH TO BE THROWN CLEAR.
BUT YOU WERE TOLD TO USE IT ONLY FOR EMERGENCIES. IS IT WORTH THE RISK?

If you use your laser pistol to blast a hole in the whirlpool wall, turn to page 10.

If you continue to struggle, turn to page 100.

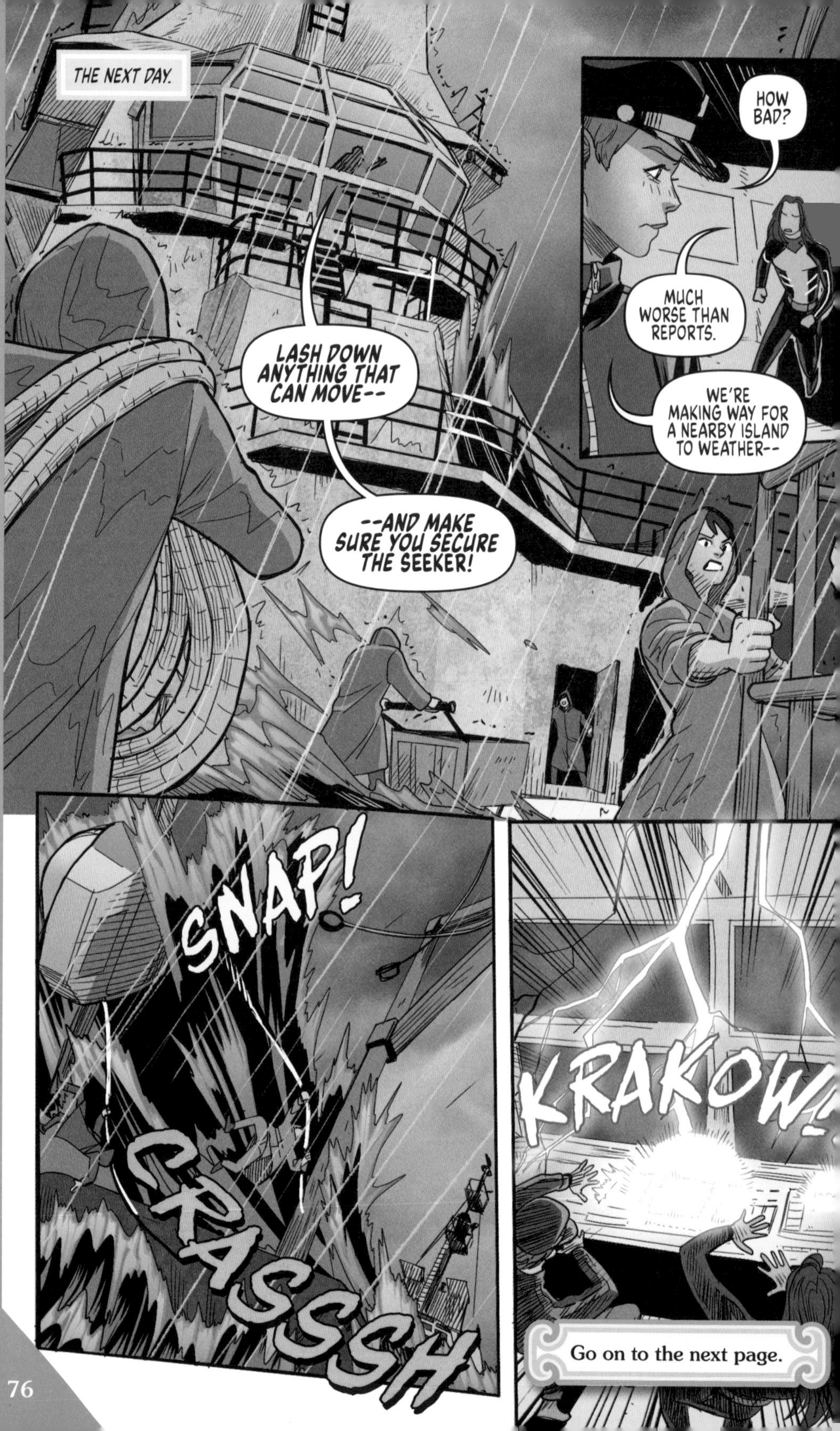
THE NEXT DAY.
LASH DOWN ANYTHING THAT CAN MOVE--
--AND MAKE SURE YOU SECURE THE SEEKER!
HOW BAD?
MUCH WORSE THAN REPORTS.
WE'RE MAKING WAY FOR A NEARBY ISLAND TO WEATHER--
SNAP!
CRASSSH
KRAKOW!

Go on to the next page.

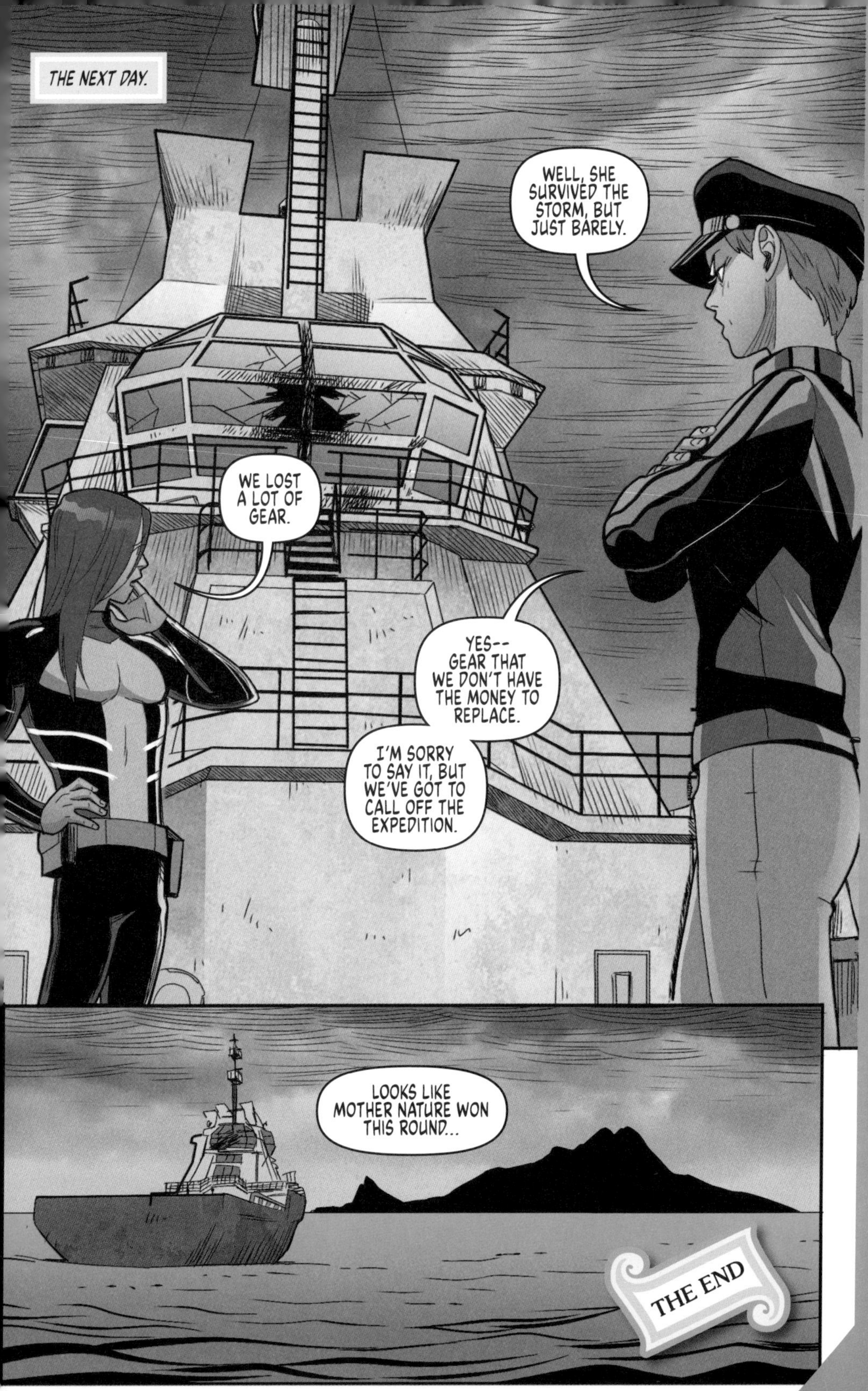
THE NEXT DAY.
WELL, SHE SURVIVED THE STORM, BUT JUST BARELY.
WE LOST A LOT OF GEAR.
YES-- GEAR THAT WE DON'T HAVE THE MONEY TO REPLACE.
I'M SORRY TO SAY IT, BUT WE'VE GOT TO CALL OFF THE EXPEDITION.
LOOKS LIKE MOTHER NATURE WON THIS ROUND...
THE END

I DON'T THINK SO.

THE WHOLE THING IS TOO FISHY FOR--

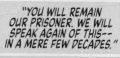

--ME!

ZZZZZZ!

I AM... DISAPPOINTED... BY YOUR DECISION, BUT I UNDERSTAND YOUR FEAR.

"YOU WILL REMAIN OUR PRISONER. WE WILL SPEAK AGAIN OF THIS-- IN A MERE FEW DECADES."

THE END

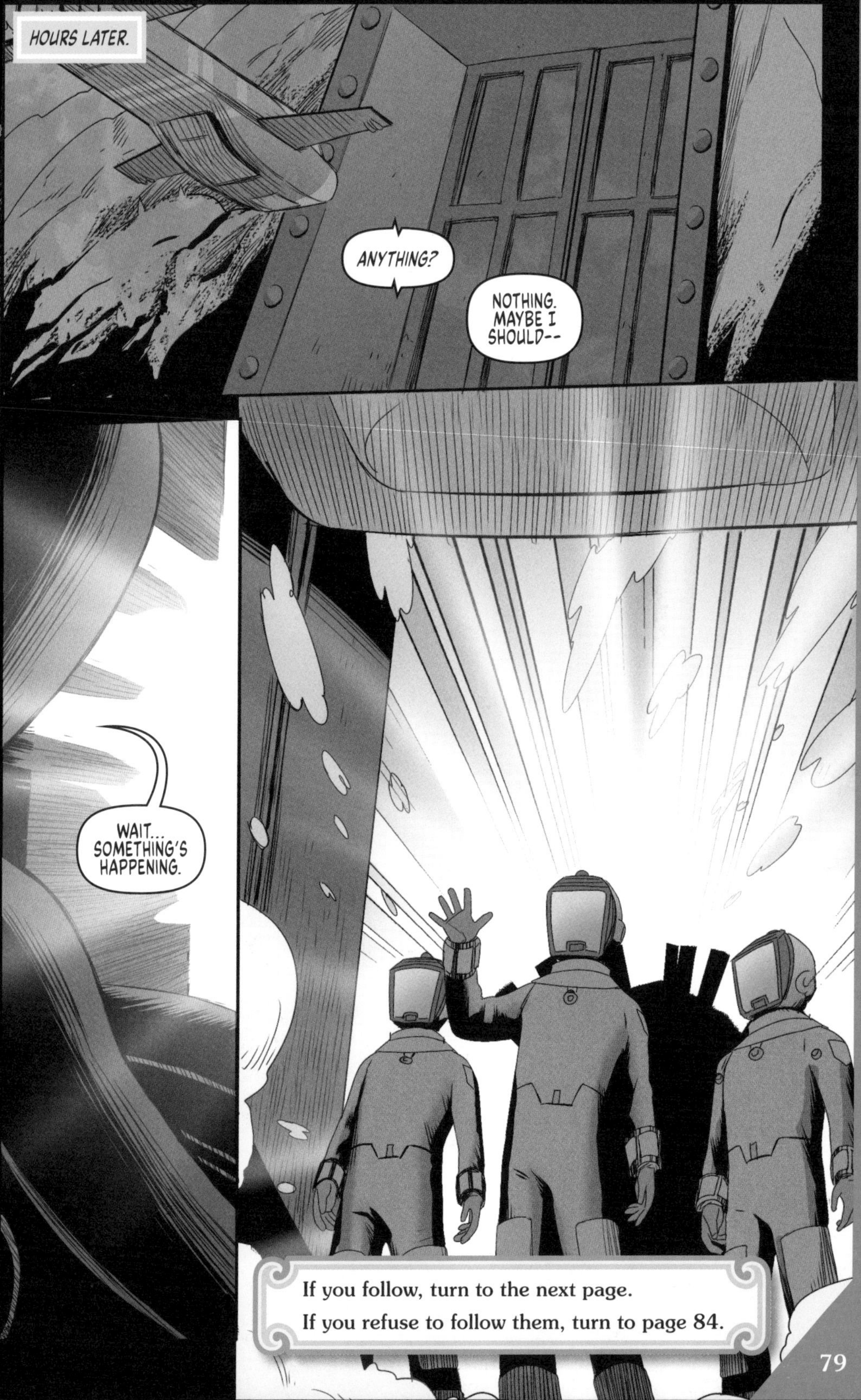
HOURS LATER.
ANYTHING?
NOTHING. MAYBE I SHOULD--
WAIT... SOMETHING'S HAPPENING.

If you follow, turn to the next page.
If you refuse to follow them, turn to page 84.

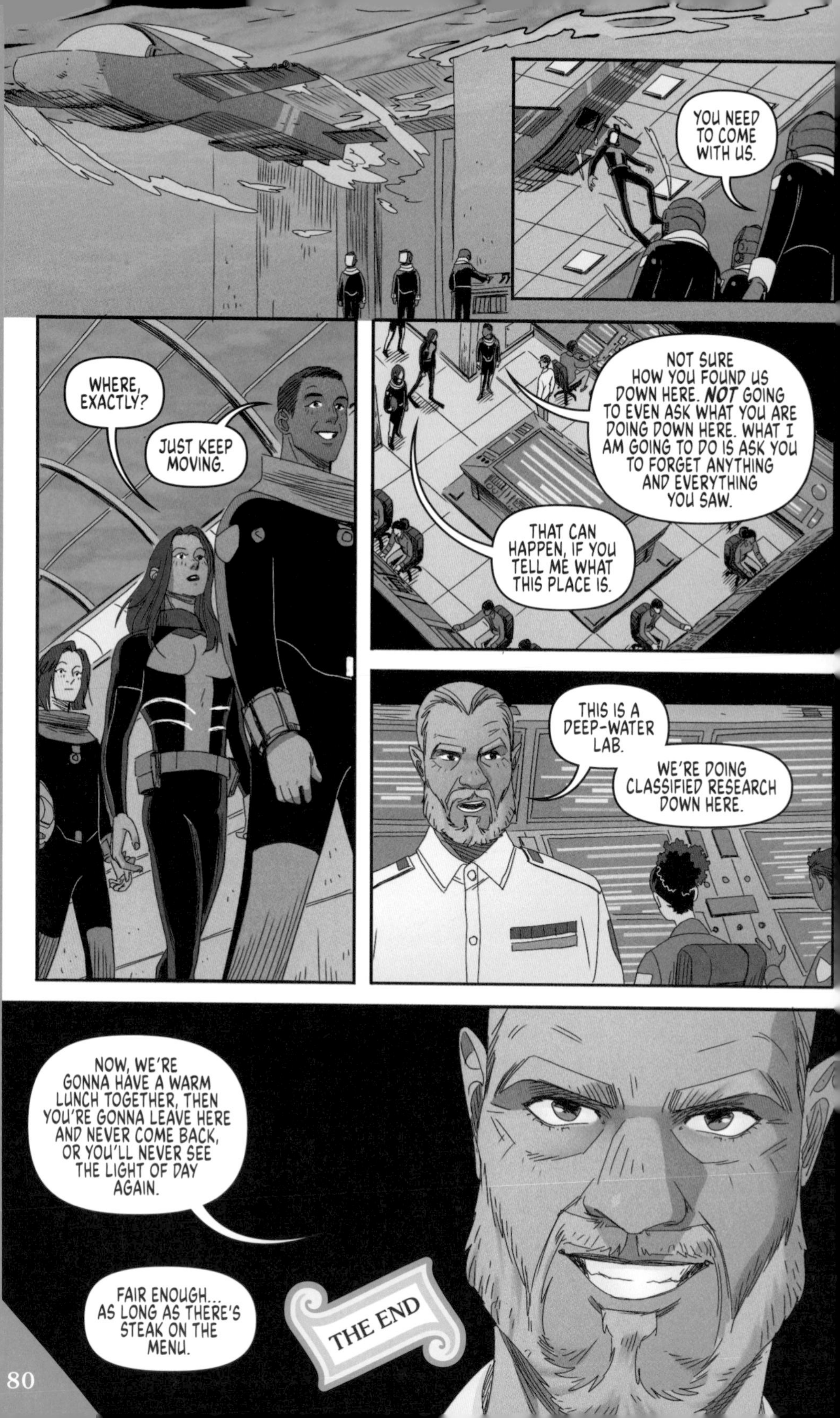
YOU NEED TO COME WITH US.
WHERE, EXACTLY?
JUST KEEP MOVING.
NOT SURE HOW YOU FOUND US DOWN HERE. ***NOT*** GOING TO EVEN ASK WHAT YOU ARE DOING DOWN HERE. WHAT I AM GOING TO DO IS ASK YOU TO FORGET ANYTHING AND EVERYTHING YOU SAW.
THAT CAN HAPPEN, IF YOU TELL ME WHAT THIS PLACE IS.
THIS IS A DEEP-WATER LAB.
WE'RE DOING CLASSIFIED RESEARCH DOWN HERE.
NOW, WE'RE GONNA HAVE A WARM LUNCH TOGETHER, THEN YOU'RE GONNA LEAVE HERE AND NEVER COME BACK, OR YOU'LL NEVER SEE THE LIGHT OF DAY AGAIN.
FAIR ENOUGH... AS LONG AS THERE'S STEAK ON THE MENU.
THE END

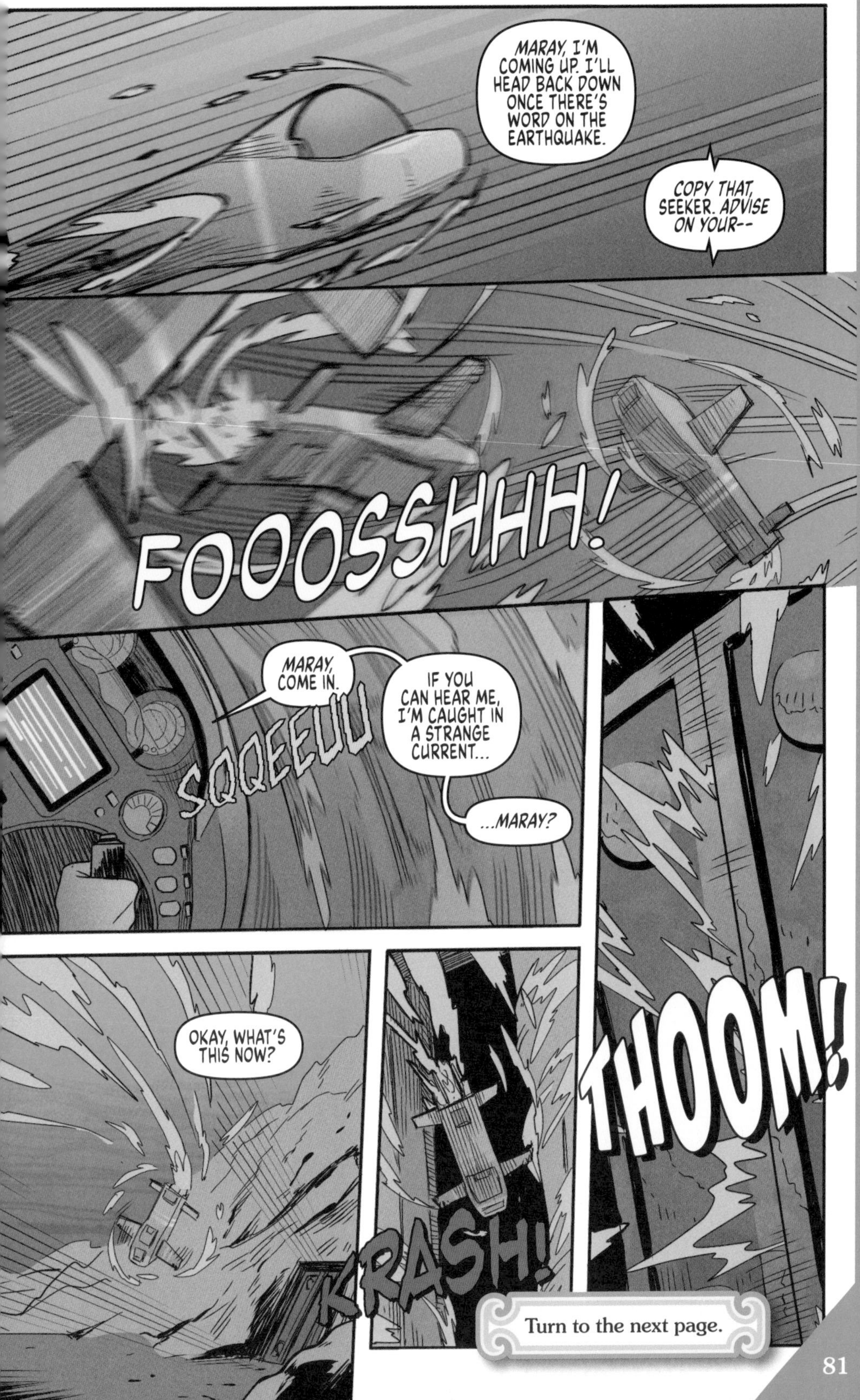
MARAY, I'M COMING UP. I'LL HEAD BACK DOWN ONCE THERE'S WORD ON THE EARTHQUAKE.
COPY THAT, SEEKER. ADVISE ON YOUR--
FOOOSSHHH!
MARAY, COME IN.
SQQEEUU
IF YOU CAN HEAR ME, I'M CAUGHT IN A STRANGE CURRENT...
...MARAY?
OKAY, WHAT'S THIS NOW?
KRASH!
THOOM!

Turn to the next page.

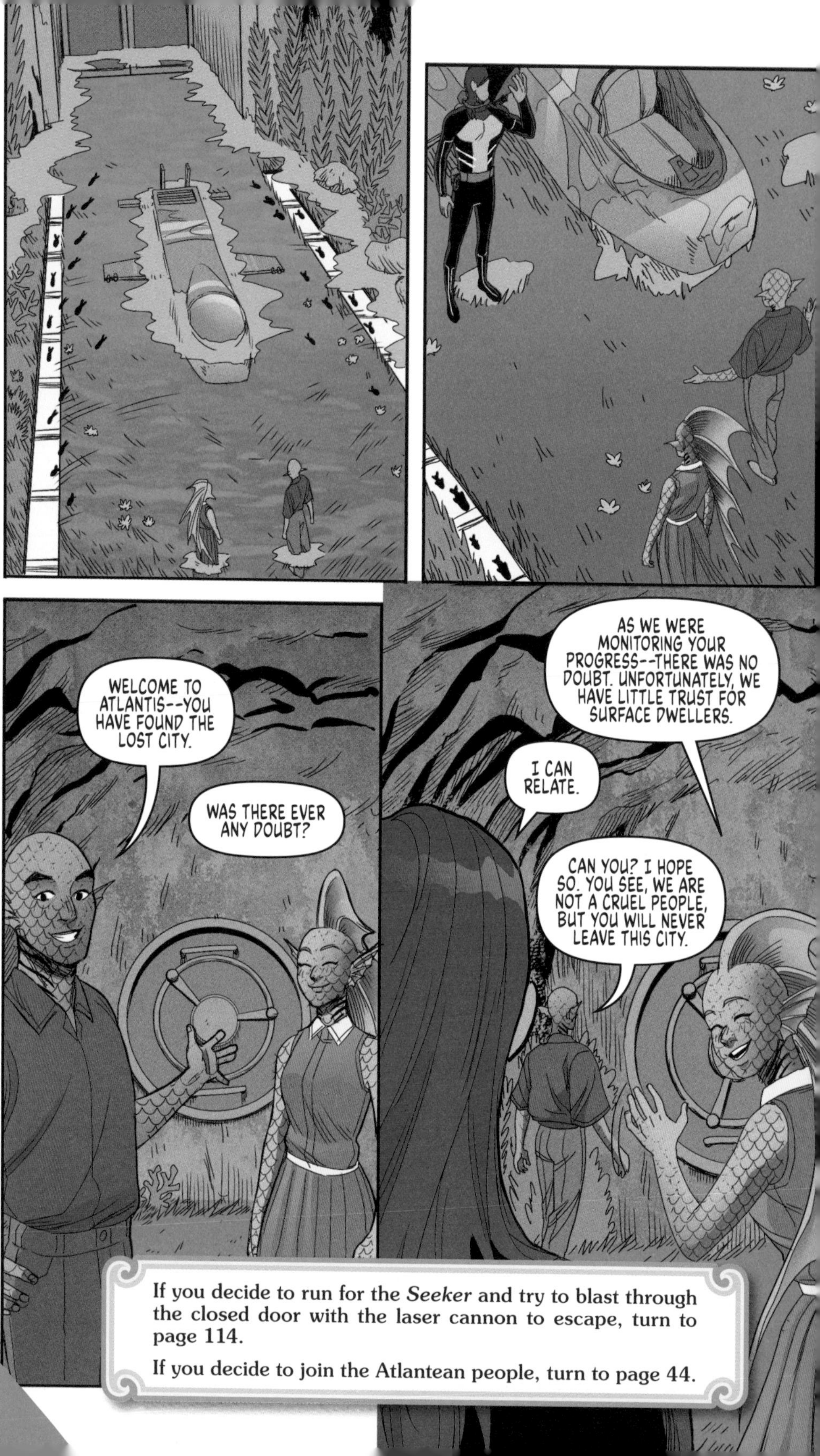
WELCOME TO ATLANTIS--YOU HAVE FOUND THE LOST CITY.
WAS THERE EVER ANY DOUBT?
AS WE WERE MONITORING YOUR PROGRESS--THERE WAS NO DOUBT. UNFORTUNATELY, WE HAVE LITTLE TRUST FOR SURFACE DWELLERS.
I CAN RELATE.
CAN YOU? I HOPE SO. YOU SEE, WE ARE NOT A CRUEL PEOPLE, BUT YOU WILL NEVER LEAVE THIS CITY.

If you decide to run for the *Seeker* and try to blast through the closed door with the laser cannon to escape, turn to page 114.

If you decide to join the Atlantean people, turn to page 44.

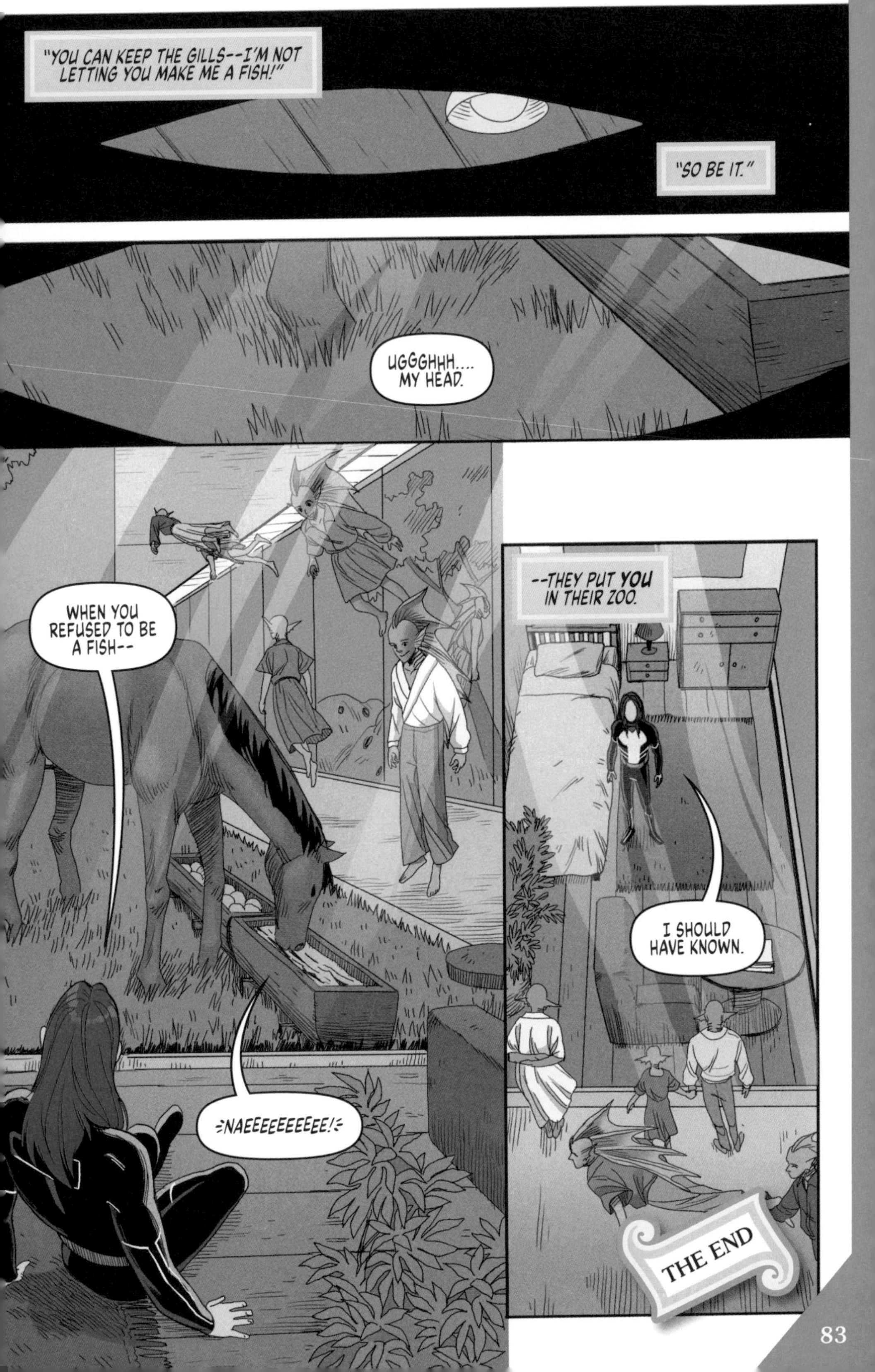
"YOU CAN KEEP THE GILLS--I'M NOT LETTING YOU MAKE ME A FISH!"
"SO BE IT."
UGGGHHH.... MY HEAD.
WHEN YOU REFUSED TO BE A FISH--
=NAEEEEEEEEEE!=
--THEY PUT YOU IN THEIR ZOO.
I SHOULD HAVE KNOWN.
THE END

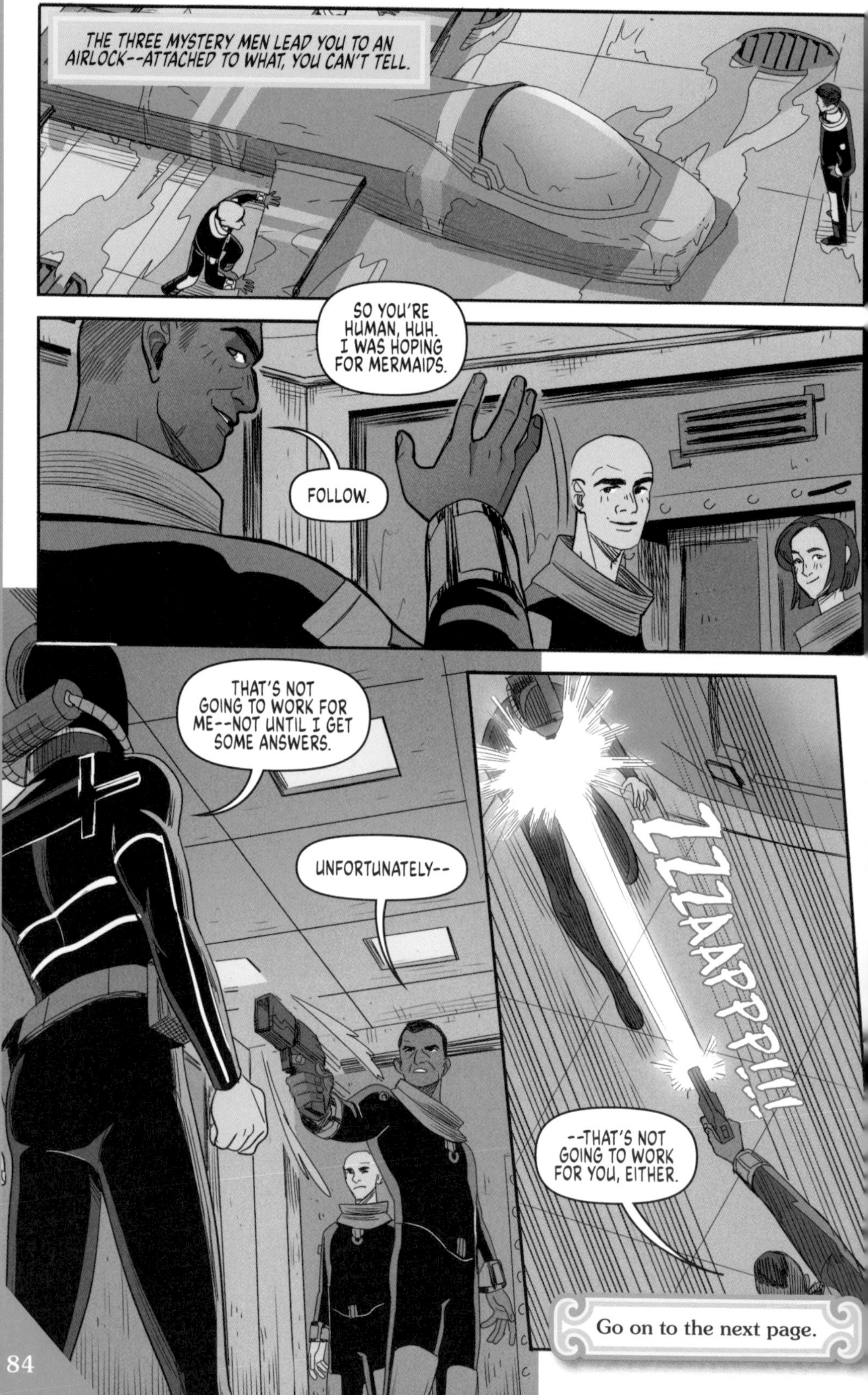
THE THREE MYSTERY MEN LEAD YOU TO AN AIRLOCK--ATTACHED TO WHAT, YOU CAN'T TELL.
SO YOU'RE HUMAN, HUH. I WAS HOPING FOR MERMAIDS.
FOLLOW.
THAT'S NOT GOING TO WORK FOR ME--NOT UNTIL I GET SOME ANSWERS.
UNFORTUNATELY--
ZZZAAPPP!!!
--THAT'S NOT GOING TO WORK FOR YOU, EITHER.
Go on to the next page.

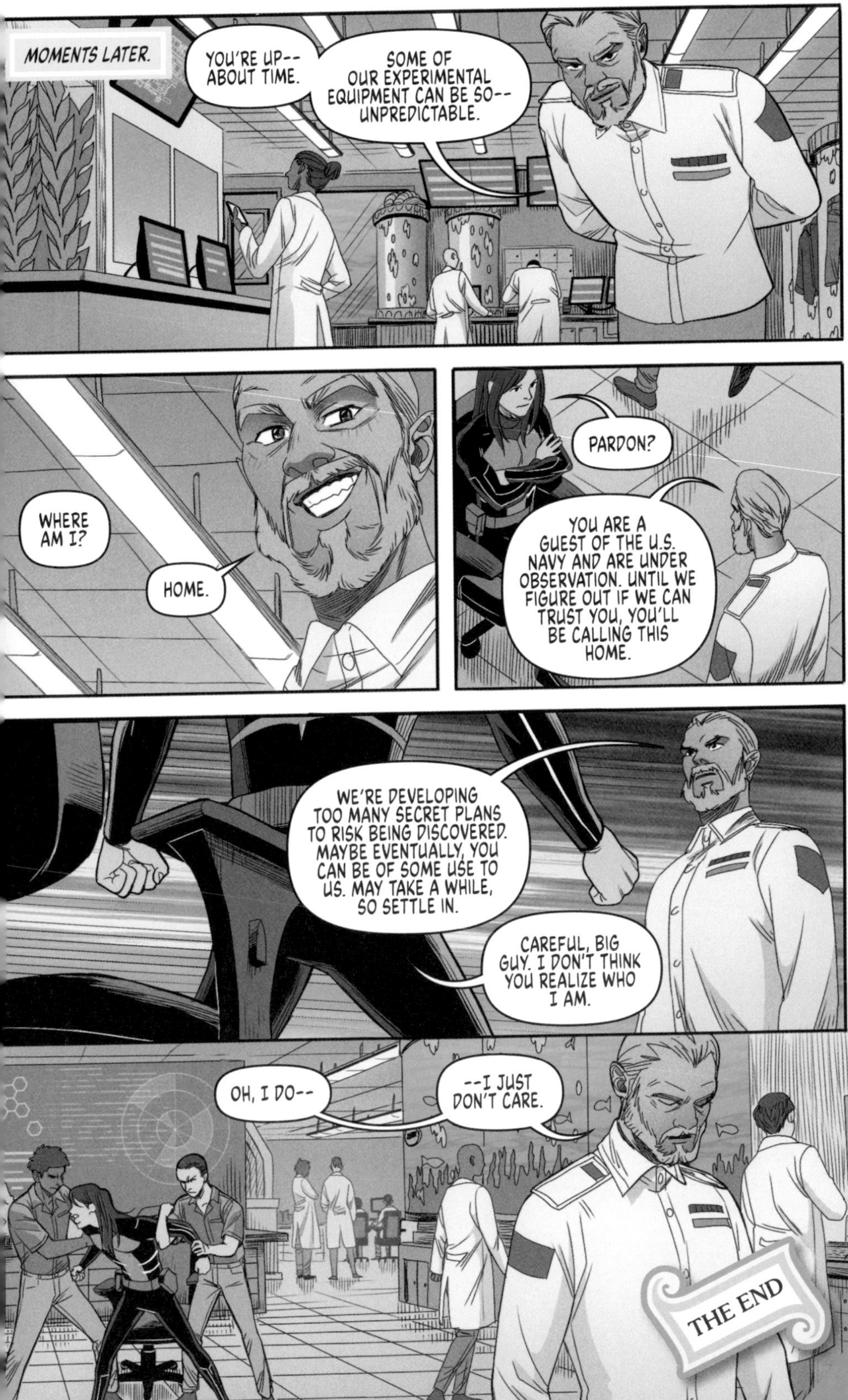
MOMENTS LATER.
YOU'RE UP--
ABOUT TIME.
SOME OF OUR EXPERIMENTAL EQUIPMENT CAN BE SO--UNPREDICTABLE.
WHERE AM I?
HOME.
PARDON?
YOU ARE A GUEST OF THE U.S. NAVY AND ARE UNDER OBSERVATION. UNTIL WE FIGURE OUT IF WE CAN TRUST YOU, YOU'LL BE CALLING THIS HOME.
WE'RE DEVELOPING TOO MANY SECRET PLANS TO RISK BEING DISCOVERED. MAYBE EVENTUALLY, YOU CAN BE OF SOME USE TO US. MAY TAKE A WHILE, SO SETTLE IN.
CAREFUL, BIG GUY. I DON'T THINK YOU REALIZE WHO I AM.
OH, I DO--
--I JUST DON'T CARE.
THE END

YOU BEGIN TO REALIZE THAT THERE ARE SOME THINGS BEST LEFT UNKNOWN.
ALRIGHT. SOMETIMES DISCRETION--
--IS THE BETTER PART OF VALOR.
COME ON, SEEKER--PUSH. YOU CAN DO IT.
SPLORCH
OR NOT.
LOOKS LIKE THIS FLYTRAP IS GOING TO BE HOME.
THE END

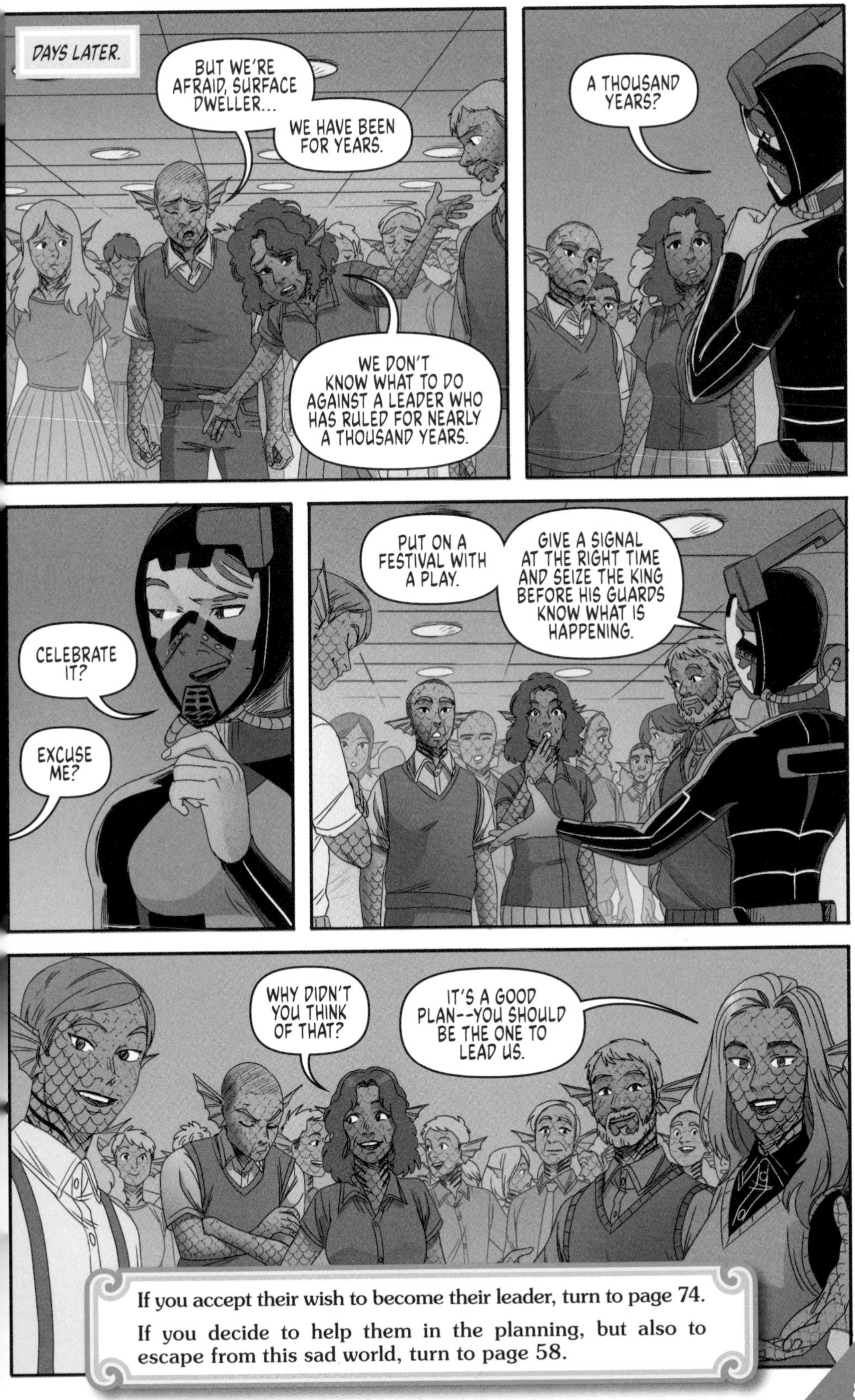
DAYS LATER.
BUT WE'RE AFRAID, SURFACE DWELLER...
WE HAVE BEEN FOR YEARS.
WE DON'T KNOW WHAT TO DO AGAINST A LEADER WHO HAS RULED FOR NEARLY A THOUSAND YEARS.
A THOUSAND YEARS?
CELEBRATE IT?
EXCUSE ME?
PUT ON A FESTIVAL WITH A PLAY.
GIVE A SIGNAL AT THE RIGHT TIME AND SEIZE THE KING BEFORE HIS GUARDS KNOW WHAT IS HAPPENING.
WHY DIDN'T YOU THINK OF THAT?
IT'S A GOOD PLAN--YOU SHOULD BE THE ONE TO LEAD US.

If you accept their wish to become their leader, turn to page 74.

If you decide to help them in the planning, but also to escape from this sad world, turn to page 58.

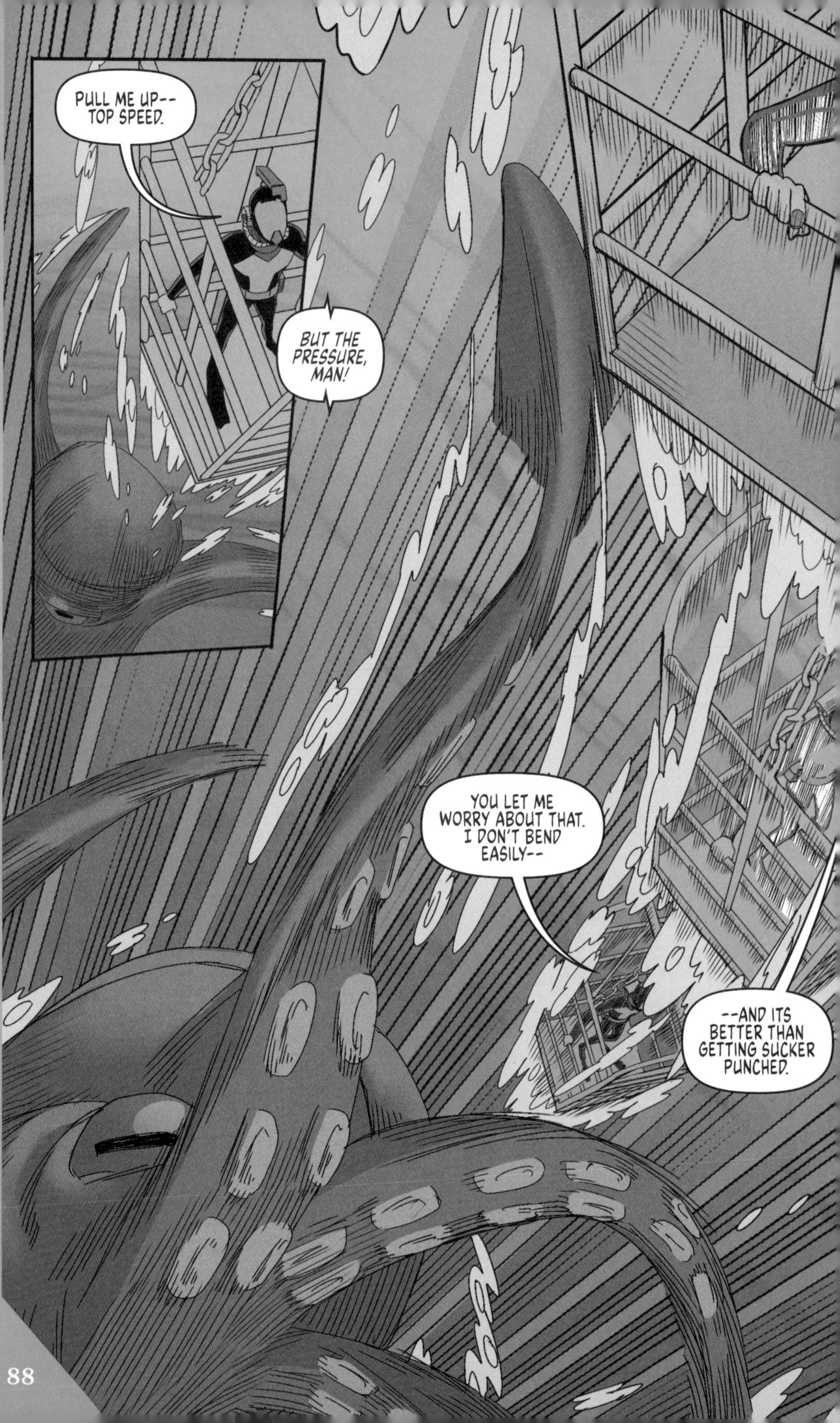
PULL ME UP--
TOP SPEED.
BUT THE PRESSURE, MAN!
YOU LET ME WORRY ABOUT THAT. I DON'T BEND EASILY--
--AND ITS BETTER THAN GETTING SUCKER PUNCHED.

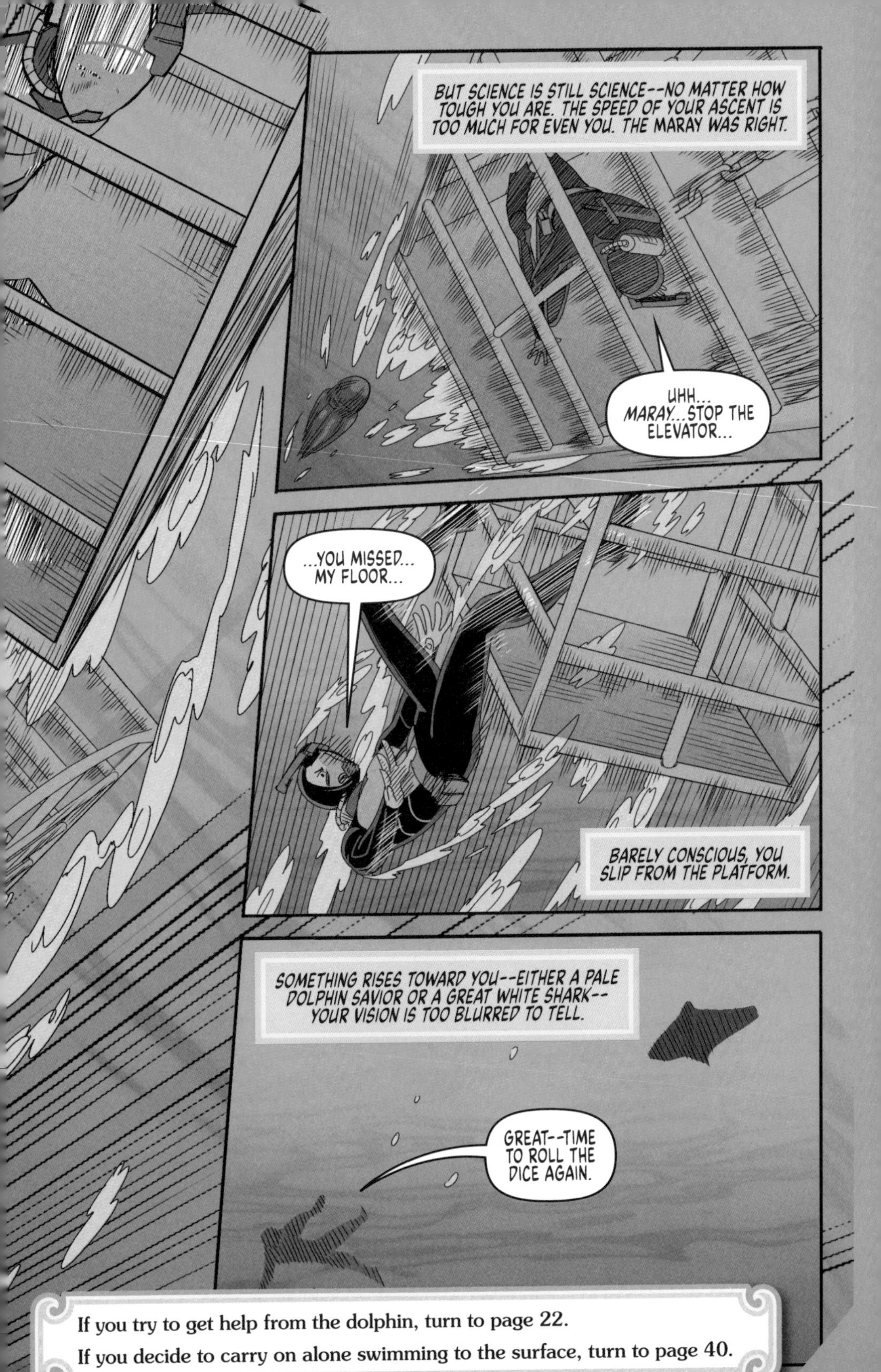
BUT SCIENCE IS STILL SCIENCE--NO MATTER HOW TOUGH YOU ARE. THE SPEED OF YOUR ASCENT IS TOO MUCH FOR EVEN YOU. THE MARAY WAS RIGHT.
UHH... MARAY...STOP THE ELEVATOR...
...YOU MISSED... MY FLOOR...
BARELY CONSCIOUS, YOU SLIP FROM THE PLATFORM.
SOMETHING RISES TOWARD YOU--EITHER A PALE DOLPHIN SAVIOR OR A GREAT WHITE SHARK--YOUR VISION IS TOO BLURRED TO TELL.
GREAT--TIME TO ROLL THE DICE AGAIN.

If you try to get help from the dolphin, turn to page 22.

If you decide to carry on alone swimming to the surface, turn to page 40.

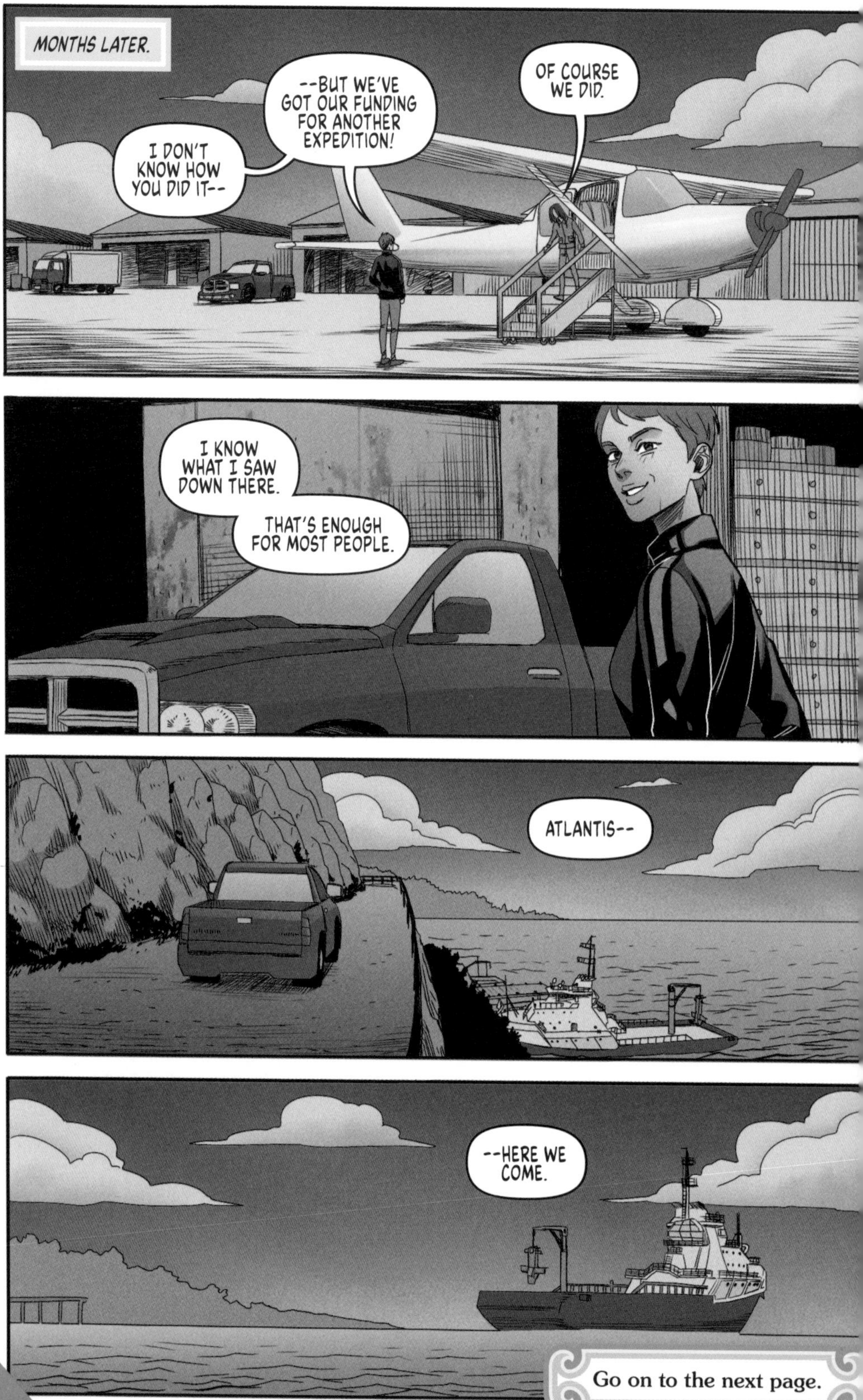
MONTHS LATER.
I DON'T KNOW HOW YOU DID IT--
--BUT WE'VE GOT OUR FUNDING FOR ANOTHER EXPEDITION!
OF COURSE WE DID.
I KNOW WHAT I SAW DOWN THERE.
THAT'S ENOUGH FOR MOST PEOPLE.
ATLANTIS--
--HERE WE COME.

Go on to the next page.

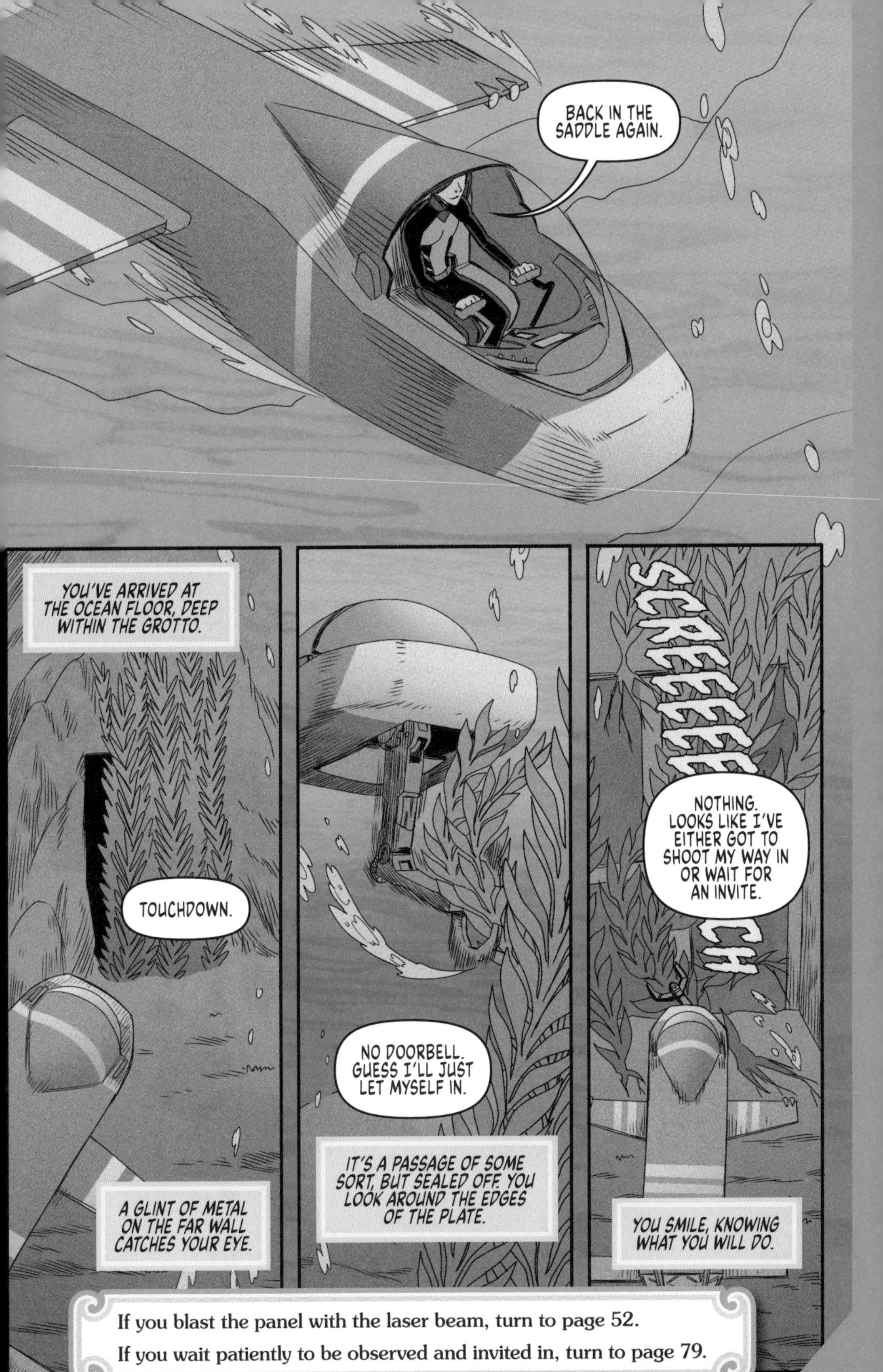
BACK IN THE SADDLE AGAIN.
YOU'VE ARRIVED AT THE OCEAN FLOOR, DEEP WITHIN THE GROTTO.
TOUCHDOWN.
A GLINT OF METAL ON THE FAR WALL CATCHES YOUR EYE.
NO DOORBELL. GUESS I'LL JUST LET MYSELF IN.
IT'S A PASSAGE OF SOME SORT, BUT SEALED OFF. YOU LOOK AROUND THE EDGES OF THE PLATE.
SCREEEECH
NOTHING. LOOKS LIKE I'VE EITHER GOT TO SHOOT MY WAY IN OR WAIT FOR AN INVITE.
YOU SMILE, KNOWING WHAT YOU WILL DO.

If you blast the panel with the laser beam, turn to page 52.
If you wait patiently to be observed and invited in, turn to page 79.

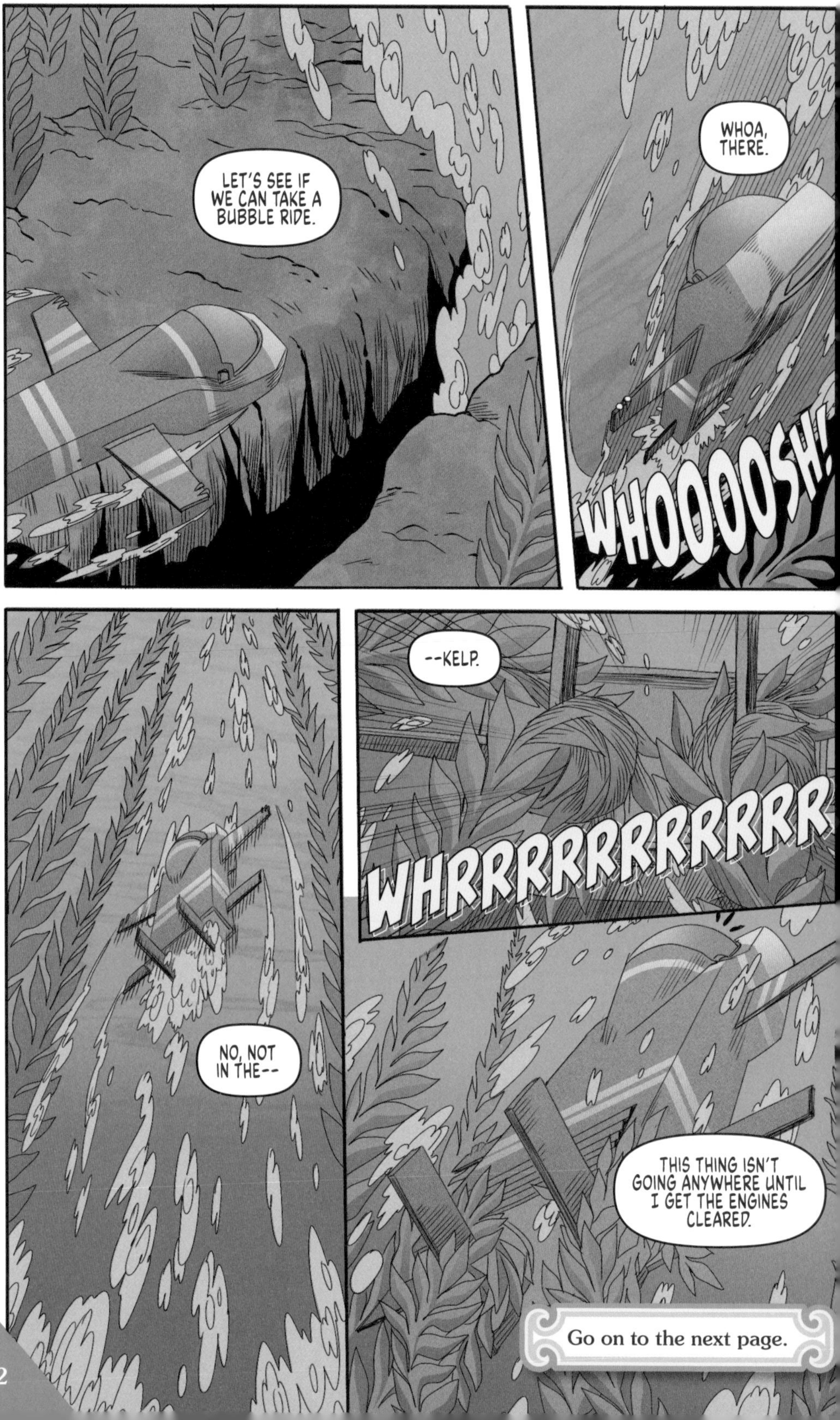
LET'S SEE IF WE CAN TAKE A BUBBLE RIDE.
WHOA, THERE.
WHOOOOSH!
NO, NOT IN THE--
--KELP.
WHRRRRRRRRRR
THIS THING ISN'T GOING ANYWHERE UNTIL I GET THE ENGINES CLEARED.

Go on to the next page.

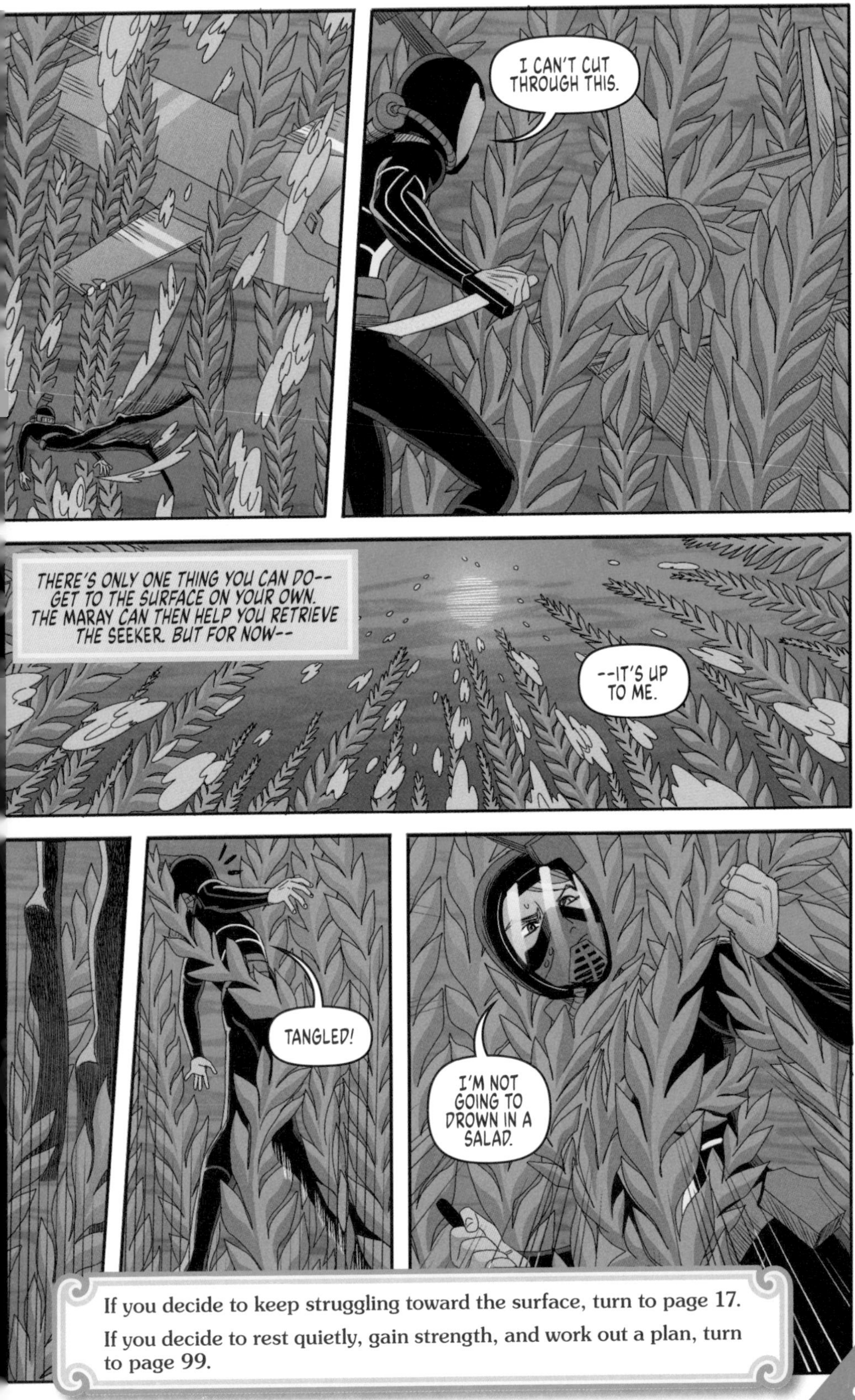
I CAN'T CUT THROUGH THIS.
THERE'S ONLY ONE THING YOU CAN DO-- GET TO THE SURFACE ON YOUR OWN. THE MARAY CAN THEN HELP YOU RETRIEVE THE SEEKER. BUT FOR NOW--
--IT'S UP TO ME.
TANGLED!
I'M NOT GOING TO DROWN IN A SALAD.

If you decide to keep struggling toward the surface, turn to page 17.

If you decide to rest quietly, gain strength, and work out a plan, turn to page 99.

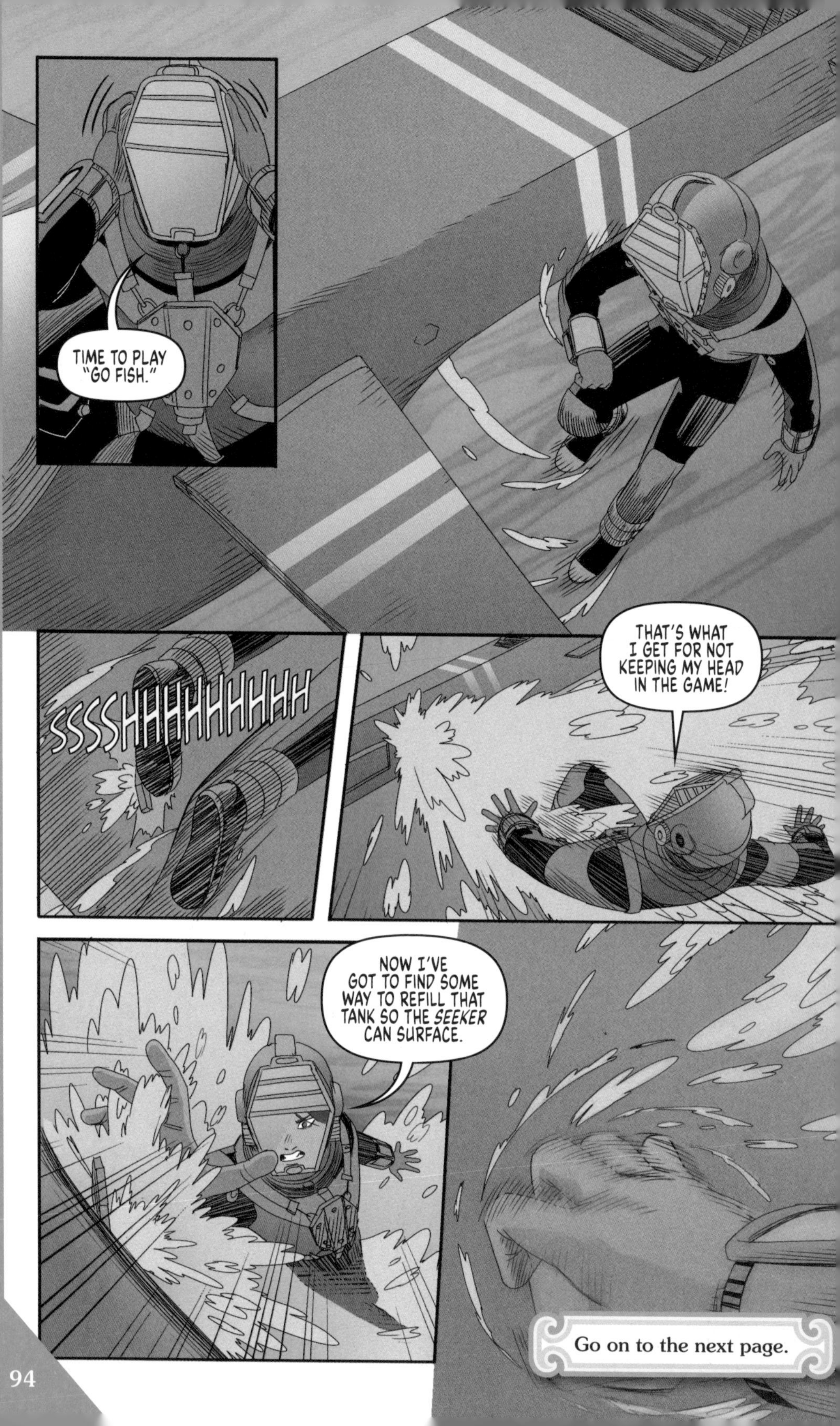
TIME TO PLAY "GO FISH."
SSSSHHHHHHHHHH
THAT'S WHAT I GET FOR NOT KEEPING MY HEAD IN THE GAME!
NOW I'VE GOT TO FIND SOME WAY TO REFILL THAT TANK SO THE *SEEKER* CAN SURFACE.

Go on to the next page.

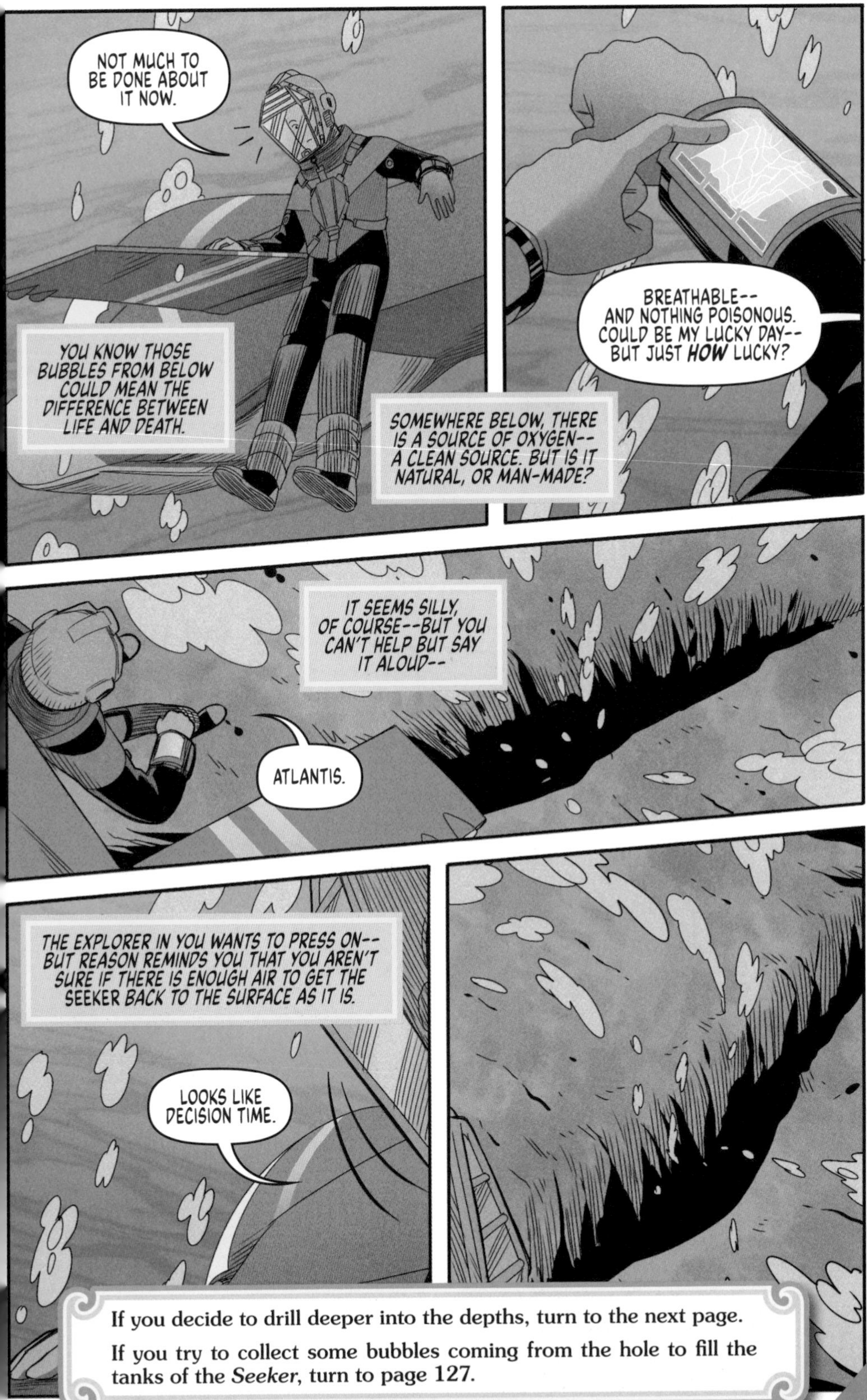
NOT MUCH TO BE DONE ABOUT IT NOW.
YOU KNOW THOSE BUBBLES FROM BELOW COULD MEAN THE DIFFERENCE BETWEEN LIFE AND DEATH.
BREATHABLE-- AND NOTHING POISONOUS. COULD BE MY LUCKY DAY-- BUT JUST HOW LUCKY?
SOMEWHERE BELOW, THERE IS A SOURCE OF OXYGEN-- A CLEAN SOURCE. BUT IS IT NATURAL, OR MAN-MADE?
IT SEEMS SILLY, OF COURSE--BUT YOU CAN'T HELP BUT SAY IT ALOUD--
ATLANTIS.
THE EXPLORER IN YOU WANTS TO PRESS ON-- BUT REASON REMINDS YOU THAT YOU AREN'T SURE IF THERE IS ENOUGH AIR TO GET THE SEEKER BACK TO THE SURFACE AS IT IS.
LOOKS LIKE DECISION TIME.

If you decide to drill deeper into the depths, turn to the next page.

If you try to collect some bubbles coming from the hole to fill the tanks of the *Seeker*, turn to page 127.

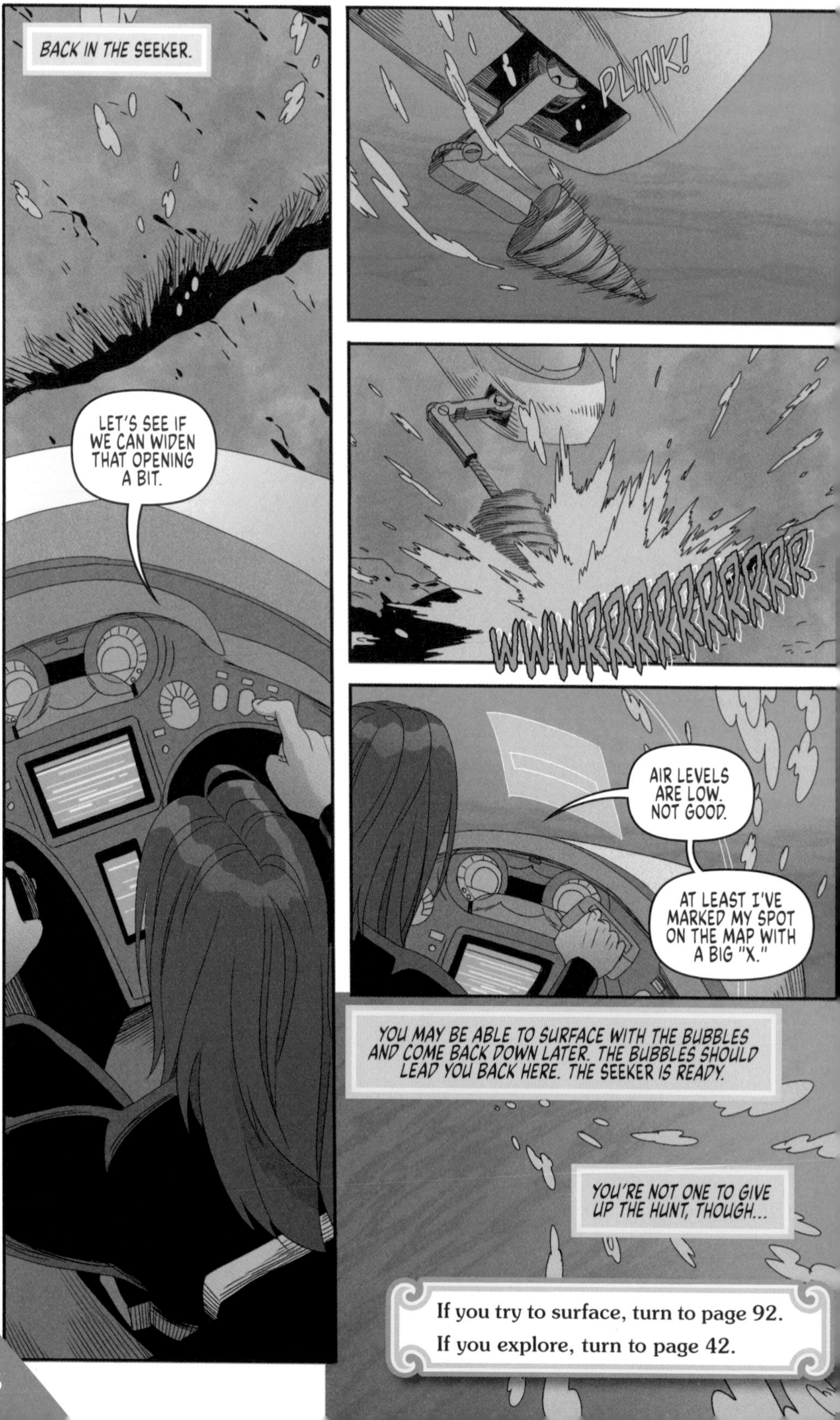
BACK IN THE SEEKER.
LET'S SEE IF WE CAN WIDEN THAT OPENING A BIT.
PLINK!
WWWRRRRRRRRRRRR
AIR LEVELS ARE LOW. NOT GOOD.
AT LEAST I'VE MARKED MY SPOT ON THE MAP WITH A BIG "X."
YOU MAY BE ABLE TO SURFACE WITH THE BUBBLES AND COME BACK DOWN LATER. THE BUBBLES SHOULD LEAD YOU BACK HERE. THE SEEKER IS READY.
YOU'RE NOT ONE TO GIVE UP THE HUNT, THOUGH...

If you try to surface, turn to page 92.
If you explore, turn to page 42.

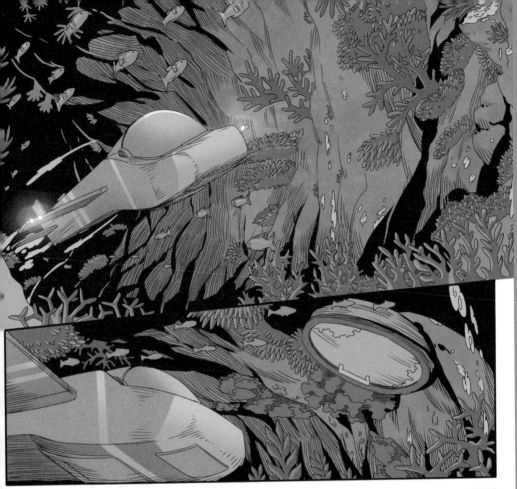

INTERESTING. LET'S SEE IF WE CAN GET YOU OPEN.

SCCREEEEAACCHH

"NOT A SCRATCH. WHAT'S IT GOING TO TAKE TO OPEN YOU UP?"

If you decide to blow the hatch open with the laser, turn to the next page.

If you decide to transmit radio communications through the hatch, turn to page 48.

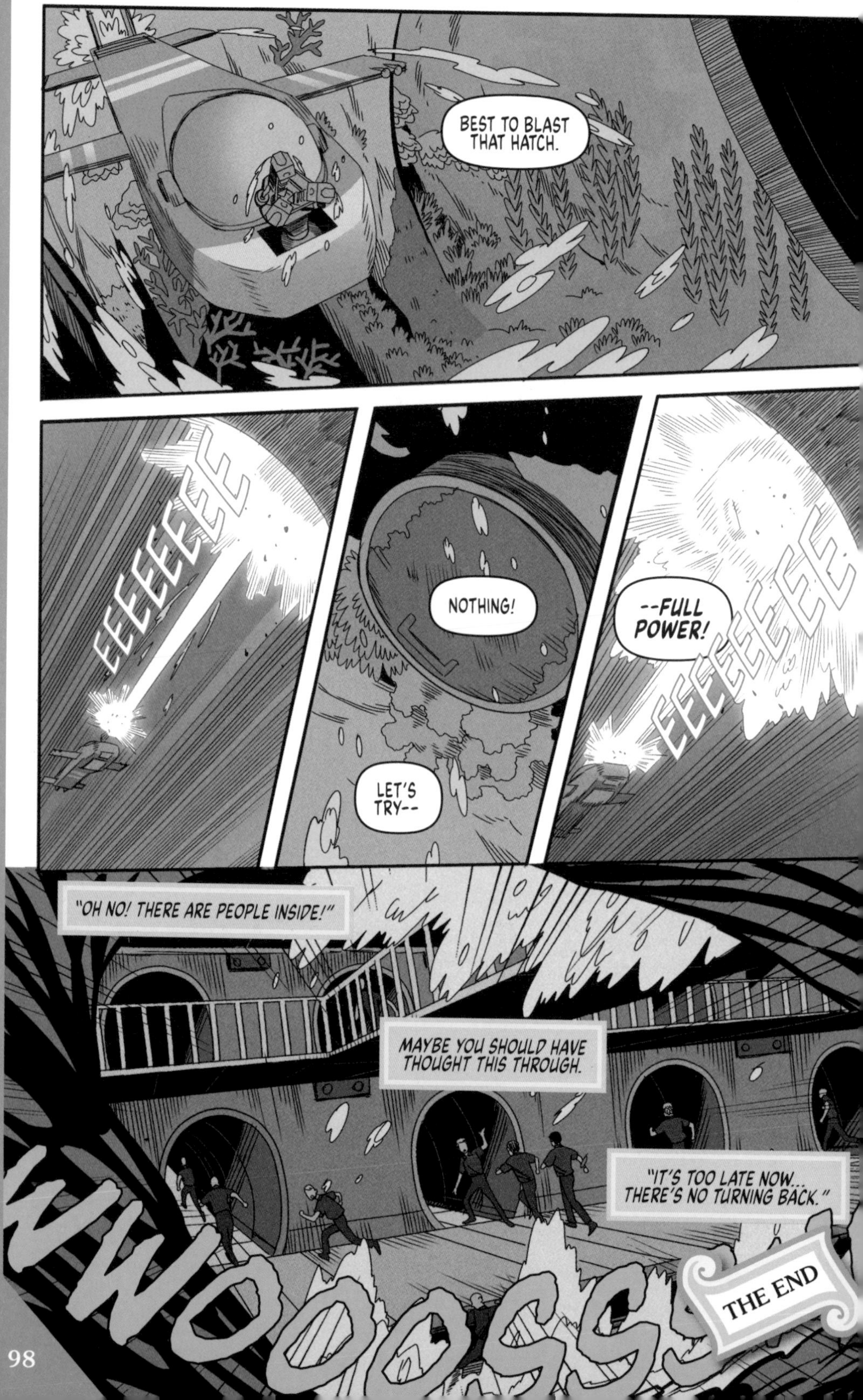
BEST TO BLAST THAT HATCH.
EEEEEEEEEE
NOTHING!
LET'S TRY--
--FULL POWER!
EEEEEEEEEE
"OH NO! THERE ARE PEOPLE INSIDE!"
MAYBE YOU SHOULD HAVE THOUGHT THIS THROUGH.
"IT'S TOO LATE NOW... THERE'S NO TURNING BACK."
WHOOOSS
THE END

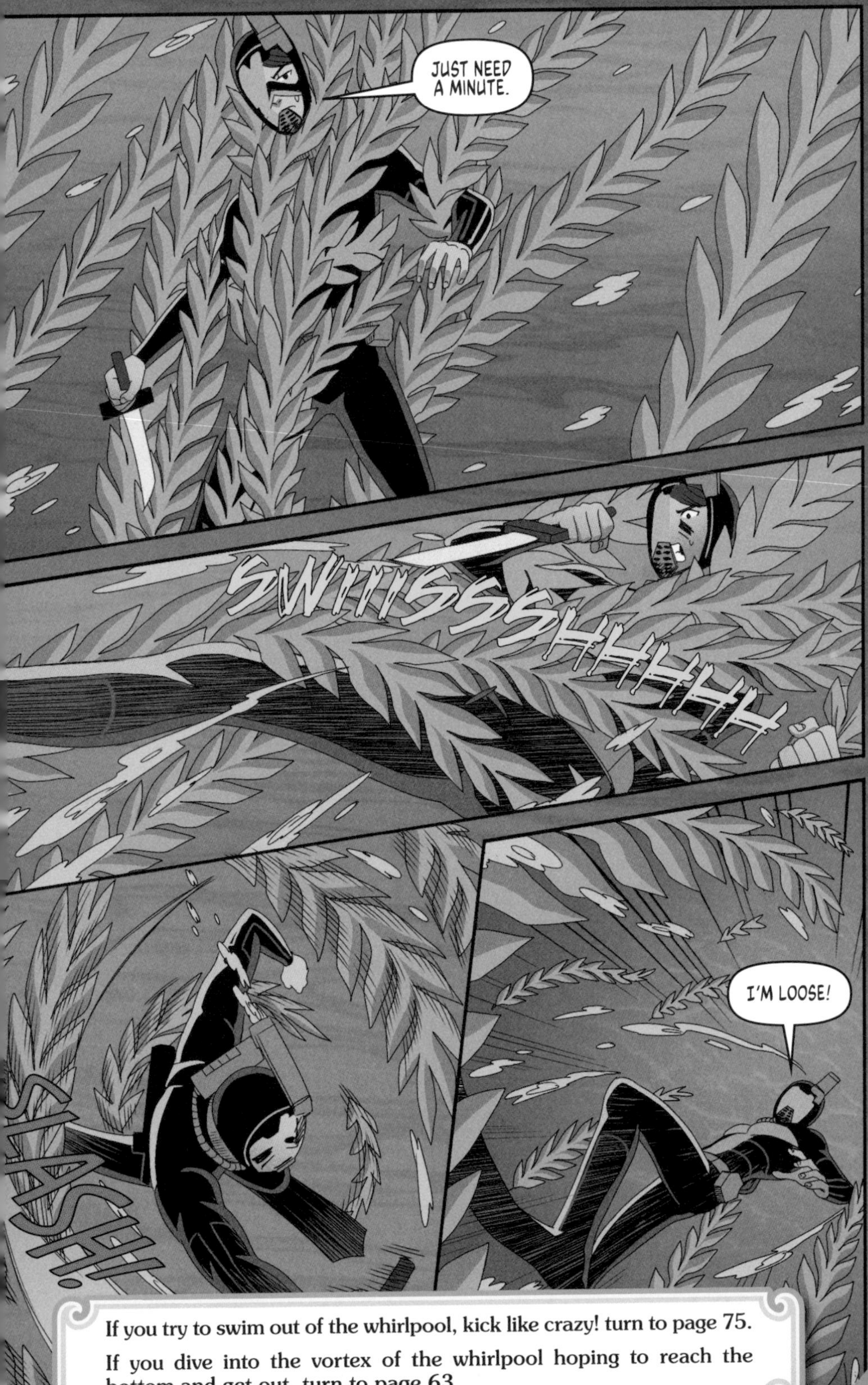
JUST NEED A MINUTE.
SWIIISSSHHHHH
SLASH!
I'M LOOSE!

If you try to swim out of the whirlpool, kick like crazy! turn to page 75.

If you dive into the vortex of the whirlpool hoping to reach the bottom and get out, turn to page 63.

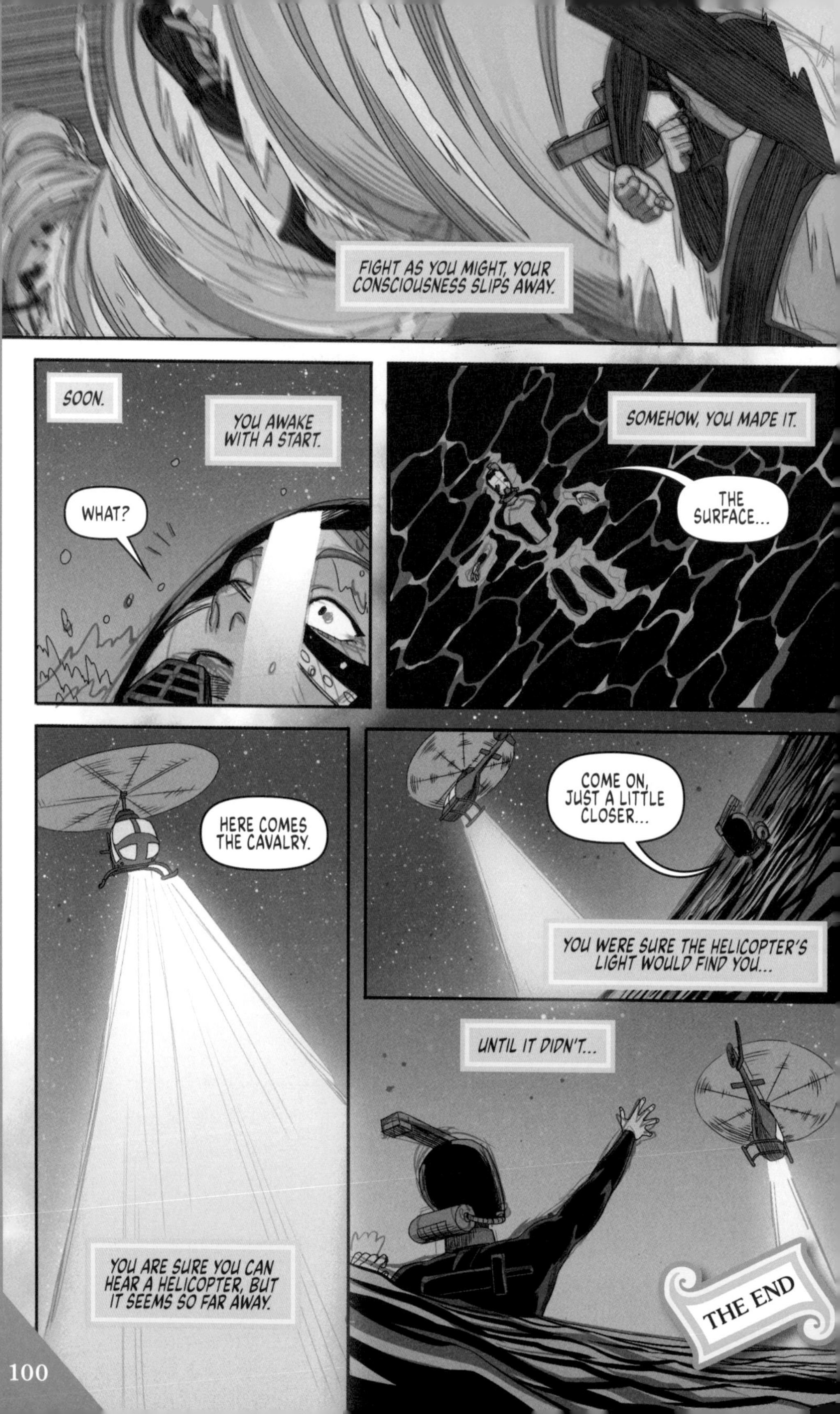
FIGHT AS YOU MIGHT, YOUR CONSCIOUSNESS SLIPS AWAY.
SOON.
YOU AWAKE WITH A START.
WHAT?
SOMEHOW, YOU MADE IT.
THE SURFACE...
HERE COMES THE CAVALRY.
YOU ARE SURE YOU CAN HEAR A HELICOPTER, BUT IT SEEMS SO FAR AWAY.
COME ON, JUST A LITTLE CLOSER...
YOU WERE SURE THE HELICOPTER'S LIGHT WOULD FIND YOU...
UNTIL IT DIDN'T...
THE END

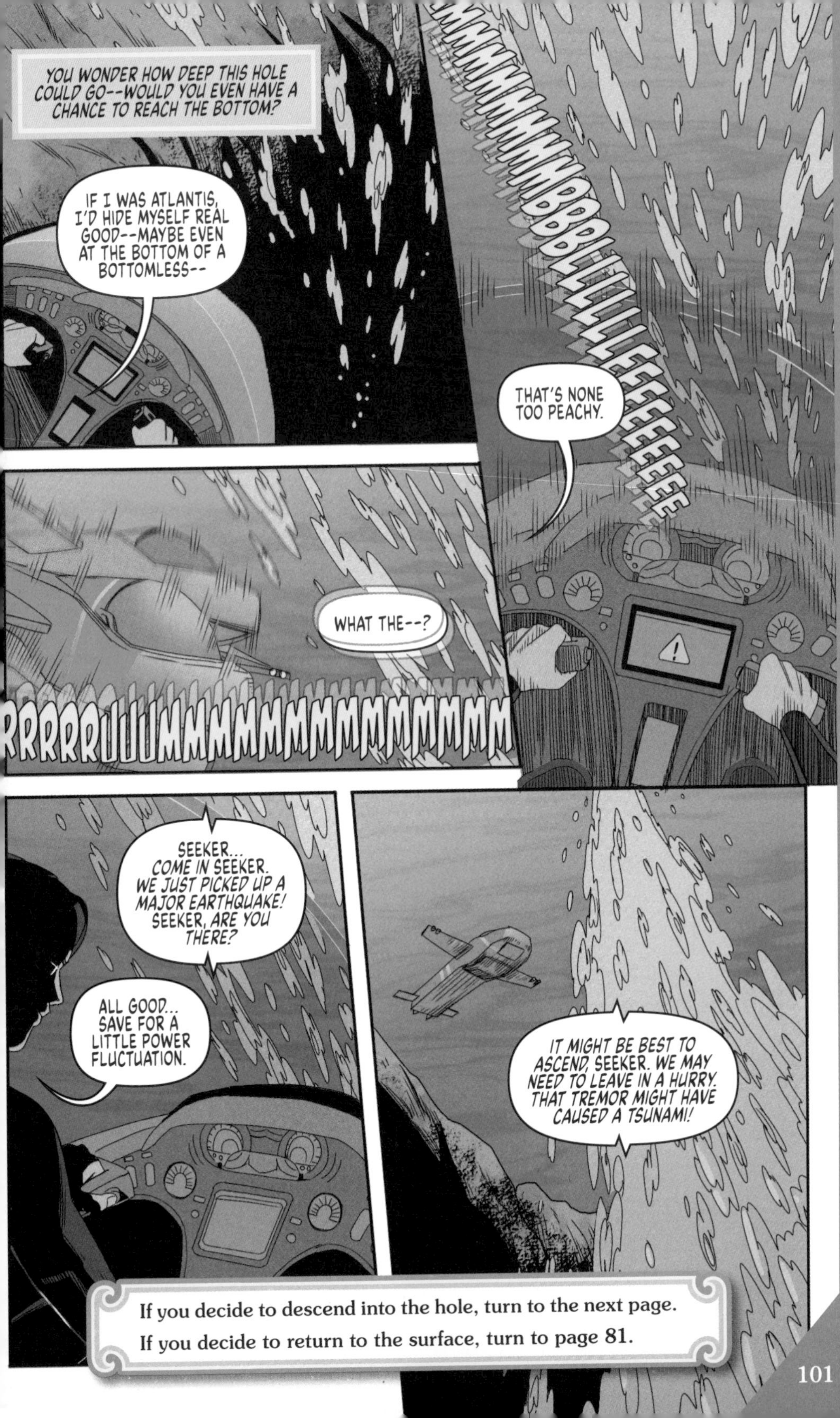
YOU WONDER HOW DEEP THIS HOLE COULD GO--WOULD YOU EVEN HAVE A CHANCE TO REACH THE BOTTOM?
IF I WAS ATLANTIS, I'D HIDE MYSELF REAL GOOD--MAYBE EVEN AT THE BOTTOM OF A BOTTOMLESS--
WHAT THE--?
RRRRRUUUMMMMMMMMMMMMMMM
MMMMMMMMMMHHHHHBBBLLLLEEEEEEEE
THAT'S NONE TOO PEACHY.
SEEKER... COME IN SEEKER. WE JUST PICKED UP A MAJOR EARTHQUAKE! SEEKER, ARE YOU THERE?
ALL GOOD... SAVE FOR A LITTLE POWER FLUCTUATION.
IT MIGHT BE BEST TO ASCEND, SEEKER. WE MAY NEED TO LEAVE IN A HURRY. THAT TREMOR MIGHT HAVE CAUSED A TSUNAMI!

If you decide to descend into the hole, turn to the next page.
If you decide to return to the surface, turn to page 81.

7,000 FATHOMS--YOU FEEL THE PRESSURE BUILDING.

8,700 FATHOMS.

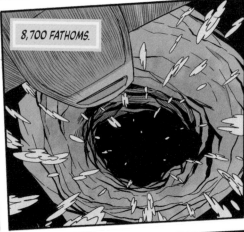

YOU MUST FIND OUT WHAT'S DOWN THERE, AND THIS MAY BE YOUR ONLY CHANCE.

TROUBLE.

13,200 FATHOMS. YOU NEED TO TRY AND REVERSE PROPULSION.

14,000 FATHOMS.

Go on to the next page.

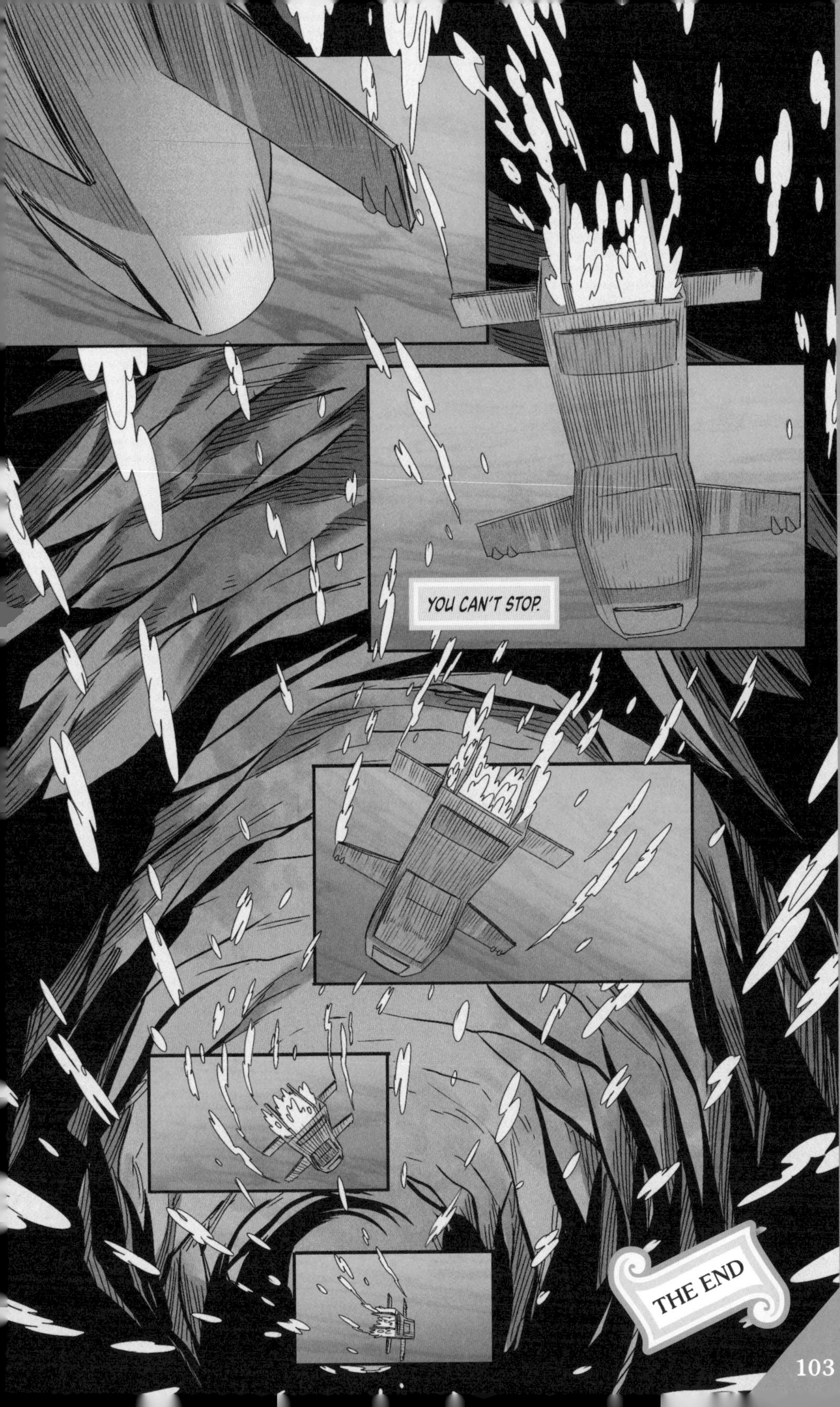
YOU CAN'T STOP.
THE END

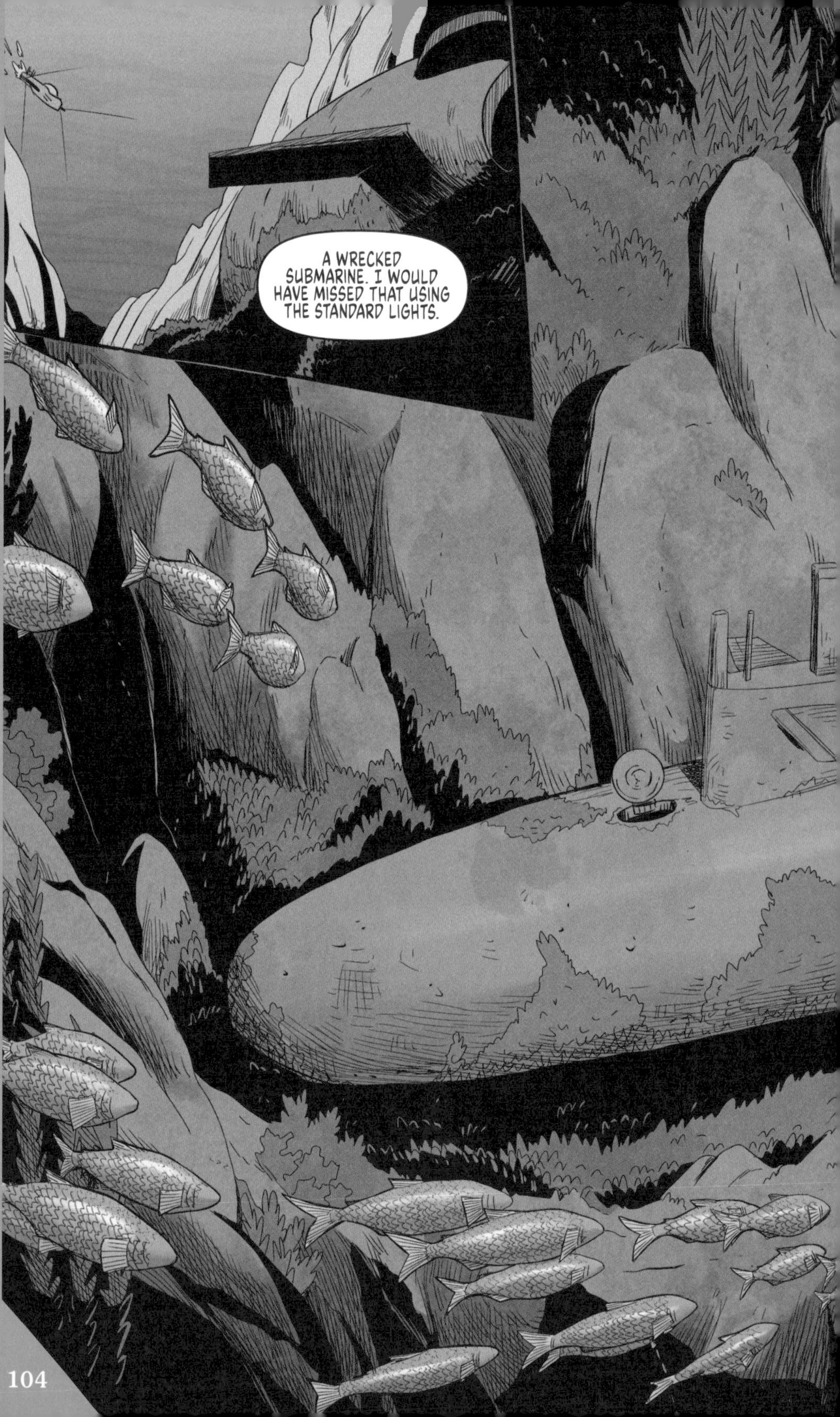
A WRECKED SUBMARINE. I WOULD HAVE MISSED THAT USING THE STANDARD LIGHTS.

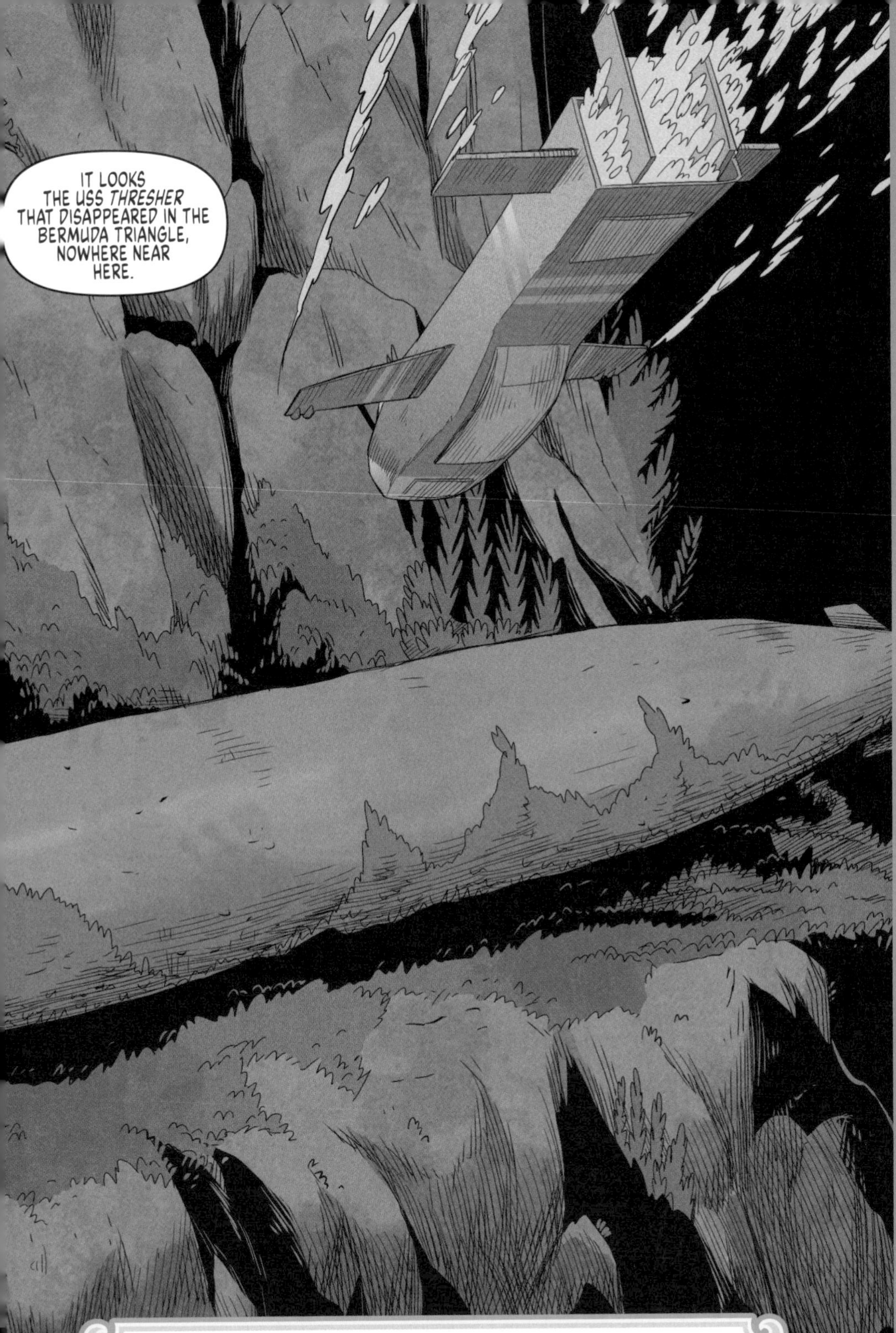
IT LOOKS THE USS *THRESHER* THAT DISAPPEARED IN THE BERMUDA TRIANGLE, NOWHERE NEAR HERE.

If you decide to enter the submarine, turn to page 61.

If you decide to cruise on through the grotto, ignoring the sub for now, turn to page 128.

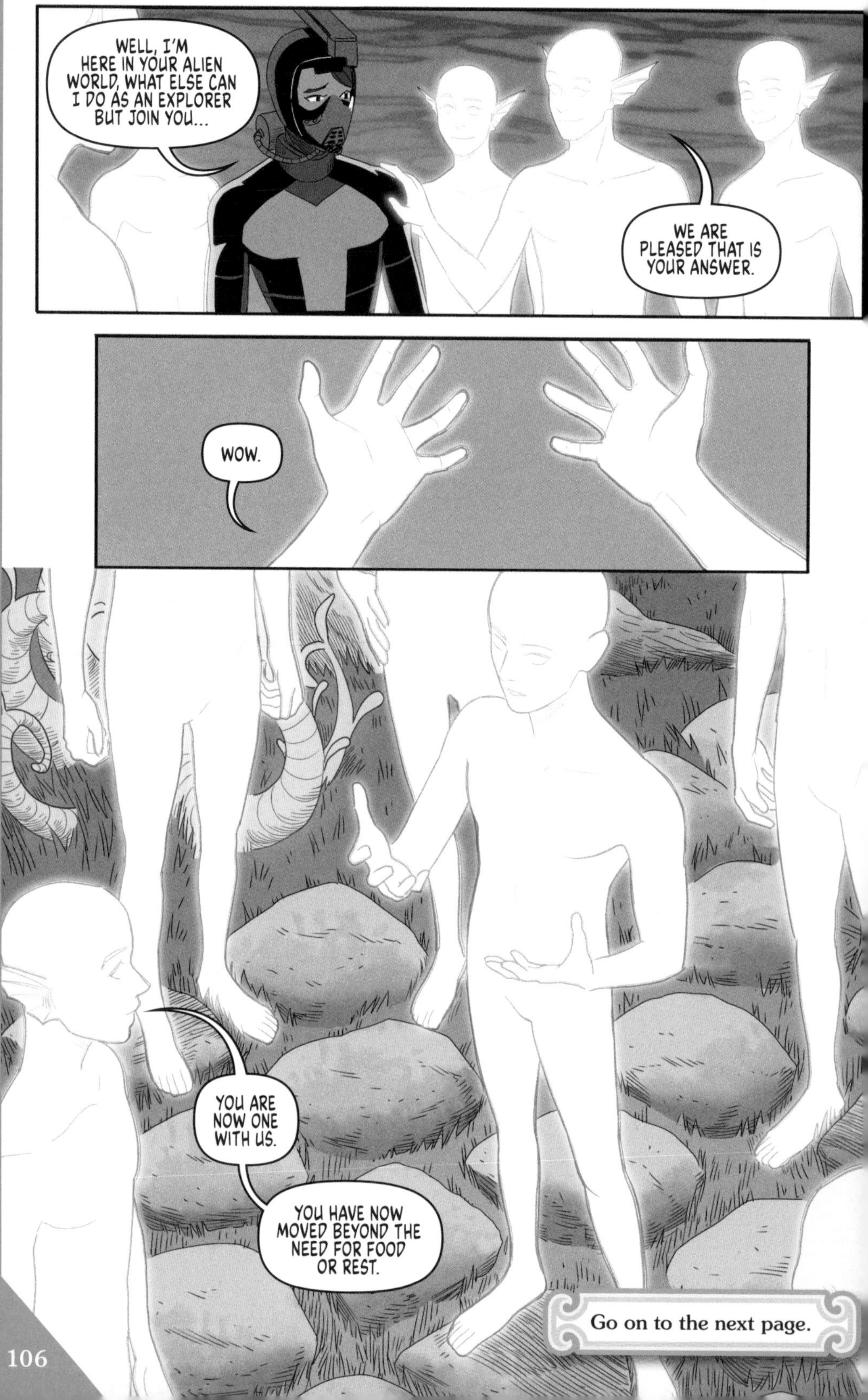
WELL, I'M HERE IN YOUR ALIEN WORLD, WHAT ELSE CAN I DO AS AN EXPLORER BUT JOIN YOU...
WE ARE PLEASED THAT IS YOUR ANSWER.
WOW.
YOU ARE NOW ONE WITH US.
YOU HAVE NOW MOVED BEYOND THE NEED FOR FOOD OR REST.

Go on to the next page.

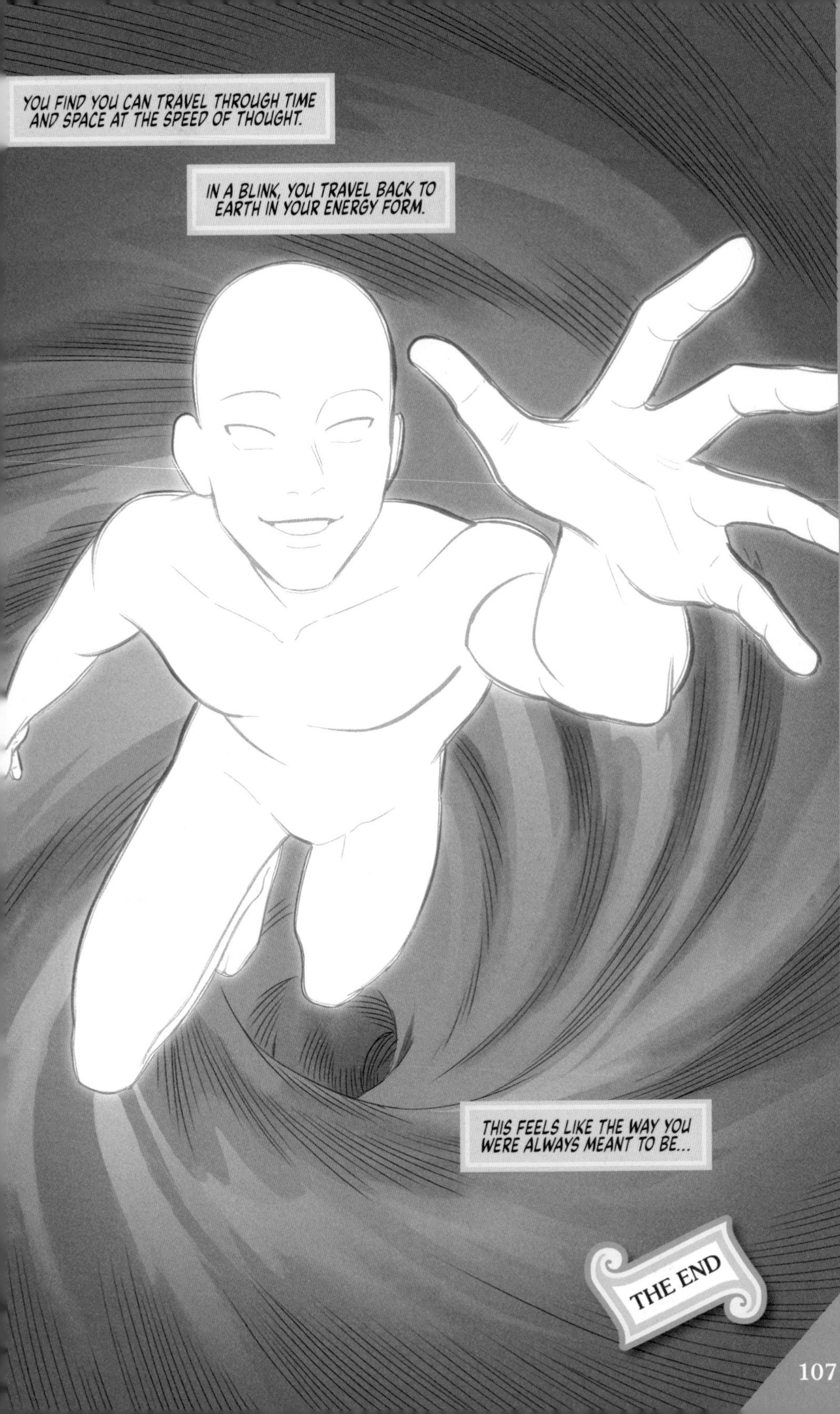
YOU FIND YOU CAN TRAVEL THROUGH TIME AND SPACE AT THE SPEED OF THOUGHT.
IN A BLINK, YOU TRAVEL BACK TO EARTH IN YOUR ENERGY FORM.
THIS FEELS LIKE THE WAY YOU WERE ALWAYS MEANT TO BE...
THE END

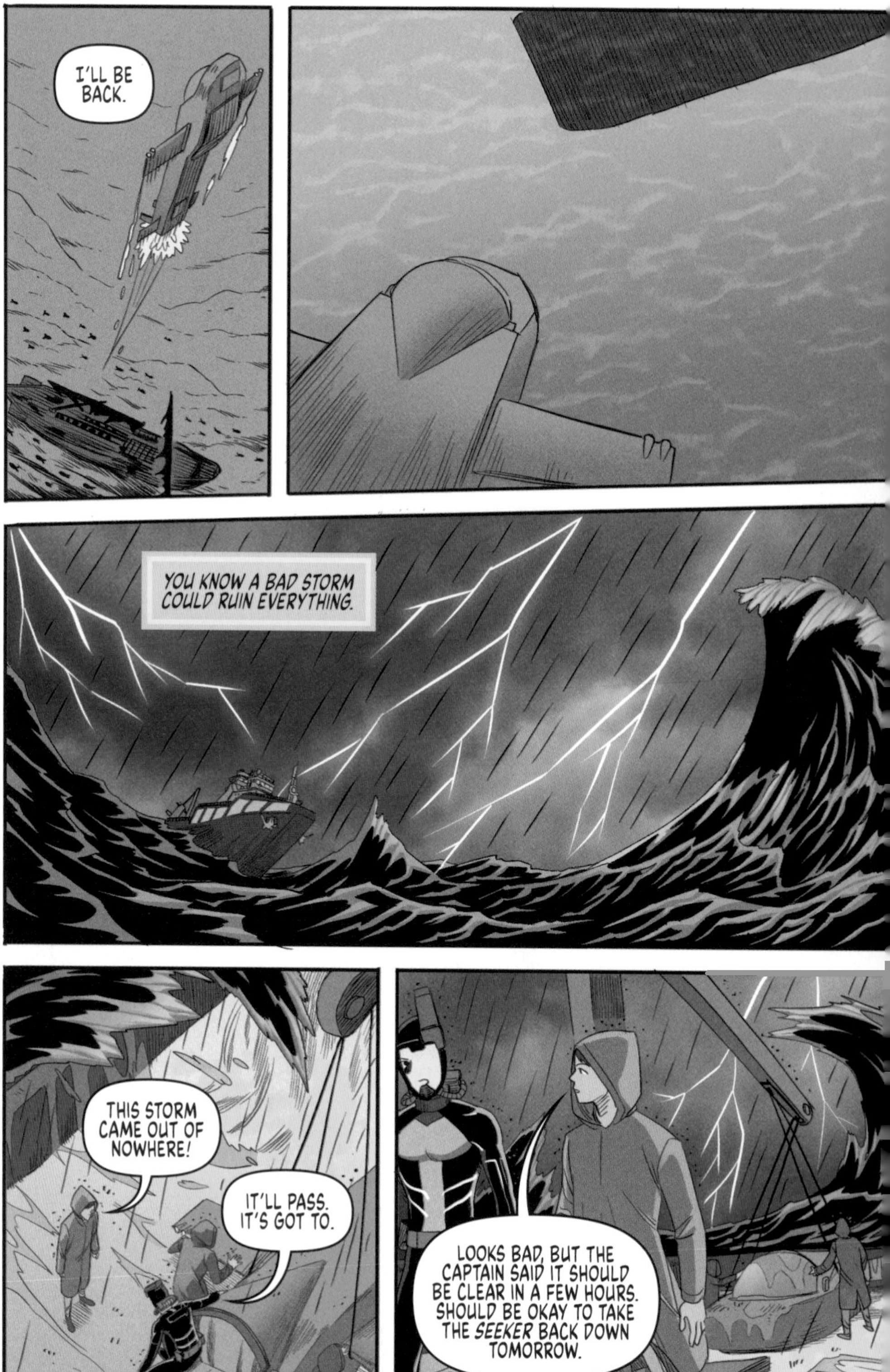
I'LL BE BACK.
YOU KNOW A BAD STORM COULD RUIN EVERYTHING.
THIS STORM CAME OUT OF NOWHERE!
IT'LL PASS. IT'S GOT TO.
LOOKS BAD, BUT THE CAPTAIN SAID IT SHOULD BE CLEAR IN A FEW HOURS. SHOULD BE OKAY TO TAKE THE *SEEKER* BACK DOWN TOMORROW.

Go on to the next page.

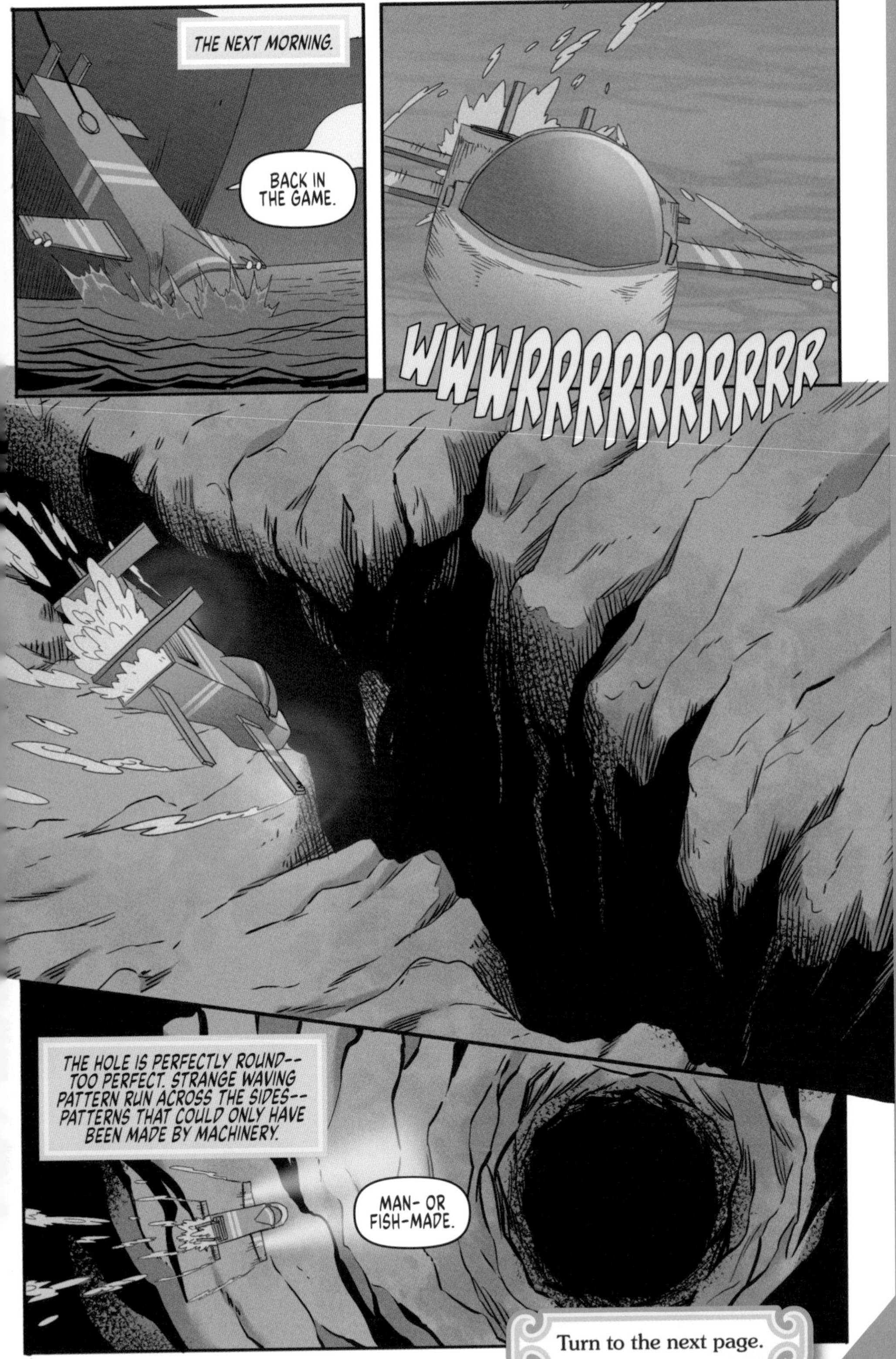
THE NEXT MORNING.
BACK IN THE GAME.
WWWRRRRRRRRRRR
THE HOLE IS PERFECTLY ROUND-- TOO PERFECT. STRANGE WAVING PATTERN RUN ACROSS THE SIDES-- PATTERNS THAT COULD ONLY HAVE BEEN MADE BY MACHINERY.
MAN- OR FISH-MADE.

Turn to the next page.

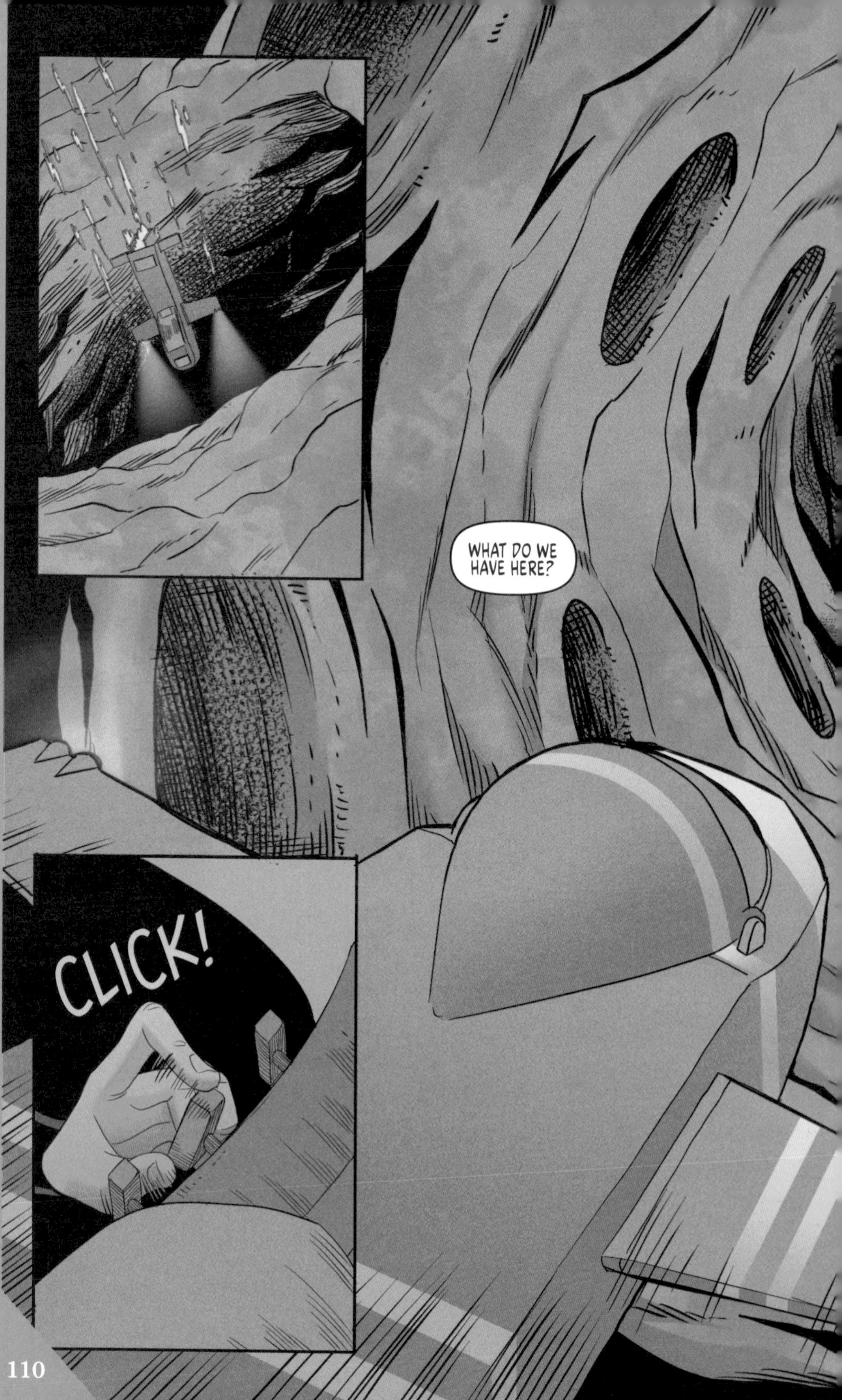
WHAT DO WE HAVE HERE?
CLICK!

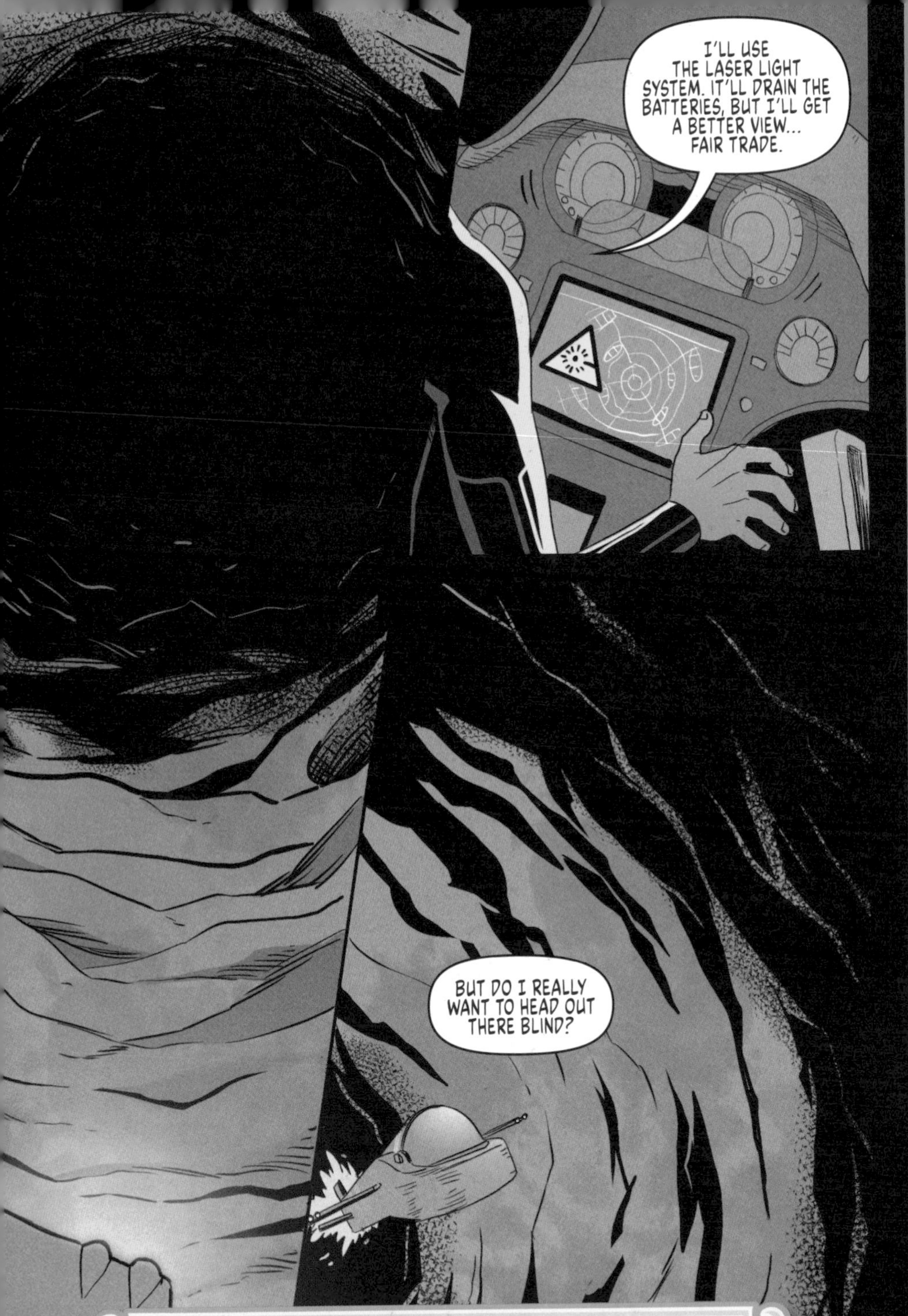
I'LL USE THE LASER LIGHT SYSTEM. IT'LL DRAIN THE BATTERIES, BUT I'LL GET A BETTER VIEW... FAIR TRADE.
BUT DO I REALLY WANT TO HEAD OUT THERE BLIND?

If you decide to cruise further into the grotto, turn to page 97.

If you decide to use the laser light, turn to page 104.

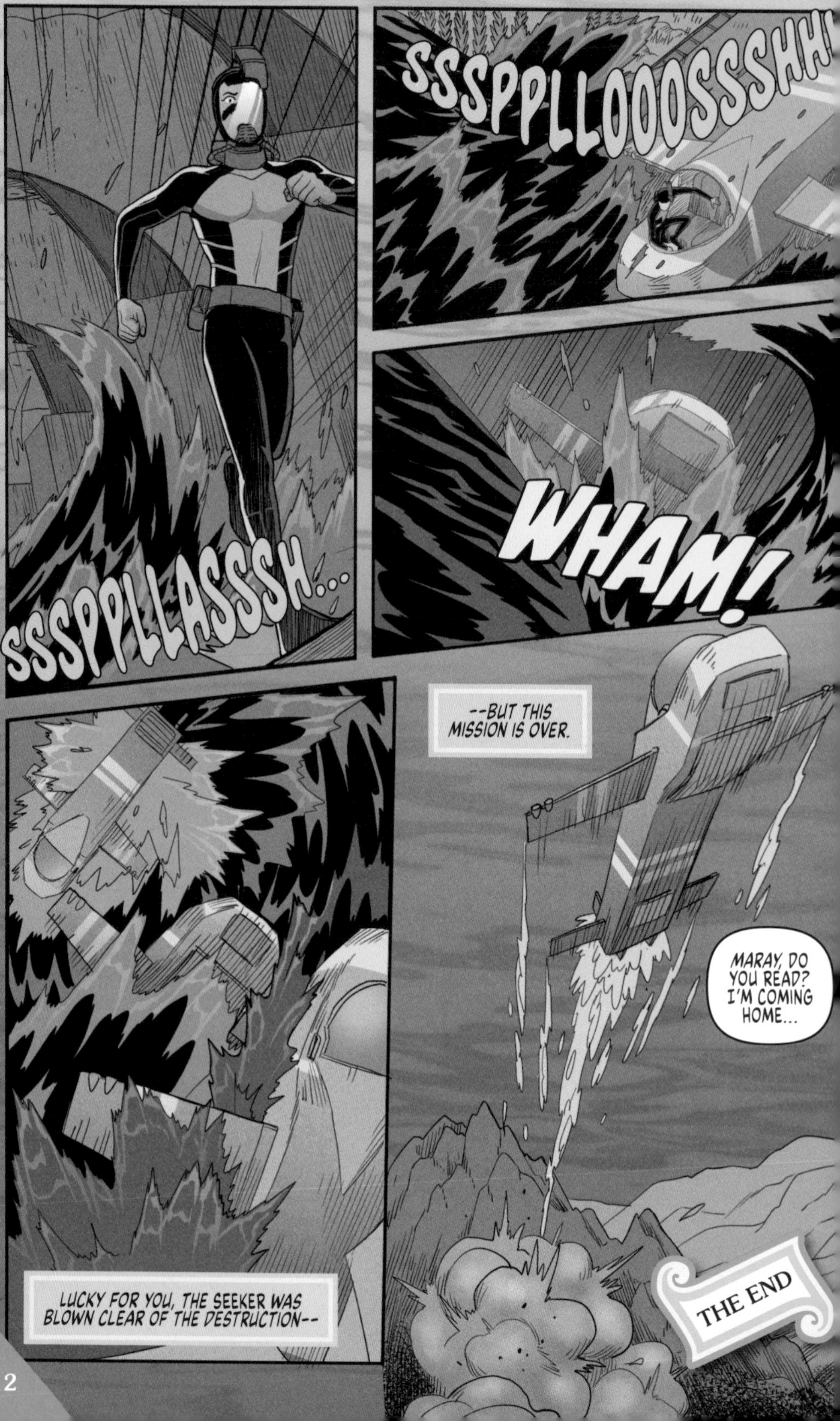
SSSPPLLASSSH...
SSSPPLLOOOSSSHH
WHAM!
LUCKY FOR YOU, THE SEEKER WAS BLOWN CLEAR OF THE DESTRUCTION--
--BUT THIS MISSION IS OVER.
MARAY, DO YOU READ? I'M COMING HOME...
THE END

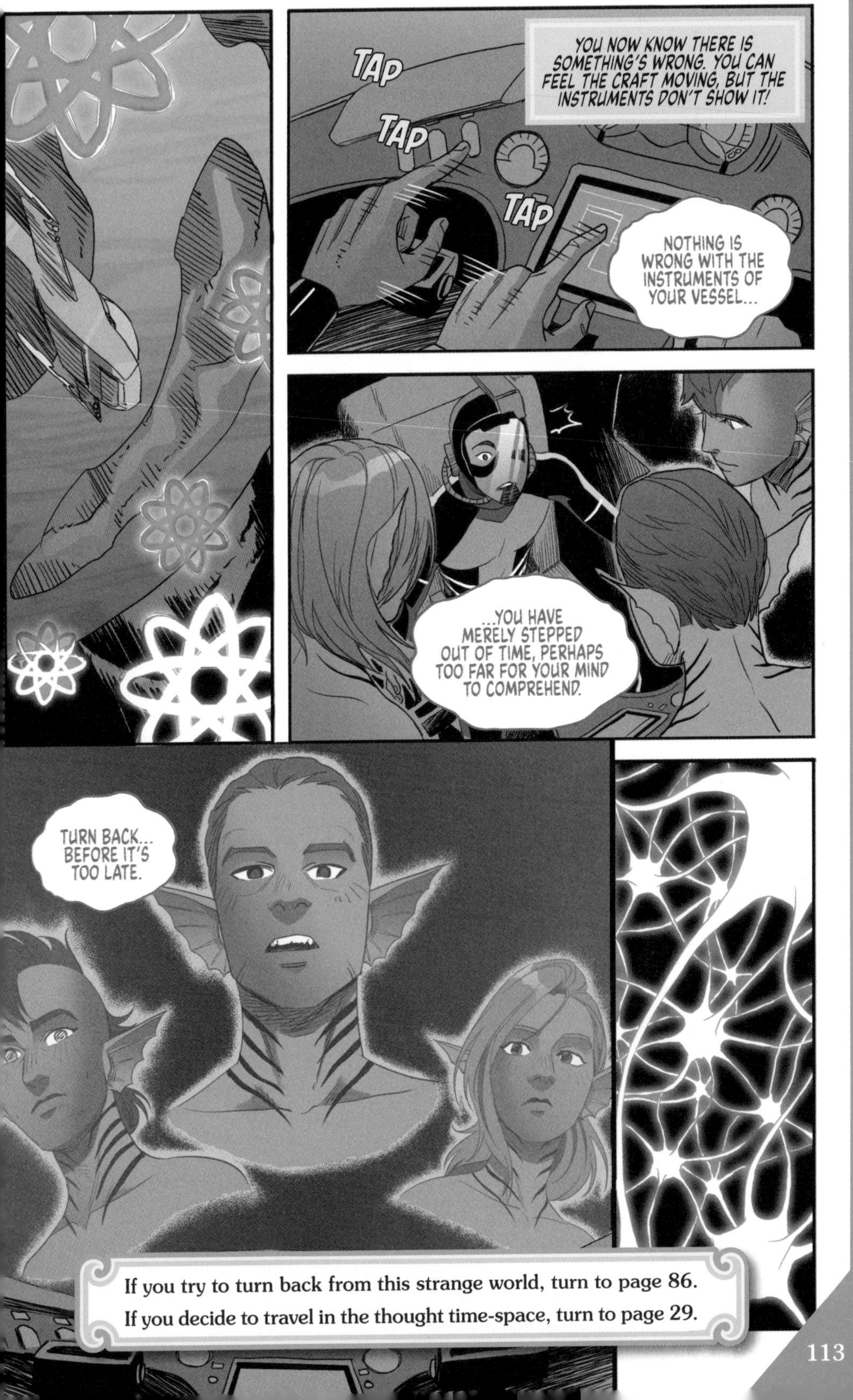
TAP
TAP
YOU NOW KNOW THERE IS SOMETHING'S WRONG. YOU CAN FEEL THE CRAFT MOVING, BUT THE INSTRUMENTS DON'T SHOW IT!
TAP
NOTHING IS WRONG WITH THE INSTRUMENTS OF YOUR VESSEL...
...YOU HAVE MERELY STEPPED OUT OF TIME, PERHAPS TOO FAR FOR YOUR MIND TO COMPREHEND.
TURN BACK... BEFORE IT'S TOO LATE.

If you try to turn back from this strange world, turn to page 86.
If you decide to travel in the thought time-space, turn to page 29.

YOU KNOW YOU HAVE TO GET OUT OF HERE!

YOU HOPE THE LASER WILL BE STRONG ENOUGH TO BLAST THE DOOR OPEN.

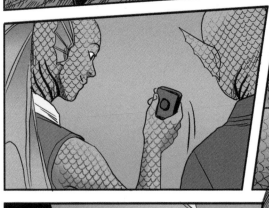

ZZAP!!!

YOU DON'T KNOW HOW THEY DID IT, BUT SOME KIND OF ELECTROMAGNETIC WAVE STRIKE JUST TOOK OUT ALL ELECTRONICS ON THE SEEKER.

YOU NOW REALIZE THERE IS NO ESCAPING YOUR FATE.

YOU ARE NOW PART OF ATLANTIS. NO HARM WILL COME TO YOU, AND YOUR LIFE WILL BE FULL.

THE END

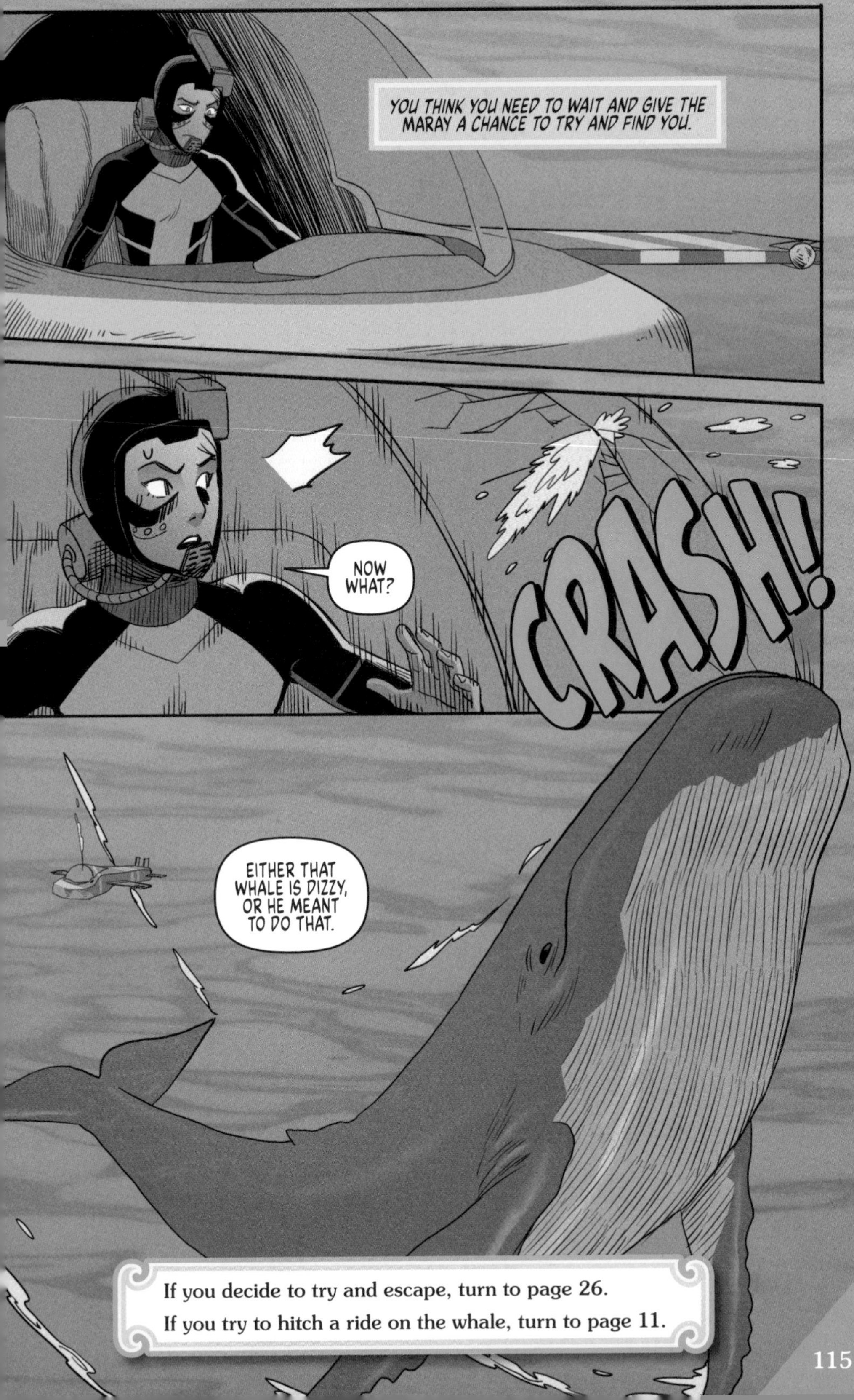
YOU THINK YOU NEED TO WAIT AND GIVE THE MARAY A CHANCE TO TRY AND FIND YOU.
NOW WHAT?
CRASH!
EITHER THAT WHALE IS DIZZY, OR HE MEANT TO DO THAT.

If you decide to try and escape, turn to page 26.
If you try to hitch a ride on the whale, turn to page 11.

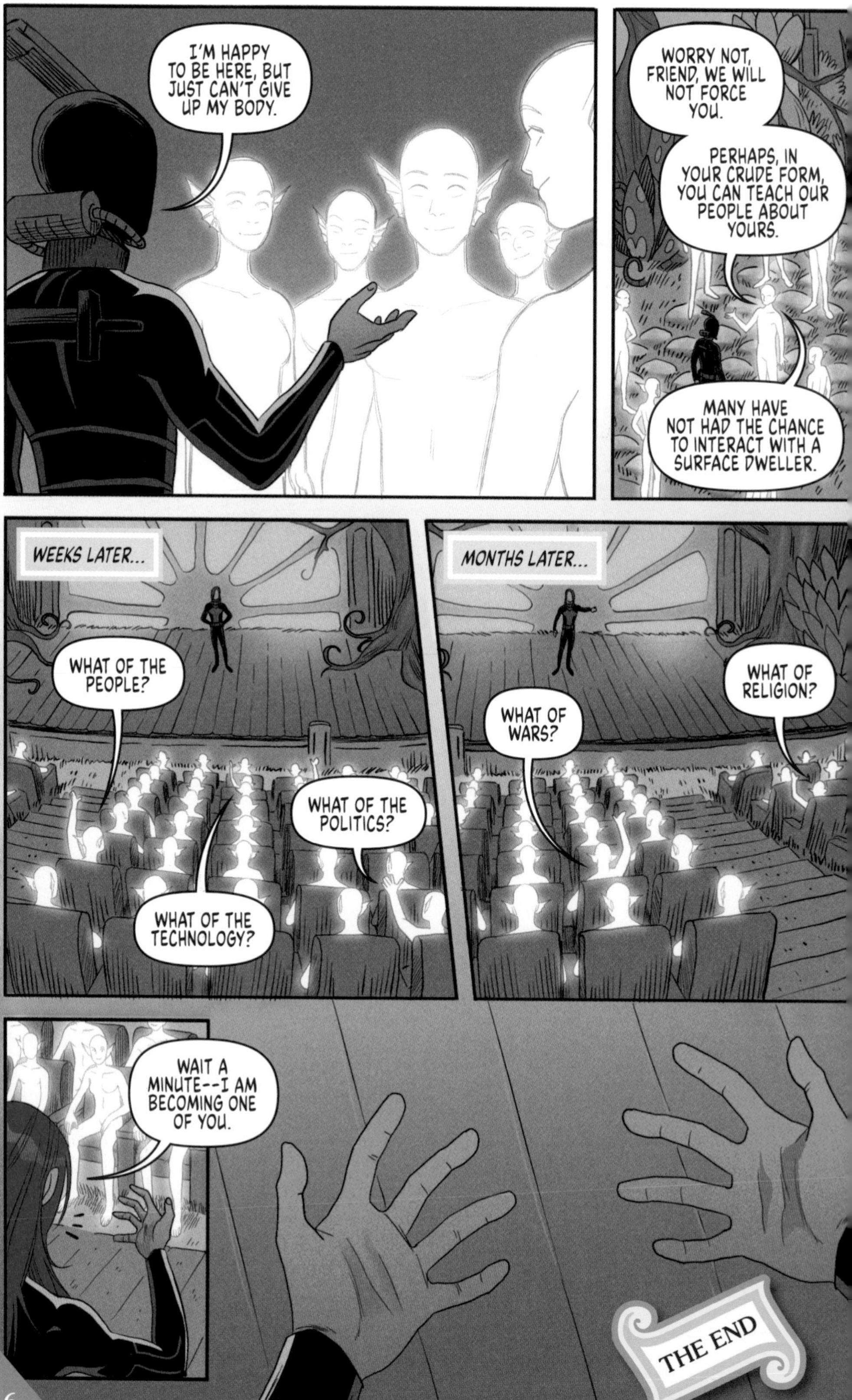
I'M HAPPY TO BE HERE, BUT JUST CAN'T GIVE UP MY BODY.
WORRY NOT, FRIEND, WE WILL NOT FORCE YOU.
PERHAPS, IN YOUR CRUDE FORM, YOU CAN TEACH OUR PEOPLE ABOUT YOURS.
MANY HAVE NOT HAD THE CHANCE TO INTERACT WITH A SURFACE DWELLER.
WEEKS LATER...
WHAT OF THE PEOPLE?
WHAT OF THE POLITICS?
WHAT OF THE TECHNOLOGY?
MONTHS LATER...
WHAT OF RELIGION?
WHAT OF WARS?
WAIT A MINUTE--I AM BECOMING ONE OF YOU.
THE END

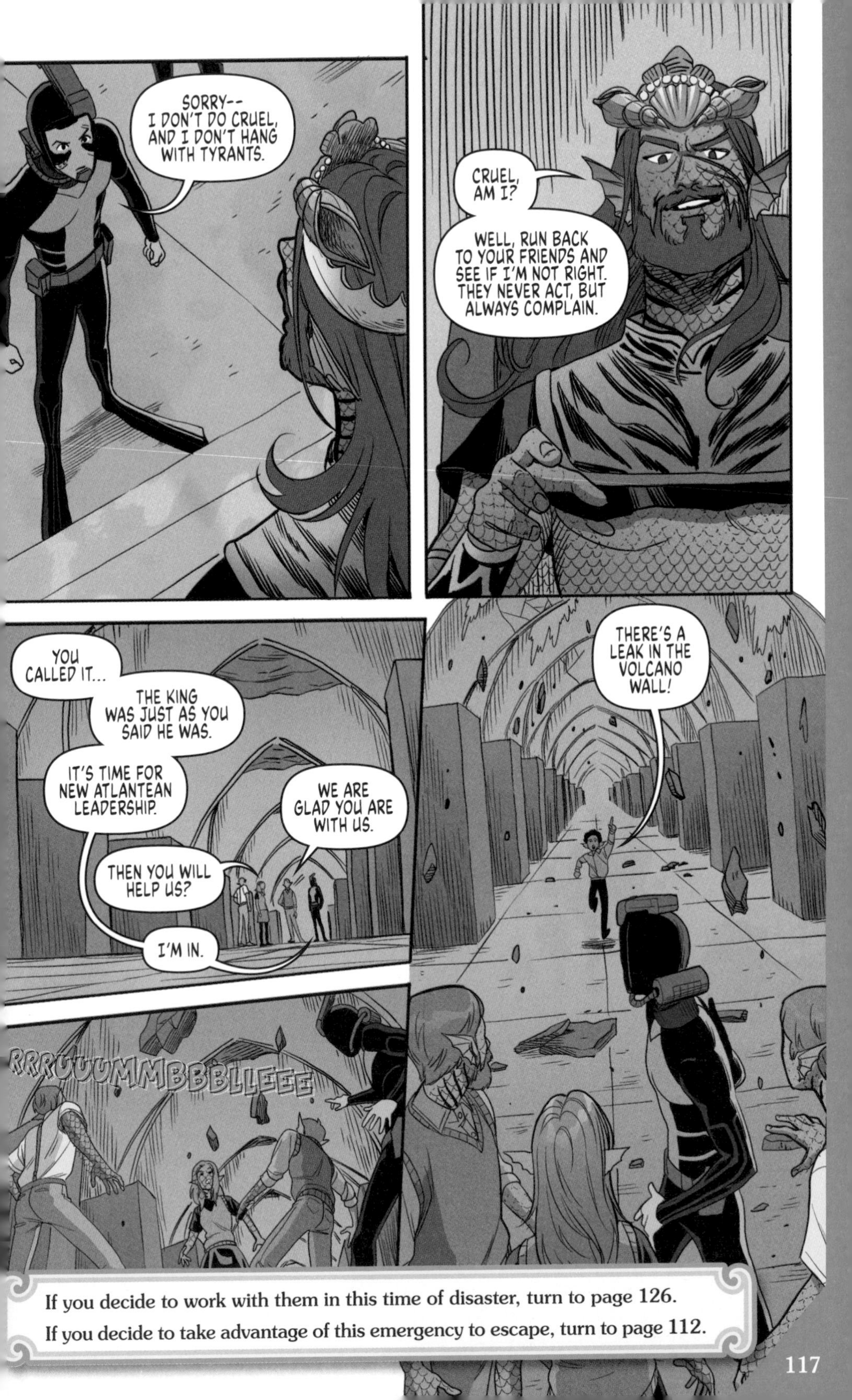
SORRY-- I DON'T DO CRUEL, AND I DON'T HANG WITH TYRANTS.
CRUEL, AM I?
WELL, RUN BACK TO YOUR FRIENDS AND SEE IF I'M NOT RIGHT. THEY NEVER ACT, BUT ALWAYS COMPLAIN.
YOU CALLED IT...
THE KING WAS JUST AS YOU SAID HE WAS.
IT'S TIME FOR NEW ATLANTEAN LEADERSHIP.
WE ARE GLAD YOU ARE WITH US.
THEN YOU WILL HELP US?
I'M IN.
THERE'S A LEAK IN THE VOLCANO WALL!
RRRUUUMMBBBLLEEE

If you decide to work with them in this time of disaster, turn to page 126.

If you decide to take advantage of this emergency to escape, turn to page 112.

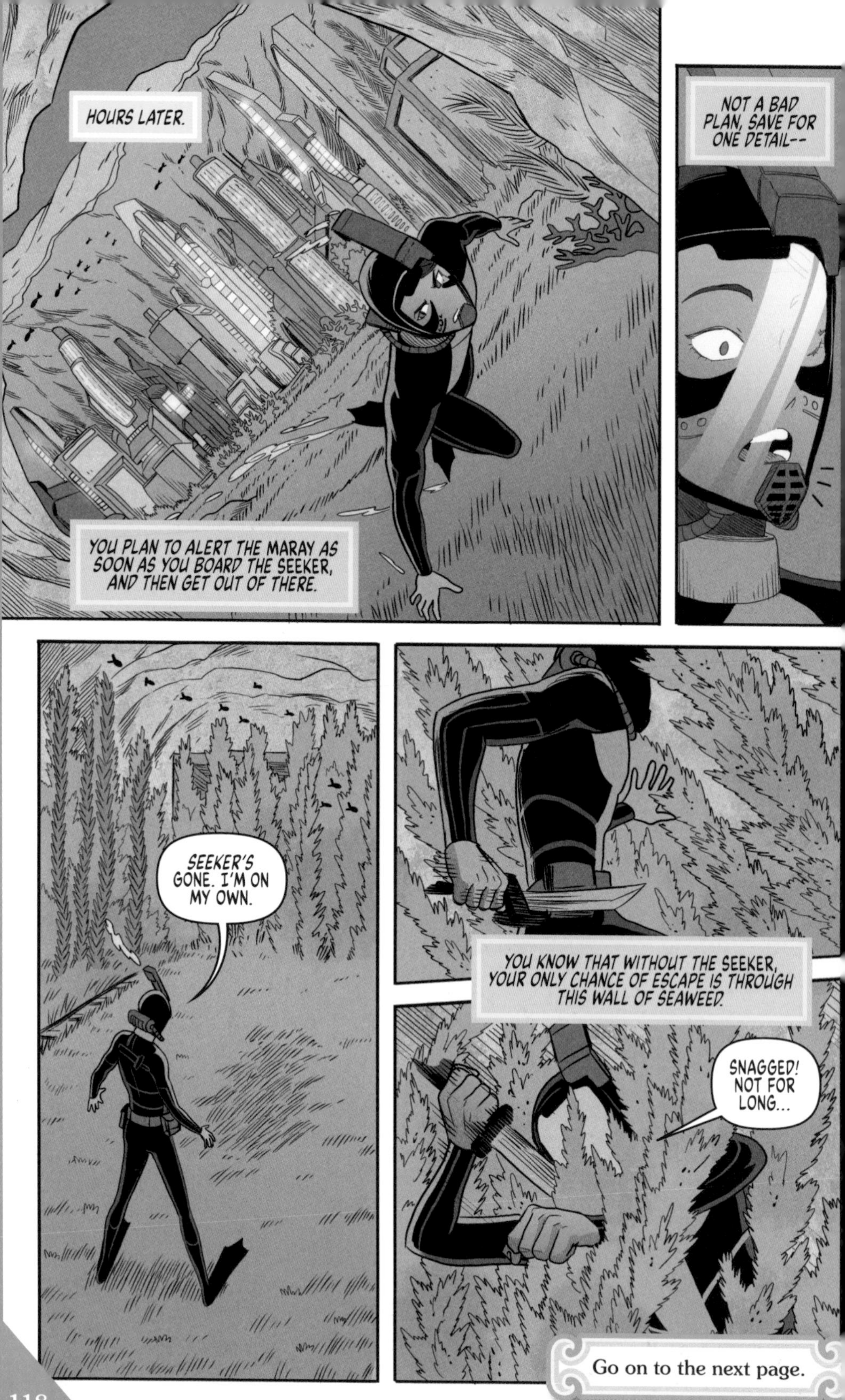
HOURS LATER.
YOU PLAN TO ALERT THE MARAY AS SOON AS YOU BOARD THE SEEKER, AND THEN GET OUT OF THERE.
NOT A BAD PLAN, SAVE FOR ONE DETAIL--
SEEKER'S GONE. I'M ON MY OWN.
YOU KNOW THAT WITHOUT THE SEEKER, YOUR ONLY CHANCE OF ESCAPE IS THROUGH THIS WALL OF SEAWEED.
SNAGGED! NOT FOR LONG...

Go on to the next page.

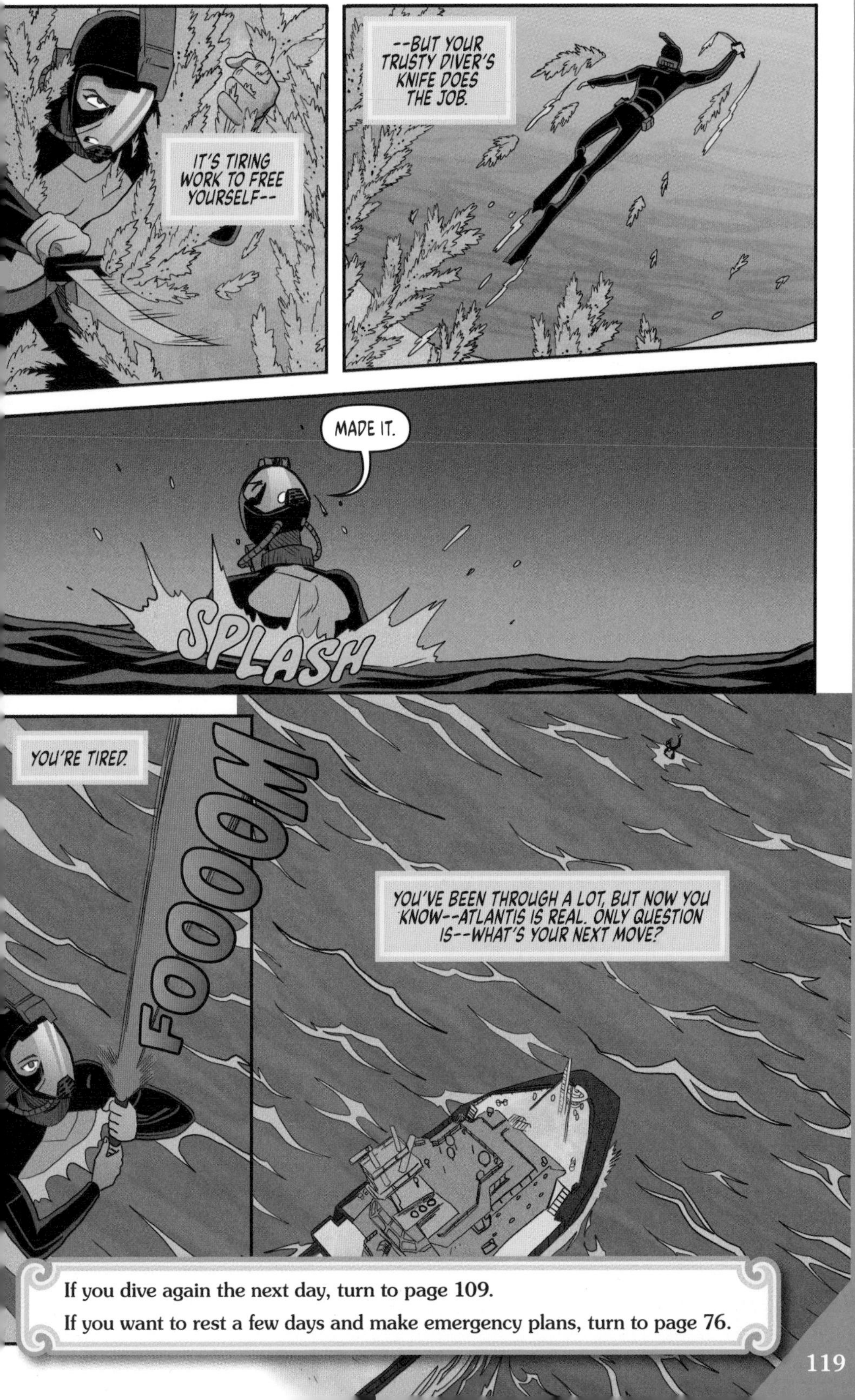
IT'S TIRING WORK TO FREE YOURSELF--
--BUT YOUR TRUSTY DIVER'S KNIFE DOES THE JOB.
MADE IT.
SPLASH
YOU'RE TIRED.
FOOOOM
YOU'VE BEEN THROUGH A LOT, BUT NOW YOU KNOW--ATLANTIS IS REAL. ONLY QUESTION IS--WHAT'S YOUR NEXT MOVE?

If you dive again the next day, turn to page 109.

If you want to rest a few days and make emergency plans, turn to page 76.

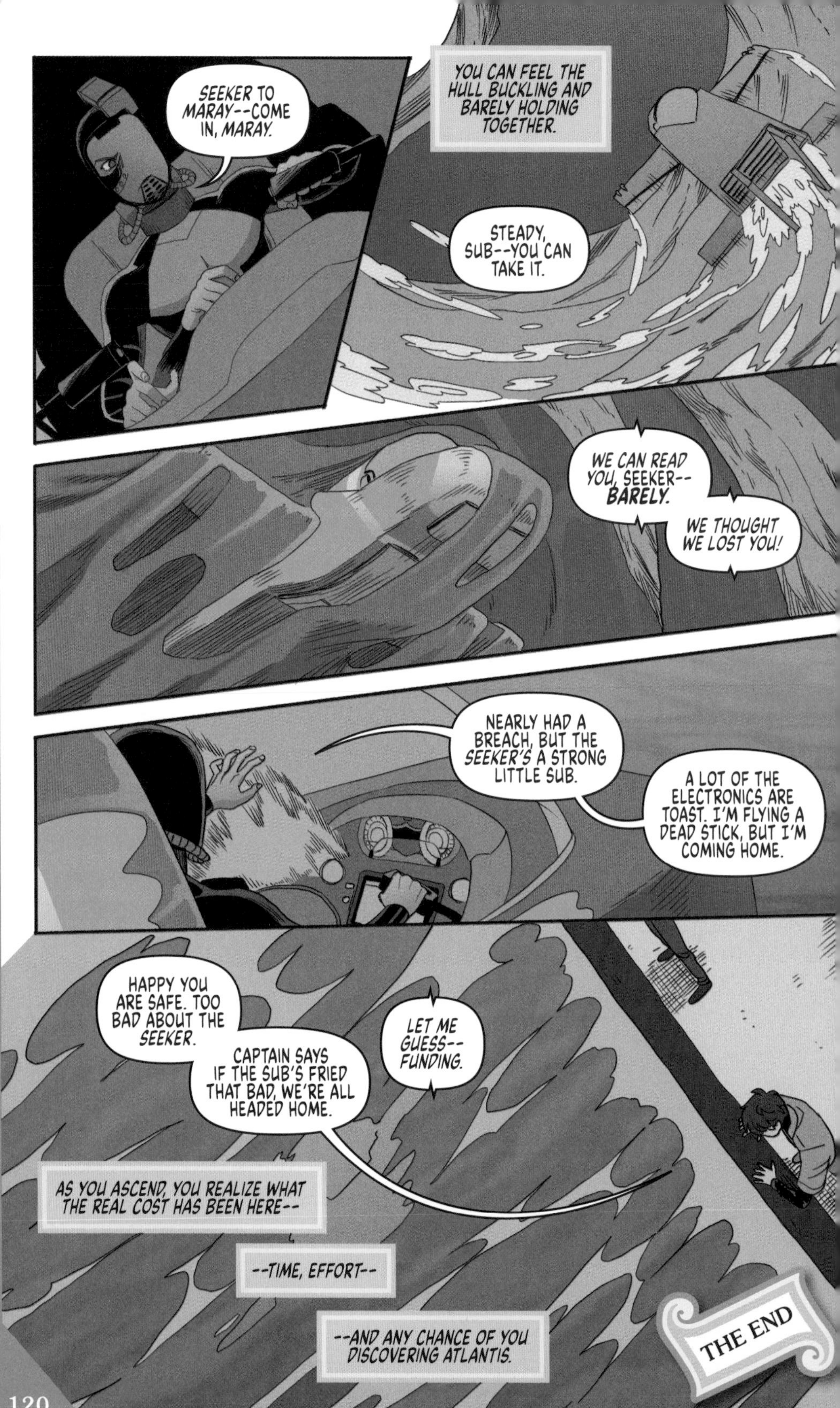
SEEKER TO MARAY--COME IN, MARAY.
YOU CAN FEEL THE HULL BUCKLING AND BARELY HOLDING TOGETHER.
STEADY, SUB--YOU CAN TAKE IT.
WE CAN READ YOU, SEEKER--BARELY.
WE THOUGHT WE LOST YOU!
NEARLY HAD A BREACH, BUT THE SEEKER'S A STRONG LITTLE SUB.
A LOT OF THE ELECTRONICS ARE TOAST. I'M FLYING A DEAD STICK, BUT I'M COMING HOME.
HAPPY YOU ARE SAFE. TOO BAD ABOUT THE SEEKER.
CAPTAIN SAYS IF THE SUB'S FRIED THAT BAD, WE'RE ALL HEADED HOME.
LET ME GUESS--FUNDING.
AS YOU ASCEND, YOU REALIZE WHAT THE REAL COST HAS BEEN HERE--
--TIME, EFFORT--
--AND ANY CHANCE OF YOU DISCOVERING ATLANTIS.
THE END

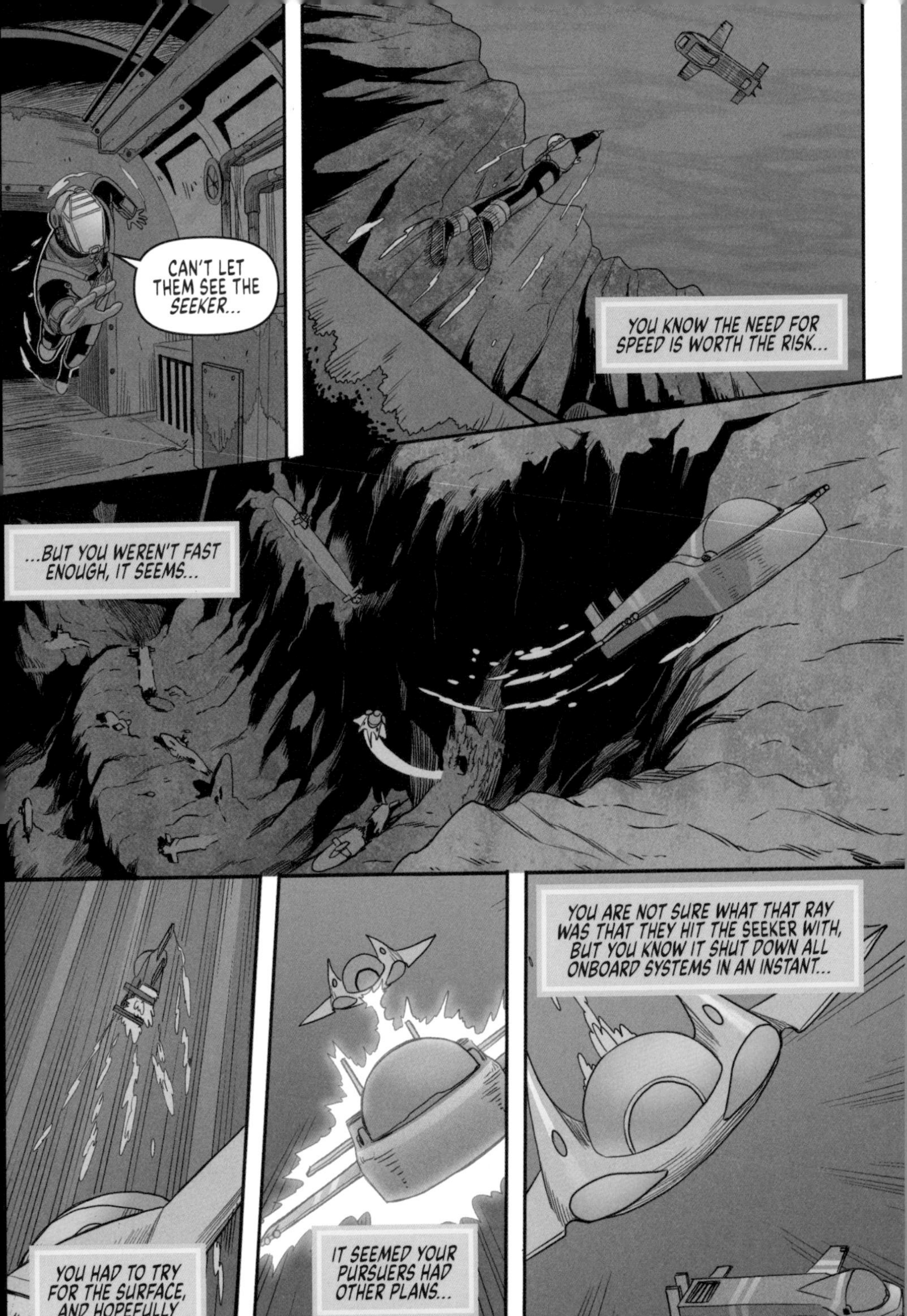
CAN'T LET THEM SEE THE SEEKER...
YOU KNOW THE NEED FOR SPEED IS WORTH THE RISK...
...BUT YOU WEREN'T FAST ENOUGH, IT SEEMS...
YOU HAD TO TRY FOR THE SURFACE, AND HOPEFULLY THE MARAY...
IT SEEMED YOUR PURSUERS HAD OTHER PLANS...
YOU ARE NOT SURE WHAT THAT RAY WAS THAT THEY HIT THE SEEKER WITH, BUT YOU KNOW IT SHUT DOWN ALL ONBOARD SYSTEMS IN AN INSTANT...

If you decide to try and escape, turn to page 26.
If you decide to give the *Maray* a chance to find you, turn to page 115.

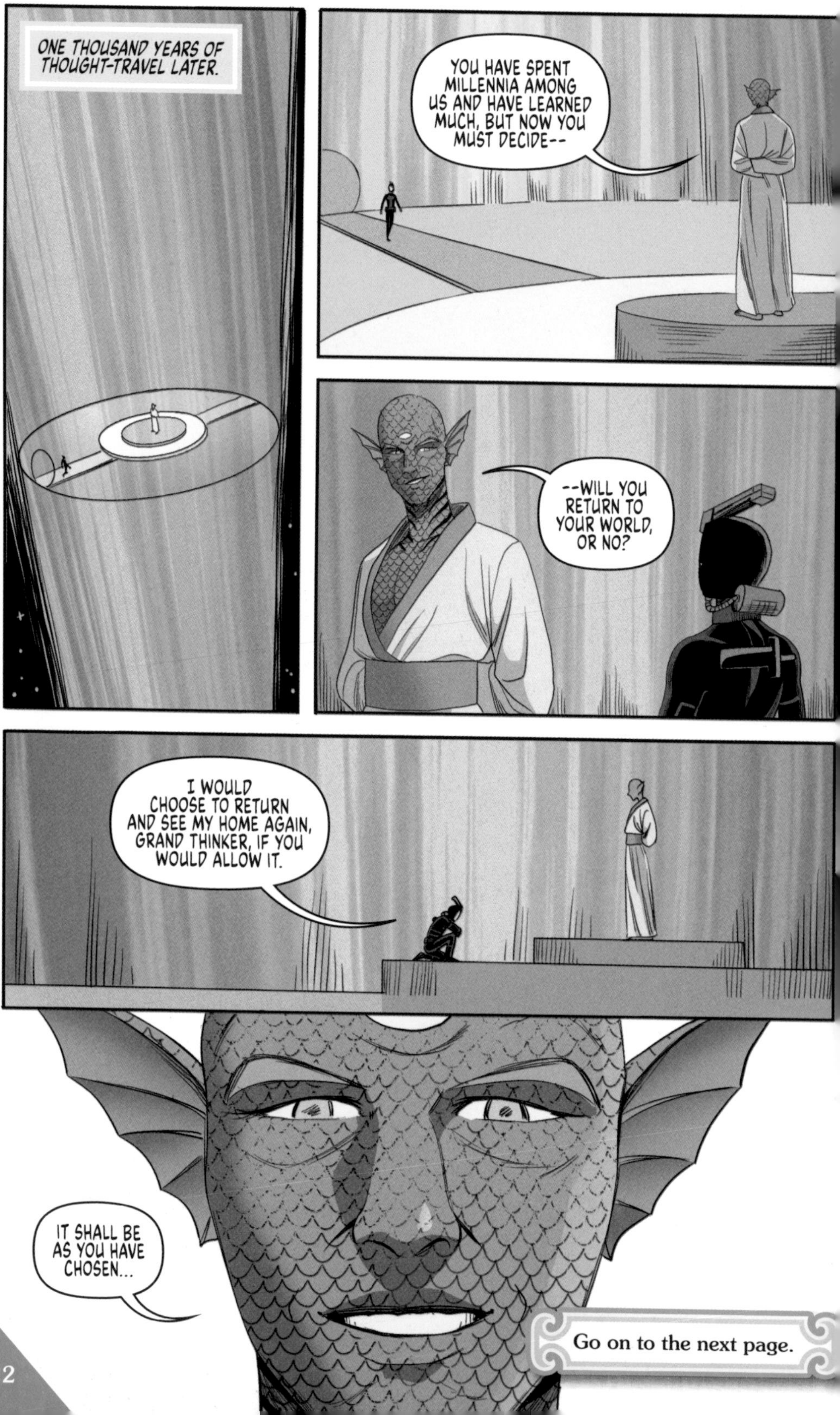
ONE THOUSAND YEARS OF THOUGHT-TRAVEL LATER.
YOU HAVE SPENT MILLENNIA AMONG US AND HAVE LEARNED MUCH, BUT NOW YOU MUST DECIDE--
--WILL YOU RETURN TO YOUR WORLD, OR NO?
I WOULD CHOOSE TO RETURN AND SEE MY HOME AGAIN, GRAND THINKER, IF YOU WOULD ALLOW IT.
IT SHALL BE AS YOU HAVE CHOSEN...

Go on to the next page.

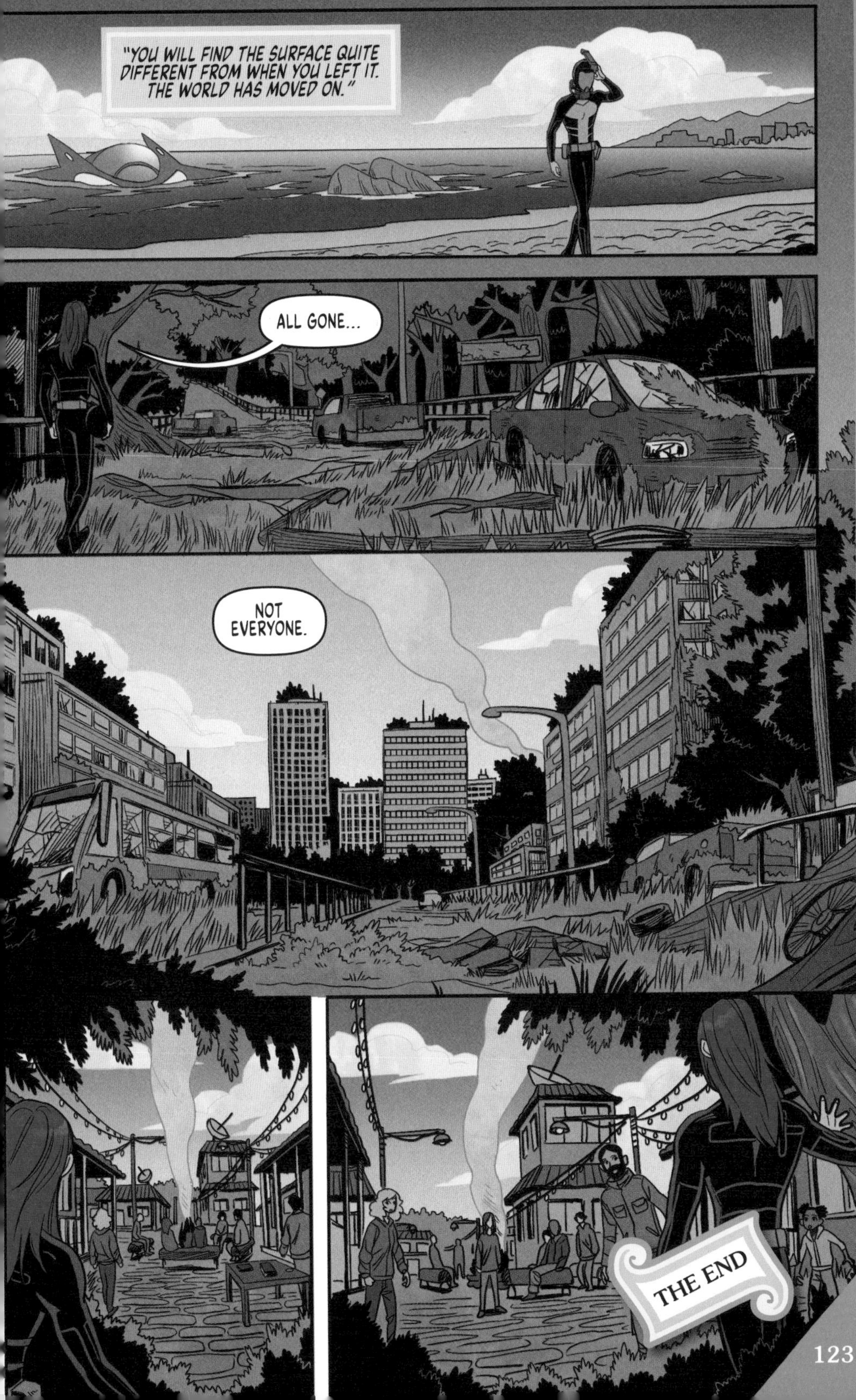
"YOU WILL FIND THE SURFACE QUITE DIFFERENT FROM WHEN YOU LEFT IT. THE WORLD HAS MOVED ON."
ALL GONE...
NOT EVERYONE.
THE END

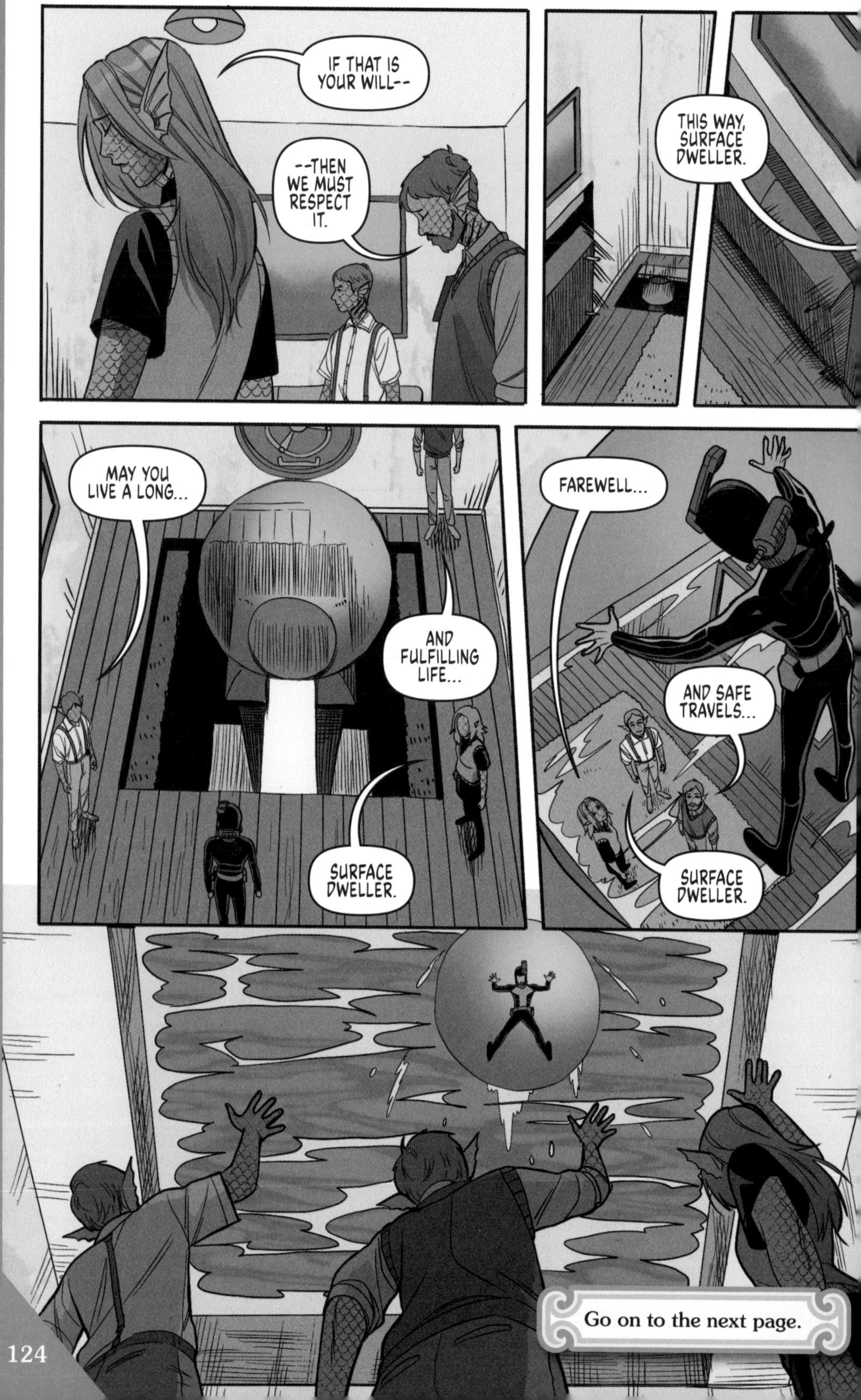
IF THAT IS YOUR WILL--
--THEN WE MUST RESPECT IT.
THIS WAY, SURFACE DWELLER.
MAY YOU LIVE A LONG...
AND FULFILLING LIFE...
SURFACE DWELLER.
FAREWELL...
AND SAFE TRAVELS...
SURFACE DWELLER.

Go on to the next page.

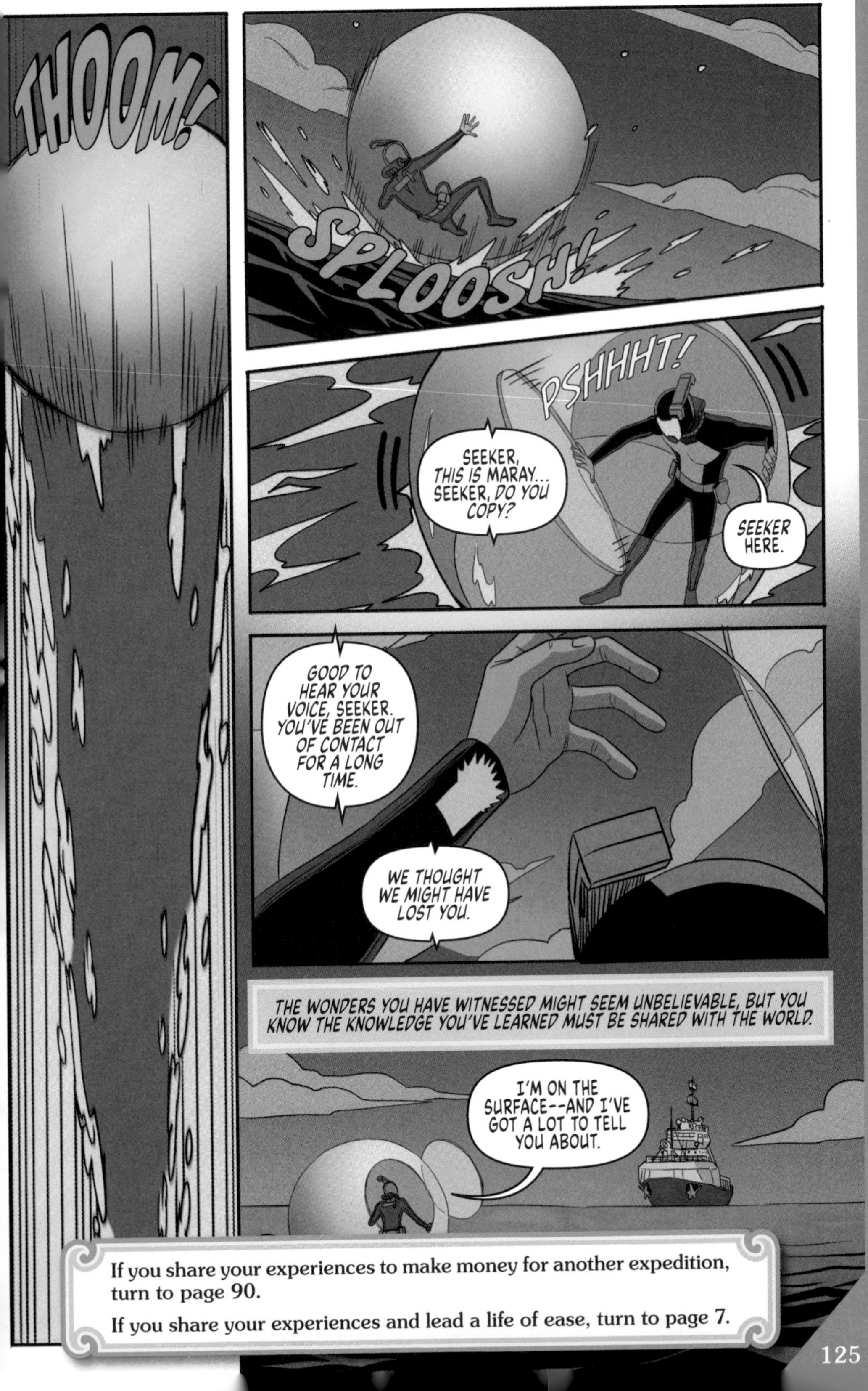
THOOM!
SPLOOSH!
PSHHHT!
SEEKER, THIS IS MARAY... SEEKER, DO YOU COPY?
SEEKER HERE.
GOOD TO HEAR YOUR VOICE, SEEKER. YOU'VE BEEN OUT OF CONTACT FOR A LONG TIME.
WE THOUGHT WE MIGHT HAVE LOST YOU.
THE WONDERS YOU HAVE WITNESSED MIGHT SEEM UNBELIEVABLE, BUT YOU KNOW THE KNOWLEDGE YOU'VE LEARNED MUST BE SHARED WITH THE WORLD.
I'M ON THE SURFACE--AND I'VE GOT A LOT TO TELL YOU ABOUT.

If you share your experiences to make money for another expedition, turn to page 90.

If you share your experiences and lead a life of ease, turn to page 7.

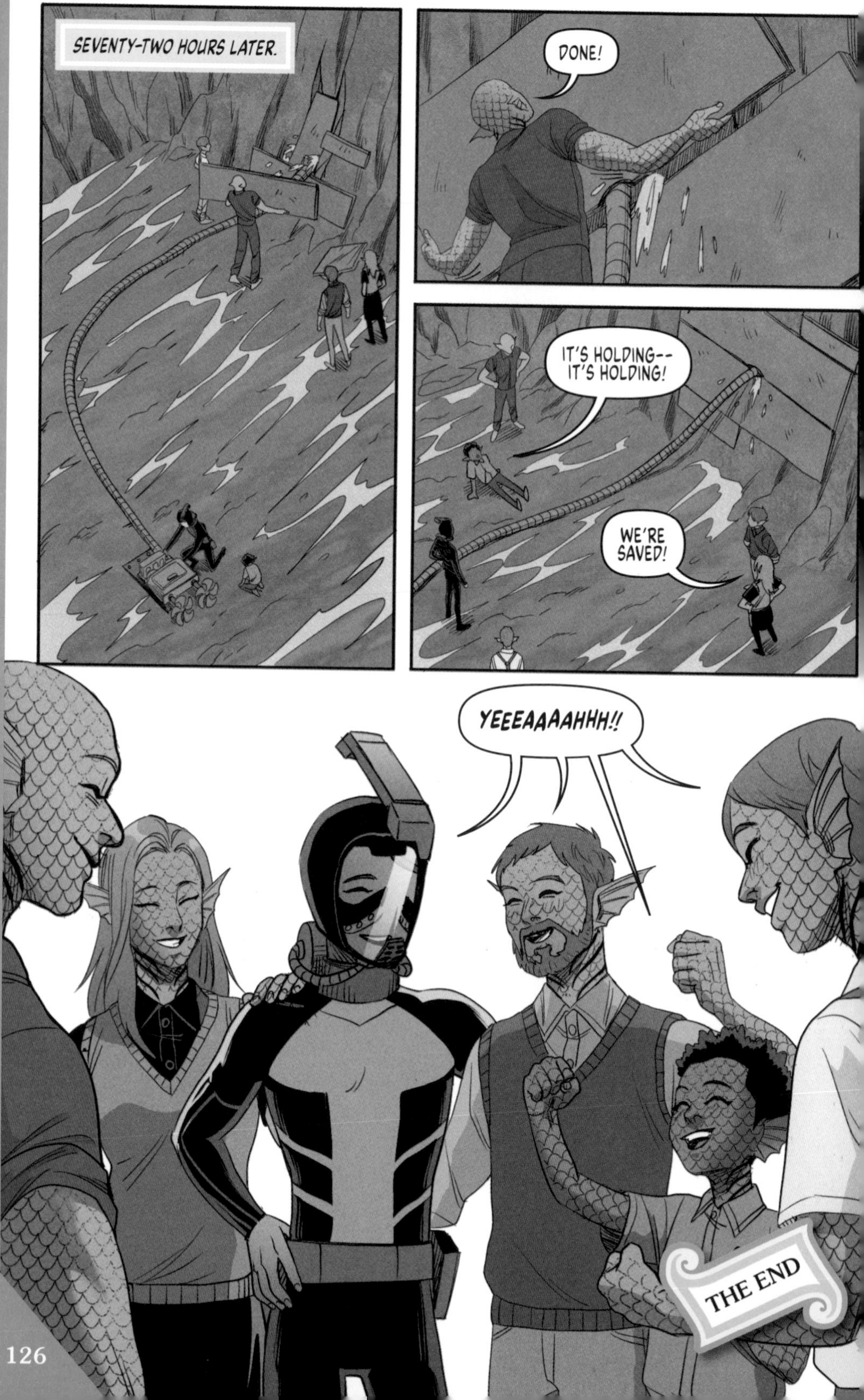
SEVENTY-TWO HOURS LATER.
DONE!
IT'S HOLDING-- IT'S HOLDING!
WE'RE SAVED!
YEEEAAAAHHH!!
THE END

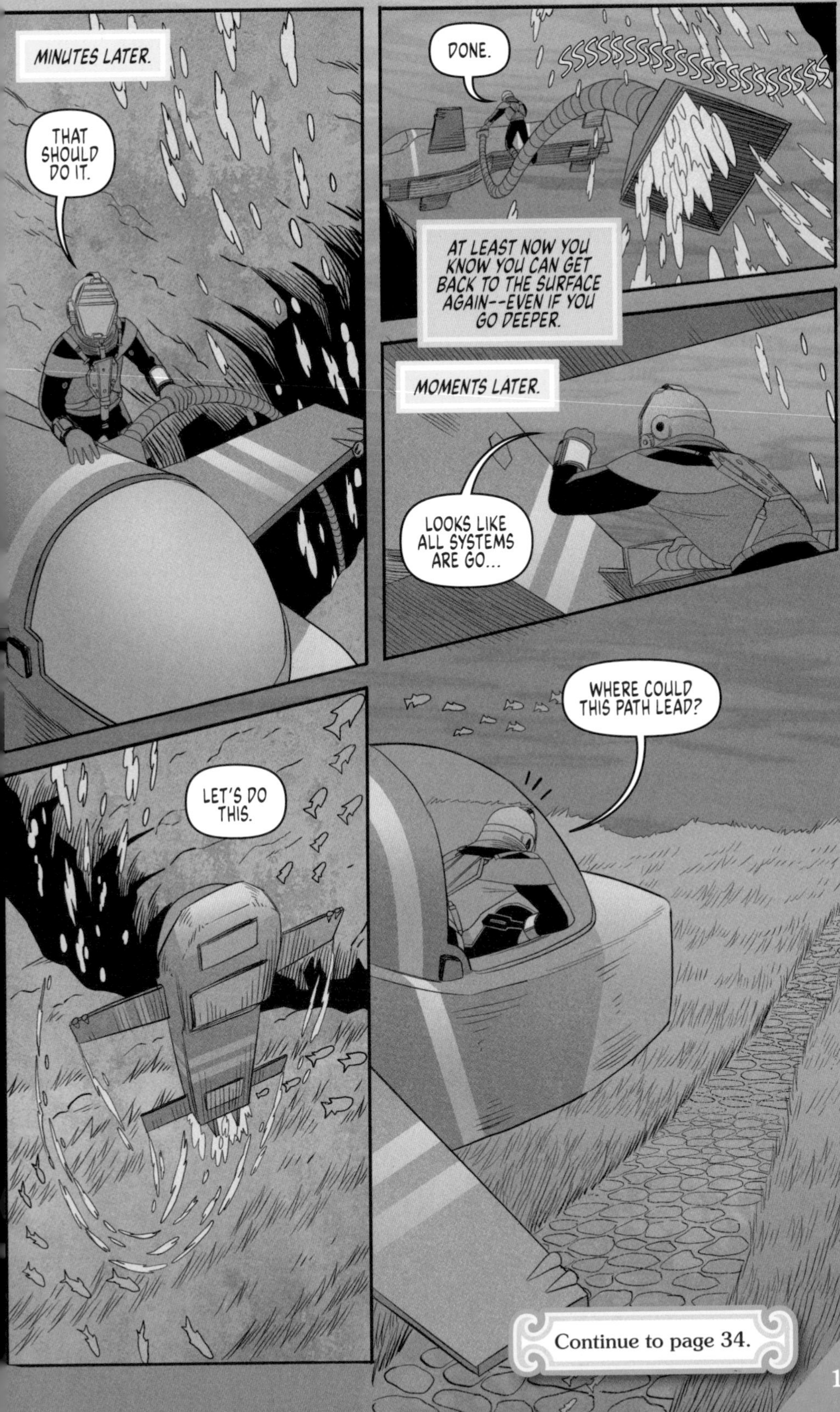
MINUTES LATER.
THAT SHOULD DO IT.
DONE.
SSSSSSSSSSSSSSSSSSSSSS
AT LEAST NOW YOU KNOW YOU CAN GET BACK TO THE SURFACE AGAIN--EVEN IF YOU GO DEEPER.
MOMENTS LATER.
LOOKS LIKE ALL SYSTEMS ARE GO...
LET'S DO THIS.
WHERE COULD THIS PATH LEAD?

Continue to page 34.

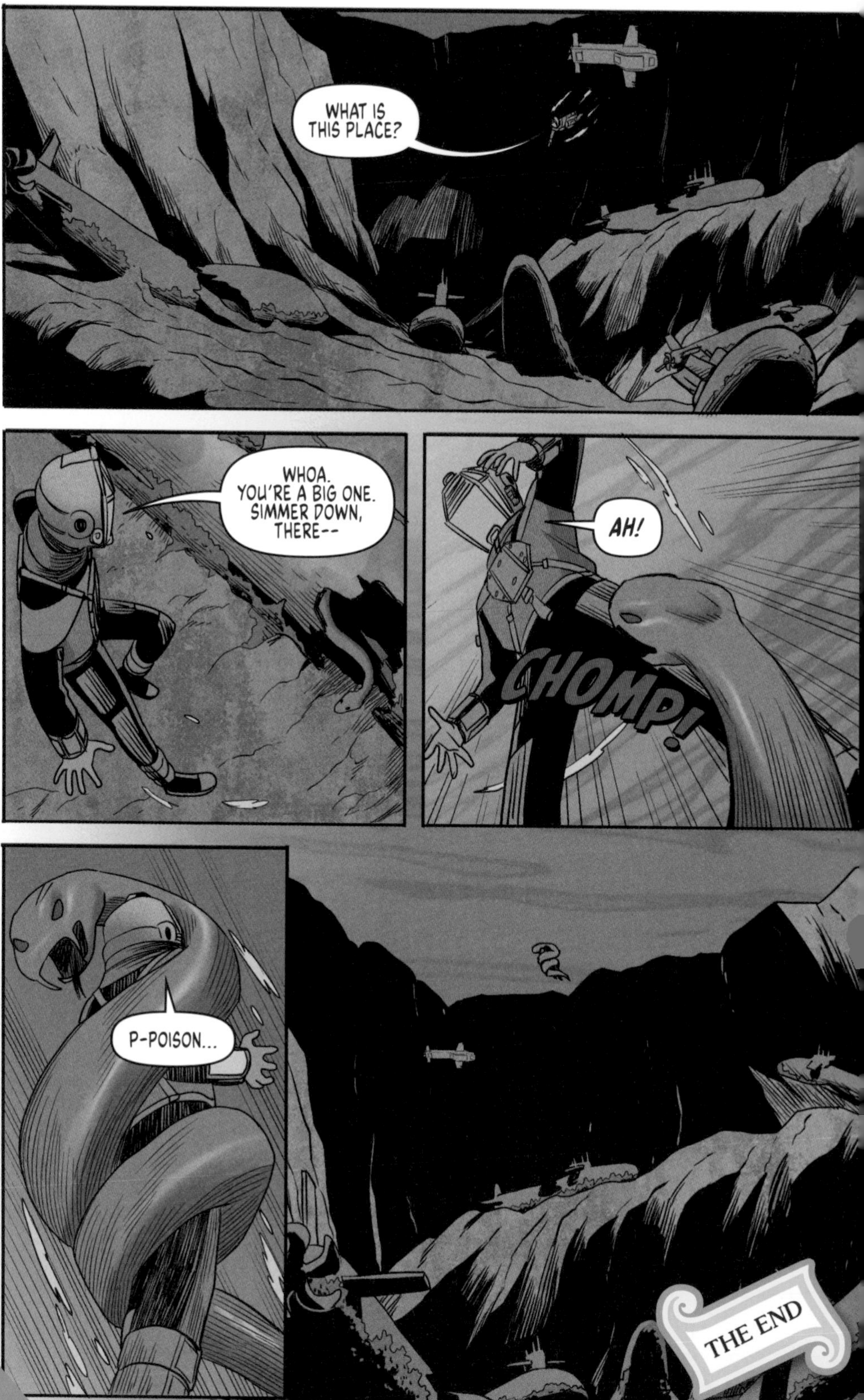
WHAT IS THIS PLACE?
WHOA. YOU'RE A BIG ONE. SIMMER DOWN, THERE--
AH!
CHOMP!
P-POISON...
THE END

CHOOSE YOUR OWN ADVENTURE®

JOURNEY UNDER THE SEA

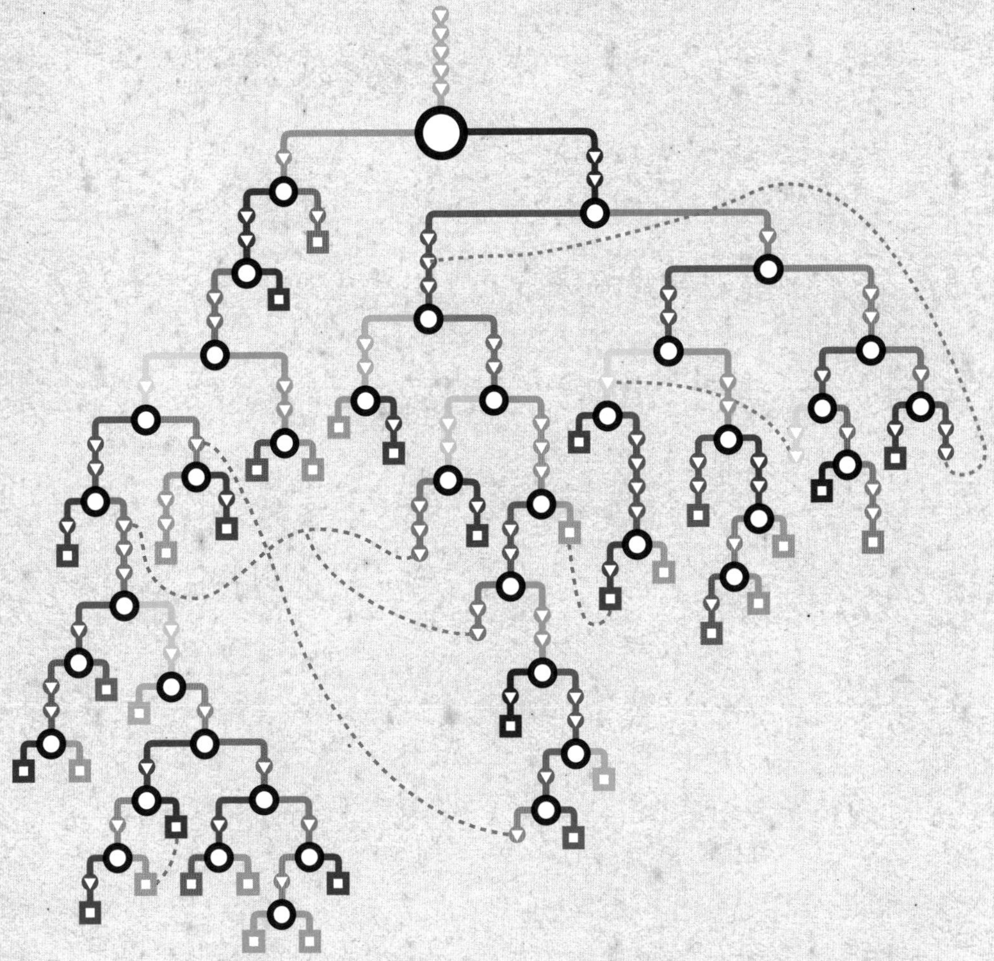

CHOOSECO

ONI PRESS

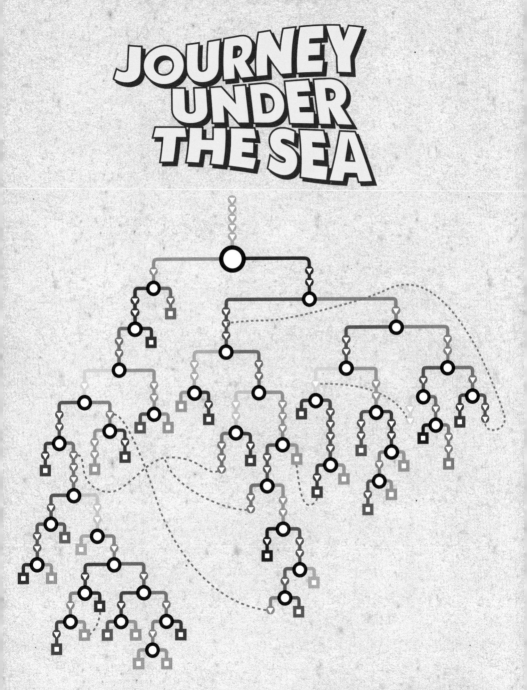

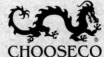

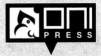

ANDREW E.C. GASKA

Andrew Gaska is an Ennie Award-winning game writer, creative director, and sci-fi author with twenty years of industry experience, Drew is also the senior development editor and head writer for Lion Forge Animation. In addition to developing STEAM education projects, Drew has adapted two classic *Choose Your Own Adventure* game books to graphic novel form. He is a freelance consultant to 20th Century-Fox, maintaining continuity and canon bibles for *Predator* and *Planet of the Apes*. The lead writer of the *Alien Roleplaying Game*, he lives beneath a pile of action figures with his glutenous feline, Adrien.

E.L. THOMAS

E.L. Thomas is a writer and game designer who has worked on numerous treatments, story bibles, and scripts for animation. His most recent credits include adapting *Choose Your Own Adventure* titles into graphic novels and co-writing the pilot for the *Orglanauts* animated series. He is the co-creator of the gaming periodical *Rolled & Told*. His additional game credits include working on supplements for the *Aliens* RPG. He lives in the Midwestern United States with his comely wife and three spoiled dogs.

DANI BOLINHO

Dani Bolinho, is the writer and draftsman for *Lobo Mau*, *Underground*, and *Desaventureiros*. Dani is also an award-winner in Japan at the Silent Manga Audition for the story *Tattoo* in 2018, and cofounder of the studio IndieVisivel Press.

PH GOMES

PH Gomes is a Brazilian colorist who has always been in love with comics, addicted to cinema, and is a father and lover of pop culture.

JOAMETTE GIL

Joamette Gil is an award-winning editor, cartoonist, and letterer extraordinaire. Her letters grace the pages of such Oni-Lion Forge titles as *Archival Quality*, *Girl Haven*, and, of course, *Mooncakes*! She's best known for her groundbreaking imprint P&M Press, home to *POWER & MAGIC: The Queer Witch Comics Anthology* and *HEARTWOOD: Non-binary Tales of Sylvan Fantasy*.